Praise for *The Human Origins of Beatrice Porter and Other Essential Ghosts*

'A brilliant, compelling exploration of familial legacies. A mythic and edifying read'
Irenosen Okojie, author of *Speak Gigantular*

'Prismatic and dazzling, Palmer's debut entrances with its stories-within-stories structure and loving portrayal of two sisters coming into their own power while grappling with family secrets and tales untold. Anansi and other folkloric figures and deities of their Jamaican Trinidadian heritage weave throughout the novel, transforming from teller to teller, from one generation to the next – at times haunting or healing, seductive or terrifying. Palmer's ever-rippling prose also shifts deftly – from magical to macabre, playful to tender, always with compassion for all'
Angela Mi Young Hur, author of *Folklorn*

'Soraya Palmer's epic, sweeping debut contains multitudes: it is tender, daring, funny and exquisitely written. It is a love letter to sisterhood that believes in the power of stories to transform. This book certainly transformed me'
Gabriella Burnham, author of *It Is Wood, It Is Stone*

'At once mischievous and warm, Soraya Palmer's voice will bewitch you from the very first page, leading you through the complexities of sisterhood and motherhood, belonging and loss'
Mina Seçkin, author of *The Four Humors*

'Soraya Palmer's characters are unparalleled and her prose is musical. Read this novel with a sibling, a cousin or a very close friend'
De'Shawn Charles Winslow, author of *In West Mills*

'Soraya Palmer weaves tales that are ancient and timeless, familiar yet new and strange. Just when you think you've pinned her protagonists down, they shift and change, slipping from your grasp like the stories themselves, like Anansi, changing form to survive the telling. I love its lyricism, the feeling of fable and oral history, one's myriad facets reflected back as through the many eyes of a spider. This book will go on to become a classic, I'm certain. Palmer definitely has my attention. A powerful story of women, powerfully and cleverly told'
Chịkọdịlị Emelụmadụ, author of *Dazzling*

'Envisions family as always in motion, careening through history, connection, attachment, discovery and warmth, with all the pain, loss and even violence that might include. Expertly paced, deeply imagined, by turns playful and heartbreaking, I love the way this novel understands that sometimes nothing will sustain us except the right story that is truer than true'
Madeline ffitch, author of *Stay and Fight*

# THE HUMAN ORIGINS OF BEATRICE PORTER & OTHER ESSENTIAL GHOSTS

## SORAYA PALMER

First published in Great Britain in 2023 by
Serpent's Tail
an imprint of Profile Books Ltd
29 Cloth Fair
London
EC1A 7JQ
*www.serpentstail.com*

First published in the United States of America in 2023 by Catapult

Book design by Laura Berry

This is a work of fiction. All of the characters, organizations, and events portrayed in this novel are either products of the author's imagination or are used fictitiously.

Grateful acknowledgment is made to the following publications for previously publishing excerpts of the novel in slightly different forms: "Anansi's Daughters" in *Calyx*, "Devil in the Shape of a Rooster" in *Calalloo*, and "Walk Like a Man" in *Ploughshares*.

1 3 5 7 9 10 8 6 4 2

Printed and bound in Great Britain by
Clays Ltd, Elcograf S.p.A.

The moral right of the author has been asserted.

A CIP catalogue record for this book is available from the British Library.

ISBN 978 1 78816 840 3
eISBN 978 1 78283 870 8

FSC
www.fsc.org
MIX
Paper from
responsible sources
FSC® C018072

*To my parents and their parents before them.*

Wild tongues cannot be tamed, they can only be cut out.

—GLORIA ANZALDÚA

If you surrendered to the air, you could ride it.

—TONI MORRISON

# CONTENTS

*Prologue*     What's My Name? A Prelude . . . . . . . . . . . . . . . . . . . . . 1

## PART I: ORIGINS

*Chapter 1*     Anansi's Daughters . . . . . . . . . . . . . . . . . . . . . . . . . . . 9

*Chapter 2*     Devil in the Shape of a Rooster . . . . . . . . . . . . . . . . . 22

*Chapter 3*     Tall Tales from Sasha Also Known as Ashes
aka the Mannish Girl . . . . . . . . . . . . . . . . . . . . . . . 39

*Chapter 4*     Once Upon a Time: Featuring Star
Scars & Dreams of Flight . . . . . . . . . . . . . . . . . . . . 57

## PART II: ESSENTIAL GHOSTS

*Chapter 5*     Sky Full a Curry and Purple Balloon . . . . . . . . . . . . 71

*Chapter 6*     Two Brothers, the Rolling Calf, and
the Wind Herself . . . . . . . . . . . . . . . . . . . . . . . . . . . 86

*Chapter 7*     Sasha & the Photograph . . . . . . . . . . . . . . . . . . . . 108

*Chapter 8*     An Unfortunate Event on Maple Street . . . . . . . . . 125

*Chapter 9*     The Human Origins of Beatrice Porter and
Other Essential Ghosts . . . . . . . . . . . . . . . . . . . . . . 152

## PART III: BEATRICE

*Chapter 10*     Lost in Her Story . . . . . . . . . . . . . . . . . . . . . . . . . . 195

*Chapter 11*     Dglo . . . . . . . . . . . . . . . . . . . . . . . . . . . . . . . . . . . . 216

*Chapter 12*     The Anansi Stories . . . . . . . . . . . . . . . . . . . . . . . . . 244

*Chapter 13*     Instructions for Communicating
with Dead Mothers . . . . . . . . . . . . . . . . . . . . . . . . 265

# What's My Name?

*A Prelude*

BY THE TIME YOU FINISH READING THIS I WILL BE DEAD AND *you, dear reader, will have forgotten all about me.*

*You see I am what they call Your Faithful Narrator, found in places the West calls fairy tales, what men call gossip, what children call magic.*

*Let me tell you a story. This one we call the first. It is a story that sounds like all the others, and yet it is also the one that has allowed for the existence of all that will come afterward—but we'll get to that.*

*In this story, two women sit inside a bar. The first one says, "Let me tell you a story." The second says, "So, tell me already!" "Okay, okay," she goes. "Once upon a time, there was a girl," she starts and looks into her drink. Her tongue starts to hang out like an udon noodle. "Well, go on," the friend says, mistaking her hanging tongue for excitement. Only the girl's tongue won't move. The girl's breath is fixed in midair. Her lips form the letter O. Her friend pricks the tongue with her fork to see what's the matter, and the tongue falls out and skitters like worms on the ground. The bartender scoops up all the pieces he can find, and they wriggle in his hands. He worries about the mess he's made. He asks the friend to fetch a jar and cap from the top shelf of the bar in order to contain the skittering tongue pieces. He looks down and notices no blood—only eraser dust.*

*The bartender thinks this is strange, but he goes to the bar to fetch his needle and thread. He begins to sew the tongue back together for the girl.*

This is a very difficult job for the man, as the pieces of her tongue keep moving. Like the tongue doesn't want to be caught. Mountains of eraser dust are flying from her mouth, getting all over the floor. Her breath stands before them. The bartender does a good job of mending except that he sews her tongue onto a piece of paper and stuffs it into her mouth. The girl and her friend rejoice as the girl begins to speak again. But every time she tries to tell her story, the words come out backward. The ending changes.

Let me tell you a story. This one will give you hope.

Once upon a time there was a girl. And this girl grew to be a woman. And this woman had the ability to conjure stories from ghosts. Now the conjure woman had three daughters who loved her stories so much that when she died it was all that she left them. Little did they know that these stories had a life before them. That this book had a life before me.

You see, the woman and her family existed in a place called Brooklyn where the maples lined the pavement, and the houses were made from limestone and brownstone that glittered like stars do under moonlight. It must have been divine providence that whitefolks refused to live on these streets, believing they were haunted, therefore leaving the most beautiful houses to be claimed by the descendants of slaves from all across the Atlantic.

Whitefolks were not entirely wrong about the haunting either. If you were to walk down these streets, you might hear the faint sound of steel drum and boom box and chickadee and pigeon. Or you might hear the chattering of ghosts—the spirits of colonialists, Ashanti warriors, slave holders, African griots, mythic creatures, and stories long since forgotten. But while whitefolks may call this a haunting, we know them to be the ancestors. After all, they only want to be able to walk through their homes like they did before their deaths—to sit in the kitchen drinking Milo, bestowing wisdom onto their children who are at risk of forgetting all about them.

Now this family lived in the only rose-colored building at the end of Maple Street. The youngest called herself Zora or *She Who Will One Day*

*Grow Up to Be a Great Writer Like Her Namesake. She could be found conjuring her mother's words into stories or if not, she could be caught, face flushed with embarrassment, fantasizing about a boy or two.*

*And then there was Sasha, the eldest, who felt her story should shine brightest for once. Commonly referred to as the Black Sheep or She Who Nearly Disappeared Until She Found Her True Self—this girl did have spunk. They say the girl had a chip on her shoulder the size of El Tucuche Mountain for nearly everyone, but particularly for her father who, legend had it, defeated a Rolling Calf with only a penknife and the power of his gaze.*

*Even with the new baby on the way, the family still fought like wolves—cunning in their ability to wound each other. The man they called Father moved out one day to live with a woman who didn't expect bread to be baked by stories. New daughters were birthed, several hearts were broken, and the maple trees were cut down and replaced with coffee shops.*

*At this point we all should've known what was coming. The scars that would form, the wounds that would never heal. It's true that Anansi stopped visiting the man's dreams at night. He couldn't tell his stories the way he used to. Images of Anansi, the Rolling Calf, and the purple balloon came and went in spurts. The wife, on the other hand, never stopped believing in magic.*

*But I will never forget the day that I first arrived in the arms of the sisters. It was the day when my two girls got me as their Christmas present. I was sitting quietly between words, inside the blank spaces of* The Anansi Stories *waiting to be unwrapped. You see, the book I lived in had been given to them by their mother, who got it from her grandmother, who got it from an Ashanti Priestess, who was there when it got made. Rumor had it that all women who tried to read* The Anansi Stories *aloud had their throats and tongues cut from their bodies like farm animals. The sisters had no idea the lengths that had been taken to keep these words alive.*

*But every night they would sit in the kitchen over Milo and go:*

*— I am Nanny, leader of the Maroons, mother of all Jamaicans! The*

*eldest, Sasha, wraps her hair in a pillowcase and holds up a shell, imagining it is an abeng. She speaks to her fellow countrymen.*

*(Please if you can, imagine you are invited to watch these girls right now. Pretend that you are a part of the enactment. Pretend you can decide how this story will end. \*Hint: The setting is a kitchen. The scene's objective is to show two sisters conjuring history.\*)*

*Sister 2 also known as Zora:* Yes, you are Nanny—lady who caught bullets in her behind and farted them out at her enemies.

*Sister 1 also known as Sasha:* Disgraceful! You are banished from my Maroon settlement!

*Zora:* Pghaw! *(farting noise)*

*Sasha:* I am Queen Nanny, the only African living in Jamaica who was never taken into bondage.

— Nanny forced the British troops to allow the Maroons to live in peace.

— This pot here represents the cauldron that burns without the use of fire. It lured the British into its waters. *(Sasha points to her mother's pot in the kitchen.)*

— The British troops try to climb up Blue Mountain but they fall right before the peak, breaking their backs in two.

— In three! One for the dupes they tricked into becoming one with their militia, two for the bloodhounds that eventually brought them down.

— Three for the bastard that killed Nanny.

*The one they call Sasha stops stirring. The cauldron turns back into a pot. The air beating beneath it becomes fire.* It was yesterday that they picked me up in their textbook and saw it plain: "Jamaica's national hero, affectionately referred to as Nanny, is of mythic status. Leading historians do not know how much of her existence has been fabricated by the oral tradition prominent in Jamaican culture. What is known to be true is that she was betrayed and murdered by one of her own, a man they call William Cuffee."

*This was the first time I ever heard that version—the one where she died. Right then, I felt the spirit slip from the ink and get cold.*

*Of course in my version, she's still alive, replaying over and over again her final battle. Sometimes she shoots down the entire British army using only one bag of arrows. Sometimes she uses her cauldron to create more arrows. Sometimes the cauldron makes a soup that is poison to her enemies, but antidote to her fellow Maroons. I could never forget that story. There are burn scars from the cauldron that run up and down my thighs. Some days, I forget what happened and then I taste the bammy and escovitch she made for Cudjoe on my tongue. I feel her handkerchief rub up against my cheek. There are scars that have faded that I feel some mornings. My hands are blistered, my breasts are chapped. But I especially love the way my two girls tell it. That is until this time—the time that she died.*

*And I know we just met, but I have a small request for you. I need you to save my life.*

*Yet already I feel your interest in me waning. You think that despite the fact that I've called you by name my words do not concern you. That someone else will pick up these words and take on the job themselves. That you don't have what it takes to save a girl like me. And because you choose to be my voyeur and sit here watching me—you too have become a part of this crime. You may have to pay for this someday.*

*But don't worry, you don't need to do much. All you gotta do is know my name.*

# PART I

—

# Origins

---

# CHAPTER 1

# Anansi's Daughters
*Sasha*

Brooklyn, NY
September 1997

THAT LEAN AND MEAN BEEF JERKY. IT LOOKS SO GORGEOUS
resting there with all the others, third shelf, second aisle where it usually
lives.

"This price oughta convince 'em, Zori. I mean it's one of the most
logical things you could buy here. Do you know how many people twelve
ounces of beef jerky could feed?"

But Zora just rolls her eyes because we already tried this routine
three times, and if it didn't work the last three times, it wasn't gonna
work now.

"For crissakes, Mom made me eat red beans with my pasta again
yesterday," I continue. "I mean she's obviously depressed because she's
had way too much time on her hands to be getting this creative with the
dinners."

"I dunno, Sasha. I thought the beans were pretty good. And
actually—"

"And then she had the nerve to tell me I wasn't getting enough protein. Well, obviously I'm not getting enough protein if we're living off this
freakin' rabbit food. Did you know babies sometimes turn orange when
they eat too many carrots? I read that in a science book, you know."

But before Zora can respond, we see Mommy and Daddy walking
down the aisle of meats, arguing under their breaths.

As Mom and Dad approach, I pipe up a little louder, pretending like Zora and I are still deep in conversation: "I mean, don't you just wanna go camping when you eat jerky? I chew on it and I go ummph! Look, feel my stomach, Mom. You'll see there's basically nothing left." I point in between and below my two bee stings where my rib cage ends. "I swear it's because we've been vegetarians way too long."

"You're being dramatic, Sasha," my mother mutters. It's like her ongoing talks on how to be in tune with one's own body have all gone to waste, and she looks away longingly at the aisle of canned beans and vegetables.

Only Dad's face is glowing with the window of opportunity. It's story time again.

"You know, Sasha, there used to be this guy by the junction who used to sell homemade beef jerky out on his stoop," he says. "Until one day he died very mysteriously. Nobody knows what happened to him, but rumor had it he became none other than the—"

"Rolling Calf!" Zora says. She's standing on the wheels of the shopping cart so she can see him better.

"Right, Zori!" he says. "You see, when a butcher dies, he becomes the Rolling Calf to pay penance for all the cows he tortured and killed in his lifetime."

As he speaks, his eyes grow large, and his voice rises and falls like a wave. Even his neck appears to stretch upward before springing back again. People in the aisles are politely trying to move us out the way, but Daddy doesn't budge.

"You could hear Rolling Calves where my brother and I grew up because they have thick iron tails that smell like sausage and clink like chains. Whenever we had the mind to be rebellious and stray against our father's wishes, we'd hear the metal, smell the pork, and know we'd gone too far. We wouldn't run off the way you kids do now—you know, foolishly."

His stories are always like this: very entertaining, so as to keep us listening till the big moral point at the end.

But after twelve years of living with the man, I feel like I've gotten to the point where as much as I love his tall tales, they never sound as good when families are pushing by us with their shopping carts, wondering why we're blocking the entire aisle. Zora, who won't enter middle school for another year, is like a puppy, anticipating his every line like it's brand-new.

Dad continues, "You see, once upon a time there was a boy and his brother. And this brother thought he could defeat the Rolling Calf alone. The boy went out to help his brother and barely made it out alive. But his brother, well . . ." He pauses. There's a flash in his eyes that always looks like lightning.

"Back when I was your age, we used to tend our own cows. You think that's real cow they're giving you at McDonald's? Cow shit is what they're giving you."

Mom glares at Dad, who quickly rotates his gaze to her knees to avoid feeling her eyes on him. Normally, his story ends with the boy luring the Rolling Calf into the ocean with the help of the hurricane and a penknife. Water is always key in these stories because, like the Wicked Witch of the West, the Rolling Calves—as well as other germ-infested meats—are all apparently afraid of cleanliness.

"Yes, clean people can't be bothered with dirty meats," Mom says.

She rubs her hands together and twists her lips when she says this, like she's wiping them clean of something. Her face looked this way when she caught the rat in our kitchen last week.

We follow our mother toward the cashier and see that she has replaced our beef jerky with raw and unsalted almond butter.

Lately I've been noticing that the families here are different from the ones who shop at C-Town. C-Town children whine a lot and fill their carts with things like Go-Gurts, Kraft macaroni and cheese, ice pops, the good bologna, peanut butter, crackers with salt on them, and white bread. Meanwhile their moms are running back and forth returning things so that their grocery bill won't be too high. Dad loves to remind us that he left his nine-to-five three years ago so we would never have to shop at places like C-Town again. This business was supposed to bring us up to speed with the Park Slope crowd and the people who shopped at the co-op. Still, it's been more than a few years, and Dad's new business has continued to flop.

Here at the co-op, families buy organic laundry detergent and tofu ice cream. The fathers are always happy to help their wives and children, picking up the most natural-looking tomatoes. Mothers look younger than they are, sometimes dyeing their hair new down-to-earth shades.

My sister and I exchange glances. The line is long.

"How come almond butter doesn't come with the crunchy chunks like Skippy has?" I ask, staring at the family ahead of us.

"I don't know," my mother says.

"Well, what's the point of peanut butter if it doesn't come with crunchy chunks?"

"It's almond butter." My mother seems distracted. She's fishing through her bag. "And where's yuh father?" she asks. "Did he take my wallet again?"

I look around, noticing that he's disappeared, but I have other things on my mind. "Then we should be eating peanut butter," I say.

"Peanut butter has unnecessary fat. Also, it releases unhealthy toxins into the body that almond butter doesn't."

I look at her for a moment.

"I think some people worry too much about fat, Mom."

She ignores this comment. Zora gives me a look. Mom keeps looking into her bag and then cautiously toward the register.

Our cashier smiles, teeth white as paint, as we approach her. My mother smiles weakly, tight-lipped, and says, "I'm sorry, but I can't seem to find my wallet. My husband's coming shortly."

The woman glances at my mother before turning back to her register.

"I'm so sorry," my mother adds.

The woman smiles widely. "Oh, that's okay. Would you mind just stepping aside for a moment then, miss?"

And then the woman just shoos my mother along and moves on to talk to the next customer. We get out of line.

Moments later, Dad finally arrives with a whole new cart full of food, and we get back in line, which is now snaking around the baking aisle.

"You didn't borrow any money from me, did you?" Mom asks Dad.

"I really don't know what you're asking me." But he says this without looking at her.

"Because I'm gonna need some money."

"I have no money for you, Beatrice."

"Nigel," she says. Her voice seems tender until the smile comes. It opens up, teeth gesturing toward him in an almost threatening manner. "You have the money."

His nose flares as he looks at her. I once saw a horse in a movie flare his nose like that. I decide to take immediate action.

"Dad, tell us the story about Anansi and his family," I say, pulling his arm, trying to get him to look at me and not at her.

At first I don't think I can get Dad's eyes to stop from squinting. But soon enough those large pupils soften into butter and widen like pancakes.

"You see," he starts, "Anansi, his wife, and their four children lived in a fancy house in Red Hills until he lost his job." He pauses for a moment, glancing at Mom before continuing. "He worked hard to keep the home life comfortable, but sooner or later the food was gone, and the family started to go hungry. He went crazy and thought his wife might leave him for a richer man, and they fought a lot. And so finally when there wasn't even a decent-sized meal for the family of rats they were living with, he cut off the right side of his buttocks, spiced it up, and served it as jerk pork for the entire family. The family loved it and had a meal for the night. Sadly, the father could never sit down again and could only sleep on his side for the rest of his life."

We look at each other silently for what feels like a minute straight.

Finally Zora says, "I don't remember the story ending that way, Daddy."

I try to cut her a look as a warning to quit while she's ahead, but she's not even looking at me.

"I mean, doesn't Anansi—"

"Actually, I remember Anansi leaving," my mother cuts her off. "I guess he just couldn't take the pressure. Started up a whole new family."

I wait for Dad's reaction. Zora doesn't wait.

"No, no, no," she says. "The wife finds out what Anansi did and starts laughing. She laughs so hard she spits it out and tells him never to work so hard again. They end up living happily ever after. Don't you remember, Daddy?"

She looks so earnest, I almost feel sorry for her.

Dad only nods silently and starts humming. My mother keeps her head up, mouth closed, as we finally emerge back at the front of the line.

Dad continues to hum as the same cashier woman asks my father if she can please help him, sir.

"Can we have all this charged, miss?" he says to the cashier, his smile competing with hers. He likes to smile with his neck arched all the way up to show off his dimple that takes attention away from his overbite.

"Sure. What will you be using?"

"American Express," he says with confidence.

The woman tries to smile as she tells him the card is not working.

"Not working?" my father asks.

"Right." She smiles. "I'm terribly sorry." And she looks like she's ready to shoo us along again.

"I've never had a problem with this card before," he says. "Please try it again." Dad's eyes are going wild, his arms are steady, and I think I can hear him humming again.

"Sir, I really don't think—"

"Try it again." My father says this like an order. A woman from behind taps her foot loudly, but my father will not move. The cashier woman seems scared, and for a minute I'm worried someone might call the police. People are already staring, and all my mother can do is bite her lip.

"Here, try this," he says and pulls out another card.

The woman smiles awkwardly. "Sir," she says, "we're a bit understaffed today. Would you mind putting some of your items back on the shelf?"

The words sting.

"Ma'am," my father says, softer now, "please try my card."

"Oh. I'm sorry, I didn't hear you say that. Sure, I'll try your card."

Her smile sinks deep into her face as she prints our receipt. Her teeth are so white they begin to look plastic. She puts the groceries into the bags neatly without ever looking down. I look away uneasily and rub my jaw.

. . . . . . . . . . . . .

Things only get worse when we get home. Dad tells us not to bother putting the groceries away—that he and Mom can handle it. This should have been the first sign that something was wrong. It was never the job of the adults to unpack the food. Mom shivers only for a second, and I figure I shouldn't let my mother stay in the kitchen alone with Daddy and his fearless eyes. But *Boy Meets World* is on now. So we make our way to the TV room next door.

"When I grow up, I'm gonna invent a country where there's no such thing as money," Zora says.

"Don't be stupid," I mutter, focusing on Shawn Hunter who is about to profess his love to Angela for the very first time.

"No, really. I'm gonna have it so that everyone will trade with each other. The farmers will trade with the seamstress people, and the seamstress people with the coal miners, and so on."

She moves to block the entire screen as she speaks.

"But who would the country trade with, moron? A country needs free trade," I say, trying to see around her head.

"We'll trade with no one. We'll be self-sufficient. We'll be Cuba."

"You'll have to trade with someone. Even Cuba knows that. Canadians trade with Cubans." I pause, letting it sink in that she's wrong.

Of course, secretly, I feel like we should be hugging at this point because I'm scared. Things are banging too loudly on the walls to just be putting them away.

I hear Dad say, "No, you don't get to put this shit on me right now, Beatrice. You blame *me* for not bringing *your* goddamn wallet to the supermarket? You have any idea how bloody hard I work each day so that I can put food down your bloody throat every night? Jesus, I ask you to remember one lousy thing."

Zora tries to drown out his yelling by shouting, "Why do people get jobs anyway? I mean if you think about it, there's really no point. No, there's just no point to life when you're not even happy. And the way I see it, I have maybe sixty to seventy years left." She reaches for her calculator on the couch. "So that means I'd be working nine hours a day, five days a week. That means that every week I could be spending time talking about, I dunno, art or something, I'm wasting about forty-five hours of every week for the next sixty to seventy years. And for the next sixty to seventy years, that'd be about 180 hours of wasted time per month. And twelve months in a year means 2,160 hours of time wasted. Ummm, 129,600 to 151,200 hours. Jesus. That's a lot of time to be wasted. That should be—I dunno, illegal."

The sounds from the kitchen are getting to me. I roll my eyes: "God, you're so freaking lazy. How would your people get anything done if they just laid around on the grass all day long? They'd all starve to death. You wanna be a writer and you really think that you'll get there by just sitting on your ass all day? Your stories are gonna be pretty boring." I regret saying it as soon as I see the look on her face.

And then we're interrupted. I hear the scream first and then the thud of a body.

Zora looks at me, holds my hand, and says, "So let's just say there was a spider."

I nod and follow her lead. This is our favorite game. "Yes. Anansi the Spider."

"He sees a calf."

"A Rolling Calf."

"He runs away."

"Or freezes stiff," I say, and we look at each other.

We tiptoe toward the door, cracking it open to peer at the mess. This time spilled soy milk runs across our musty old carpet. There'll probably be a huge stain tomorrow, and Mom'll fuss and make us clean it up again.

"But what if he finds a window?" Zora asks.

She's still standing in the doorway, but her eyes are closed.

"Yes, a big window with silver panes," I continue.

"He opens the window."

"He takes a step outside."

"A web is there."

"To catch him."

"He's safe now. Home free."

We open our eyes and look at our mother. Bits of tofu are all over the new shirt she bought when she took us to Bobby's last weekend. She's shaking on the ground, screaming up at my father who stands like a steel crane over her bent frame.

"Yuh want to buy new china set for yuh girlfriend, well go right ahead. Move right in with yuh nasty white woman. Calling every night saying, 'I'm stuck at the office.' What kinda foolishness dat? Ent? So doh bother accusing me of usin' up de money."

"I don't know where the hell you get that from. The bloody shit I put up with, Beatrice. Between your fucking paranoia and your over-priced vegan crap. Look at this food, Beatrice."

He shakes a box of soy macaroni and cheese in her face, and I think he might make her eat it, cardboard and all. "I mean for bleeding Christ, I can't eat this crap!"

"So dat's yuh excuse? Yuh work like a dog so yuh can bull yuh coworker?"

We shut the door. Maybe there is nothing left to say. But Zora's looking at me to be the older sister for tonight.

"You see in the web," I begin, "Anansi gets bigger and stronger. The web can't hold him."

"This is his land now," Zora continues, "outside the big silver window. He lands on his feet and he's okay."

"At least until school starts."

"Or church."

"And he has to go back across the window."

"And the Rolling Calf is there."

"Well, maybe the calf is asleep," I offer.

"Yes, it's daytime now, and Rolling Calves have to sleep in the day because they're like vampires."

"And Anansi is safe again."

"Yes. Safe. Home free."

But the kitchen is a mess. We creep behind the doorway with the next crash that sounds like the bottle of vodka sauce that smashed the counter a week ago. Now there are more tomatoes splattered on the floor. It looks like blood on my mother's arm, but I don't wanna think it could be anything other than tomato. My mother's arms shake furiously, her knees banging into each other, making a hard bumping noise, and I wonder how badly she hurts.

My father leaves the kitchen with a pack of Marlboros in hand and stops to look at us. "Look, you know how your mother can get," he says. His voice trails off as he places his hand on the wall above him. "You should go help her—the two of you," he says.

"Yes, Daddy," Zora says.

I say nothing and stare at his feet.

He turns away from us to walk out the front door, pausing every few moments to glance at the mess he made.

"Come help me," Mom says after he leaves. We walk over slowly to further assess the damage. She has all the primary colors across her skin. A mix of bruises, wounds, and food. She shines brightly beneath the kitchen's overhead lights.

"Mommy," I say, and I try hard to keep any strong feelings from entering my voice.

"Let me tell you a story," she says. Her arms and legs are still sprawled on the floor, like she's doing a yoga position.

"Maybe you shouldn't talk," Zora says.

"I'm okay," she says.

"Mommy," I repeat. I can't think of anything else to say.

"No, I'm okay," she says again, and we help her to sit up and lean on me and Zora for a while. Her food or bloodstains get onto my overalls, and I'm fine with that. I don't really want to hear a story about what my father did to her in the past or how he's still a good man and still our father or why I caught her crying out for God in the bathroom a week ago.

But instead she goes, "You know why we call them Anansi stories?"

It catches me off guard.

"Because they're not real?" Zora suggests.

"Of course they're real. All stories are. But did you know that they used to be known as Tiger stories?"

We did not know, and so we shake our heads in unison.

"Tiger has always been the vainest of them all," she says.

Now when my mother tells stories, she sings them. She taps her feet in time with her words, but her feet look so tired and caught under food that we tap our feet for her.

"Now Tiger was always naming things after his own inflated image." Fast taps. "Tiger lilies, tiger moths, tiger sharks, and so on. And every night before the children went to sleep, he wanted the children to tell one another Tiger Stories. And Anansi was sad because he thought he might go his whole life being called small, someone to be stepped on while people walked to work—without even the acknowledgment that they took a spider's life." Slow taps.

"So he said, 'If I can prove myself to be a warrior, will you let the stories be named after me?' And the forest itself broke out in hives of laughter, shaking the ground, causing Anansi to bow down in shame. A spider is weak. A spider breaks under doorways and under feet. Tiger said, 'Bring me the snake, and I will let the stories be named after you.' Tiger, of course, said this as a joke, knowing that the spider could never overpower the snake. A snake is clever. A snake is strong. A snake eats raw eggs whole for breakfast. But still, the spider felt he needed to try. So he tied a noose to string Snake up; he dug a hole to stick Snake in;

he made a fly trap and stuck an egg in it. But Snake outdid him every time. And for a while Anansi thought, 'Well, if Tiger thinks I'm weak, and Snake thinks I'm weak, and Rabbit thinks I'm weak, then I must be weak. Small. Meaningless.' Then he thought, 'Guess I could give this one last try.'

"He said, 'Snake. I'm sorry I keep trying to kidnap you. I only wanted to prove to the rest of the forest that you were the longest animal in the kingdom.

"'But of course I'm the longest.' Snake was indignant.

"'I bet you're not even longer than that bamboo stick over there.'

"'Bring it to me,' Snake said. 'Carry over the stick and I'll prove that I'm the longest.'

"Anansi did this, and Snake started to crawl out of his hole. 'But how can I trust you?' Anansi asked. 'How do I know you won't keep sliding up and down the stick to make yourself seem bigger?'

"'Tie my tail so I can't move.'

"Anansi did this. He said, 'Now stretch so long and far that you have to squint your eyes a little.'

"Snake did this, and as soon as Snake closed his eyes, Anansi tied his head to the bamboo.

"The forest became still and quiet, and all the laughter in the world stopped for an entire moment to honor Anansi. The spider had now outsmarted both Snake and Tiger. And from then on, these stories have always been known as Anansi Stories," my mother says.

But I am still upset.

For a while we sit where we are—our mother propped up against us on the dirty floor like she needs us to give her life. Zora's the first to change positions. She collapses into my mother's lap. Muffled sounds come from her mouth. My mother lifts her face to wipe the water falling from her eyes.

And then it's my move; I stand up. I open the paper towels and wipe up the soy milk and tomato sauce on the floor where we are. Zora is braver and brings the paper towels to my mother's face and arms. I put away the tofu, carrots, and kale before coming back to sit by them. I finally look at her—her clothes still a mess but her face dry.

"So what is the story saying, Mom?" I ask. "Are you saying that they'll always be bullies, but we should keep our chin up until the day we can fight back?"

I'm feeling sick of stories. I don't see a warrior in my mother's stretch pants and tank top. She just looks old. Tired. Tomato stained.

My mother strokes my cheeks before holding my face in her hands.

"No," she says, "I'm saying that Anansi is a woman."

And then we are silent.

# CHAPTER 2

## Devil in the Shape of a Rooster
*Zora*

Brooklyn, NY
April 1999

"MOMMY, WHAT'S A CONDOM?" I ASK.

"What?" she says.

Mom's cooking now, which means she'll be pleasantly distracted for at least another four hours—which means I'm more likely to get a nod and a grunt, less likely to get a beating. She's been cooking and walking around the house a lot lately considering how big she's been getting, what with my new sister on the way in eight weeks or so, according to Sasha. It's a particularly good time to talk to Mom since Sasha's got basketball practice after school all week, leaving the kitchen to be championed by my mother and me alone.

Mom's looking after a pot of callaloo on the stove, swizzling the okra and bhagi and coconut milk faster than before.

"Remember that scene in *The Mask* where Jim Carrey starts making balloon animals?" she asks without looking up from her pot. "At one point he pulls out a condom instead of a balloon. That's what a condom is."

Her body looks small and oval like an egg, her copper forehead glistens like pearls from the heat of the burner.

"Oh," I say, but I'm sure there's more to this question. "It's for Sex Ed., Mom."

Mom takes a paper towel to wipe the pearls off her forehead and closes her eyes. She looks like she's somewhere else now. She's been doing this a lot lately—getting distracted in the middle of cooking or having important conversations with her children.

"Mom?" I ask.

"Get me some water," she says.

"What's wrong?" I ask as I fill a glass from the sink.

"Just a little headache," she says before taking a long exhale.

This is the fifth "little headache" she's had this week. Must be because of the baby.

She stops swizzling and sits down on the kitchen stool and beckons me over to the stove.

"Come learn to make callaloo while yuh father not here. You know how he love to quarrel about Trini-people food. It soon finish, but at least yuh could learn to swizzle. Learning to use de swizzle stick is a lot more important for adulthood than knowing about condoms. Trust me."

I go to stand in front of the bubbling liquid.

"Now plenty people like to use a blender for callaloo. Don't fall into that habit. It's lazy and a hard one to break. Proper callaloo should be swizzled."

I put the stick in my hand. With hesitance I start to rub my hands back and forth around it, trying to get the rest of the callaloo and okra to turn to mush under the weight of the wooden eight-pointed star. The stick keeps slipping from my fingers; it won't just stay in place and mash the food like it's supposed to. My hands are quickly becoming tired, and the solids left in the pot aren't looking any mushier.

"But Mom—"

"Besides, ah don't like what they teaching yuh in these liberal American schools. American boys like to do experiments on young Black girls, yuh understand? Think about that before asking me to go by this one and that one house for dinner."

When my mother starts to feel on edge her dialect switches from New York to Arima so fast you think you're talking to two different people—which is true. My mother in the United States and my mother in Trinidad are often two different people. Lately, she talks about Arima more than usual. Sometimes about the baby. Rarely about Dad who's away on business again. He hasn't been home in three weeks.

When I get back to my room, I take out my journal to write words to try and understand my family. The word that comes up most often is "sacrifice." I write: *Sacrifice is waiting three weeks in a row to watch the latest* West Wing *episode with your father like he promised before he left for Europe.*

When I get into bed, I think about Jay Robert Ellison from school. Kids in my class call him Rabbit Tooth because his parents can't afford braces, and his teeth stick out kinda funny. But I dunno, I mean he smiles so rarely that when he does, it's like he's sharing his secret with you, and you feel like you know him. People look up from what they're doing when he walks down the halls; every step like an accident. Dad would probably call him rude because of how his pants swing so low, but I know the real reason—he's just overcompensating. He has eyes the color of tree bark and nicely shaped hands (soft but not dainty), long and thick fingers that look good for holding, fingernails that seem groomed, and bright copper skin like me and my mom's.

But now my thoughts are being distracted by how shadowy the room is. My room is darker lately since Sasha spent all summer begging Mom and Dad to sleep away from me and be in her own room. Mom and Dad think I should be preparing for my soon-to-be role as big sister. Dad told me I should be happy they finally gave me my own bed, but my covers seem too big; the sheet corners look like the heads of animals coming to eat me.

But I guess the one good thing about nighttime is that no one else can see me. I keep my hands crossed on my stomach, not letting them anywhere near my lower area. Still, I imagine what it might feel like to have my hands travel there. Like maybe Rabbit Tooth would ask me for a pencil and then take my hand instead. He'd smile at me for about an hour with wide questioning eyes before leaning in, letting the air between us feel sparse, causing us to breathe harder. Now I'm hyperventilating with all the lack of oxygen in the room, and I like it that way. I anticipate the feel of his lips for the first time. Are they coarse or smooth? Chapped or wet? Will I feel his teeth? His tongue? He comes closer before leading me into the broom closet. And that's when we do it.

. . . . . . . . . . . . .

"Doh go past Miss Douglass's stoop else jumbie go ketch yuh," my mother yells at Sasha and me the next day after school. We're not allowed to go more than three buildings past ours, and so we usually end up sitting on the stoop of our building, content just watching other people's freedom. We like to count the number of Black boys we're not supposed to talk to because their pants hang an inch or more below their waistline. But this time I have something to tell Sasha. I'm panting with excitement.

"I gotta tell you something," I say as soon as Mom goes inside.

"Wait, hold on. What do you think about this one?"

"I dunno. Two inches?" There are more important things on my mind.

"Oh, please, it's gotta be three at least. Wow, to the knees." Sasha points at a different boy across the street. "I wonder how they walk like that," she says.

I have to admit it's a curiosity that we share.

"So what does it feel like to be kissed?" I say, inching toward her.

"I wouldn't know, Zora." She crosses her arms and looks up to the sky while she speaks.

This fact surprises me because Sasha's already a freshman in high school. I mean I'm only in middle school, and I still know plenty of people who have been kissed.

"How do they say it feels?" She glances down at her feet now, attempting not to seem too interested in my answer.

"Actually," I say, slowly trying to prepare her for my big news, "it happened."

I watch eagerly for her reaction. Nothing.

"Just once though," I continue.

Still nothing.

"Today I asked Rabbit Tooth at school how to get rid of the hiccups, and he said I needed to get them knocked out of me. So I let him punch me in the stomach."

"You what?" She finally looks at me.

"Well, what else was I supposed to do?"

"Not that!"

"And then I started crying because it hurt so much. And that's when he kissed me."

"He did what?"

"He said he was sorry."

"Lord, Zora. What do they teach you in that school? You know you can't be letting people punch you in the stomach." She pauses and strokes her chin like she's about to lecture me before smiling. "So was it a good kiss?"

"Yeah, I mean his tongue was pretty warm, which was good since I was cold. His lips seemed pretty strong—not too soft like some shrimpy kid would have."

"Well, that's something, I guess. Did he hold you good?"

"Not really. He stroked my cheek with his hand at one point. That felt good. Like we could just be kissing forever."

"You wouldn't be, trust me. He was probably resting his hand on your cheek while he thought about where else he could put it."

"Like my hips?"

"Like your ass, Zora."

I turn around to see Mom coming from inside the building. She's walking slowly, belly first.

"We're not hungry, Mom." The bald-faced comments always have to come from Sasha.

Mom sucks her teeth and holds up the cordless phone rather than say anything about Sasha not being hungry after she slaved for hours cooking dinner so we wouldn't starve to death. She's too tired to discipline.

"It's yuh father. When yuh finish talk to him, come and get yuh dinner."

Daddy was supposed to call us on Tuesday. He looked me straight in the eye right before he left and said that we'd talk every Tuesday because Tuesday's our day. But he didn't call on Tuesday or Wednesday or Thursday. Today is Friday.

"Yes, Mommy," I say.

Sasha takes the phone and hands it to me. "You first."

She sounds kind of angry now, but I'm trying not to overthink the situation.

"Zori?" His voice booms like a radio host's would, and I can't help but smile.

"Hi, Daddy."

"Your mother tells me you and your sister have not done your homework yet for the night."

"After dinner, Daddy."

"Zora, you're about to be a big sister now."

"Yes, Daddy."

"Time for you to start taking your work more seriously."

"Yes, Daddy," I say and then, "So like, where are you anyway?"

"Germany. And trust me, it's no vacation or I would've brought you with me."

"Oh. So when are you coming back?"

"As soon as I can. Look, reception here's not great and it looks like I'm being called back into a meeting. Be sure to give your sister and mother a big hug and kiss from me."

"Don't you want to say hi to Sasha? She's standing right here."

"Yes, well, just tell her I have a meeting to run back to and that I'll talk to her soon. Take care of your mother for me while I'm gone."

He hangs up. I look at Sasha and think about if I should tell her what he said or if it will hurt her feelings. She told me once that right before Dad left for business, he and Mom got into this big fight and that it was scary. Mom and Dad fight a lot, but what was strange was how shaken up Sasha seemed.

"Dad says he'll talk to you later. He has a meeting," I say, but Sasha just rolls her eyes and starts walking inside.

"Well, did you want me to tell him you really wanted to talk to him? Cuz I could do that, you know."

"Whatever, I'll just talk to him when I talk to him, you know?" And then she just goes inside like it's nothing not talking to Dad when I know she must want to like I want to. Plus during dinner Mom and Sasha are both quiet. Mom leaves before finishing her dinner to go and lie down. "Headache," she says and is gone for the rest of the night.

Later I start to think about all the ways I can move my hand inside myself to feel something, but my hand never makes it more than three inches below my belly button. In my head we're still in a broom closet. Rabbit Tooth strokes my hand gently before slamming it into the wall behind me and tying it back with rope.

Now he's locking me up inside the basement of his parents' house for days. One night he walks loudly and determinedly down the steps carrying a laundry basket. He drops his basket as soon as he sees me, scattering dirty clothes all over the ground. He runs past the washer and dryer to my tied arms and legs. And then without untying me, he starts piercing with his "you know what"; he goes in on me till he's finished.

. . . . . . . . . . . . .

On Monday I spend the whole school day trying not to say or think about anything that will send me straight to Hell. It's harder than it sounds. Like I could swear when Mrs. Bolax asked me to tell her the slope of $-6x$, she was really asking if I still believed in God and why I would be so disrespectful to Him in my own father's house.

I see Sasha sitting on our stoop after school. I'm unsure if I should tell her about my dreams or my feelings about Satan. I examine her face, searching for signs of treachery in her veins. "So," I say, "you ever feel like you're going to Hell?"

"All the time," she says, kicking her feet up and down on the steps of our building.

"Do you ever feel like you're being possessed by a demon that makes you do bad things?"

Sasha looks up from her feet, cross-eyed like she knows what's up. My body freezes, and I wonder if I've been caught.

But instead she says, "I ever tell you the story about Incubus?"

"Incubus?"

"He's a demon that lies on top of the woman when she's sleeping."

I feel my body getting hot. I don't want to sound too eager for information. I can't figure out how much she knows."Well," I say, trying not to look at her too hard, "what does he do to her?"

"You know what," she says with that same cross-eyed look.

"Then how does the woman get rid of him?"

"I think you can probably sprinkle salt on him, and he'll go away."

"Huh," I say, not sure what else to say. I watch the girls playing double Dutch across the street. "So what'd you do in school today?"

"Mom's getting in late tonight," she says, not looking at me. She seems upset. "She's meeting with my teachers. They're probably going to tell her that I'm failing math, but whatever."

"Oh." I'm not as good at playing Big Sister. "Wanna watch a scary movie?"

"Yeah, sure," she says and nods.

We go through Dad's closet of grown-up movies we're not supposed to know he has and find *The Exorcist*. It starts kinda slow until we get to the part where her bed is shaking—no, more like convulsing. I feel something crawling inside me. The little girl's face looks so scared. Until it starts to look like someone else's face. Like her own fear and evil thoughts are wriggling out her body, spreading across her bed, and seeping back inside her face—keeping her prisoner until the Devil swallows her whole. I don't wanna keep watching and neither does Sasha.

"Maybe we should turn this off before Mom catches us," I say.

"Yeah," Sasha says. "It's kinda boring anyway."

"Right," I say. "So boring."

I start to turn away toward my room when she goes, "You know, I had a dream about the Devil once."

I look at her, saying nothing.

"He took Dad."

"What do you mean he took Dad?"

"See, in the dream, me and him were talking in the kitchen, and his eyes got all red. Then his skin started growing feathers. Actually, I couldn't tell if it was his skin or just his sweater. He started talking, but no words were coming out. Just these clucking sounds like a chicken. Then I'm looking at him, and I realize he's not my father but the Devil— in the shape of a rooster."

"Devils can't be roosters."

"Devils can be anything. Then he just flies away."

"Roosters can't fly, Sasha."

"That's only because we won't let 'em. What do you think would happen if we stopped feeding them so much? I bet a rooster could fly just like any other bird if we didn't train 'em to get so fat that they could hardly walk. I mean all they can do is to peck out each other's eyeballs just to survive."

"But why would—"

"Look, the point is he just flew away. He left us to take care of Mom all by ourselves."

Her voice is shaking.

"I dunno, Sasha, maybe it didn't mean anything."

"Yeah maybe." She thinks about it. "But I think it means Dad's having another affair."

"No way. Mom forbade Dad from ever going back to that girl in Berlin."

"That's what she thinks."

"I guess so." I shrug, not really wanting to hear her explanation.

I mean there's no way Dad would cheat on Mom again.

"Is that why you didn't want to talk to him on the phone?"

"I mean think about it." She ignores me. "He leaves us in the dream, but he's too cowardly to do it as a man. He's gotta do it as a chicken. That's what cheaters do, you know. Cheaters cheat because they want to leave, but they're too chickenshit to say so. Then the other person gets mad and ends their marriage. It's like it's out of the cheater's hands or something."

"I guess. Look, I think we should go to bed now. Mom'll be home any minute."

"Sure, whatever." She shrugs.

We both just sit there until I feel my heart beating faster.

"Well, good night," I say finally and start to walk toward my room.

All I need to do is focus on making sure my room is safe, but when I get there, I'm hesitant. *I'm not scared*, I say, *I'm not a baby*, but I check the closets and behind the curtains for anything that might be lurking there. I mean that's just common sense. My windows are shut, but the grate for the heating vent has been permanently broken off. I find nothing in my closet but my stuffed animals and Barbie dolls, so I turn off the light. I touch my comforter, trying to believe in its inability to move. My thoughts are all over the place. Like I keep thinking about what Sasha said and if Dad really did go back to that girl in Berlin and how mad Mom would be if she found out and when is he coming back anyway? I take out my journal and write: *Sometimes I wonder if the difference between God and the Devil is that with one we sacrifice our bodies and with the other we sacrifice our freedom. I just wish I could remember which was which.* I put my journal away and start thinking about Rabbit Tooth and if he could've found out about my dreams somehow like maybe I wrote something about it when I was doodling, and he saw it and that's why he won't talk to me.

And then I start to think about Rabbit Tooth in the basement. I'm still there tied up when his footsteps grow louder. Now I can feel my head thudding back into the wall that I'm tied to. I can't tell what keeps pushing me so hard as Rabbit Tooth's barely made it past the washing machine. And the sound his dryer's making is like a bunch of screams trying to get out of there. I open my eyes and my bed is vibrating. No—shaking as though being moved, thudding loudly into the wall. Like the Devil's come to teach me a lesson. As soon as the feeling reenters my legs, I run all the way into Sasha's room without looking back.

"The Devil's coming for me!" I'm out of breath.

"What? What time is it? Get Mom," she says, half asleep, half angry. She has sleep issues too. I crawl beside her on the bed, ignoring her sleepy protests, and lean in close to face her.

"The Devil's coming for me," I say again. "I think it's because we watched *The Exorcist*. Did he come for you too?"

"Zora, are you sure about this?" she says. But she sits up anyway, realizing that this is serious.

"Look, Sasha. I mean the walls were screaming and coming in on me. And it wasn't a dream. The Devil really is coming for me. Maybe this is a premonition that you should be saving me or something."

"Yeah maybe." She thinks about it for a moment. Then she lies back down like she's going back to sleep.

"Sasha!"

"What?"

"So are you going to save me from the Devil or what?"

"Sure, sure." She sits up again and rubs her eyes. "So here's what we'll do. We'll perform an exorcism."

"All right," I say, but I'm a little hesitant.

"Hmm." She turns on her desk lamp and goes through the books on her bedside table. "Remember that story Mom told us about her cousin that they wouldn't let out of the house? She just played in her room by herself all those years," she says, still leafing through her books.

"No."

"Mom said the girl was possessed by Satan."

"Did they get rid of him? Because if they didn't, then you really shouldn't be telling me this story."

"They had to take her to a seer."

"What in the hell is a 'seer'?"

"I'm trying to find the book Mom gave me last Christmas. The one with all those ghost stories." She holds one up. "Here it is!"

"Hey, that's my book! Mom gave it to me because I told her I was writing a story about the Rolling Calf for school," I say and snatch for it, but her arms are too long, and she holds it high above my head.

"You'll get it back. I think it says what a seer is." She reads the gold-painted lettering across the cover, *The Anansi Stories.* Then she opens up *my* old-fashioned fancy leather covering. "Ahh, chapter two: 'The Seer.'" She starts scratching her chin like she's some sort of detective. "It says here that a seer is someone who sees things that other folks don't. They can cure people of ma-ladies, both real and imaginary."

"What's a ma-ladies?"

"I'm pretty sure it means you're sick."

"And what's an imaginary ma-ladies?"

"Good question." Sasha continues reading, "Ahh! To rid of a demon, slap the host several times to get the demon's attention."

"It doesn't say that. Let me see that." I try to grab the book from her hands.

"Or you can thrash a cocoyea broom across her face. It says they're made with bunches of coconut fronds tied together."

"You're not going to hit me with a broom, Sasha."

"Okay, okay. The other thing we could do is to smoke some special herbs."

"What—like drugs?"

"Or you can wrap yourself in a blanket that has the scent of another man's ghost."

"What?"

"Or a woman's ghost, I'm guessing."

"Why would I wanna do that?"

"Demons are very territorial, Zora. They can't be sharing blankets with any old spirit that walks along."

"You're not making any sense, Sasha. I think we need to call a priest."

"Hmm, let me look at you," she says and begins pulling my eyelids up to my eyebrows.

"Ow!" I say and slap her hands away.

"No. No demon yet. You're still you," she concludes, unfazed by my slap.

"How do you know?"

"If a demon was inside you, your pupils would be more cloudy looking—like a man was inside them, maybe."

"I don't even think you know what you're saying at this point."

Sasha gets up and goes into her closet and brings down her heavy wool blanket.

"Look, Sasha, you're not listening to me. The demon's not even in me yet. It's in my room. All these instructions are about how to get a demon out of a body. How will we get the demon out of my *room*?"

Sasha stops between her closet and her bed, dropping her blanket on the floor as though finally catching up.

We run into my room, stopping in the doorway for a few minutes, afraid to go inside. Sasha's the one to finally flick on the light switch. The room is quiet now; my bed is stationary. I remain in the doorway. Sasha examines the walls, running her hands up and down the sides and puts her ears to the walls to see if she can hear anything.

"He's not in your walls," she decides.

"How do you know?" I ask.

"Lord, Zora, stop asking me things!" Sasha throws up her arms in frustration.

We hear footsteps coming from down the hall. Our mother stands in the doorway—the look on her face makes her five feet taller than she was when she handed us the phone the other day. She's carrying her swizzle stick, the eight-pointed star at the end of it twirling in the air. She doesn't say anything. She's waiting for us to come up with a good explanation that won't result in us getting a beating.

"Mom." Sasha steps in front of her, ready to give it a try. "Zora heard the Devil in here earlier." She whispers, "We think he's in the room with us right now."

"You children were supposed to be in bed from 10:30."

I can tell that this isn't the explanation Mom is looking for. Her voice is gaining heat. She's tapping the stick lightly against her palm now.

"We're sorry, Mom," I say and bow my head a little to show her that I mean it.

"Come here," she says.

I walk slowly toward her.

"You too, Sasha."

Sasha doesn't say anything this time, just walks up right behind me. Mom holds the stick up in the air, and I duck down on instinct, waiting to feel the lash. When I don't feel anything, I look up. Mom's just staring at us. Her eyes are small and squinted—just big enough to show us her anger. She's biting her lips like she's trying to stop herself from saying something. I can't decide one way or another, but I don't think I've ever seen her look this way before.

And then the sounds come. The things are beating on all four walls. It sounds like things dying, like things crying out to be saved.

Sasha moves closer to me like she's gonna take my hand but doesn't. "Is that what you heard?"

"Shh," says my mother. She puts a finger to her mouth and walks toward the wall. She moves to sit down on my bed, looking like a deflated balloon. "Hmm," she says. The shaking keeps going and going. Sasha puts her hand on the wall so she can feel the vibration. I stay close to Sasha for protection. Mom just sits there, putting a hand to her belly like she's protecting my new sister from the shaking too. The screaming and thudding finally get quiet after a while. And then it stops.

"You know"—she looks up at the ceiling like she's talking to God—"it just might be de Devil." She starts to rub circles around her temple like she's trying to rub him out. "Your father's going to be living in Europe for the next few months," she says finally.

We look at her.

"On business," she adds.

No one says anything for a while. My mother eventually gets up and walks toward the doorway before turning around.

"Come," she says.

So we sleep in Mom's bed that night, all four of us. Mom snores in between us while we shield her and the baby from harm on either side. I decide not to give her any more information about the seer. Wouldn't want to worry her. I stay awake, trying hard to only hold on to thoughts that will protect my mother, but the others come anyway. I take out my journal and write: *Dear Mommy, sometimes I wish I was strong like you, but other times I wish you were stronger.*

I close my eyes and pretty soon I'm in the basement again. The machine's not running, and there's dirty laundry all over the floor. I hear Rabbit Tooth's leather boots coming down the stairs. He's wearing a nice autumn-brown sweatshirt that brings out his eyes, and he's carrying a whip.

I tell him, "Not now, Jay. This isn't a good time."

"Is it ever a good time?" He smiles at me. He strokes my cheek gently with his left hand, cracks the whip on the floor with his right. He comes closer, breath heavy, smelling strange. His lips are maybe half an inch away from my neck. And for the first time I notice a large rock on the ground near a pile of socks. There's glass all around us.

"What's that?" I ask him.

"The window's broken. You're not cold, are you?"

I look up at the one window I can see from where I'm tied. It is indeed broken, and it is indeed cold. I start to get scared like I should get out of the dream, but I want to know where this is going.

"Someone's coming to join us," he says.

I start to wriggle in the rope he's tied me with, trying to get loose.

"Look, Jay, I think I want to go—like for real now."

"Look." He points to the windowsill. And it's my dad. He's come in the shape of a rooster. He looks at me, real disappointed like. I'm feeling pretty embarrassed. Dad looks over at Rabbit Tooth. Leans his wings and puffy chest in closer. And then he eats him; just gobbles him up limb by limb. At this point I have to wake up.

When I come to, I hear a sound. Not a scream this time, but a murmur. I get out of bed, careful like so as not to wake the others. But right when I walk toward the walls, it's like they get silent. I press my ears to the faded chipped paint and listen. I hear something soft that doesn't quite sound like the Devil. But it sounds like something. It is a thing like singing.

"Who's there?" I say, a little scared.

I hear it again. I feel like I should be praying, but I can't think of what I could possibly say to God right now that wouldn't sound stupid.

"The Devil's back?" Sasha comes up behind me, making me jump.

"Shhh!" I say, not wanting to wake Mom.

"What?" she whispers.

"I heard something," I say.

"What?" she says again.

"Just something," I say. "Like singing."

"What you mean, 'singing'?"

"Shh. Listen." I point to the wall.

Sasha puts her ear close to it and listens. It's silent a moment and then we both hear it. I can't put my finger on what it sounds like, but I know I've heard it before.

"Hmm." Sasha starts to scratch her chin.

"Yeah, I was gonna pray, but . . ."

"Sounds like a pigeon," she decides.

Once she says it, I feel silly. It does sound a lot like the noises pigeons are always making outside my window.

"It's not a pigeon, Sasha," I say, although now I'm not so sure.

"Hmm," Sasha says, scouring the walls.

We both notice the empty heating vent in the corner. "Ahh of course!" she says. "The birds must've got in through your heating vent. Just as I suspected."

"You never suspected that. You—"

"All right, all right," Sasha says, throwing up her hands.

We hear the sound again. Sasha's right, it could definitely be a pigeon. But it sounds like something else too. The singing sounds almost human.

"What if it's not a pigeon?" I say, getting scared again.

"Hmmm."

"I'm thinking maybe we should pray."

"Okay," she says. I let out a little sigh of relief. I wait for her to tell us what to do next. "Well," she says, "there's that song we learned that time in Sunday school about the great speckled bird. We could sing that. That's kinda like praying, right?"

"Yeah, sure," I say. "Except I don't know any of the words."

"Yeah, me neither. Except for the part that says the bird's name is recorded in the Bible."

"Hmm. Yeah."

"Or we could just sing 'Like a Prayer' by Madonna."

"Yeah, that sounds better."

She nods, takes a deep breath, and starts in a few pitches too high. "Mmmmmmm!"

I join in with my out-of-breath-like rasp. "Aaahhhhh!"

"Mmmmmaaaaaahhhh!" we sing in unison.

I look back at Mom, who is still sleeping peacefully, her snores underscoring the chorus. I look out the bedroom door, imagining my stuffed animals trying to peek from around the corner in my room to see what all the fuss is about.

From the window, the sky is the bluest it's been all week. People walk the streets below us, pushing laundry carts, collecting cans and bottles from the trash for quarters like always. Outside looks just like any other day.

The walls start to shake with birds or girls or something else altogether as we sing to them.

# CHAPTER 3

# Tall Tales from Sasha Also Known as Ashes aka the Mannish Girl

*Sasha/Ashes*

Brooklyn, NY
May 1999

### 5/3/1999
*Four Weeks Before the Baby Comes and Changes Everything*

So this is about two weeks after Mom spins this elaborate bedtime story—the one where Dad's in Europe on "business" for like the ump-teenth time. Dad still calls every week or so saying, yeah, he'll be back to see Zora star as Lady Liberty in the school play, yeah, he'll be back to talk to my teachers and find out where all this "backsliding" behavior's been coming from. Yeah, I heard Mom yelling at him on the phone about missing parent-teacher conferences. He didn't want to talk to me. Don't worry, it's not like I care to be sitting behind those rose-colored lenses. But with the new baby coming at any moment, there isn't much space in the house. Even with my own room, I still have Zora bugging me like every five minutes for everything: *What does it feel like to be kissed? What does it feel like to be a woman? What does it feel like to drink beer in the park with high school girls and not get caught?* Zora doesn't get that I'm really not into all that. We used to be like two peas. But in the last few weeks, even she doesn't see that I'm changing.

## 5/6/1999
### Dad's Wardrobe

My favorite room in our house is Dad's study. Mom put all his clothes and stuff in there so that she doesn't have to sleep with it every night. She had me help her move his entire dresser and medicine cabinet into his office. No one goes in there except for me. I go in there like two, three times a week in between doing homework or running errands for Mom when she's lying on the sofa because of one of her latest "dizzy spells" and Zora's off in space obsessing over some boy who barely acknowledges her existence or some other dumb shit.

Back when he was around, Dad used to come home from work late to find me in his wardrobe fast asleep under his cardigans. He would pull me out his closet, put me in his lap, and say, "I thought I sensed my shadow in here." But not anymore. The last time he found me like that was right before he left for "Europe."

"Didn't we just give you your own room? Maybe Zora would be more appreciative," he said, eyebrows all raised, lips curled into a dough-nut twist.

But still, whenever I'm in my father's study, it's like I'm in my own little world that no one can enter but me. I have this whole ritual I go through every time I'm in there. First, I sift through his work sweaters: Calvin Klein crew necks modeled after the Bill Gates "smart and casual" look—20 percent off at Burlington Coat Factory. Then there's the burgundy striped ties he got at Bobby's—five ties for the price of three. These I wear with the Syms Burberry cuff links and the Payless Oxford-style dress shoes, 60 percent off original retail price if you buy them in August for their Back to School special. I step outside the closet with big slow strides so his Oxfords don't slip off mid-step, and I look in the mirror.

But something's not quite right. For starters my plaits are too long and wiry looking. I used to undo them every chance I got, but Mom likes to fuss too much. Second, my face is too small, too bony—aside from my cheeks, which look to me like a cherub's. My chin looks like the letter *V*.

My eyelashes are long like I took a curler to them—like I'm *trying* to look like a girl. It's embarrassing. My bee stings are turning into giant plums that plop around in front of me wherever I go. I like to bend my knees so that I can only see myself from the neck up. This helps sometimes.

I'd like to say I'm reminiscent of a young Denzel Washington or a *Pulp Fiction*-style Samuel L. Jackson right now. But something's not quite right. I open the left mirror cabinet: Benadryl (for Dad's allergies), Mom's extra stash of Excedrin, which she's been taking like every night now for the past few weeks, meclizine, which she takes for her dizzy spells, and extra floss. Behind all this I find the shaving cream—the Taylor of Old Bond Street kind. I know how to beat it real fast so it lathers right up into foam and looks like whipped cream from when he used to let me do this last step for him. Then he'd finish the shave himself with a razor.

When it comes time for me to do my face, I put a butter knife to my cheek to wipe off the foam. After a while the cream slides slowly off my face and onto Daddy's shirt, which I then have to wash before Mom finds out. Afterward I use the set of grocery bags I have stashed by the mirror to dispose of the evidence. I throw the bag out on the corner when I'm running errands for Mom who's *tired of having to carry the whole household while we just sit there not lifting a finger.* It's okay, though, because that way I can replace the tub of shaving cream before anyone can notice.

### Later on 5/8/1999

So there's this thing that happened in Dad's study two days ago. I don't wanna talk about it. Well, maybe I do. So I'm admiring my clean shave in the mirror and feeling kind of pleased with myself, when I look into the toilet bowl. It's awful: horrible, evil, red blotches are desecrating the white bowl. It's hard to say whether my mother will be excited for me or whether she'll strap me down and lock me up for becoming a "woman."

Not that I'm going to tell her. I'm not one of those girls who's trying to cheat puberty either. I would never wanna be a boy, but I don't know that I'd ever want to be a woman. Boys just want to pound each other to the ground and laugh every time they hear a fart or the word "boob," and girls think that's funny. That almost makes girls worse. Like the other day we were all sitting around in the park, and Crystal asked Joey who he thought out of all us girls would give the best head. Joey said Vicky would cuz she can put a rubber band on a pickle with just her tongue. She was the only girl who could do it when we all tried last summer. But then Jerry said, no Sasha would cuz she got those big Black-girl lips. I wanted to knock him into next Tuesday, but I played it cool and said his dick was probably so small it'd be like sucking on a toothpick. Meanwhile Crystal had already dissolved into laughter.

5/10/1999
*On the Curse of the Red Clap*

Nobody can believe that I'm turning fifteen soon and only just got my period. Shay refers to it as the Red Clap. I remember Mom told me once that your period can be your privilege or your sentence, so you'd better use it wisely. And to be honest, it's been kind of a pain lying to her about the whole thing. Like I've been using my lunch money to buy the pads that I now gotta throw out along with the shaving cream. Plus the cramping's been real bad, but she keeps getting on my case about helping out more before the baby comes, so I just put some rice in a sock with a rubber band and microwave it and keep it underneath my belt to help ease the pain.

5/11/1999
*Even More on the Curse of the Red Clap*

So get this: the week I get the Red Clap just so happens to be the week of the annual spring potluck at school. You think this shit's too ironic to be true? Well, fuck, so do I, but it happened.

Like right when we're at the school entrance and trying to get inside,

Mom goes, "I know." She's gripping on to my jacket sleeve pretty hard, and I'm not sure what's coming next. I think she's probably about to slap me, but instead she says, "It's beautiful," and kisses me on the forehead. I'm confused, but I try to smile cuz I think maybe Mom's a changed woman, and this is all that's gonna happen to me tonight. That was until she says something to Mrs. Harpy—mother of Kimberly Harpy and president of the PTA—the one Mom calls Demon Harpy behind her back.

I'm sitting down about to enjoy some mac and cheese with some string beans when Harpy taps her glass and announces that Mrs. Porter (my mother) would like to make a toast:

"Ladies and gentlemen!" Mom begins in the voice she uses for white people—overly enunciated words with long pauses like maybe she thinks the stretching out of every vowel will thin out her accent. "My daughter"—pause—"has recently"—tears well up in her eyes— "become a woman!"—wipes tears. It's quite the performance, but the smirk out the corner of her lips lets me know that this was her revenge plan all along, and I have to say I'm impressed by how well the punishment fits the crime.

Shit looks particularly bad because Shay's sitting two tables away with her eyes turned downward and when Shay's too embarrassed to even look at you, you know you're never gonna live this one down anytime soon. Of course she might've just had her head down because her grandmother made her wear that girly red sundress. She kept twitching and kicking her legs—like that would change something. Meanwhile, I kept trying not to stare at the way she stayed flexing her calf muscles as she kicked her legs back and forth, back and forth, until her grandmother reprimanded her.

5/12/1999
*About Germany*

I walk through the park a lot now to clear my head. I think about shit like my mom and why she didn't just have the abortion. I know I'd never have a baby if my husband was off screwing some Eurotrash ho in Germany or wherever the hell he really is. Zora still acts like this shit's not happening, but she wasn't there when the bitch called, and I answered the house phone. Dad had already answered from his office line in his study, so I hung up and picked up again real slow, putting my hand over my nose so they couldn't hear me breathe. Dad was sweet-talking his woman in some half-English/half-German tongue.

Of course it turned out that he heard me anyway. I figured that out the next morning when he knocked me across my face and slammed me up against my desk. Then I was late to school cuz I had to ice my cheeks so as not to get those funny looks at school or get sent to the school social worker again.

Anyway, Zora doesn't get that the man's probably been two-timing Mom since before we were born. A part of me always feels like even if Zora did know the whole truth—like if I took her aside and told her everything like I used to—that she'd still wind up taking his side and leave me alone to clean up his mess with Mom while the two of them went traveling the world telling stories together.

I can tell stories. Like just last month I told Mom I joined the basketball team so that I could hang out with the girls in the park. Mom doesn't believe in curfew, so she clocked forty-five minutes for the amount of time it should take me to get home. So if I'm home more than fifty minutes after "practice" lets out without an official note from the "coach," I get the switch. But it's worth it. This way I get to hang out with Shay and her crew. I met Shay in the park a couple months ago. She's a few grades above me at school so we never talked until that day, but I did notice her walking past my locker once, dressed like Salt from Salt-N-Pepa. Shit was fly. She even gave me the head nod when she caught me looking.

First time she invited me to sit with them, they were sitting on the stones by one of the miniature waterfalls, drinking bottles of Busch Light like it was their own backyard. Shay's overall straps were hanging over her waist, and through her black and yellow skate tee I could see no plums.

"So you're Sasha," Shay says, eyeing me up and down. "We're like two giraffes," she said, because we were both tall and made of bones.

### 5/15/1999
### *About the Two Giraffes*

So for real, I think Shay and I are becoming real friends now. Once in a while she'll leave her crew to walk me home through the park to eat ice cream with her and her grandma. Her grandma's from Ghana, and whenever I see her, she gives me a FanIce ice cream pack, and I give her a new HitClip so that she can stay current *with all the racket kids are listening to these days.* Her grandma told me about all the words both Jamaican and Trinidadian patois share with her language, Twi. Like "unnu" or "unu" is the plural word for "you" as in, *what unnu pickney doing sittin' pon de television while dishes stay rot pon de sink?* And "buller" or "bulla man" for "penis," "sex," and "faggot," as in, *a bullet inna a bulla man go a long way.*

### 5/17/1999
### *On How I Discovered Plum Wrapping*

The first time we're in her room she locks the door and pulls me onto her bed.

"I know you're curious," she says, and I wonder if we're gonna kiss. I don't know if I feel excited or sick to my stomach that she would even dare. Her skin smells like rosewood and cardamom. Her breath smells like Bubble Tape. Her eyes are mischievous slits. She takes off her T-shirt. Her plums are being flattened by ACE bandage wrap and held together with masking tape. She smiles when she sees me looking at her chest, and she tries to take my hand, but I snatch it away. Suddenly I'm not sure I'm up for the challenge.

Shay throws her head back and laughs. "You can touch it," she says. "They don't bite." I look into my hands nervously. I was hoping for a bit more romance before this part.

"Besides," she says, "I only date femmes."

She can tell from my shrug that I have no idea what she's talking about.

"Girly girls. Not butches like me and you."

My chest tightens when she says that. I look away, trying to focus on the floral pattern on her bed, the swirls making my head hurt.

"Look," she says and peers away from me toward the ACE bandage wrap in her hands. "I only brought you in here cuz I thought you'd wanna try. Wrapping, I mean. I could show you."

I feel my face get hot. "What makes you think I'd wanna try that?"

Actually, I do know why. It's cuz of the time we were all talking about who had the nicest plums (she calls them titties), and I said that she did because you could hardly see them. I said I liked the way her torso looked sturdy and fit like a man's, and then the other girls laughed.

"Look, just because I said that I'd like to be smaller up here," I say, pointing to my plums, "doesn't mean that I'm like . . ."

"A dyke?" She sighs, puts her hands on her knees, and stares me down, cold. "My father hates them too, you know."

Her emphasis on the word "too" causes me to wrap my hand around my stomach.

"My mom's probably wondering why I'm not home for dinner. I should probably go," I say.

But as soon as I get home, there I am in the mirror: upset at the sight of those hanging plums. I wonder if she's right about what she said. *Butches like you.* So the next day in school I say, "Okay." She smiles and says, "Friday."

Shay tapes her plums down with tape every morning before school in the McDonald's bathroom. She has to untape them before her grandma gets home from volunteering at her church at 5:00 p.m. Shay taught me that if you take the pill every day without taking the placebo, you can stop getting your period forever. "Worst day of my life," she says. "Looked in the toilet and thought I would die."

I smile in recognition.

"All right." I take a deep breath. "But no peeking." I take off my shirt. She unrolls the ACE bandage slowly. She holds my arms out, and my body jumps a little as she circles around me with the wrap, her fingers pressing into me, reaching across my plums for a split second. She gives me a Hilfiger button-down and some jeans to try on.

"You look good," she says. "The Bulldogs are having a party to celebrate making it into the playoffs. You should come."

"Isn't that a college party?"

"Don't be such a pussy, Sasha. You'll never get laid."

She got me there.

"Butches gotta be fierce. In fact, I got a new nickname for you: Ashes. Sound deadly, don't it?"

### Later on 5/17/1999

I get home and Zora's yelling, "Where have you been?" the second I walk through the door.

"Yeah, yeah, yeah," I say, walking past her into my room and slamming the door. I can't handle her. Not now.

Of course a few moments later there she is lurking in my doorway, holding an envelope. She comes and sits on my bed. "Sasha?" she asks.

"Zora, can't you see I'm not in the mood?"

"It's just . . . you seem so mad lately. And you're never around."

I can see she needs some kind of reassurance from me that shows that things are still okay, so I say, "You know that girl Shay from my school? You hung out with us once at her grandma's house?"

"The one who dresses like a man?"

"Yeah, Zora. That one. What do you think about her? Like, what if I dressed like that?"

"Like a man?"

"See, Zora, this is exactly why I can't tell you things."

"No, Sasha, you got to," she says, almost pleading. "Look, you were right," she says and hands me the envelope in her hand.

It's addressed to our dad. It has no return address, but it was probably sent internationally based on the postage.

"It was in the trash. Can you believe it? That she would write a letter. *Here?*"

"Let me see that," I say, grabbing the envelope so I can examine it properly.

"I was waiting for you to open it, so should we?"

"I don't know. Maybe there's things you're better off not knowing."

"What's that supposed to mean?"

"Look, can we talk about this later? I got a lot of studying to do if I wanna keep Mom and Dad off my back."

The other thing I should probably tell you is that there is in fact another thing that happened just a few days ago. I can't seem to get this one out of my head. I'm walking out the park near the white side when I see someone who has to be my father getting out of a car on Prospect Park West and entering an apartment building. One of those buildings where white people like psychiatrists and pediatricians with home offices live. Dad's wearing the Calvin Klein crew neck with some khakis and sunglasses. That's all I could see.

5/19/1999
*So I Decide to Tell Zora*

"I saw Dad."

She moves closer to me and puts her hand on my arm. "Where'd you see him?"

"By the Bandshell."

"When?"

"Few days ago."

Nods.

"Was he with anyone?"

"Dunno."

The conversation doesn't go much further. We watch *Scream* to get our mind off things. Mom cooks pelau for the third time in a row. The taste is dry and ricey.

The next day after school Zora says, "Let's find him," and so we stand by the building on Prospect Park West.

"We don't give out tenant information," the doorman says and escorts us back outside.

5/20/1999
*Searching*

I start walking down Prospect Park West every day after school to see if I can find him. When I don't, I think about Shay instead, the feel of her calf muscles next to mine.

5/21/1999
*Today Mom Found Out That I'm Not Really on the Girls'*
*Basketball Team So Now I'm in Some Real Shit*

Also, she says Dad's coming home. I can't tell if she's for real or not.

5/22/1999
*She's for Real*

She made us clean the walls with vinegar this time. Maybe I never saw him in the park after all.

## 5/23/1999
### *The Night of the Party*

Is when we decide to make the plan of all plans: me and Zora are pretending that we're staying over at Amelia's—the Christian girl with all the cats. See Amelia's been owing Zora this favor ever since Zora let Amelia copy her Spanish homework for like a week when she was out with the flu. Now in exchange for this favor, I gotta take on all of Zora's chores until the baby comes, but that's pretty much a walk in the park for me since I'm basically grounded anyway, except for tonight. Zora puts a doo-rag over my head and pulls out the pinstriped button-down from Dad's closet instead of the horizontal stripes I was initially gonna go with. Girl has taste.

When we finish, Zora stands before me, admiring her creation.

"Well, you did it," she says. "You look like a man."

"Okay, okay, but do I look like Denzel or what?"

"I wouldn't go that far."

"Samuel L. Jackson?"

"I don't know about all that, Sasha. Maybe Marlon Wayans. Maybe," and then, "So you like her, don't ya? Shay, I mean."

I roll my eyes in response.

"It's okay. I mean if you're going to Hell then so am I." She smiles.

You gotta smile back at her for that.

"Thing is, we're cool cuz we both like to dress all butch or whatever—you know, masculine-like."

Nods.

"But she says she only dates girly girls."

"Sounds like a conundrum."

"Exactly."

"Maybe dress like a girl for a night, get her all excited, and then say, see it's the inside that counts."

"That's corny, Zora."

"I dunno, maybe she likes that gushy stuff. I know I would."

"You and me are different, Zora. The biggest sin you ever committed was about getting in trouble watching *The Exorcist*."

Zora has this look like she's gonna say something, but she just gets quiet instead.

5/24/1999

*The Aftermath: Where Shit Really Hits the Fan*

The party was all right. Shay spends the whole night talking to some cheerleader with braces.

"Yo, white girls are so easy," she tells me when we leave. "All it took was for her boyfriend to leave and a double shot of Malibu, and she was ALL over me."

We're standing alone on the curb while she smokes a cigarette. She tries to give me the pound, but I just roll my eyes and shift away from her.

"She's probably just using you." I try to sound real casual and look out at the cars so she can't read my face.

"Oh don't be mad just cuz you ain't got game, sis. You just wanna sit in the corner and wait for the girls to come to you. Femmes expect butches to be like men—only nicer. We gotta make the first move."

"Don't call me sis."

"Whatever."

I leave early even though the plan was to spend the night out so as not to ruin our whole alibi. I could go to Amelia's, but I don't wanna have to deal with Zora asking me how it went and all that.

So I go home. I walk inside, and there he is standing in the kitchen with a Marlboro and a glass of whiskey in hand.

"Daddy?" I get closer, wanting to poke him to make sure he's real.

"Sasha," he says. His voice is tired. "Would you like to explain to me what you're doing walking in at this hour?"

"Nothing . . . I mean I was over at Amelia's with Zora, but I felt sick, so I came home."

And that's when he looks me up and down assessing the button down I took from his closet, the Knicks cap I borrowed from Shay the day before. I shield my face just in case a slap is coming.

"We'll talk about this tomorrow," he says. "Get to bed before your mother hears you. It's a school night."

### 5/26/1999
### Dad's Home

Like nothing's changed. Mom seems happy he's here, but quieter too. His first day back and it's like they've stopped fighting altogether. Of course they don't really talk much either. If he walks in the kitchen, she leaves to use the bathroom. If she's lying on the sofa watching *Touched by an Angel*, Dad goes out for a smoke. I'm glad because it means he probably hasn't had the chance to tell her about me coming in late last night dressed like a man. I wanna say things like, "Where the hell have you been?" but he's the first to speak.

"Let's go for a walk," he says.

We walk through the gardens the way we used to, and I feel lucky that he took me and not Zora, like maybe I can be his favorite too. Of course, I also feel pretty tense knowing that he could snap at me at any moment, call me a mannish girl or a sodomite—or worse. As we walk, he points out the technical names for flowers, saying things like "The peonies here are part of the Paeoniaceae family" and "It's too bad the Cherry Blossom Festival is over and done with at the gardens this year. I would've loved to take you there." His voice has this new zest to it. I try to listen for that turn to the sharper tone, the one where he emphasizes all the consonants—something to signal that things are about to change so that I'll expect it before he throws me to the ground.

We exit on Ninth Street, and I know that it's happening. We take the elevator to the eighteenth floor. Inside the apartment, the AC is on high, and it smells like too much air freshener and dog hair. But there's also a real hardwood floor (instead of carpet) and a real marble counter.

Also, the expensive-looking couches don't have the plastic covering over them the way that ours do. There is a real porcelain bowl with real fruit to eat and candles that have been taken out of their wrapping so they can actually be used for light and not just for decoration. And there's a dog. Certainly not a Caribbean household. I look at everything in the apartment before I look at her.

"Aren't you going to say something?" my father asks me in his trying-to-be-polite-around-whitefolks voice.

"Oh, it's nice to meet you, Mrs. . . ."

"Call me Adaliz," the woman says. She holds out her hand with painted fingernails. She's wearing a red cashmere sweater and khaki slacks. She has long blond hair that reaches to the middle of her back. Not nearly as pretty as Mom. Probably makes good money, though, from the looks of things. She asks me if I want any chocolates. She says she brought them all the way from Belgium. I say nothing, but Dad says, "Of course she does," and stuffs some in my palms. The woman looks real nervous suddenly, shuffling back and forth, rubbing her hand around her stomach in slow meditative motions. It takes me a minute of staring at her hand-over-stomach to realize that she's rubbing what looks a lot like Mom's belly bump a few months in.

"How long has she been living there?" I ask when we leave.

"Don't tell your mother about this," he says, taking out a cigarette. "She's just an old friend I like to visit from time to time."

"Oh, so why'd you want me to meet her anyway?"

"I thought you should know a woman as accomplished as her. Graduated third in her class from Oxford. You need to start thinking more seriously about your future at your age. Needless to say that nobody is impressed with your academic performance as of late."

I mumble a response.

"Speak up, Sasha."

"Thank you, Daddy," I say.

"You're welcome. And don't repeat any of this to Zora. She's too young to understand."

"About going to college?"

"Don't be smart, Sasha."

## 5/28/1999
### *Since That Day I've Started Finding New Ways to Sneak Out*

Sometimes one of them will catch me, and I'll get the switch, but that's about as bad as it gets, and it probably would've happened anyway based on how I've been doing in school. My progress reports will come through the mail any day now and not only am I already failing math, but I'm only pulling a C in Chem and U.S. History. Dad hasn't really been on my back cuz of the deal I guess we made. The one where I say nothing and he holds off on giving me the switch or the belt or the swizzle stick for a while. Turns out the reason he knew about me is that doorman. Guess he doesn't know that Zora was there too. Zora's not sure if we should tell Mom about what happened. Yeah, I told Zora eventually.

## 6/1/1999
### *My Last Entry for a While*

At some point I decide to tell Mom. I run all the way home, ready to tell her everything. Like maybe if she knew, this time she'd leave him for good. But I get inside and there *he* is, holding *my* baby sister. Mom's standing right beside him with a sleepy grin on her face. Mom's doula and midwife are sitting on the sofa holding some paperwork. Zora's there too, gazing in amazement like this child's the second coming or something. If you ask me, she's the ugliest baby I've ever seen: a bald and wet-looking bundle with giant eyes and puny alien-looking limbs.

"Come give your new sister a kiss," Mom says.

"Don't you want to hold your sister?" Dad asks.

I wanna say no, but my tongue feels frozen so I just stare at the thing. With all the crowding around it and with Zora poking at it like it's pudding, I decide to stay put. Another sister. Lucky me.

"You've got to be fucking kidding me," I say. I storm into my room before either one of them can run after me with the swizzle stick. I lie on my bed for a minute, then two. Nobody comes. "Well, shit, maybe now they'll finally treat me like the older sister for once. Can say whatever the hell I want."

Still nothing.

Eventually I get hungry, so I have to go outside. In the living room, Zora's holding the baby and making stupid faces. Mom is on the couch looking zonked out of her mind. And Dad? He's on the floor, Mom's feet in his hands. He looks up at me and puts a finger to his lips. "Your mother needs her rest," he whispers.

He motions for me to sit by him. His beard has grown out with bits of gray scraggle. His broad arms look flabbier, more tired.

He strains a smile. "How about I let you two take over," he says to Zora and me before walking into his room and closing the door.

"You ready to hold her yet?" Zora asks me when he leaves.

I look at Zora hesitantly and then at the alien. I wonder how long it will be till Dad sneaks off to his other baby—the whiter one. I wonder how long it will take him to leave us altogether. "All right," I say and attempt to hold her. The baby feels less alien-like now that she's in my arms. She opens her mouth into an O, yawning, stretching tiny baby fingers toward me. "She's okay, I guess," I say, hiding a smile.

"Things will be different now, Sasha. You'll see." She has this wise-older-sister look on her face that I've never seen her wear before.

After a few minutes of me holding the baby, Mom starts to stretch and opens her eyes. She smiles at us being sisterly toward one another. "Look who's returned," she says, pointing a lazy finger at me.

She looks pretty worn, but there's a grin on her face.

I look from the baby to Mom, deciding if I should just say it, when Zora steps in, stealing my thunder: "Dad's cheating again. This time it's serious."

"Zora!" I say. I can't decide if I'm mad that she beat me to the punch or if I'm suddenly thinking that telling Mom is a bad idea.

Mom just shifts, then yawns. Says nothing.

Zora keeps going. "There's letters, too. We think he got her pregnant."

Mom laughs a little girl's giggle that transforms into a loud cackle. "So I see he twenty-woman and dem finally catch up with him, ent," she says, still laughing. "Just hush nah child and let me see my baby."

I bring my new sister toward her. She takes her from me, stroking her face and head.

"A mistress with a baby on the way?" She laughs again. "Maybe now he'll learn," she says.

"Aren't you even mad at him?" Zora asks.

I don't say anything, but of course I'm wondering the same thing.

"More important things on my mind," she says. "You might understand it one day."

We both look at her, confused. She reaches her free hand toward us, beckoning. "Then again, I hope you won't," she says and smiles.

I can't figure out if it's the baby or the fact that Zora's news holds some kind of redemptive power over Mom—freeing her from worrying about what she's always known to be true, but the woman looks positively giddy. Still, if you were just watching us all huddled around the baby with sleepy grins and didn't know our story, you could take a picture, call us, "The new mosaic American family"—the perfect Kodak moment.

# CHAPTER 4

# Once Upon a Time:
## Featuring Star Scars & Dreams of Flight

Discovery Bay, Jamaica & Brooklyn, NY

1975–1997

THIS ONE WILL GIVE YOU HOPE.

See, once upon a time there was a girl. And this girl grew to be a woman. And this woman had the ability to conjure stories from ghosts. Now this conjure woman fell in love with a man who could see beneath her scars. He believed in magic once too.

You see, the man and his conjure woman—they weren't always like this. No, once upon a time the two kissed, they fucked, and talked long into the night while he tried to trace the shape of burn scars across her back. His favorite was the one in between her shoulder blades. It looked like a cartoon wave. The first time he saw it, he asked her if he could ride her wave down to Jamaica and bring her back some curried crab while he was at it.

Beatrice laughed. "What a Jamaican tink he know about that? Curry crab is a Tobago ting." I could tell she was pleased, though, because she got up to change the record without draping her robe over her back.

He couldn't have known that this was the first time she had done this: allowed herself to be naked with a man she just met with the lights still on. He would probably never know about the number of times she'd dreaded this moment: the one where his voice becomes a gasp, where his eyes try not to cringe. He would never know that she had only ever been with one man other than him—a brief episode with the library clerk on

Grand Army Plaza. And of course there was the rape at fifteen, but she doesn't count that on her list anymore.

It was something in her unreserved strut to the record player singing lyrics from the Mighty Sparrow's "Jean and Dinah" that gave away her pleasure to be with him. "Dance with me," she said. It was the shuffling of her feet in fuchsia slippers that made him say yes. Her lack of pretense, her ability to get lost in sound like she'd never been humiliated enough to get called "shy."

Beatrice didn't realize how big a feat it was for Nigel to surrender to her in dance. Nigel's hips swiveled awkwardly, fighting against words that threatened to gaze, that threatened to comment. Soon his hips turned smoothly, his feet shuffled to meet hers. His eyes were a swing set, following the way her body twirled like ribbon. Girl was unreal. One minute her limbs would be flying through the air in all kinds of directions. Next minute she'd land on the carpet soft like a cat, shuffling around in her fuchsia-colored feet.

Let me tell you a story. This next part is what we call the foreground.

See, our fairy tale begins in 1983 when Nigel, our not-quite-valiant knight, was working as a custodian at the JP Morgan Bank on Empire. The man grew up dreaming of flight, having taken care of his immobile and diabetic mother for the past ten years. Each day back home in Discovery Bay would more or less start and end the same: one shot of insulin through his mother's arm. At 8:00 a.m. he would carry her to her rocking chair on the veranda so she could admire the scenery. Usually she'd wind up eyeing the mangoes on the tree three yards away, and he'd climb up to get her one.

After a few hours of breathing deeply the mountain air, remembering the way her husband used to sit at her feet with his guitar some nights singing, "Blessed Assurance," Nigel would recite to her sections from the Bible. Typically she asked him to read sections about the afterlife so that she might prepare herself to die with a light and holy heart. In the middle of breathing, Nigel would offer her arm a second injection of insulin. For supper, she asked for saltfish boiled three times. It no longer tasted like saltfish after the third boil, but it was her way of making a sacrifice (salt) without consciously admitting that she was doing so. She could still say that she was eating saltfish after all. At this point came her third shot of insulin. Then back outside for more breathing and the singing of hymns to bring up memories of her late husband. Subsequently came the final shot in the shoulder before tucking his mother into bed.

Every day ended for Nigel with him opening the box of things that belonged to his father before he killed himself—the day he lay down on his company's conveyor belt and became one with the molten cryolite. This was three years after his firstborn was found dead in a hurricane lying in the arms of another man. It was also the night the news spread that Australia had become the world's largest producer of bauxite aluminum followed by Guinea. Rather than get laid off with the hundreds of others, he'd decided to play God.

He was supposed to join his father at the factory after graduating from secondary school, but after a man becomes chopped liver and seared heart, it's not surprising that his son would begin to make other plans. His mother, of course, did not mind his company in the least.

But in all this, I must admit that it was hard for me to watch him like this.

You see, I was sitting in the blank spaces of a story, waiting to be remembered. I recall being everywhere, being unable to move my limbs. I'd say it was almost like watching a car crash. Only it wasn't like watching. Humans have this ability to watch the crash, watch the numbers rise and fall like stocks: 24,000 killed today, the news might say. Today it's only 12,000. What a shame. Turn to watch the sunset instead. Enjoy that.

I apologize for getting personal, as I know you came here today to read a fairy tale.

This is the part of the story where the miracle occurs.

This particular miracle occurred for Nigel while he was writing by his windowsill. Writing, after all, is the place where miracles tend to happen.

In this moment, Nigel swore he felt a mist coming up to his lips. The mist grew hot and burned his lips. He jumped back and saw that it was a giant ball of fire. The ball turned out to be Ole Higue.

For those who may be unaware, Ole Higue is a woman who flies through the sky like a fireball and sucks your blood, leaving you with embarrassing hickies. Also known as the soucouyant, Ole Higue is deathly afraid of salt: sprinkle a whole bottle full on your front door and she will stop to count each and every grain.

In this case, however, Ole Higue did not come to suck on the neck of our dear Nigel, but instead, motioned for him to climb on her back. Now Nigel shuddered at first, knowing that Ole Higue rarely comes in peace. But the thought of flying on someone's back, even if that someone was a satanic bloodsucking fiend, was just too enticing an offer to pass up. So he grabbed on tight and ignored the heat as they bolted out the window and flew upward toward the moon. Bits of overcooked skin (either hers or his) kept flaking off his hands as he tugged, but he couldn't help but be seduced by the feeling of burning stars passing him by. The air soon got thin, and his nose started to bleed, but he got the feeling that it would all be worth it in the end.

It was cold on the moon, not at all like Swiss cheese. Ole Higue patted his head and left him there. He sat on the moon feeling bored. He kicked himself for his lack of appreciation for this life-changing happening, thinking, Ah moon! Ah humanity! He spent a good forty-five minutes of pacing, of trying to make sense of things, of feeling bored and depressed, of kicking himself for feeling bored and depressed before he saw her: the spirit of Beatrice. You could recognize her by the ocean- and star-shaped scars across her neck, her back, her shoulders—one in the shape of a cartoon wave. Nigel, of course, did not know that this would soon be the love of his life for the next two years, the mother of his children for twenty-two, and his deepest regret till the day he would die from an aneurysm at the age of eighty-one. All he knew at this moment was that she was the kind of woman that Neruda wrote about. He tried to talk to her, but the words got stuck somewhere in his throat. The spirit of Beatrice came closer to him. She had one particular scar on her neck that at that moment (and never again with the real Beatrice) looked to him like the Statue of Liberty. And then she vanished. Ole Higue returned to bring him home.

The next morning, Nigel awoke with a plan. He marched into each and every business establishment in Discovery Bay, Montego Bay, and Ocho Rios demanding work. After a few months, he was sent to a rum distillery where he was able to make a decent-enough wage to hire a woman to come cook and clean for his mother thrice a week. He saved up for the next few years until he had enough money to fly to America. He left his mother a note that read "Apologies" and nothing more.

When Nigel first arrived in NYC, dimes in his pockets, ideas in his head, and no time to write, he set out to fulfill yet another humble dream: become the first Black president of J.P. Morgan. Of course when he first asked for the job, they laughed at him and told him he could sweep the floors instead. But rather than give up, he brought each man in the office coffee every morning and went without eating dinner four nights a week until they gave him the job of maintenance man. He would stay up all night doing research on accounting and third-world economic development and leave it under the doorway of the director with a note that said "Always Ready to Serve." And so it was that after a late night's work of sweeping and research, Nigel had caught the director coming out of the bathroom and very bluntly explained to him that the future of their organization was dependent on him. The very next day he was offered the job of bank teller before six months later landing the job of J.P. Morgan's vice president.

At least this is the version Nigel tells his children years later. In reality, however, Nigel never got hired by this particular bank. In fact, after the third time chastising him for leaving notes under managers' doors, they felt compelled to let him go. When he first met Beatrice, she encouraged him to enlist in community college, and he was able to transfer to Hunter two years later. Following this, he was offered the job of bank teller before becoming branch manager of the Brooklyn credit union within four years. When he told his daughters the fairy-tale version years later, he always tried to smile, though they could tell that beneath the skin, he was trying to forget the parts of the story he couldn't will himself to say out loud just yet.

Flash forward to the moment where they first meet on October 3, 1983:

Beatrice parades through those bank doors like she's a carnival float. She's determined to open her very first American bank account. She smiles at Nigel's red custodial suit on her way up to the fourth floor. It makes him look warm like Christmas.

First thing Nigel notices is the scar on the back of her neck that shines like a star. It reminds him of something. He doesn't say what.

"Does it glow in the dark?" he asks her.

She shifts uncomfortably. "Like the butt of a lightning bug."

So here's the other beginning. You see, our fairy tale actually begins in 1978, three years after Beatrice stepped off her plane in JFK, ready to make a name for herself. This meant three years of sleeping in a cot in the hallway of her mother's cousin's Flatbush apartment, three years of repenting from her short stint in teen rebellion, and three years of being exiled from her family for illicit behavior, in which time, Beatrice vowed never to disrespect God's house again.

Beatrice was a girl who always strived to be chaste and pious enough to be saved from a dungeon (or her mother's cousin's apartment as it were) by a prince (or a man with a job at the very least). She was sent to America by a not-quite-evil, not-quite-step mother who, nonetheless, nearly burned her only daughter alive for sleeping with a wrong one— but we'll get to that.

Now to show God that she meant business, our dear Beatrice would recite passages from Corinthians, chapter 6, every morning before tea. She joined the most stringent Catholic church she could find and only befriended those who seemed even more devout than her mother. This was a full-time endeavor. She walked through the rows of high-rises and skyscrapers like it was Babylon and she was sent there by God Himself to set things straight. She marched down Forty-Second Street, Wall Street, and Flatbush Avenue with her Bible over her crotch. This way no man would be able to gaze at her golden prize without remembering that she was a woman of God.

And whenever thoughts of the flesh did enter her young mind, she would kneel to pray. She prayed while waiting for the subway to City College. Just stared into the eyes of the giant platform rats and dared them to interrupt her time with the Lord. She prayed before classes. She prayed after classes. Anytime her thoughts drifted from the teacher's lecture to making grocery lists for the weekend or to the nice-looking young man (or the occasional woman) in her vicinity, she would get off her desk and kneel on the ground. Her teachers would pause occasionally but would usually continue on with their lectures. This was how she knew she was doing God's work.

The only time she didn't stop to pray was on her fifteen-minute walk home from the train station to her apartment. She avoided getting down on her knees in the middle of her walk for fear of being pickpocketed. She was sure the good Lord would understand. She settled on sneering at the impure men who stood on street corners gawking and calling out to her without the decency to at least address her as empress or sistren as they once did on Ariapita Avenue. *Hey, shorty, hey, mama, and hey, hot titties* were how they addressed her here in Flatbush. Her mother called occasionally, warning her to marry an American before it was too late and she died a barren disappointment to everyone.

Flash forward to December 3, 1983, where our story first began, Nigel's studio apartment: the room where they first make love. (Now I know you're probably wondering how Beatrice went from kneeling every time she had an impure thought to sleeping with her soon-to-be husband before marriage. It's an important question, which we'll get to eventually, though not now.)

"I saw you in a dream once," he says before it happens. "Ole Higue brought me to you and you shined like the Statue of Liberty."

"Sounds like her to do a thing like that," she says and blushes in spite of herself.

First comes more dancing before lying side by side. She kneads his scalp with her forefingers. Tries to push distractions out his mind. Like worries about his mother. The woman he hired to take care of her has been stealing fruit and silverware, but at least she shows up on schedule, and his mother has someone she can talk to. Beatrice's hands move down to his neck, down farther to twirl her fingers around his long chest hairs. She teases the breastbone till he moves her hand away and kisses it.

"Wait," he says, "just wait." His body shifts away from her.

*But shit I've waited long enough,* she thinks, and she has. So she pulls his weight—all two hundred pounds, nearly 60 percent muscle at the time—on top of hers. Her frame seems fragile as a doll's house from his perspective. But her tiny limbs maneuver his from underneath with the grace of a gymnast. Her legs stretch back to meet her ears, her arms pound fists into his back like Tarzan's. Her voice hollers words she didn't know she had. Words that should've been beaten and broken down into gibberish after more than two hundred years of bondage start rushing out her mouth like she's an Obeah woman: ɔdɔ, tumi, nyankomade. Nigel breaks into a sweat. Keeps his eyes focused on her wavering breasts, her fleshy thighs. Screams loud into her face, "Fuck, this is good." He closes his eyes, trying to take in her breath, the way her hands are wrapped tightly around his ass. But then the other images come: the way his mother's face must've looked when he wasn't there that morning to inject her arm with her first shot of insulin: cheeks run over with worry lines and age. Maybe the woman he hired to replace him wouldn't bother to bring the mango for her one day, and she'd drop down dead just to spite him.

And then there's his father's body. The one they buried in the backyard underneath their family tree. Cheaper than a casket, and it meant he'd always be near his wife to listen to her songs. His skull face grows back its fleshy cheeks and weathered skin just in time to curl his lips and narrow his eyes into an expression of absolute disgust: *Yuh leave yuh own muddah to die by sheself so yuh can become yankee and jook a coolie woman?*

Now we will go to November 3, 1984, to the day they say "I do."

This is the part we call the happily ever after. It is the moment in fairy tales where stories end. Unfortunately for you, however, this is no ordinary fairy tale, and their story is only just beginning.

For their wedding day, Beatrice made her dress by hand out of old satin curtains. She'd taken the idea from *The Sound of Music*. She'd spent the morning of the ceremony singing the words to "My Favorite Things" and then to "Jean and Dinah."

Flash forward to January 2, 1985, to the room where her belly starts to swell.

She thinks of all her plans: try every famous pizza place in NYC at least once. Get a master's degree in something, anything. Flash forward to morning sickness, spending nights at home afraid of how the baby will come out. She tries to read all the books on mothering. Gets sick and skips to the pages with pictures. She tells her priest about her worries. He tells her to do a rosary and six additional Hail Marys, says that God is a forgiving God, but she might be testing his patience. And yet she can't seem to get the dreams to stop coming: the baby comes out with no head; the baby's head knocks her clitoris right off; her vagina becomes a dishrag. Flash forward to thoughts like, What if he's a boy with big dreams and a big mouth who winds up missing? Gets found in the river days later with wolves or police at his feet? Flash forward to what if she's a girl left alone one night after puberty hits, liming with her cousin and no one stops to think what he's capable of?

Flash forward to August 28, 1985, SUNY Downstate Medical Center where the first baby is born.

The doctor takes the baby away and she's relieved. She doesn't want to hold her yet. The baby's hand is like a monkey's paw: alien to her. She tries to remember the number of exits in this hospital. Six? Seven? She could make a run for it when Nigel's in the nursery with the baby. Wait for the nurse to leave.

Now let's go to December 26, 1985.

Beatrice grows the face of an older woman. Except she's not old.

Just tired. Doesn't remember to apply the cocoa butter to herself every day, and so her skin appears rough with a ghostlike ash. White patches hover over her long slender fingers, her face, her tiny belly. She works long hours; she's still not used to the cold. Nigel doesn't understand. Or perhaps he's just busy—with a freshly ruptured dream to nurse every month or so. The good luck will come to him later, though not with her.

Flash forward to Beatrice and Nigel who proceed to make love in forced pieces. Look at Beatrice who grows distracted, her eyes fixating on a certain star or if not, she's kneeling by her bedside, whispering prayers long into the night. Her attention moves away from the curves of his body, the crease of his back. She stares at the star as though she's waiting for it to do something. It doesn't.

Flash forward to Nigel who hasn't been promoted yet. He'll be a bank teller for another two years. No time to write. Hasn't looked at his journal since the baby came. He tries to remember that she is his. Wants her to know his father. Wants her to hold his machete. Hasn't called his mother in weeks. Can't afford to fly her down to meet her grandchild. Dreams about flight. Stops going out for runs cuz it's cold, and he has to be in by six or she'll holler about women's rights, how mothering's a job, how she's not cut out for this, how she wants to go home and see her mother. He should've played the field some before getting married. Back home, girls used to smile and offer to buy him drinks. Who is she to be the uppity one? To withdraw from him? Takes another drink. Buys Cuban cigars. Buys knockoff Italian suits. This is the life he was meant to lead. His mother will be proud.

Of course Nigel doesn't yet know that his mother will be dead before he ever makes it back to Jamaica. By that time he'll be too jaded and preoccupied with work to feel the presence of her ghost.

Flash forward to 1997 when Beatrice looks at her wedding album in the bathroom after telling her daughters the story of why we call them Anansi stories. She decides to put the dress on. Takes the cross off her neck, grazes it along her thighs, imagining the sensation of digging—the sputtering rhythm of blood making lines and shapes across her dress.

She doesn't do it of course, settles for throwing the cross in a drawer and spilling red wine all over the gown. She'll use this moment to justify throwing the dress out into the dumpster while Nigel is away on business.

This isn't the hopeful story you were looking for, I can tell. I'm sorry I couldn't change the ending for you. But I believe there is always another route promised when going back to the start. Look back and you might find Nigel smiling and longing to be held. Here he believes there's still a chance for him to be reunited with his mother. Here he thinks back to his stories; he wonders which story will be his daughter's favorite. He dreams of turning his childhood stories into books to be read by the children that aren't yet his. Turn back and you just might be able to rewrite history, you might be able to rewrite me.

Here Nigel is visiting Beatrice's grave. He has a new wife now, and he hasn't spoken to Beatrice in years. He tries to push her out his mind as much as possible, but she enters anyway: as he makes his morning coffee, as he sleeps beside his new wife, as he tucks the daughter they share into bed. Now he wriggles his fingers into the dirt by Beatrice's coffin, puts it in a jar, and labels it "Lightning Bug." He keeps the jar in a drawer in his desk at work. He never tells a soul.

There are nights when Nigel will shut himself up in the bedroom and blast "Jean and Dinah" on the record player. Nights when he dances around, hoping to feel her spirit.

Here Beatrice allows Nigel's fingers to trace the constellations and ocean waves that have formed on her neck, her back, her shoulders, moving up and down her spine like the tide.

Here he has just invited her in. She can tell that he wants more. To know her secrets. She hopes he doesn't ask her how she got her scars. She holds her breath. Looks up to the ceiling, trying to see God's expression. Beatrice tries to see her mother. Considers the promises she made to them all before she left Trinidad to start her life anew in His eyes. She starts to pull away from him, ready to say "Good night" and do her six Hail Marys on her long walk home as penance. But then no one had ever been able to look at her scars and make her feel like that before. Like maybe the scars were always supposed to be right where they were, engraving permanent secrets and histories beneath her skin.

"My mother says that God gave me these scars to remind me of my punishment," she says.

Nigel laughs. "Punishment for what?"

But she dare not say.

And so he draws her to him, puts his hands on her neck, lets them travel down the top of her spine.

"But didn't God say that 'Just as a father has compassion on his children—'" Nigel begins.

"So the Lord has compassion on those who fear Him," she continues. It was from Psalm 103. She's pleased that he knows this.

"He is mindful that we are but dust."

*Yes,* Beatrice thinks, *how could God have such high expectations of dust?*

And so Beatrice unzips her church dress with ease, like she's a natural at unzipping dresses in front of strangers. She looks at him with the eyes of a hunter, walks toward him slowly.

"I'll show you all of my scars," she says, "if you promise to dance with me."

Nigel smiles nervously. He extends his arms toward her, clumsily holding her waist. "There's nothing I want more."

# PART II

Essential Ghosts

# CHAPTER 5

# Sky Full a Curry and Purple Balloon

*Zora*

Ocho Rios, Jamaica
December 1999

INSIDE MILLIE'S STAND SIX TABLES: ONE LONG RECTANGLE and several squares all covered in red and green for Christmas. Out of the six, four are empty. An elderly couple wearing matching rainbow shorts and straw hats sit at one of the larger squares fit for a party of five. The lights above us spray a pale yellow around the space. The radio plays "Santa Ketch up inna Mango Tree"—one of the few Jamaican Christmas songs I actually know all the words to. Our waiter with confident black skin, dark as licorice, has eyes that avoid my father's lighter ones. He sits us down at the smallest table. I keep my notebook and pen close at hand. I write: *Sacrifice is sitting down like a lady at the restaurant your father took so much trouble to arrange before you go asking if you can go out and "explore."*

..............

"Don't be spoiled, Beatrice," Daddy says. "You don't come to Jamaica to eat veggie patties and the same gerbil food you give them in the States. You come here to eat curry goat. And oxtail."

My mother just looks at her menu, anxiously twirling what Aunty Shirley once called "coolie" hair. "Maybe we should ask the kids if they'd rather eat at the Veggie Hut down the street." My mother tries to read our bellies by staring at our stomachs.

"They'll eat curry," my father says and puts down his menu, ready to order.

What Daddy forgets is that before Mommy converted to the macrobiotic life, she used to make us curry goat all the time. In fact, Mommy says that Daddy isn't the best chef when it comes to homestyle cooking because he's been spendin' too much time sleepin' with that bitch from Berlin—"and everyone knows dem German gyals cyah cook curry." Of course Daddy says it's just Mom's Dougla blood that makes her pretentious around the cooking of curry. I'm still wondering what the both of them meant.

So this is my mother's recipe for curry goat: "First take three pound of goat from that man with the black gums and the bald head—you know the one who calls you 'sugar cheeks.' Thyme and scotch bonnet from the fat man who also makes the nice jerk pork. One lime. Plenty onion and garlic. Two tomato and enough green seasoning to coat the goat. Potatoes are optional. Don't forget to salt. Generous pinch of amchar masala and several pinches curry powder—half price off at the discount store on Flatbush. Don't go to the old man who likes to look down yuh tits sometimes.

"You mustn't forget to wash the goat first with water and vinegar. Must rub it real good with the powder and seasonings and let it sit. Don't take it out the fridge for at least another hour. Better to leave it overnight. And when yuh cooking the thing, don't forget to watch it close lest it burn. Don't try to add water lest the fat not soak up the whole flavor and it come out soup instead of curry."

At least that's what she used to say before she had an affair with modern dance and a book called *The Return to Afro-Veganism*. Around the same time she stopped cooking oxtail and started boiling soba noodles and brown rice with our callaloo instead. Around this same time, her voice got softer and her footsteps lighter. I write: *Sacrifice is your mother shutting you out so you don't have to watch her doubled over and in pain, on her knees from the headaches and the dizzy spells that seem to be getting worse by the day.*

..............

Mommy and Daddy ignore us, arguing quietly over books. Every once in a while, Mommy reaches over to Kayla who keeps trying to take the pacifier out her mouth so she can cry some more.

"But don't you feel like Mr. Wright's portrayal of us was a bit too reductive?" my mother says.

"The man's gay."

"No, that was James Baldwin," my mother corrects him.

"They were both gay, Beatrice, so that doesn't explain much."

"Richard Wright's not gay, Nigel."

"They were all gay; you can hear it in the writing."

"Nigel, that was—"

"All gay. And he was a communist. A man who never had to grow up in the fields with nothing to brush his teeth with but a piece of sugar cane, and he calls himself a 'proletarian'?"

My father's eyes look so faraway for a second before he fumbles through his messenger bag to take out his copy of *Live Life Genius*: "Walden Henry Benedict—brilliant."

He reads the back of the book, "'Walden Benedict is a *distinguished* professor—not one of those Obeah hacks that go around mixing legitimate science with absolute nonsense. Benedict has advised two U.S. presidents and more than sixty CEOs across the country.' This is something you should read, Zora," he says to me. "That is if you want to get a real job and not live off your husband the rest of your life and then try to call yourself a feminist like your mother does."

My mother breathes loudly but says nothing, pushing the pacifier back inside Kayla's mouth while she sits snug in her high chair. My mother closes her eyes a moment and taps her forehead, like it hurts. When she opens her eyes again, her left foot starts to shake; the whole table vibrates.

Whenever my father talks like that, my whole body clenches with the words I wish I had for him. I haven't yet learned how to open my mouth to articulate the things my churning stomach can say so well. I write: *I love you, Daddy, but I'm afraid your words will pound me till I'm dead.*

.............

Other white families come into the restaurant, and the space is soon filled with shuffling Tevas and Birkenstocks. From our table, I can see many feet for me to watch and many long arms carrying trays of stew chicken, jerk chicken, and my favorite—escovitch. Of course none of the food is for us. I'm getting tired of sitting at the table, and my head is starting to spin. The drone of the air-conditioning makes it hard for me to sit still. There are other kids in the restaurant now walking around. I want to go outside but settle for holding my notebook tighter against my chest.

.............

Sasha clears her throat and asks in that loud but controlled voice we practiced together if she can order an appetizer.

"Of course," Daddy says as he tries to wave over the men who are busy helping a family who came in twenty-five minutes after we did.

"I told your mother we should've gotten reservations. It's no wonder that a place like this would now have us waiting."

My mother taps her foot against the table leg once and then stops.

"But trust me, it'll be worth the wait. They had the best curry goat you could ever eat at this restaurant. Celebrities from all over the world would come to eat here. When I was young, we'd never be able to get into a place like this." My father looks out at the other tables and closes his eyes as though lost in memory.

"Why are they serving the white families before they serve us?" Sasha asks. I nudge her hard with my knee and look away, not wanting to look like I'm a part of that statement.

My father opens his eyes and holds up a glass of water like a warning before setting it back down on the table. "Don't get it confused, Sasha," he says. "Don't become one of those people your mother worships that blames race for everything wrong in the world. You say you want to make a change in this world? Become a lawyer, start a business, but don't you ever let me hear you make excuses for yourself. Nothing in this world is worse than a Black man who lets a white man tell him what he's worth."

"Or a Black woman, Daddy," I add, hoping he won't mind.

"Yes, of course, Zora. Or a Black woman. Now, are you three hearing me?" I nod quietly. Sasha looks away from the table where she can roll her eyes without punishment.

"What's that growling sound?" I ask, looking around.

"It's the baby, you idiot," Sasha says and glares at me. "She sounds hungry. We should at least get something for Kayla, don't you think, Daddy?" Sasha asks.

"Yes, of course, dear. The waiters saw me and as you all can see this is a very busy night for them."

But I can tell that his mask of calm is becoming difficult for him to carry.

"It's cold in here," Sasha says. Nobody answers.

I write: *Sacrifice is watching your father's skin turn to leather, knowing that leather is what happens to animals whose skin is destined to be taken.*

. . . . . . . . . . . . .

Another white family walks in and is seated at the largest table. My father hums "The Ballad of King Matthias" by Antonín Dvořák and smiles, looking ready to order.

I stare at the white family ordering food. Daddy shows no reaction at all. The mother at the other table is busy taking pictures of the scene. The Rastafarian colored beads in her hair slap against her broad shoulders. The girl looks around my age. She seems bored like me. Watching her makes me want to wander off with her, see if we could maybe become friends outside of this place. The girl tells the waiter in her perfect New England accent that she is not afraid to try the jerk chicken. She is ready for spice.

At our table, we hear new sounds coming from Kayla's stomach, like the sound of Mom's oxtail soup bubbling. Still, I have no idea where all the noise is coming from when all she has been putting in her stomach since we got there is water. But out it comes from the pit of that baby's stomach like a volcano—a belch: it's loud and horribly inappropriate. Daddy glares sharply at my mother as though he's waiting for her to make the baby say excuse me.

"The baby's hungry," my mother says.

"Take her outside." My father says this as a warning.

"Don't be ridiculous."

And right there in front of the entire restaurant, my mother unbuttons her good church blouse, pulls out her breast, and begins to feed the baby.

My father's heavy hand begins to pound the table. His voice is sharp and jagged like a broken vase. "Beatrice, you better get that bloody child out of here before I silence that mouth you like to use so much."

"Watch how you talk to me out here, eh Nigel."

Kayla stops feeding and starts to cry. I sit on my hands to help fight the urge to cover the baby's mouth.

"Beatrice, I'm gonna give you to the count of five, and I swear to God, nobody will even think to call the police fast enough to save you."

My mother looks from her husband to us, her children. I look down to my journal so that neither can try to read my face as a sign of loyalty. I write: *Sacrifice is going to sleep and watching your mother drown. In the dream, I sit by the bathtub, holding on to my mother's hand, unable to pull up her body. In my free hand is my bloody tongue, which has been cut out as a sacrifice for my indecision.*

I finally look up to see Sasha shifting her feet under the table to distract herself. My mother turns to the waiters who pretend not to see her and then finally to the family sitting next to them with the little girl who looks about my age and is staring at my daddy like he's some kind of monster. My mother realizes that my father is right—there is no one here to save her. So she picks up her baby and carries her outside, like Kayla might help keep her afloat.

The white girl whispers something to her mother that I can't hear before being told not to point at my family. Her father tries to distract his family by making jokes about the food.

"The chicken here is pretty spicy, huh, even spicier than the food in Mexico," he says between long sips of water. "Maybe we can ask to get some more water . . . Uh, waiter!" he says, laughing, "I hope you don't mind us, the food here is great! I was just hoping we could get a little bit more water for the table . . . I guess we're just not used to this. I hope that's not a problem."

"This is Jamaica!" says the waiter. "No problems here."

"Daddy, can I get something else?" asks the little girl. "I can't eat this food."

"Yeah, why don't you bring something a little less on the spicy side for my daughter but something . . . authentic, if you can. Right, Sydney?"

"Can I just have french fries?" she asks.

"Like I say, no problem, everyting irie," the waiter says in his perfect tourist accent.

The family laughs as the waiter shuffles away, pretending not to see our family.

Daddy excuses himself to go to the restroom. The little girl just stares at him. He walks back into the room looking above our heads as he sits back down. He smiles at my mother who returns with Kayla asleep in her lap. She does not smile back.

The waiter brings the other table their fries before finally making his way over to the only Black table. I'm not sure whether he came to throw us out for making a scene or bring us our food to get us out sooner. The fries smell good. I reach for Sasha's hand but she's too busy rubbing them together—a thing she does when she's feeling tense and about to have what her school counselor calls "a bad spell." My head feels light with hunger.

"Is everything all right, ma'am?" the waiter asks. He looks only at my mother.

"Yes, everything is quite fine," my father answers.

My mother curls her lips slowly into a small smile. She rubs her head like it hurts. Her feet begin to tap.

"Yes, I think we'd like to start with a round of drinks. My wife and I, we'll have the rum punch, two rounds of sorrel for the girls, and some hot milk if you don't mind. As you probably heard, we have a crying baby on our hands. Tap water is fine, but no ice please." The waiter only nods.

............

There are times I want to hear my mother tell me a story. Something in the way my whole body shakes and my lips quiver with anticipation of the words I don't know are coming, because as she says, these are not her words to own. Some goddess or old person called an ancestor lets her borrow them, and after she speaks them the words are gone until she needs to tell her story again—only to be remembered by her children. In fact, she says that if we keep very still and quiet, we can feel the dead walk among us. Some people can even be trained to see them.

But it is usually our father who is the storyteller.

"Tell us the story about the two brothers who fight the Rolling Calf in the hurricane," Sasha says because it's her favorite.

The very first time I remember witnessing my father's storytelling, he performed it like a whisper so that nobody—not even Sasha—could hear us. He told me the story of the artist in Jamaica who set his own house on fire so that he could paint the flames. I write: *You can tell by the way his eyes jump forward as he tells us how he once walked to the butcher shop after school with his brother, saw the butcher's head in a saucer, saw his chain wrapped in blood, that this was never just a story.*

My father hesitates, staring from the backs of his hands to the white tablecloth. "Okay," he begins. "Once upon a time there was a boy and his brother . . ." His voice trails off. He asks the waiter in his best imitation of an American accent for another glass of water.

"Why don't you tell us the one about the purple balloon?" I ask because it's my favorite.

"Yes." My father's lips curl up slightly into a weak smile. "Why don't I? Well . . ." he begins and clears his throat. ". . . They say there was once a town where all the dreams were kept in pretty boxes." His eyes grow in size and look up to the ceiling where I imagine his story is drifting high above him, trying to get back inside. "The keys for these boxes got lost in the ocean years ago and, because nobody knew how to open them, the townspeople kept them hidden. This way, little children wouldn't find them and have their hearts all twisted up inside, realizing they had been missing their dreams all this time."

At this point, Kayla has started making noise, and Mom gets up from the table and starts to walk her around the restaurant, circling around waiters and families, patting Kayla's back till her cries become whispers. I'm worried this will distract Dad from his story and start up a whole new battle but it doesn't. Instead Dad looks right at me: "There was a little girl, however, and this girl was around your age, Zora. She used to ask her parents so many questions about the dreams that were stolen from her that they grew tired of her pestering, know-ing they could never change her situation, and left her in a field of acorns with nothing but a book of fairy tales. They couldn't decipher the words in the tales anyway. Maybe this would help answer some of her questions."

He holds up his hands in the shape of a book, and I can see a little glimmer come back to his eyes as he orchestrates his hands to move in time with his voice. At this point, Sasha and I know that our plan is working.

"And in these fairy tales, women had the power to fly. They would fly around the land protecting it from harm, and the men would pray to them like goddesses. The girl studied these stories every night. Some-thing about them kept calling her closer to the sea, as if the keys them-selves wanted her near them. She knew what she needed to do. She would become a fairy herself." Now Dad clasps his thumbs together so his hands look like wings. His eyes follow his wings back up to the ceil-ing. I look over at Sasha to see how she thinks Dad is doing, but she is busy looking worriedly at Mom and Kayla. I look over to see a smiling Mom bouncing Kayla in her arms as they swerve between tables. Dad goes on, paying no mind to our now divided attention.

"And so she began to hide in dumpsters, stealing the newspapers that everyone in the town had forgotten how to read, and tried to use them to create her wings. But the seabirds warned her that times had changed since the Land of the Fairies. Children had become too heavy to fly. She would probably drown if she tried to spread her wings across the sea. But she didn't lose faith. No, she would use words from the newspapers to create stories to send out to the seabirds, who would spread her message: that she was prepared to fight to get the magic back in her town. And soon enough she was known as the only girl in all the land who could write. And for a while she felt almost satisfied . . . until . . ." And then Dad looks back down from the ceiling and closes his eyes. He opens them again, seeing the restaurant and staring at the blond European-looking couple seated next to us. "Until . . . I forget how the story goes, actually, something about a purple balloon."

I look to Sasha who looks back at me. We shrug, not knowing what to say next. But then she puts her hand on the table next to mine. She nods for me to continue the story.

"Yes, Daddy," I say, hesitant at first. "Until the day she stepped inside that small no-name store that sold nothing but purple balloons."

"Yeah," Sasha says. "Small balloons, large balloons. Balloons in the shapes of trees and stars and moons. And one balloon, larger than them all that was in the shape of wings. The wings were so big that they took up the entire store. She was afraid that if she were to truly blow up this balloon, the windows might explode from its very size. As you can see, this was no ordinary balloon."

"No, in fact, this was a magic balloon," I whisper. "The storekeeper wouldn't say where she got it, but she told the girl she could have it for a price."

"'But what do I have to give you?' the girl asked." I do this part using my squeaky voice. "'I have only the dress on my back and this book of fairy tales. Or I could sell you my hair,' she said, showing the woman her long locs."

"Wait," Sasha says, pulling my arm. This is her favorite part. Her face scrunches up as she tries to speak with the kind of croaky voice she imagines the old woman to have: "'I have no use for your ugly matted hair. Nor do I care for these rags you call a dress. But I have heard throughout this town that you can write. I find it . . . peculiar that any-one so small could ever write the way that you do. For as you know, no other woman in this town has this power, so I'd like to know, what will you write for me?'"

At this point, Mom and Kayla sit back down. Mom pats Kayla's back in a rhythm and hums quietly to herself. I imagine that she's doing this for us, providing us with background music, although I know that this probably isn't true.

Sasha keeps going: "'If you can write me a word so beautiful that I forget how ugly this moment is that we're sharing—that I am talking to a girl who can read better than I can, who at twelve years old calls herself a fairy while I at eighty-five am stuck here, forever in this shop, I may consider a trade.'"

I clear my throat. "My turn," I say. "And so the girl thought and she thought. Finally, she felt the pulse of an idea come rushing through her blood into her fingertips as she raised her hand to write in pure de-light. It was the most beautiful word. But as she lifted her arm, ready to write down this magnificence, the storekeeper raised hers as well—with a knife, cutting the girl's hand right off. The girl screamed in horror, but the storekeeper laughed. 'Now I will have the hand the people in this town have been calling magic. Now I will be the only woman with the power to write. Here's your balloon,' the woman said, and she threw the little girl out of the store."

I nod in Sasha's direction so she knows it's her turn to take over: "Yet the girl did not lose hope. She took the balloon with one hand and one bloody stump, knowing that the women who came before her had sacrificed much more. She walked to the edge of the ocean, taking one deep breath, and said to God, 'My Goddess, I have found you or perhaps it is you that has found me. I have come to tell you that right now I am choosing to live.' She blew and she blew and she blew, until not only did the balloon expand to be greater than the size of her village—"

"But now the balloon had carried her with it—across the sea and to America!" I say, cutting her off. Our voices are now racing each other's, trying to be the first one to finish the story.

"Where although she never became a true fairy, she worked really hard until she learned to write with one left hand and became one of the world's greatest female novelists," Sasha continues.

"Where she lived happily ever after," I say.

"Well, mostly happily ever after, anyway," Sasha adds.

"Yes. The end!" I smile triumphantly.

"Yes, Zora. Yes, Sasha. That's right," Daddy says. His voice is quiet and his smile smaller. He flicks up his forefinger to ask the waiter for another glass of water. "No ice this time—and a slice of lemon, if you don't mind."

I pick up my notebook to write: *Sacrifice is when the girl lands her purple balloon, knowing that it's too late to go back to Fairy Land but not knowing whether she can stay. Wondering, whose dream was it that told her life would be any easier in America? Wondering, so how does it feel to be free?*

. . . . . . . . . . . . .

Now the families that were at the restaurant in the beginning have left. Others arrive instead, with banana-peel hair that magically dances every time somebody opens the door. Kayla's crying so hard her face starts to look like a tomato.

"Everybody's staring at her because she won't stop screaming," Sasha whispers.

"They had the best curry goat you could ever eat at this restaurant," my father says again. "I used to be very good friends with the people who owned this place. They must've left a few years ago now."

"Daddy." Sasha takes our father's hand. "You're too good for this place."

It was a bald-faced move for her to make.

My father nods with his eyes on the table. "Let's go," he says.

My mother is the first to stand up and pick up the baby. We all follow suit. It is at this time that the waiters come rushing toward us.

"But sir! Your food is right here!" one says.

He holds the curried goat on a plate that glows in the yellow light. The curry smells the way Mommy used to make it but better because I am hungry. The smell is so thick I can taste it. My father picks up the fork from the table and sticks it into the meat delicately. He lifts the fork to his mouth in slow motion, watching the waiters' expressions change from smiles to gasps as he takes a bite of the food and chews slowly for a moment, before spitting it out onto their platter. The waiters step back, aghast, in unison.

"Ugh!" my father says. "I'm sorry, but my family will only eat curry made by your previous chef, James Graham, who I can tell by the watered-down flavor here is no longer with you."

"Sir, this is extremely good local curry—"

"Yes, I'm sure, see, my family is made up of real Jamaicans including myself. We're not some tourists you can fool with this garbage." And then Daddy just turns and walks away.

My mother glides past them, holding the screaming Kayla in her arms. Then she turns toward them with fire in her mouth: "You oughta be ashamed of yuhselves," she says. When my mother gets angry, she conjures her past and heritage through her tongue.

"Allyuh Negroes spend so much time washing de white man's ass, yuh tink it's yuh own reflection." Her words grow faster, angrier: "Allyuh tink yuh gonna get big tips from dese whitefolk? Well, let me tell allyuh, white people doh give a shit about no niggas—not a shit. De next time yuh tink so just turn on de television—yuh notice how dem bathroom made from tile while yuh using de latrine to teach yuh classes in? That's when yuh know yuh in Jamaica—that's how yuh know yuh a nigga."

The waiters say nothing. Instead, they fumble, clumsily trying to bus the dishes filled with goat and oxtail from our table before retreating to the kitchen as quickly as they can.

I look back at the staring crowd and smile widely. My mother sighs and breathes heavily as though wiped out by the words that just ran through her. Dad doesn't look directly at Mom, but I can tell that he is proud, or he would've said something to challenge her. Sasha shakes her head at the crowd, rolling her eyes. When I see her do this, I decide to roll my eyes too. I'm not completely sure what Mom meant by her words, but I want to be a part of the moment the rest of the family seems to be sharing.

I smile all the way out of the restaurant. Sasha folds her arms across her chest. I write: *And everybody will be there telling each other stories they heard echoed from the water in their veins. And it'll say, if you were really listening you would know that you were already born free.*

.............

The ride to the hotel is slow. All anyone can hear are mosquitoes and the sound of Dad exhaling cigarette smoke into the purple night. Nobody asks what we're planning to eat for dinner now that Dad spit in our food and Mom yelled at our waiters. We end up with bread. Just sit in the Volvo, parked in front a bakery, devouring the hardo loaf in silence. When we get to the hotel parking lot, Dad pulls over and says, "Guess we made it."

Sasha hurries out the car and keeps walking toward our hotel room. My mother leaves with Kayla. I reach to open the car door before Daddy taps my shoulder. "Zora?" I can tell by the way his eyes are twitching like they're about to pop from the dead sockets they're kept in that he wants to tell me a story.

"Yes, Daddy."

"Do you want to hear what really happened to the girl in the purple balloon?" he says, lighting a cigarette.

"Yes, Daddy." I climb to sit beside him in the front seat.

"Now what I'm telling you may shock you, but I'm pretty sure you can handle it. You handled yourself like a lady today. I was proud of you."

"Yes, Daddy. I'm ready." It seems like the right thing to say, but I can tell that my father's hand is finally shaking a little, making my hand shake too. He continues though, blowing smoke into the car, talking to his rearview mirror.

"You see, the story"—he pauses—"it was actually about a boy. A boy whose hands were made to choose between mining bauxite for aluminum and . . . and anyway, I only told you it was about a girl because—I mean, this story, it could be about anybody—and it is in fact about all of us—but this boy, who was only a few years older than you are, Zora, he tried to fly away in a purple balloon . . . and he never really made it to America."

I wait.

"The balloon got stuck somewhere, nobody could find it."

I wait again for him to continue but all he says is, "Okay, Zora. Get inside before your mother worries."

I go back to the hotel room to sit on the balcony with my journal. I pick up my pen and think hard about what words I should write for my father. I try for a moment, my mind fighting to create the perfect ending to my father's story until—I put the pen down. I realize I have nothing more to say. Instead, I creep outside my hotel room to the back with the pool and crawl around in darkness looking for branches to build a—well, all I know is that I don't need to cut off my hand just to create a purple balloon. No, I'll make a canoe instead and leave it outside the car door for my father to see when he's finished trying to recapture his dreams for the night. That way he can travel the currents to find his childhood, and he can meet me there. Not just me but all the people he left behind when he got on the balloon to come to America.

# CHAPTER 6

# Two Brothers, the Rolling Calf, and the Wind Herself

Discovery Bay, Jamaica
October 1973

ONCE UPON A TIME THERE WAS A GIRL. AND THIS GIRL GREW to be a woman. And this woman had the ability to conjure stories from ghosts.

But this story isn't about her.

No, this story is, incidentally, about the man that she loved. A man that, perhaps, you think she should not. A man that, perhaps, reminds you of other men: your father who went out for cigarettes and never returned; your husband who is currently fucking your nanny. You'd probably like very much to hate this man, but what kind of storyteller would I be to let you?

Let me tell you a story. This one will test all your definitions for love. Please if you can, imagine that this man was once a boy. Imagine that this boy once loved to make his father proud almost as much as he loved to create stories.

This boy, whose name was Nigel, would say that his father taught him two things: (1) Never walk to the butcher man shop when night come. (2) Never trust the Wind. Said that if you weren't careful, the Wind could trick you into believing you could fly and then you would belong to her forever.

Course the boy and his brother, Harold, they did both. Decided to play a game of chicken the night that Hurricane Gilda hit on

October 16, 1973. If you were alive then and living in or around Discovery Bay, you would know that this went beyond general fool-fool behavior. This was because of Old Man Toby, the butcher man who was killed by duppy and so turned into Rolling Calf to haunt the streets come nightfall.

Course I know that Nigel and Harold had their reasons for being fool-fool. Both had this feeling eating away at their cores that their manhood was at stake. You see it was the night before Gilda swept through Discovery Bay, when I, Your Faithful Narrator, watched as our dear Nigel got caught at the dinner table with lines from "Bartleby, the Scrivener" cut out and glued onto his Bible—right in between Psalms and Proverbs. Their father spent six days a week, ten hours a day over at the Kaiser Bauxite Company. Came home late each night with clothes that smelled of melted aluminum and sweat—with hands that could take on new forms on a daily basis: blisters in the shapes of hexagons, pentagons, and squares. All he asked from his children was for quiet at the dinner table and diligence with their studies of the Lord. So when they went around the table to read from Psalms as was ritual and Nigel read, "Ah Bartleby! Ah humanity!" instead of Psalm 40, the room went silent. Amos then proceeded to leap from the chair in the fashion of a great lion, grabbed his youngest by the throat, licked him with his good belt, and made him spend the night on the grass with the chickens.

That night, Nigel felt the wet grass scratch against his cheek; he felt the warmth of the full moon hover over his torso, his limbs, heard the erratic shrieking and squawking coming from the roosters, when he heard something else: a movement coming from the bushes, a shadow crossing the moon. Nigel sat erect with machete in hand when the shadow emerged with a hunched back and horns atop its head. Nigel's breath quickened and became shallow as he held the machete tighter in his fists, wondering if the beast in the bushes was in fact the Rolling Calf. After all, every parish in Jamaica had one. According to his father, the Rolling Calf was a butcher man who had sold his soul to the Devil and was now made to pay by the almighty Himself. "Remember this now. No matter what him look like pon daytime, de Rolling Calf more mad than man. And him always a look fi eat fool-fool bwoy pickney, like fi unnu," his father would say. Though Nigel did not like to admit it, the image of the Rolling Calf was a frequent haunting in his mind.

And on this very night as he saw it approaching, his hands began to shake. He heard the rattling sound of chains dragging across the grass, jingling like a bell. Nigel closed his eyes and crouched as low as he could, shivering in the eighty-degree heat. He peeked from one eye and looked above the shadowy grass. The creature towered above him, a head like a duppy's and gnarled horns like the Devil. Nigel knew he could no longer hide. After all, it's said that a Rolling Calf can smell a small boy's fear from at least six kilometers away. And so Nigel tried for bravery and snarled at the beast. Unfortunately for Nigel, however, his snarl came out as more of a whimper. The beast lunged at Nigel and Nigel screamed for his mother. And then the beast did a most curious thing: it proceeded to laugh—just held on to its sides and howled. Nigel looked up to see his brother, Harold, with branches looking like horns atop his head.

"Yuh tink me duppy, breddah?" Harold said, still cackling.

"No . . . I . . ." Nigel began, but lost face before completing the statement. Harold was two years older and a good foot taller than Nigel. He knew it best to let him have his laughs if he could help it, though he held the machete upright, just to show him that *he* was not the woman of the bunch.

"Mi see yuh not ready for what mi come fi do," Harold said, regaining composure.

"A weh yuh a seh?" Nigel asked.

Harold removed the branches from atop his head and put his hands firmly on Nigel's shoulders: "Tonight you shoulda stand up to Big Boss. Show him de one story you show me the oddah day. The one bout de boy who fly a New York inna one purple balloon."

Now it was Nigel's turn to laugh.

"Yuh mad or what, breddah? Tomorrow mi wah sleep inna mi bed."

Though secretly he was elated that his brother remembered his story.

"Yuh shoulda tell Daddy bout de prize yuh get from Mrs. Edwards. It de best story inna all de tird form. Yuh know a thing like that mek yuh get scholarship to go a foreign. A dis yuh want?"

Nigel tried to hide his blushing.

"Him nuh know how good yuh are," Harold said, and Nigel turned away so he couldn't see him blush.

Harold and Mrs. Edwards were the only two people whom Nigel had ever shown his writing. Harold would give him pointers on how to read it: "Puff out yuh chest some, nuh man," he would say. "Show dem idiots yuh mek from steel."

"A dis yuh want fi tell mi?" Nigel asked now.

"Nuh man. Mi come a formulate plan. Mek wi show Daddy wi more man than even him."

*But who could be more man than Daddy?* Nigel thought. After all, this was the man who took him to hunt down barracudas for dinner, who taught him to hide along the coral reefs until the barracuda came by and then whack the thing over the head one time with a machete and carry it to shore with his bare hands.

"And how we fi do that?" Nigel asked.

Harold said this next part in front the full moon so that Nigel could see him enunciate each and every word: "Mek wi bring back de head of de Calf," he said. "De Rolling Calf."

Nigel fell silent a moment and yet he was still curious. "How?"

"Old Man Toby," Harold said. "Mek we leave tomorrow pon dusk."

Nigel felt the air close in around him as his brother said these words. Course everyone knew that Old Man Toby was rumored to be Rolling Calf ever since the night that Little Kevin was found dead outside his shop after going to pick up some goat for his Aunty Sonia one poor Sunday. Nigel and Harold's mother had forbidden them from traveling anywhere near that shop ever since.

"But what if—" Nigel's voice stumbled.

"Shh," Harold said, walking toward his brother, his tall stocky frame glimmering in the moonlight.

"Trust mi."

When Nigel returned to his room the next morning, he found his father sitting on his bed, going through his illicit Herman Melville passages that lay hidden inside his Bible. Amos's lips scowled as he flipped through the stories that Nigel had written himself, appropriately placed in the Book of Daniel—the verses illustrating how sinners bring on Babylon because of their own self-indulgence.

"Father—" Nigel uttered by way of apology.

But his father rose a finger to stop him. "Yuh good, son," Amos began. "Cyah seh mi understand it all nuh man, but yuh good." He put his hand on his son's shoulder and squeezed it.

Nigel's lips spread into a grin. He couldn't remember the last time his father paid him a compliment.

"Problem is yuh not that good."

Nigel stopped smiling, knowing that this was probably true.

"You know, in my day mi haffi travel two hours from home to go a school fi offer A-Level and upper sixth course yuh need fi go University. Even won big award from mi teacher making mi tink mi some kind of special."

Nigel bowed his head at this, realizing that Harold's compliments about his story were probably meaningless.

"You want fi know what dat hard work get mi?" He towered over Nigel now with a devilish sneer on his lips. Nigel winced, preparing for another beating before his father began pacing across the room.

"It get mi on de wait-list fi UWI two times before mi decide fi move on fi learn trade. Because no matter how smart unnu pickney tink you is, we still only have one real university in dis here country. You haffi be de best of de best to get into that one. And yet you see how I work? You tink I like going to work sixty hours a week to provide for unnu pickney? It is the Lord who get me through this, yuh hear? The Lord. Yuh fifteen year old and not you nor yuh brother know how fi fix sink or door for yuh mother. Yuh could barely climb tree fi fetch mango or coconut. You spending all yuh time reading and not God word, mind you. If yuh ask me is like raising a bunch of woman."

He said this last word with so much disdain, Nigel could feel himself shrink underneath his father's gaze. But also, he wanted to know what his father thought of his stories.

"You want prove mi wrong? Name three Jamaican writers who ever amount to anything in this country. Name three and I wrong."

"I—" Nigel searched his mind. "Ah doh know, Father."

"You doh know?" Amos smiled. "Yuh tink mi doh wah see yuh succeed? Yuh doh tink if mi could, me nuh send fi yuh already?"

"Yes, Daddy."

"All right," Amos said, standing up.

"Daddy?"

"Hmmm."

"Yuh really like mi story?"

Amos smiled at his son but did not respond—just walked out the door and left Nigel alone with his thoughts.

And so Nigel decided that Harold was right. There was only one way to prove themselves to their father.

He remembered his father's last words of the Rolling Calf story went like this: "In order fi kill de Calf mek sure yuh carry de sand and sea salt inna di bag wid de leather bullwhip, and de penknife. But de most important ting is de water. Yuh see, when de butcher become Calf, him dry up. Dere always be de one part of him dat want set free of himself. Like him only want to end de burning—dat need to be reborn without him sin and monster face. It said dat de Rolling Calf dat prove himself to God may be forgiven and thus separated into him two true selves—de man and him beast. Dem also say dat de Calf believe dat by plunging himself into de sea, him will get back him human side. But it not so. No, yuh see God rarely change Him mind on evil. For de most part, de Calf dat plunge himself inna de sea will dissolve wid de tide, taking wid him him humanness. Whatever left go crumble pon de shore looking like pile of cure meat."

.............

So here's the second story. You see, if you were to ask the Calf, he would tell you that he's not as bad you might think. No, the Calf is no manifestation for the shadows you used to confuse for duppies as small children. He is not a stand-in for the men your mother warned you about. He's more like the crocodile is to the egret, the fly to the cow's eye, the mosquito to your blood and sweat. The Rolling Calf is not evil. After all, ghosts rarely are. Perhaps he is even a necessary fixture to purge out the Babylonian chaos by scaring little children who run off in the middle of the night—there to remind them to behave themselves and listen to their fathers.

Truth be told, I feel sorry for the beast. After all, there is no rhyme or reason for those who get called to be seers, to be tricksters, to be Rolling Calves. Still, most humans will swear up and down that the Rolling Calf is what happens to men who sell themselves to the Devil.

What I do know is that I was there the night that Old Man Toby was turned. I had watched him from his ceiling. He didn't notice me. He had come home from working late in his shed, standing over the cow he had just sliced open. He held his machete like a sword, ready to cut off her head when her eyes opened up to him and glowed like the full moon. I watched as her tongue fell low on her lips. Her tongue was black and rough. The blood from her mouth streamed onto his shed table like a fountain.

Old Man Toby's machete dropped from his hand and onto the floor. His face was like an ice sculpture: frozen in time. The Calf walked toward him, wagging her tail, exposing her flesh. The calf bit into his shoulder, dug his teeth into the man's neck and sucked. The bite is different from Ole Higue, which feels more like a hickey than a true beast attack. Different still from the white man's vampire in that the Calf's black tongue burns like coal. I saw Ol' Man Toby's face change from fire red to black as cow tongue as he screamed.

Had Old Man Toby seen his own face transform, his soul might not have been able to take it. His skin grew fur, black as feather, all around his torso and limbs. His eyes grew large and swallowed his pupils in a pool of red.

The scream coming from Old Man Toby's lips, at first, was a human's scream. This scream grew to a growl, to a bellow, to a sound no earthly being could make. The sound was what could only be described as monstrous—except that if you listened closely, beneath the bellowing growl, underneath the monstrous pitch, was the sound of a soul trapped inside its own terror. The sound of it made my body shake like a rattle.

Old Man Toby collapsed in exhaustion and closed his eyes. In this moment, he swore he saw his mother. She wore a bright floral church dress and a wide-brim hat. She looked so peaceful as she lay flat against the reclining chair. I watched her smile as wide as her hat as her son devoured her body piece by piece.

Old Man Toby woke up in a sweat. He gasped for air and hoped against hope that last night was all a dream. He turned over to reach for a glass of water when he saw it: the cow head next to his pillow.

After the screaming, Old Man Toby did what any God-fearing duppy would do. He got on his knees and prayed. As if to say, *though mi faith get tested, ah will always remain yuh true disciple.* Yet he heard no answer. He saw a swirl of smoke in front his face and wondered if it came from the spark he felt glowing like an ember inside his heart.

. . . . . . . . . . . .

Now Harold and Nigel climbed the five kilometers past bamboo bottom, past the caves where the duppies go to rest, around the Windsor loop and into town, where they approached Old Man Toby's butcher shop. From the outside, the shop looked like it always did: a bright red sign that read TOBY'S MEAT SHOP was nailed to the front door. Tree frogs' throats ballooned out wide as palm leaves from the surrounding bushes, and the crickets rubbed their wings together. The Wind Herself was like a constant tease: one moment she was a breeze, a gentle caressing of hands like their mother's when tucking them into bed; the next she was a whip, which was also like their mother's hands. As they arrived at the door of Old Man Toby's shop, the Wind Herself turned silent, and all the boys could feel was heat. It enveloped them like a fog.

Inside the shop, marbled meats swung slowly from iron hooks, sounding like sighing. The chain links appeared to surround the boys: dragging down from hooks to scratch the floor. Others coiled up like serpents in the corners, and the boys threw small rocks from the ground to make sure they didn't slither. Nigel's hands shook and Harold's lips trembled. Their throats dried out so that they could not speak. Neither could admit to the other that they were having second thoughts. That is until Harold stumbled into the back of the store where a sink ran hot water over dirty knives. Harold felt something dislodge in his belly and work its way into his throat as he saw it: the Rolling Calf's head lying atop a bed of banana leaves. There were streams of blood running out from underneath the head and off the plate, over the countertop, and onto the floor.

"Nigel, come quick," Harold whispered.

"What is it?" Nigel said before putting his fingers to his lips in disbelief.

The Calf with the severed neck and the hanging tongue batted his long lashes at them bashfully.

The boys' stomachs turned, and their hearts beat loudly.

"Mek wi find new way to impress Big Boss, yes?" Nigel said and Harold nodded.

"Leh we go, nuh man," Harold said and they went. But before they did, Nigel bent over to pick up a small coil of chain link and hid it in his pocket. To this day he still can't tell you why he did this. Occasionally a younger brother does something to upstage the older one. To show that despite size and age difference he is indeed the alpha.

As the two brothers exited the butcher shop, the Wind Herself had become heavy and gray. She swirled around their faces gently, but ever present. It was as they walked out that Nigel noticed a shadow. "A who-dat?" Nigel asked, his hands shaking.

But out of the shadows appeared Oscar from down the road.

Nigel's fear turned to anger as he saw Oscar's lanky frame. "Weh di rass you want?" Nigel asked. Now normally, Nigel was never this confrontational. But right now, Nigel is thinking of something that happened about a week ago. Nigel had gone down to the river telling his father he was there to catch some crayfish for dinner, knowing full well he was going to write stories, when he saw two male bodies snaking the bush beyond the river, slithering on top of each other, one boy's eyes scrunched up as if in pain. They seemed too busy in their sin to notice Nigel who moved between the trees to get a better look. Instinctively, Nigel picked up a rock to throw at their heads till he recognized the "Harder, faster" moanings of the half-naked, hairy-backed boy to be his brother. The rock trembled in his hand. He tried to make his voice sound deeper, more menacing-like as he said, "Eh, batty bwoy! Move from mi bredda dey." It came out more a quiver than a shout, but it got their attention.

Nigel heard the gasps and the rustling of clothes and a "Blood fiyah" coming from his brother until Harold realized who was threatening him. At this point Harold glared boldly back at his younger brother. The ripples of muscle showed through his unbuttoned blouse, reminding Nigel who the strong one was. Nigel decided to direct his attention to the other boy instead: a thin, red-skinned boy with too much grease in his hair. Nigel could tell the boy was afraid, because he refused to make eye contact, just pulled his clothes on in a silent hurry. "Move fast, batty bwoy," Nigel said. His voice had gained heat from seeing the boy look so weak. He looked again at his brother who walked toward him slowly.

"Yuh nuh see nothing, yuh hear?" Harold said to him.

Nigel said nothing, just tried to look back at his brother without wincing.

It was then that Harold grabbed Nigel by the collar and held him close, pulled out a scaling knife from his pocket and grazed it lightly against his brother's neck. Nigel struggled against him and felt the roughness of the blade pinching. The red-skinned boy looked at them in shock.

"Walk home, Oscar," Harold said to the boy. And then to Nigel,

"Yuh tink yuh can romp wid me, boy?" Harold's breath smelled of licorice. "Mek yuh breathe a word of dis and mi go cut yuh good, yuh hear?"

"All right," Nigel said. Tears began to form, not so much from fear as out of anger. He really thought he could outdo him this time.

"Good," Harold said and let go.

This was a week ago. Now here was Oscar again, waiting for his brother. Nigel was fuming, but before he could say anything, Harold said, "Watch yuhself, yuh hear?"

"All right," Nigel said, his hands up in surrender. "Look, mi sorry 'bout the other week, yuh hear?" he said to Oscar and put his hand out to shake his. Oscar took the hand reluctantly.

"So whaa gwaan, breddah?" Oscar asked them.

"Nothing, breddah. We going home now."

"Come, look at the sky," Nigel said, pointing a finger upward. The sun had long since dropped below the mountains, and the clouds puffed out gray and amorphous. The Wind Herself picked up her pace and swirled quickly, wrapping herself around their bodies, making them trip as they walked. "Leh wi go home." Harold nodded in agreement.

And so the three boys turned to make their trek back up the hill to their homes and walked in silence. Nigel glared at the two boys, observing his brother's walk and trying to find a clue in his seemingly masculine gait, his large arms, his stone-cold stare. He couldn't see anything in him that seemed different from any other boy that he knew. This troubled him.

Harold avoided eye contact with either of them by focusing on one large cloud in the sky. The cloud seemed to have merged with the other clouds, making one giant blanket of gray. The Wind Herself began to relax and hovered above them as a wet breeze. A mist cooled around them. Amidst all this tension, a little shower would be nice, Harold thought to himself.

.............

Here's the third story. You see, what Harold didn't tell his brother Nigel that night on the grass in the company of chickens was that Harold was keeping secrets of his own. It started with photos of Jimmy Cliff in *The Harder They Come*—the billboard photo of Jimmy wearing a leopard-print shirt, a cowboy vest, and a French beret. And that voice, let me tell you! Solemn church organ meets a voice so pure with sweetness, so raw with pain you wouldn't know he was only twenty-one when he wrote "Many Rivers to Cross." Harold would hitch rides to Ocho Rios nearly every weekend so that he could watch the film again and again—hands clutching tight the seat in front of him, guzzling down his Kola Champagne, trying to create a permanent mental picture in his mind of Jimmy's neck when he sang—the way his muscles loosened and constricted, the way he made love to Elsa on the beach, the way he rode his bicycle through town without a care in the world. He wanted him. Wanted him bad.

One evening, he came home from his latest excursion to Ocho Rios to find his father staring at a crack in the wall.

"Daddy?" he asked.

But his father only continued to look at the wall as though Harold had said nothing. Harold proceeded into the kitchen where his father sat, staring. As he drew closer, he noticed that his father's good shirt was ripped from the elbow down and that there was blood dripping from his arm like a leaky faucet onto the floor.

"Daddy?" Harold asked again. By now he was afraid. He knew better than to ask his father what had happened, but he knelt beside him on the dirty floor and put a hand out tentatively—not on his father's arm exactly, but hovering next to it in the air.

"Yuh must promise me something." Mr. Porter finally spoke.

"Yes, Daddy."

"Yuh mother is not to know about this."

"Yes, sir."

"Yuh brother, neither. Yuh know how him get." By this he meant that his brother, Nigel, was sensitive. Both a crybaby and a woman. Harold beamed in spite of himself now, knowing this meant his father must like him at least marginally better than Nigel.

"Yes, sir," Harold responded, trying to hide his smile from his father.

His father looked at him now. His eyes were completely empty of feeling. It is the look your eyes have when they've just been frightened to death.

"The Rolling Calf was here," his father said.

"Where?" Harold's eyes widened as he looked around the house, frantic.

"Right dere so." He pointed outside the window right beside the wall they were staring at.

Harold noticed the salt around the windows now and on the floor in the corners of the room they sat in.

"Did you—?" But Harold was too scared to finish the sentence.

"Yes," his father said. "Mi cut him once wid me machete, and him fall down, splat!" He clapped his hands together. "Mi drag him body inna mi truck and drag him pon de ocean and him vanish."

Harold looked at his father in awe. He tried to imagine being so brave.

"Them might look tough, Harold. But a little salt and water and them nothing but a ordinary cow."

Harold looked at his father's arm bleeding and went to fetch him a washcloth and a bottle of iodine. He put the rag on his father's arm tentatively at first, unsure of how he might react. Would he beat him with his belt for touching his arm without permission? But his father only continued to stare at the crack in the wall. This crack had always been there, mind you, but the longer his father stared, the more Harold wondered whether there was something different about this crack—something his father was seeing that Harold somehow could not. His father had this ability to just look at a man and know when there was a demon inside him. Know if a woman was practicing Obeah just by looking at her. Know when someone had been cursed. Know when someone looked tough but was nothing but a batty bwoy.

Now Harold pressed down less tentatively on his father's bloody arm. His father put out his arm, and Harold flinched, thinking he might slap it away, but instead he took Harold's hand and held it there.

"That thing," his father said, "it get me." His eyes were still empty, but his hands trembled in Harold's grasp. "Mi get him in de end, yes, but de ras still get me good. Him cut me up wid him horn."

What was most alarming to Harold in this moment was that he had never heard the man curse before.

"Daddy," Harold began, trying to think of something that could comfort his father, but he thought of nothing, and the word just hung in the air.

"Come." Mr. Porter looked at him now. "Help me clean this up before dem two women get here and start fuss."

And so it seemed quite logical for Harold to complete the job his father had started: find and kill the Rolling Calf. He originally thought to find the Calf on his own. After all, his father had given him enough information to complete the deed himself. But as much as he hated to admit it, it would be good to have a partner in crime. Just in case anything went wrong. He was sure that his father would assume it was he who killed the beast himself, while Nigel sat and wrote a story about his near-death experience.

And of course, there was also the chance that they may not succeed in altogether killing the beast. Harold heard his father's voice ring in his ears: "If yuh cyah tek him head, then tek him tail. Yuh see, him chain-link tail is part a de Calf core self. Him need it fi feel like calf, fi break him victims in half. To destroy de tail, mek sure fi submerge it inna de salt water. Just remember dis: chance is, him gon come after yuh for what is his."

..............

In all these years, I still wish there was something I could have done to warn them. As the teller, I feel responsible for my endings, powerless that I am to change them. But first, let us return, if only momentarily, to Old Man Toby who was trying, at this very moment, to ignore the spark growing inside him, the smoke rising off his tongue.

You see, Old Man Toby went to work that morning just as always, chopping every animal in sight but swine. He could smell the blood and carcass on his clothes as he left the shed to travel to market. He felt a hunger—no, a burning grow inside him. Like his heart lit ablaze. And when he arrived at his shop, his customers came and left, their faces frozen in horror. It was then that he looked in the mirror and saw his eyes change from brown to fire red. How his tongue looked the color of tar. His chest shook and sweat as fur appeared all over his body. He walked outside his store and heard a child scream. But when he looked, he saw nothing but desert. He felt the chain drag behind him, felt a drumbeat where his heart should be, heard a voice tell him to run, and so he ran. Ran toward the wind. Ran toward the sea. Felt the hunger start to sear. Felt the fire start to burn.

As he ran, he witnessed boys and girls lurking on the street, when, of course, they should have been at home. Teenagers fornicating on the side of the road when they should be studying God's word. Couples smoking ganja and listening to the music by Rastas and other godless people using the Lord's name in vain. Perhaps God brought him here in this form to restore order in a world that had not seen morality in a very long time. He smiled, feeling like his old self again. And that was when he saw them: three little boys walking and loitering like heathens. And two of them smelled like battyman.

............

It was then that the boys thought they heard something. A chain rattling, cracking against tar road and tree trunk. It's true it smelled of sausage, but not of any sausage you've ever eaten. You could smell the things they put inside it—the things you pretend aren't there when you devour it with stewed tomato or jerk sauce—you know which parts I'm referring to. I won't get into it. I'll just say that besides the smell of insides, it also smells revoltingly familiar. You are now aware that the Calf was once human. You're aware he could be you.

The smell of fire came next and then the sight of the beast. Blood rose from the Rolling Calf's nostrils like heat. Pus dripped from his mouth. The horns atop his head were gnarled and knobbed as tree trunks—much larger than the fake horns on Harold's head earlier. His eyes swirled like lava, his chained tail snapped the ground and the earth separated into minerals. Nigel realized that the Calf had probably come for the rest of his chain. Instinctively, Oscar moved closer to Harold and put his arms around him. How were they supposed to wind up victorious in their mission with this lanky batty bwoy in their way? And more importantly, why did it always seem to Nigel that he was never enough for his brother? Nigel watched their embrace in disgust for just a moment, when he had a thought: why not teach this batty bwoy a lesson once and for all? He slipped the chain-link tail into Oscar's knapsack, knowing that all he would have to do once the Calf began to chase him was to stab it him the leg with the penknife and then drag him into the sea. Oscar would be fine, of course, and hopefully all the wiser.

And yet with one swift movement, the Calf charged into Harold and Oscar with his horns, and they toppled over. The boys began to run. The boys began to scream.

. . . . . . . . . . . . .

Old Man Toby moved closer to batty bwoy number one and two to try and explain to them of their sins. Of course, no English words came out his mouth. Just fire and sounds whose only purpose must have been to put fear into man. The Calf snarled at the boys, pointing his horns at them for effect, and then battyman one and two fell to the ground and rolled around like girls.

He heard his tail crack the grass. He charged the two boys with his horn, and they scattered. He followed the boys into the bush. The third boy who had taken the rest of his chain disappeared in the bushes opposite the battyman. He'd deal with him later, of course. He decided to start with the red-skinned boy, and he pushed him down with his horn. His initial plan was only to preach to him, but there was a hunger growing inside him. He opened his lips to the boy's arm. The red-skinned boy began to cry. Just a taste, he said to himself. A taste won't kill him. A taste will only teach him a lesson. But ooooh! Tastes so good! Better than sweets! Better than the touch of a woman! The blood filled him now. His body began to cool down. As if he were swimming in the ocean. Like a wave breaking overhead. Like the sun setting over his eyes. As though he were swimming in the middle of a rainbow. He could feel the boy's limbs breaking apart against his teeth. Felt the bones crackle and pop inside his mouth. Felt them swish around inside his belly.

.............

Was like Oscar'd never heard the stories before. You never run from the Rolling Calf. But then Harold started running too. Watching his brother roll around on the ground, screaming, he felt a growing horror inside him and he worried he might throw up. He ran toward the Calf with his bag of sand and salt water in hand. When he caught up to where they had fallen, he cried out at the sight before him: it was Oscar lying on the ground barely conscious and bleeding as the Calf took a bite from his left arm.

The Calf looked up at Nigel to see his bag of sand. Steam evaporated off his hanging tongue. His breath smelled of smoke and rotten meat. The Calf was quickly approaching him now. The steam and the smoke came together to make wind and, you remember what I told you about the Wind, don't you? Well, on this day the Wind Herself wore a steel-blue dress. She ran circles around the Rolling Calf's eyes and mouth, scaring the flies and mosquitoes away from landing there. Nigel thought of his father's warning—and yet the Calf seemed scared, too. His fiery breath wavered in the breeze as he shook from side to side. The Calf tried to sink his hooves deeper into the earth for balance from the wind. Nigel thought that maybe his father was wrong—that maybe the Wind was a sign of something—like a miracle—or at the very least, a good diversion. Nigel used the opportunity to stick his penknife into the ground while Harold attempted to carry Oscar into the bushes to hide.

And then came the rain.

It started as a leaky-pipe kind of drizzle before coming down at a steady pace. Small puddles transformed into pools all around them. Nigel took out his whip and tried to herd the beast toward the ocean only a few kilometers from where they stood. The Calf looked afraid. His fire was dying. All that came out his mouth now was smoke. He began to cough. His horns began to shrink. The Wind Herself swirled around his face like a small tornado.

Now Nigel used this opportunity to gloat—to consider that maybe fathers didn't actually know everything. Sometimes they existed only to make you feel less than. He took out his penknife and lunged at the Calf like it was his sword. The knife grazed the Calf's neck and blood spurted. He was whimpering now. Nigel laughed: "Yuh see here?" he sneered at the Wind. But Nigel didn't notice the hot air become cold, the Wind's shy laugh as she opened her arms to the sky, her blue dress flying upward, turning gray, turning black—how her dress was ripping up stones and wood planks off houses, how cheap folding chairs took flight. Nigel stood transfixed to the pieces of steel blue creating moon shapes in the air. Didn't anybody ever tell him not to push against the Wind? She's unpredictable. Hurricanes and tornadoes come out of nowhere they say and it's true. She'd never admit it to anyone, but underneath all that bravado, all she really wants is a little recognition—for the world to know that even the Wind gets a little lonely sometimes. It's no wonder she feels the need to be everywhere at once.

Meanwhile, Harold picked up Oscar, heading for the hills. The Rolling Calf came charging right after them, leaving Nigel to admire his lunge. The Calf threw his horns at their torsos, and the boys screamed.

And then came the Wind.

The Wind Herself took the Calf and the boys into her bosom and flew. She flew them up over the moon. She flew them up over their neighborhood and over their homes. They saw chickens in trees and duppies sleeping under children's beds through the windows. Harold held on tight to Oscar. He kissed Oscar's arm above where it had been bitten. Oscar leaned into Harold's chest. They took a deep breath and closed their eyes.

This is the part we call the final act, in which our villain is vanquished. Unfortunately for you, however, his defeat brings little joy. It was in fact, Old Man Toby himself who prayed that Jesus would come for him that night. On this night the Calf saw huts flooded and sinking down into Babylon. Saw himself fly over the ocean. Saw the moon glow like Heavenly light. The Wind Herself dropped him down into the sea, and he could feel himself burning. It made a hush, hu-shh sound like a hiss. He felt his horns break off into the water and watched them float along the current. He felt his fur wash off his skin. Saw bits of fur float all around him. He felt himself melt into the ocean. It was at this point that he realized he could no longer feel his body. "God, please tell me the plan," he said before disappearing into the sea.

.............

The Wind Herself forced Harold and Oscar to drink from her teat. In their last moments, the two lovers drank in mango peel, baby powder, Milo tins filled with pennies, hair grease, butterfly wings, and nail clippings. And when there was nothing left to swallow, they were made to swallow Wind. She got inside of them, in their lungs, in their bellies until they were finished. Just two bodies tossed and found by the side of the road before church on a Sunday.

.............

Nigel watched his brother fly up over the trees with Oscar and the Wind before disappearing into rain. Nigel waved his arms frantically, trying to call out Harold's name, but the Wind took his words every time. All that came out was "Har" and then the shooshing sound of the Wind in his ears. His body sank down into the earth until he felt warm again, until he thought, *Maybe this isn't really happening* or *Maybe she'll take me too.*

Yes, Gilda went hard that night. Mud swallowed houses. Goat and cow slipped and broke their necks. Puddles became lakes and rivers with tree branch, human limb, and uneaten fruit drifting around like dead fish. Houses became seashells and got swept away. Wind wasn't angry. Truth is, girl was just hungry. Swallowed six people whole and spit them back out as bones. Harold, Oscar, and Old Man Toby were only three.

..............

Do you know what it's like to watch someone get swallowed whole by a hurricane? I do.

In order to paint you a picture of my experience, I'd like for you to first close your eyes. Imagine for a moment that it is you that has been forced to record everything, to empathize, at least momentarily, with the other side. Imagine Hitler's *Mein Kampf* running up and down your aorta while *The Diary of Anne Frank* pumps through your lungs. Imagine you are forced to enjoy the satisfaction an oppressor has in taking down her prey, eviscerating organs, popping them in her mouth like canapés—and yet you are also forced to watch as you yourself are being eviscerated, while someone else enjoys the show.

Because when I think of the Wind, I can't help but remember how beautiful she looked—even as she snapped a man in half, plopped him into her mouth, and chewed his bones out before licking her lips. Even then, all I could do was admire her handiwork. Even I found myself laughing along as her throaty chortle teased the leaves. I couldn't help but notice how Oscar's and Harold's bodies wrapped together in flight looked like a swirl of watercolor within her grasp.

You're judging me, but you forget how hard it is to be relentlessly called to witness. That there are times when a girl wishes to do more than tell stories. I'd like to remind you that the part where I ask you to save my life is coming up before you know it. I hope that you'll come prepared.

But first, let's take a look at Nigel. Now Nigel will wind up spending the next forty-five years trying to write this story. He will try to describe the Wind's eyes that day: Were they blue or gray? Did she smile at him before taking his brother in her arms and smashing him into the trees? He will write words and then delete them until the story of what happened replaces what actually occurred. *Using the wisdom of my father,* he will write, *I alone defeated the Calf. It ended with a swift jab in the neck with my penknife. But alas, it was too late for my brother.* This is what he tells his parents late that night. It is what most townsfolk believe to have happened. It is what gets written in the official police report. It is what gets written in Harold's obituary and eulogy delivered by none other than Nigel Porter himself.

After the incident, Nigel's father will take to working longer hours at Kaiser. Amos's once sporadic pep talks for Nigel quickly deteriorated into grunts in the doorway with a nod and a tip of his hat in Nigel's direction. The dimness in his father's eyes told Nigel that his father might not have known, but at the very least suspected that Nigel was keeping something from him about the death of his son.

Now, if possible, try not to be too hard on our dear Nigel about the keeping of this secret. Because the truth of the matter is that the actual memory of what happened that night could have killed him had he let it. At times, stories need to be reinvented just to get through the telling of them. Imagine how much more tortured Nigel's soul might have been had he told his father and mother and the room of people who listened to his eulogy at his brother's funeral that he in fact held himself responsible for the death of his brother and his brother's lover? Why, he might never have had the strength to leave for America, pursue his own business, and live. His story, instead, might go something like this: *After the death of his brother, Nigel decided to take his own life—jabbing his neck with a penknife until it stuck.*

Nigel's retelling of his defeat of the Rolling Calf will, in fact, become one of Nigel's "famous stories"—the kind his daughters will tell their children's children about. How their father's eyes grew large, how his voice rose and fell like a wave. *Once upon a time,* their father would say, *there was a boy and his brother.* Many have suspected that there is more to this story, but none have ever been able to come up with any tangible proof. Unless, of course, you are paying close attention to the way he tells it.

If you look carefully at Nigel as he tells this story, you may pick up on the flash of lightning in his eyes, the storm that never left him. You may hear the crack in his voice as he repeats his brother's name, "Harold." Sometimes he holds a hand out as he says it—like maybe this time he can grab him from the Wind's grasp. Like maybe this time it won't be too late to save him. But most who listen will just hear a story—the kind told at night to scare children out of disobeying their parents' wishes: *Whenever we had the mind to be rebellious and stray far against our father's wishes, we'd hear the metal, smell the pork, and know we had gone too far,* he would say.

Now Oscar, on the other hand, has been imagined out of Nigel's story entirely. When they find the bodies wrapped into one another early on a Sunday morning, everyone will assume it was the Wind's doing. They will turn their minds away from the interlaced fingers, one boy's head resting on the other one's chest, and the Calf's tail—the metal chain wrapped around their torsos, pulling them into a close embrace.

# CHAPTER 7

# Sasha & the Photograph

*Sasha/Ashes*

Brooklyn, NY

June 2002

SO I'M LOOKING IN THE MIRROR WHEN I REALIZE IT: I WILL never ever look like Denzel Washington. With my long girly lashes and my chubby-ass cheeks, I still look exactly like a twelve-year-old girl. I squint my eyes shut, hoping that when I open them again, I'll look somehow different. Like my chin will somehow be more round, less pointy. Like my lashes will magically uncurl and shorten. But of course, when I open them, I still look exactly like me. And to make things worse, I got a huge-ass zit on my forehead.

Shit is especially bad because today is the day that I get to see Shay, which will be the first time I've seen her in like two years since she's been off in Atlanta at some all-girls school. She'll probably see my zit and run all the way back to Georgia. I take out my mom's concealer and think what's worse—Shay making fun of me for wearing makeup or Shay making fun of me for having a zit?

I sigh, take a deep breath, and look into the mirror. "So, Shay, I've been doing some thinking and . . ." But already I feel like an idiot. First time I'm seeing her in two years, and imma start off with, I've been doing some thinking? Lord, get it together, Ashes.

I close my eyes, and the moment is perfect. Shay'll come in wearing that Knicks jersey that always makes her skin pop. Our hug will extend and linger between us. My arms will fall from her shoulders to her hips to her lower back. She'll look up, surprised. I'll inch my lips closer to her lips. She'll inch her lips closer to my lips. I'll avert my eyes. I'll stall. I'll stall. I open my eyes. I take another breath. "So, we've been friends for a long time and . . . I've been doing some thinking."

I sink into the boxes on the floor and sigh. Maybe I should just call and reschedule. I pound a box with my fist till it breaks into pieces of cardboard. I pull out my blunt and lighter from my pocket. As soon as I exhale, I feel my heart slow. Thank God Mom took Zora and Kayla to get their hair ironed by the Dominicans. Plenty of time to air the place out with how long the wait times always be.

I'm nearly finished with the blunt when I notice that inside the box I broke open with my fist is a photo of Dad. The photo is worn and colorless. Dad looks no more than fifteen years old—a whole two years younger than I am. In the photo, he's standing in front of a river with a barracuda in hand like a giant trophy. He's sitting next to another man that I imagine to be his brother. His possible brother is tall and muscular, making Dad look a bit lanky—maybe even scrawny. My uncle is smirking at me from the photograph like he's up to no good.

The only thing my father has ever said about his brother is that he was killed by a hurricane—or the Rolling Calf, depending on his mood as he's telling the story. As I examine the photo, I notice another man with copper-tone skin staring at my father and dead uncle from in between the trees. I bring the photo closer to my face to see it better, when I hear a knock on the door.

"Not supposed to be in here."

I jump at the sound of her voice. It's Zora, hands on her hips like she's in charge of shit.

"You guys are back early," I say without looking up.

"There was a long-ass wait, and Mom was complaining about how she had a headache again," Zora says. She looks around the room then, sniffing the air like a puppy. "And uhh, you might wanna air this room out before Mom comes up here. It stinks."

"So tell her not to come up here." I shrug.

"I'm not your lookout girl, Sasha. Not anymore. I'm over it." Her voice is strained.

I roll my eyes and walk over to the window. "Did you come in here just to tell me that?"

"No. Shay's waiting for you. She's downstairs."

And now I'm pissed. "Seriously, Zora? You should've led with that," I say, getting up and straightening out my clothes.

Zora shrugs. "Look, I'm getting sick and tired of—"

"Okay, okay, goodbye, Zora," I say and I'm off.

When I finally see Shay, I barely recognize her. She's gained some weight and has a lot more muscles than I remember her having. I can tell that she has all her hair shaved off underneath her Knicks cap. But most surprisingly—there's a beard on her face.

"Well, dang, don't just stand there," she says and opens her arms to hug me.

When I do, I feel everything coming back to me, and I hide my face so she can't see me blush. She still smells good—like rosewood and cardamom. I want to stay there longer in between her arms, but she pulls away and looks me over.

"Wow," I say, taking a good look at her.

"I look different, I know," she says.

And she did. I can't tell if I'm feeling angry, intrigued, or something else altogether. But before I can say anything, I hear the loud bass that is my mother's voice calling me from the living room.

I walk over to see her sprawled across the couch with an ice pack on her forehead.

"Mom, you good?" I ask, concerned. I wonder if it's her headaches. They seem to be getting worse by the day—longer and more intense every time she has them. I wonder if it has something to do with Dad announcing he's marrying the German home-wrecker through that hideous wedding invitation we got in the mail last week.

"Bring me back some Excedrin from the store for me please," she says, ignoring my question.

"I can't, Mom. I'm going out with Shay, remember?"

My mother sucks in her breath and points a finger at me.

"If I were you," she says, "I would be very careful of the friends yuh keeping, yuh hear me?"

"Oh, God, Mom, goodbye," I say and start out the room.

"Sasha," she says again.

"Yes, Mom?" I turn around, trying not to show the annoyance in my voice.

"The Excedrin."

I roll my eyes and walk out behind Shay without saying another word.

We walk silently at first, rounding the corner, and away from my mother. But once we're out of sight, we both start grinning and hug each other tighter than we ever have before. I wonder if we'll kiss, but she pulls away before I can consider making a move.

"So, where we going?" I ask, feeling shy around her for the first time in a while.

"Like I told you on the phone," she says with a smile, "it's a surprise."

We get to the park, and I think, of course this is where she would take me—just like old times. We start making our usual route and see the Drum Man selling his djembes like usual, trying to make small talk, asking Shay how the family's doing now that she's back in town.

My heart starts speeding as I think about what I want to say to her. I've loved you since the day I met you—no. I think we should be more than friends—no. I've been doing some thinking and—no. Lord, Ash, get it together.

As we walk by the lake, we hear someone blasting Vybz Kartel. Shay starts swinging her head from side to side, vibing with the music. I want to vibe with her but settle for watching her nervously instead. And then I ask the question I don't want to but feel like I should.

"So, are you like a . . ."

"A man?" she says, looking to the concrete and shoving her hands down deep inside her jersey pockets. "Becoming one—slowly but surely,

I guess." She grins so wide on the last word that her teeth start to look bigger than her face, and I can tell that she seems happy.

"So, how'd you do it?"

"Listen, man, it's a process. They made me see a doctor then a shrink and then a motherfucking psychiatrist. I can walk you through it, you know . . . if you want."

"If I want to what?"

I feel my temperature rising.

"Ashes," she says. "I don't know how to explain it, but it feels . . . different. Being a man. Like you feel like you're finally you again, you know what I mean?"

But I didn't know. "You know, sometimes I think I don't really wanna be a man or a woman."

"Then you're fucked," she says.

"I'm saying."

And we laugh.

We enter one of the trails that goes by the water and makes you feel a little more like you're in the woods. We continue walking the path for a while in silence until I break it with the inevitable: "So like what do I gotta call you now anyway?"

"Call me Shay," she says, and I have to smile at that.

"So what, you mean you not gonna pick a new name?"

"Guess I'm just waiting for one to come to me."

"Hmm," I say, thinking for a moment. "How about Shane?"

"C'mon, that's such a white-boy name, Ash."

"Fair enough."

As we walk, I notice how quiet everything seems in the park. There are no other people walking our path and all I can hear is the sound of the stream beside us. I wonder where all the birds are. The water looks green with algae.

Silence and then: "Shawn?"

"Nah."

"What's wrong with Shawn?"

"Too basic. I need a name that's gonna make me stand out."

"Well, you don't need a name to do that," I say and then I look away, realizing I might be blushing.

There's silence again and then: "So like what does this mean for like . . . ?" I want to say us, but I can't quite get the words out. Does this make her straight now?

Shay turns to me at this point, putting her hand on my shoulder, and I feel a current run through me. "Nothing's ever gonna change between us, you know that, right?" she says.

"Sure," I say, although I'm not, and then she lets go of my shoulder, and I wish I hadn't spoken so soon.

As we're walking through the trail, I realize I no longer recognize the path we're on. Even though I could swear we've walked this path together before probably like a million times, it looks somehow different now. Like the dirt path seems to have shrunk to nothing, and there's a bunch of overgrown bush in our path. The trees look a lot taller and wider than they should be for Prospect Park, and there are weeds everywhere that we keep needing to step over.

"Umm . . . not that I don't trust you, Shay, but where the hell are we going?"

"Relax," she says with a smirk forming on the edge of her lips.

"I don't know, Shay," I say and just as I'm about ready to dip, the bushes separate.

I look up to see the gates of a graveyard. The sign reads BROOKLYN FRIENDS CEMETERY.

"We're here," she says.

"You taking me to a graveyard?"

"You gonna like this, I promise," she says.

And yet I hear the sounds of birds and insects that I don't know the names of creating a lump inside my chest. "Are we even supposed to be in here?"

"Look, don't bitch out on me now," she says and climbs over the fence. "I got you." She holds out a hand for me and pulls me up to the top of the fence.

When we get to the other side, I have to admit that it's beautiful. We're surrounded by stone sculptures of angels and animals, and there's a bunch of blue and purple flowers all around us. Even the tombstones sparkle like diamonds from the way the sun hits them.

"Okay, you got me, this is nice," I say.

"You were so scared," she says and holds her belly, chuckling.

"Hey, don't blame me for having doubts—you took me to a fucking graveyard," I say, but she keeps laughing.

We go to sit down in between the sculpture of the angel and the porcupine when I hear a noise coming from the grass. Is it a squirrel? Is it a rat? Is it some psycho lurking for us in the bushes? But already I know in the pit of my stomach that it doesn't sound like any of those things. It is a sound like rattling.

"What the fuck is that noise, Shay?" I want to grab her hand, but I don't.

"Hang on," she says and goes to investigate.

As she leaves, the sound gets low and far away until my anxiety begins to subside. I start to think about the other thing I've been dreading. Well, here's my moment, I guess. I take a deep breath. "Shay, there's something I've gotta tell you." I sigh and pull out Dad's photo from my pocket. I took it from the study when I left the house. I don't know why, but the image of my father and dead uncle holding a barracuda seems comforting now. There's something in the eyes of my uncle that seems somehow knowing. As I'm looking this time, I notice how nervous my father looks. Where my uncle puffs out his chest, beaming into the camera, my dad's eyes are off to the side—like he's looking out for something.

And then I notice something else: the copper-tone man behind my father and uncle is no longer staring at them. His eyes are now turned up to the sky. And there is a large silver chain around his neck. Not like the chains men wear to look like they got money. They were the kind they put on the necks of people who looked like me in order to drag us here. Of course this picture had to have been taken sometime in the seventies judging by my dad's age in the pic. I blink and look at it again. The chain is still hanging from the copper man's neck. It is wound so tightly it looks like he should be choking, but he's not. I put my finger on the photo like touching the chain will tell me something, when I hear something else.

"Coast is clear," Shay says and plops down next to me on the grass. "Damn, Ash, you look like you just seen a ghost."

"You know, I really don't like being in the park this late," I say, zipping up my hoodie and pulling my arms up around my knees.

"Here. Maybe this will help," she says and lights a blunt.

"Oh, thank God," I say, taking it from her. I feel my body relax with the first exhale. "So why'd you really bring me here, Shay?"

"Shh," she says, putting a finger to her lips. She lies down on the grass and motions for me to do the same. As I lie next to her, I feel her breath moving in time with the wind. The sun is spread across the sky like butter.

"This cemetery has the best sunset in the whole city—hands down," she says. "Plus, nobody knows about it so it's like Brooklyn's best kept secret."

"It's really beautiful," I agree.

I feel her body come closer to me, and I feel like this is my move. I tilt my head toward hers, but her eyes are still on the sky. I inch closer, and she looks at me startled for a moment. Our lips touch for just a second. She pulls away.

"Wait," she says.

"Look, I know what you're thinking," I say, "but before you say anything, I've been doing some thinking, and honest to God, the whole becoming-a-man thing doesn't even bother me. I mean sometimes butches do go with other butches—and honestly Shay, I just need you to know that—"

"Sasha." Her voice turns to gravel. "I met someone."

My heart stops beating. "What do you mean *someone*?" I say, although I know exactly what she means.

"Sasha, I—" she starts, but the words stop in her throat.

"You called me Sasha," I say because she never calls me that.

"Ash," she says, "I'm sorry."

"You know we've been walking around for at least an hour now. You could've said something."

"I know. I know. Look, I'm sorry. What else do you want me to say?"

"Nothing," I say and hand the blunt back to her. "Anyway, it's getting late."

"Oh c'mon, Ash. Don't be like that."

But I look away from her. "I gotta go," I say and get up.

"You don't even know where you're going," she says.

But I start walking, hearing her call my name over and over till it sounds like wind.

As I get back onto the path that led us to the graveyard, I notice that the sun has finally gone down and been replaced by a cold breeze. The park always looks different at night: shadowy and dark. The people who live here come out with their carts, and all you can hear is the heavy breathing of strangers, newspapers fluttering, and crickets. The same stream from before now looks lit up by the moon. I stop for a moment and take Dad's photo out again. When I look now, my dead uncle is standing next to the copper-tone man instead of my father. The copper-tone man is holding my uncle's hand. Their hands are tied by the iron chain that was previously around the copper man's neck. My father is standing behind the two of them now. His eyes are a swirl of red. I drop the photo to the ground, feeling my body get cold. All the sounds of the park get quiet until I hear nothing but wind.

But then I hear the sound again: a rattling. Like a chain being dragged across the ground. I start to run toward the nearest exit through the skating rink only to end up right back in front of the cemetery. What the fuck? "Shay?" I whisper. Then I call louder, "Shay!" my voice shaky. And then I scream it, "Shay!" "Shay!" "Shay!" until my voice is a rasp.

"Ash!" I finally hear in the distance.

I see her shadow down the hill and run toward it, stumbling onto the ground. She runs the rest of the way, and we hug.

I feel myself start to cry.

"I'm so sorry, Ash," she says and pulls me toward her. "I'm so, so sorry."

We stay there in the embrace for a moment, feeling the moonlight on our backs.

"Let's get out of here," she says, and I agree.

As we walk back toward my place, the wind lifts, and there's a heavy heat in the air. There's no one on the streets except for the occasional dollar van and a couple kids playing Sean Paul on someone else's stoop.

When we get to my house, she turns to me, and I already know what she's going to say. "I love you more than anything, you know."

"I know," I say and give her a kiss on the cheek. "Good night."

I decide to take a deep breath before entering the house. I sneak inside and hear the television playing *Touched by an Angel*—which means Mom is home—which means I'm in some real shit. I try to slide past the living room to my room on tiptoe so she won't hear me.

"Sasha?"

Shit. Too late.

"Come in here, Sasha. I can hear you."

Mom looks like a shadow in the dark hovering over the sofa.

"Do you know what time it is?"

I sigh. "Look, Mom, I wasn't doing anything—I was just—"

She holds up a hand to stop me. "Where's my Excedrin?"

"Shit."

"What?"

"Sorry, Mom—I forgot."

"So instead of helping your mother, you decide to go off gallivanting with your friends while you leave me here to die."

"Good Lord, Mother. You're not dying."

And that's when my eyes adjust to the light in the room. There's a broken vase by the sofa. Books and dirty dishes are strewn about on the floor.

"Mom, what's going on?"

Mom shrugs weakly.

"Is it Dad? Is he here?" He hasn't lived here in over two years, but it's still my instinct to want to go into fight mode.

She shakes her head.

"Not Dad."

Her words are forced, like it's hard for her to speak.

"Have you been lying here this whole time?" I say and start to pick up the lamp and plates from the floor.

"Headache," she says.

"These are beginning to seem like more than headaches, Mom. We should take you to the doctor."

I look back at her, and her face looks drained. Weary.

"It's nothing," she says.

"Bullshit."

"Watch your mouth, child. Ah could box you yet."

"Why didn't you just ask Zora to get you the Excedrin?"

"Then who would watch Kayla?" she says. "Besides, I asked you to get it."

"I know. I'm really sorry, Mom. I'll get it now."

"It's too late for that," she says. "Just come be with your mother."

I walk toward her tentatively and lift the blanket up to her chin and then move to lie beside her.

I feel scared about what's happening. But there's something else I want to ask her. "Mom?"

"Hmm."

"What do you know about Dad's brother?"

Mom sighs. "Not now, Sasha."

"Please, Mom," I say. "Did Dad ever talk about him?"

"No," she says. She rubs her finger around her temple as she speaks.

"Okay," I say and sigh. I look away from her, ready to get up and go to sleep defeated, when she stops me with her hand on my shoulder.

"Except for this," she says. "Say they found his body tied up with another man."

I open my mouth wide and stare at her a moment. "You mean he was—?"

"Like you, yes."

"I was gonna say murdered, but okay."

"Him own father kill himself shortly after."

"Jesus."

"Language."

"Do they know who did it?"

"They say it was the hurricane, but . . ." She pauses to rub her other temple with her hand.

"Here," I say and move to rub her forehead with my hand.

"Some say it was the Devil."

"Oh, please, Mom. Don't tell me the Devil got him for being gay or some shit."

I look away from her to roll my eyes.

"No." Mom stops my hand from massaging her forehead. "The one who did it—you could say he was kind of like a Devil," she says, finally.

I think about the rattling when she says this. "Did they say how he did it? Was it with a chain?"

She looks at me sideways. "Why you so curious?"

"I found a photo in Dad's study."

"I see," she says and wraps an arm around me. "Well, I'll just tell you this. The amount of time yuh father try and write de story about he and his brother, yuh know there must be something he eh ready to tell as yet. To tell yuh de truth, I tink he still scared."

"Of the Devil?"

"Of himself, child," she says and then yawns and stretches her legs out at that. "So," she says, "did you have a good time with your friend?"

"Not really."

Mom looks at me for a moment and then says, "To be honest I always thought you could do better than that one."

"Oh please, Mom. You just want me to end up with a man."

"Not all love is easy, ent?" she says, and I wonder what kind of love she means. She strokes my forehead softly for a moment and says, "But when you find it, the whole earth will stop to celebrate you."

.............

I get upstairs to my room to find Zora waiting for me.

"Someone was out late," she says.

"Zora, I'm really not in the mood," I say, walking past her to my bed.

"What's wrong?" she says, walking toward me.

I look from Zora to the back of my hands and then back to Zora again. I don't know if it's being rejected by Shay or being chased out of the park by my uncle's ghost or possibly the Devil—or maybe it's Mom's headaches that seem like more than headaches, but I just fall into Zora's arms and sob.

Zora looks back at me in shock but eventually puts her arms around me and tilts her head on my shoulder. "Shh," she says. "You're okay now. You're okay. You're okay. You're okay."

.............

The next day I decide to go over to Dad's for dinner.

"Way to drop a bombshell, Dad," I say, referring to the wedding invitation. "Zora's pissed by the way."

We're eating a flavorless roasted chicken and mashed potatoes that Dad's woman must have made. She keeps flashing her wedding hand in my direction to not so subtly show off her rock.

"We spoke to Zora," Dad says. "She said congratulations."

"Well, you know I'm not gonna say that, right?"

Dad gives me a steady gaze. Dad's woman just looks away. Their child is playing with her food, singing to herself.

Dad breaks his stare to smile at his bride-to-be. "Didn't I tell you that Zora would take it better than she would?" Dad says to his woman, and his woman just nods.

"I'm sitting right here, Dad. And anyway, no, she's just pretending to take it better than me. She came crying to me about it last week."

"We did think of you when designing this, you know," Dad's woman says to me. She's waving her hands around her face wildly as she speaks, her diamond sparkling under the chandelier. "It was hand-painted and then digitized by this young gay street artist I met, Sergio. Brilliant young man."

I roll my eyes and spit out some bland potatoes into my napkin. I think instead about what I came to ask them.

"So, Dad," I say, "have you ever told Addy and Madeleine here the story about the two brothers and the Rolling Calf?"

"Ooh!" Dad's woman says, clapping her hands. "One of your father's famous stories. I'd love to hear this."

"Maddy might be a little too young for this story," Dad says, wiping his lips with his napkin.

"She'll love it," I say, perhaps a little too mischievously.

"Sasha," he says, his voice oscillating between annoyance and a warning shot.

"C'mon, Dad," I say, "you love to tell stories."

Dad sighs and looks to his fiancée, realizing that he is stuck. "Once upon a time," he begins, "there was a boy and his brother."

Dad's woman's eyes light up like a jack-o'-lantern as he speaks, and I fight the urge to slap her. Their child is currently making a mashed potato monster on her plate while her parents do nothing to reprimand her.

"The two brothers were so close that some would say the two even shared a body," Dad continues, "but at a certain point, the brothers began to compete as brothers often do. The older brother was often shunned at home and called a girl. The brother became jealous, bitter, and went off by himself to fight the Rolling Calf."

As he speaks, I notice it has just begun to rain.

"Sasha, would you like to tell them what the Rolling Calf is?"

"Soul of a butcher," I say, through bites of chicken.

"Yes, Sasha, a tortured, *godless* butcher," he adds, emphasizing the word "godless" while he looks at me. I notice in his eyes what looks like a flash of lightning. Outside the window, I hear thunder. "You could hear Rolling Calves where my brother and I grew up because they have thick iron tails that smell of sausage and clink like chains."

"Oh, so this story is about your brother," I say, smiling.

"So one day, the boy goes out to find his brother," he says ignoring me, "but as he does, the sky begins to tear. A hurricane is coming."

"Ooh! How exciting!" Dad's woman says and grabs her child. "It's raining right now, just for us—do you see that, Maddy?" His woman points to the window emphatically. Maddy ignores her.

I'm having a hard time paying attention to Dad at this point as the rain keeps getting louder, steadier. It's starting to sound like it's coming from inside the house.

"When he does find his brother, he is at the edge of the ocean, being backed into the sea by none other than the Rolling Calf himself."

The rain is pounding so hard against our window, I'm worried it might break the glass. I notice from the corner of my eyes, the water seeping in from the windows. I don't know why I say nothing.

"The boy is afraid of the Rolling Calf, yes, but he is more afraid of what may happen to his brother."

As the rain pounds harder, I notice that Madeleine is no longer staring at her food, but at the window.

"It's just thunder, honey," her mom says, but Maddy is transfixed by the sound of the rain.

As I listen, I realize that I'm hearing it again—the sound of a chain rattling.

"Do you guys hear that?" I ask, feeling a familiar cold running through me.

"So cute," his woman says. "The two of them, afraid of a little rainstorm."

"Hmm," Dad says, barely noticing. He's absorbed in his story now. "The boy jabs the Calf with a penknife and drags him into the ocean. But alas, it was too late for his brother."

At this moment, I stop hearing the words my father is saying. I feel something sink to my stomach, something rise in my throat. I get up.

Madeleine joins me at the window, and we both look out into darkness. It's hard to see anything besides lightning, but then I see on the wall next to the window, that picture of my father and uncle. It's framed right next to a baby picture of Madeleine. I don't know how it got there, but in the photo my father is standing behind my uncle, looking stern. My uncle has his hand outstretched in the air, but the copper-tone man, who was holding his hand the last time I looked at it, is gone.

I reach to touch the photo, when my dad stops me. "How'd this get here?" he says, taking it from me.

"Is this Uncle Harold?"

"How did you get this photo, Sasha?" Dad's voice turns to glass.

"What do you mean, Dad—it was right here on your mantel."

"Yes, but how did it get there, Sasha? And don't be smart."

"Nigel, what is this about?" His woman walks over to join us.

"Addy, have you ever seen this photo before?"

Dad's woman looks lost.

"I'm giving you another chance to explain yourself, Sasha," he says.

"What are you talking about, Dad? You saw me pick the photo up right here." Of course truth be told, I'm feeling confused about how it could have gotten there when I definitely dropped it in the park last night.

"Nigel, come sit down and let me make you some tea," Dad's woman says. "And Sasha? Why don't we call you a cab home? It's late and raining. Your mother must be worried sick."

I want to say something slick about what my mother might be more worried about than me walking home in the rain, but I decide to hold my tongue.

"Yes, it's time for you to go," Dad says, and I can tell he's trying to remain calm in front of his woman.

But I feel a fire rising in me. "What happened to your brother?" I say.

"Sasha," Dad says, "I'm warning you."

I feel the water getting inside my shoes at this point, and I wonder why no one else is trying to keep the water from flooding their house.

"And what happened to the other guy in the photo?" I say.

Dad says nothing, just slams his fist on the mantel till the photo crashes to the floor. The glass splinters. Dad looks at me like he wants to pound my face in, but he doesn't. Instead, he looks from me to the floor, which is covered in rain. Our shoes are all soaked. I look with him to the photograph on the floor, and as we look, the faces of my father and dead uncle are surrounded by water, their faces sinking into rain until all I see are two pairs of eyes, soaked in red.

# CHAPTER 8

## An Unfortunate Event on Maple Street
### *Zora*

Brooklyn, NY
March 2003

IT WAS LIKE THE END OF A JENGA GAME, THE WAY SHIT JUST fell apart. Our family foundation had been fading slowly for years, and yet when it all collapsed, it seemed to happen all at once. The first piece to fall apart after Dad moved out was Sasha.

See, one day Mom's going through Dad's old study that we've been using as a storage unit, looking through our three-year-old clothes to see if there's anything that might fit Kayla. Little does she know that Sasha's been using the room as a secret make-out spot since she started talking to Mel about a week ago. And I'm supposed to be the lookout girl. This is my job. But lately I've been feeling like Sasha only wants me around to help her get out of trouble. I mean she's going off to college in a few months, and you'd think she'd wanna spend some time with her sister who's always had her back, who's like her other half—or at least that's what she is to me. Instead, she's been spending all her free time with Mel—this rich white girl from Brooklyn Heights/wannabe hoodrat who I know Sasha's only keeping around for two reasons: (1) Mel's older brother's weed connections. (2) Shay'll be graduating from college and moving back to NYC in a few weeks, and she thinks she can make Shay jealous.

So when I hear Mom stomping down the hall with a box of clothes in one hand and a cocoyea broom in the other, I decide not to say anything. Just let her waltz right in there to find a half-naked Sasha and

Mel rolling around between old photo albums and boxes of stuff. All I can hear from my vantage point of the living room is hissing and cursing sounds like a serpent coming from my mother, the white-girl screams like nails on a chalkboard coming from Mel, and the sounds of thrashing coming from the cocoyea broom—Mom's weapon of choice. I run into the room in time to see Mel run past me to the front door half-naked while Sasha just lies there silently, her back flinching every now and then against the thrash of the broom.

I peek in to try and de-escalate, but Mom looks to me like a monster woman—her hair stringy with sweat, her eyes burning like fire. Mom, of course, has always gone off the handle, but lately she's seemed more intense—always complaining about getting headaches and dizzy spells, which make her meaner and swifter with her swipes.

I walk out the room and sit on the sofa to take out my journal. The social worker at school tells me she's glad I like writing so much—that it will help me to connect more with my feelings. I tell her I'd rather not connect to them at all—that lately I just want to write about magic like what if I became a superhero like Buffy the Vampire Slayer—stuff like that. Write the first thing that comes into your head when that pen is in your hand, she says. I tell her she'll be sorry she said that, and she laughs. The journal she gave me is leather, and the paper in it looks old and mystical. I write:

*The cocoyea broom is made from several pieces of coconut fronds tied together. Great for sweeping backyards, front yards, and thrashing the back of your sister till it looks red and black like a ladybug that got crushed under your foot. My mother tells me that the cocoyea broom was once used to free people and places from evil, which only makes me wonder what evil she thinks my sister's back must be responsible for to end up like a bug under her foot.*

I come in to check on Sasha hours later, and she's still in there, hunched up on the ground like a four-legged creature, surrounded by empty bottles of 151.

"Sasha?"

Her head bobs up and down in response, as though to a song.

Her speech is slurred with liquor and hard to understand. I don't think I've ever seen anything so scary. That is until she left.

So by the time Mom says she wants to take us out to dinner, Sasha's already been MIA for eight days. It's just me, her, and Kayla.

"You know they're saying that fake meat's just as bad as real meat. Maybe even worse," I tell her. I can tell by the fact that she's wearing her dancer pants and shirt that don't match when she doesn't even teach today, that this isn't really the time, but I can't help myself. "They say it's because the isoflavones can mess with the production of estrogen in your body."

Mom just gives me a look. "I think I'll have the sesame chick'n. What will you have, Kayla?" she says to her and not to me.

"Chicken!" Kayla says. "Chicken! Chicken! Chicken!"

I want to tell her that it isn't real chicken, but I decide it isn't worth the effort.

She looks nervously at Kayla who keeps banging her spoon on the table. Usually Mom says something like, "Behave yuhself, else I feed you to one of dem jumbie on the corner," but this time she doesn't. This should've been my warning that something was wrong.

"I'm going back home to Trinidad," she says. And then, "Don't ask for how long."

"What?" I say.

"Remember when you and Sasha kept asking me to go and find out what's going on with all these headaches and dizzy spells. Well, the doctors—they found a shadow in my brain."

My body freezes.

Kayla keeps talking, but her voice sounds muffled and faraway. "Mommy, why can't I come to Trin-dad?"

Mom sighs and runs her hand along Kayla's forehead.

"Shadow?" I can hear the sounds of feet and shuffling plates all around us, couples laughing. I start to feel dizzy.

"They say it started as little moles underneath my fingernails," she says, examining her hands. "That's why I couldn't see them. But then it metastis . . ." She struggles to finish the sentence.

"Metastasized," I say.

"What yuh know about all o dat, child?"

"The internet."

I feel myself losing patience. Why does she sound so calm? Why haven't the doctors said anything?

"Did they say if you need surgery?"

Mom sighs again.

"Chemo?"

"Are you sick, Mommy?" Kayla keeps butting in.

"Hush nah, child. I'm going to be here for a long, long time."

"Well, I think you should get a second opinion before you make any decisions." After all, people get misdiagnosed all the time.

"Why you think I'm going to Trinidad?"

"What are they going to tell you in Trinidad that they can't tell you here?"

"If I'm going to die, it's not gonna be in the cold. I won't die in the cold."

My mind goes blank again. She keeps talking, but I stop listening.

Mom says I was born in the snow and that when I was little I would try and run out of our old apartment building barefoot in the middle of a blizzard, and that's how come I like the cold so much. Whereas she came out at the start of a six-month drought. Before she died, Granny said the drought happened because her daughter had the power to absorb the moisture and heat of the whole world and keep it for herself. Ever since her first winter in New York with no heat in a drafty Flatbush apartment, Mom's been planning her escape route out of here and back to the place with only two seasons: rainy and dry.

"You hearing me, Zori?"

"What?"

"Steups," she says—the sound Mom makes when she sucks her teeth.

"Sorry, Mom. I'm listening."

"I say they want me to do some surgery I can't afford. Not with the insurance yuh father left me on. And it'll be cheaper there. Need to see if I can find Ma. She hard to reach these days. Don't like to talk on the phone. Think she disconnect it. But if anyone can tell me what it is I have, is she."

Ma is Mom's grandma on her mother's side. She's a retired general physician as well as a healer and Shango Baptist. Dad calls her the Obeah Woman. She's 104 years old. One time Mom says she saw her heal her neighbor Eddie who was basically paralyzed from the neck down. Everyone said the paralysis happened after his wife hired an Obeah woman to put a spell on him for chatting it up with some twenty-something-year-old waitress in town. Either that or it was muscular dystrophy. Either way, he came back from his session with Ma hours later, walking and talking like he never got laughed out of parties for his lazy eye and calves that sagged down low at his feet.

"So you're going to get the surgery in Trinidad then?"

"Didn't I just tell you I'm going to find Ma?"

"She's 104, Mom."

"Course I can't tell she about me and yuh father. Yuh know how that woman feel about divorce."

"Mom, are you even listening to me?"

"Can I come, Mommy? Can I? Can I? Can I?"

"Shut up, Kayla," I snap, and she begins to whimper. Mom cuts her eyes at me.

"No, child. You'll have to stay with your father and he woman."

"But I wanna come!"

The sounds from the nearby tables are getting louder again: the chatter and giggling are almost deafening.

"Mom, why did you bring us here?"

"I just thought—"

"You thought what?"

I feel something rising in my throat that needs to get out.

"Zori." Mom reaches out a hand to me and then touches her head like it hurts.

I feel guilty that I'm getting upset now, knowing that she's hurting. "I'm sorry, Mom."

Mom says nothing and looks back at Kayla. "Yuh father wants to spend time with you, child. Don't you want to spend time with him? Besides, over there they have a likkle girl your age. And a dog. Remember how much yuh loved Aunty Nelsa and Uncle Mark's own dog? This one is even cuter."

"How would you know?" I say before she cuts her eyes at me again. "Anyway, I thought that Shango couldn't cure cancer."

"Americans always worried about cure. Is not a cure. Is through prayer and herbal remedies that certain things can be revealed. And who knows? Maybe it's not really cancer. And if it is, she'll know. She never tried to cure anything outside of her abilities a day in her life."

The one time I met Ma was the only time me and Sasha went with Mom to Trinidad when we were little, and she agreed to take us to the beach. She kept telling us to stay close to the shore, and we kept not wanting to listen. I remember thinking how strange it was that a woman as small as she was could yell so loud.

"Help me spirit, Mama Dglo," she said to the water. "Rid me of darkness in your castle below."

"Why was she doing that?" I asked.

"That day was supposed to be a real tough storm," Mom said. "Two boys drowned later that night in the same spot that you two children was swimming in. She was talking to the ocean to make sure it took care of you while you was there."

. . . . . . . . . . . . .

That night I spend hours searching through the yellow pages for the profiles of various doctors as well as their addresses, their reviews, and price lists. Dr. Woodworth looks like a winner with a specialization in neuro-oncology and an average wait time of only twenty-eight minutes.

He doesn't accept any form of insurance, though. His ad says that every patient is his top priority. First consultation only $959.99. I try to wrap that number around my head: 959. Then I don't want to think about it anymore, so I start watching *Buffy the Vampire Slayer* on TV. The Scooby Gang convinces Buffy not to do a spell to try to get rid of her mother's cancer.

"The truth is, the mystical and the medical aren't meant to mix, Buffy," Giles says. And she just accepts that. Her mother will die, and she'll have to grow up without her. I want to kick Giles in the head for that. I think maybe it's good that Mom's going to Trinidad. Maybe only magic can save her.

Kayla comes into the TV room during the scene where Buffy runs out the magic shop at superhero speed to defeat the cobra monster and save her sister Dawn—the one she can save.

"You shouldn't be watching this," I say, before pulling her onto my lap, wrapping my arms around her tight. We watch as Buffy runs toward the cobra monster in a long black trench coat and large hoop earrings. Her face is so determined. Her hair is golden perfection. We know that Buffy is going to win because she has to. She yanks a chain from a gate and straddles the cobra monster, strangling him. The cobra monster's eyes go from golden brown to gray. His reptile skin turns the color of ash. It's revolting. Kayla's eyes are transfixed to the screen. She squeezes my hand tight. The scene ends with Buffy punching the cobra's mouth over and over and over and over as though somehow this will keep her mother from dying. I understand this. We skip the part where Buffy and Dawn return to the hospital to find their bandaged mother is still sick. Like maybe not watching the ending will change it. And then we fall asleep like that on the couch until morning.

When I wake up, I sneak into Dad's study to call the first doctor I find in the span of like thirty pages that actually takes her insurance. A woman answers the phone. She sounds exhausted.

"Yes?" she says.

"Is this the office of Dr. Myers?" I ask tentatively.

"Yeah, can I help you?" Though her tone doesn't sound as though she wants to hear my answer.

"I'm trying to make an appointment for my mom. She thinks she might have brain cancer. I'd like to have a second opinion."

"Dr. Myers doesn't do second opinions," she says and sounds as though she might hang up.

"Well, you see my mom was just told she might have skin cancer that spread to her brain and now she's saying she's going to Trinidad to see her great-grandmother who's 104 years old. I mean this woman's been retired for the last forty years. So, if there's any way Dr. Myers could see her—"

"Next available appointment is August first," she says.

"But that's three months from now."

"Would you like to book the appointment?"

I stop, breathe loud into the receiver. The line dies in my hand.

I call about fifteen more doctors before I find someone who takes her insurance and can see her this week.

When I go into Mom's room to tell her, she's already started packing.

"Mom, what are you doing?"

On her bed is a small duffel bag with a few summer dresses, a bikini, citronella oil for mosquitoes, a painted figurine of Saint Jerome, a sun hat, and a family photo album.

"What does it look like, child, I'm leaving."

"Does Sasha know about this?" I say, crossing my arms and trying to look larger than I am.

Mom looks smaller than usual sitting on the edge of her bed, staring at her room as if for the last time. Her forehead is dripping small beads of sweat underneath a bright yellow head wrap. Around her neck is the silver pendant with the turtle she sometimes likes to wear.

"I left her a voicemail," she says.

"Seriously?"

"Zora," Mom says, rubbing her forehead, "I doh have time for Sasha and she back talk right now. Ah tiyad. Just tell Sasha I'll call."

What the hell is wrong with you? I want to say, but I don't. I just roll my eyes and look away so she can't see me wipe the tears from my eyes.

"I made an appointment," I say without looking at her, "to get a second opinion."

"Zora—" she starts, but I stop her.

"If you don't like what they have to say, I promise to back off."

"That's not how this works, Zora."

I place my hand on her knee and squeeze it. "Please, Mom," I say.

Mom looks at me for a moment and finally nods. "You know you remind me of someone I used to know," she says.

"You're changing the subject."

"She was the only female chieftain the Taínos ever had."

"Okay, so you didn't actually know her then."

"Course she was the only one to give that boy Columbus a run for his money."

"You know, because the Taínos have all been dead for five hundred years."

"What I'm saying is that you have a little warrior in you yet. I'm going to need you to keep Kayla safe while I'm gone."

She moves to put the last of her dresses in her suitcase, and I move to stop her with my hand. "Don't go," I say.

Mom takes my hand in hers and kisses it before placing her dress back down on the bed. "Let's go see this doctor," she says.

.............

We arrive at the office and immediately I want to leave. The wallpaper looks like it's from the 1950s—all faded with paintings of giant green leaves. In the waiting room, there are mothers with crying babies and somebody yelling at the nurse up front about not paying to do a lab she never asked them for.

"I think I must be in Hell," Mom says, looking up to the ceiling fan whirring above us.

I try to think of something cheerful to say but settle on "It'll be okay," although I'm not sure that it will. I squeeze her hand tightly. She doesn't squeeze back.

"Who is dis doctor yuh taking me to anyway?"

"They have very good reviews, Mom," I lie. Really there was only one review I could find anywhere, and all it said was that the people were rude, but that the wait time was better than most sliding scale clinics.

"Steups." Mom sucks her teeth.

I try to think of something to take us out of being in a waiting room with faded wallpaper that may or may not have been changed in the last fifty years.

"Mom?" I say.

"Mm-hmm."

"Did Ma really talk to the ocean when we were little to make sure we didn't drown?"

"Yuh children still alive, aren't you," she says.

"But how—"

"She was talking to Dglo."

"Right," I say. "And Dglo's the healer right?"

Mom sighs and takes my hand in her lap.

"Mama Dglo is who we call the mother and protector of all things water—including little girls like you," she says and smiles for the first time all week.

"What about mothers?" I ask, but she doesn't answer.

"Uh, Beatrice Porter," a nurse says, "the doctor will see you now."

. . . . . . . . . . . . .

The doctor is a very young and pretty brunette with diamond studs in her ears.

"So how are we today?" she says cheerfully.

"Terrible," Mom says.

"We got some bad news, doctor," I say. "She thinks she might have skin cancer that spread to her brain."

"Well, that is bad news," she says.

Leafing through my mother's paperwork, her nose and eyebrows crinkling into a frown, she says, "So I received the paperwork from your previous doctor, and it says here that you refused the surgery."

"Tell my daughter how much that thing you want me to do will cost me." Her voice simmers with indignation.

"Well," the doctor says, still looking through Mom's forms, "you would have to talk to the front about the details, but it looks like it would be about—"

"Five thousand three hundred fifty dollars," Mom says, cutting her off. "Five thousand three hundred fifty dollars is what it would cost me."

My heart stops at the number.

The doctor clears her throat like she's about to speak, but I interrupt. "But she has insurance. I don't understand."

"She doesn't understand." Mom throws up her hands.

"Zora," she begins. "Yes, your mother's current health insurance is able to cover about 60 percent of the procedure—after the $2,000 deductible that is."

"You hear her?" Mom looks at me.

"Why can't they cover the other 40 percent?" I ask.

"I'm sorry, but you will have to talk to your insurance about your coverage. Now if you would like to discuss the procedure—"

"I tried to explain to my daughter that there was nothing you could do. Seems she needed to hear it for herself." Mom crosses her arms around her chest, her face smug.

"Nothing until you get the tumor removed," she says. "And judging by how far the cancer has spread based on these scans, Mrs. Porter, you should probably do that soon."

I notice that the doctor is now inching backward toward the door. As though this isn't what she signed up for when she agreed to help people like us.

"I'm sorry there isn't more that I can do," she says.

I'll say, I want to say, but instead I just look back at her without blinking.

My mother sucks her teeth.

The doctor clears her throat. "Look, I know that sometimes this type of news can produce a bit of a shock to the system," she says. "If you want, I can set up an appointment with our therapist. I'm sure this is a difficult—"

"No," Mom says.

"Mrs. Porter," she says again.

And the more she repeats my mother's name, the more it sounds like someone else's name—the name of someone I wouldn't want to know. I take Mom's hand and help her up and out of the office.

..............

That night, Mom says she's leaving, and Kayla just bawls and bawls. Mom lets her. I refuse to let Mom see me cry, partly because I don't want her to know how mad I am and partly because I want to seem strong for Kayla who I then have to rock slowly and whisper, "Hush, hush," to until she falls asleep three hours later. When she does, I surf through piles of books until I find it: *The Anansi Stories.* The last time I remember reading it was when Sasha and I used it to try to exorcize the demon from my walls four years ago.

As I flip through, I find a drawing of Anacaona. It says, "Anacaona: fierce warrior who led thirty-one battles of colonial resistance." In the illustration, she's wearing a crown of grass. A string of seashells falls around her waist. I wonder if this is who Mom thought I reminded her of earlier, if she really even looked like this. In her hand is a spider, which seems beyond strange until I notice something else: around her neck is the pendant that looks exactly like my mother's. I feel a shiver run through me for a moment until I decide to flip the page. I look instead for the story on Mama Dglo where she saves the girl from the evil man, and then carries her down to her underwater castle, making her immortal. "In order to be saved by Dglo," it says, "find ocean water, wear colors of the sun, ask Mama Dglo to come to you. Whisper, 'Help me spirit, Mama Dglo. Rid me of darkness in your castle below.'"

. . . . . . . . . . . . .

When we get outside the new house the next morning, Adaliz Austerlitz is standing there with her and my father's child. The only time I've ever met her before today was at their wedding. Other than that, whenever Dad would come to see us, it was always at a neutral spot like the park or some nice restaurant to ease the blow of him leaving us for a white woman. Of course Dad used to have Sasha over from time to time until Sasha refused to spend time with them last year after some fight occurred that she never told me the details of. But he never brought me or Kayla. Not that I would've wanted to be brought there anyhow. Anyway, Sasha told me all about her: "It's awful. She just smiles at you all the time. She's not even pretty. I thought guys only left their wives for women who were prettier than their real wives."

But she is pretty. Her sun-bleached hair is all blown out, which I figure she's probably done just to impress me, and it works.

"The infamous Zora," she says. "We meet again."

Our hug is awkward. Her smile is unnaturally wide. Sasha was right about that. Kayla holds on to me, pulling my arm, acting shy. And then another little girl with puffy hair and honey-colored skin stands next to Dad, her arms wrapped around his waist.

"Now I'm sure you remember your sister Madeleine," he says, trying to keep smiling. Kayla holds tighter to my arm.

"Hi," Madeleine says with wide eyes.

"You girls are around the same age," Dad says to them. "I'm sure you'll have a lot to talk about."

Kayla looks up at me, perplexed. I don't know what to do.

"Your father tells me you like Coney Island. Maybe after you girls get settled, we could all go for a walk on the boardwalk?" Adaliz says, her smile still lingering on her lips.

A snow-white labradoodle comes out and barks at us, jumping in front of Kayla. Kayla smiles and lets him lick her hands.

"This is Sebastian," Adaliz says. "He's very excited to meet you. Down boy. Sit. Sit," she says, beckoning the dog back into the house.

Dad follows his woman and their dog, carrying our things.

Madeleine's still just standing there, staring at us, all sweet-like.

Kayla lets go of my hand and walks up to her before I can think to do anything about it. She stares that girl right in the face, says, "You're not my sister. Also, your hair looks like your dog's hair. And not in a good way." And then she walks into the house before the little girl can say shit.

The new house is one of those Cosby-like brownstones except it's nothing like the Cosbys'. All of the wood is dark, making the house seem gloomy and haunted-like. The details in the walls are supposedly very Victorian.

"Isn't it lovely?" Adaliz says, and she's glowing. And then, smiling at Dad, "Yes, the Brooklyn brownstones are one of the few instances in which I retain some faith in American architecture," she says playfully, letting her fingers linger around Dad's neck.

To me, the brownstones on our side of the park are nicer—bigger, older, and prettier than the ones in Park Slope.

"I keep telling her she needs to go to Europe so she can see all they have to offer," Dad says. "Maybe this summer, Zora?"

I think I'd rather go to Trinidad, I want to say, but instead I smile and say, "Sure."

"Well, I'll let you girls get settled. I think you'll be happy with your room, Zora," Dad says.

Of course, not five minutes after I start unpacking my things Kayla's already knocking on my door.

"Absolutely not," I say as she jumps on my bed.

"I want Mommy."

Kayla's eyes start to water then, and I sigh, reluctantly pulling her close to me. "She's just going away for a little while. We're gonna stay with Daddy for just a little bit. Think of it like a vacation. Tomorrow you can play with Sebastian. And Madeleine—"

"I hate her," she says, hands turned into fists.

"Shhh! Not so loud." I take her hands into mine until they begin to un-ball. "Me too," I say as a whisper, though I know that I shouldn't. Kayla only smiles.

"Zora?" she says after a few minutes. She lays her head in my lap. Her braids are dry and loose from not being retouched in a while.

"Hmm?"

"Is Mommy really sick?"

"Shh. Come, Kayla, your hair is a mess," I say.

"Nu-uh, Zora. You make it look ugly."

I take the castor oil and brush from my desk and ignore her. "Hush," I say, trying to say it the way Mom would've. "Mommy ever tell you the story about Mama Dglo?"

"No stories! More Buffy!" Kayla wriggles in my lap as I try to pass the brush along the parts in her scalp.

"Mama Dglo is the mother of the sea." I ignore her. I can tell that she's only half listening, but I continue all the same. "She protects all women and girls—just like you, Kayla. She takes them down under the sea where they sleep and play until they're well again. When Mama Dglo's in the water, the color of the ocean changes from green to blue. It feels just like magic. Make her smile and she'll heal you. If not, she'll make you her prisoner for this life and the next one. She lets you play with her treasures and read the books in her cave. That's where Mom is going. She's going to be healed. Don't you want her to be healed?"

"No. *I* wanna be healed."

"You are healed. Dglo came to you in your sleep when you were little, and she healed you."

"Baloney," she mutters, and I laugh.

"Stop! You messing my hair!" Kayla says and pushes my hands away. She rolls off my lap and lies down diagonally, her arm splayed across one side of the bed and her leg across the other.

I sigh, looking at her half-plaited head with several of my attempted braids sticking straight out her head like horns. "Just for tonight," I say.

I try to sleep, too, but end up staring at the spaces surrounding my new room. The spaces stare right back at me: the walls are long and wide, white and bare. I can hear Sebastian pacing in front of my room, panting. I try not to hear the murmuring coming from Dad and Adaliz, but I do anyway. "Just give them time to adjust," I think I hear her say. She sounds so reasonable, so nice and understanding. I can picture her hands around his neck and shoulders calming his fears and then going to sleep in his arms. Right then I wish I could drive my bed through the walls and into her skull. And then I close my eyes and see Mom. She's smiling on a beach in Trinidad. She shows off her dancer's body in a bikini and a wraparound skirt. She beckons me toward her with an outstretched arm. I run toward her to take her hand, but when I do, her fingers are like tissue paper and crinkle in my hands. I look up, and her gums have turned to black. Most of her teeth are missing. I wake with a start, worried that my thoughts might be seeping into the open where Kayla might feel them. But I look over, and she's still fast asleep, small body spread wide all over my new bed.

I take out my journal and write:

*Once upon a time lived Mama Dglo who ~~tried to save the world but~~ ~~ended up having to babysit her sister who only symbolized pure destruc-~~ ~~tion instead~~ they say was captured by a good man who wanted to make her his wife by stealing her memories of the sea. But each day at dawn she would take off her skin to enjoy the sun before plunging back into the ocean with her snake tail. Mama Dglo would look out at the sea every night not knowing why she kept feeling the urge to run out to her fire es-cape ~~and dive headfirst onto the open fire hydrant six flights down~~ and run through the dirty street water and play. One day her daughter finds her mother's memories in a box and ~~smashes them~~ shows them to her. Mother doesn't even blink an eye, ~~just takes off her skin and jets. Daugh-~~ ~~ter doesn't want to admit this, but she understands why her mother leaves~~ ~~without saying goodbye. Her daughter can't openly admit how much she~~*

~~wants to be held by her mother.~~ ~~She doesn't want to be the thing that holds~~ ~~her mother back but she also wants to be the one thing her mother can't~~ ~~live without~~ says, *I'm sorry I ever thought I could be happy without you.* *I'll never leave you.*

. . . . . . . . . . . . .

Sasha doesn't show up again for another week. When I find her, she's with some girl I don't even recognize, by a miniature waterfall in the park looking high as fuck.

"Not even the Devil himself could drag me to that hellhole," Sasha says when I ask her to come back with me to the new place. "I'll talk to you later, Lex," she says, and the girl gets up to leave.

"Oh c'mon, we could start our own place," I try.

"Oh for the love of God, not that 'let's start our own country' bull-shit again."

And we smile.

"So where are you staying anyway?"

She gestures in the direction that the girl just exited. "Her name's Lex."

"New white girl?"

"Nah it's not like that. We're just friends is all."

"Sure, Sash."

"Nah, for real though. Her family's just very sympathetic to our whole situation—I mean they probably think Mom's a total whack job, but whatever."

"Uh-huh. So whatever happened to Mel?"

Sasha looks away, coughs, and goes on like she doesn't even hear me. "Yeah, see, whitefolks don't ask questions. They believe in democratic family shit where the kids make the decisions with the parents. They won't call Mom and Dad if I don't want them to."

"They should. They could be charged with kidnapping."

"Don't be so dramatic, Zora. I'm eighteen for crissakes. I'm an adult now."

"Without a job or a future."

"Oh for the love of God, Zora!"

"Okay, okay, whatever."

"Anyway, I have a plan. I'm going to stay at Lex's country house with her and her grandparents for the summer. Then I'll be at Hampshire. If I get in, that is."

I want to tell her that I miss her, that I need my big sister, but instead I say, "Mom has cancer."

Pause, deep breath, and then: "I know. She called me right before she left. She asked me to come to lunch, but I told her I was busy."

"You didn't, Sasha."

"She didn't want me to come, trust me. She gave me like fifteen minutes' notice and then said she was going to Trinidad to do a couple tests."

"Well, she's in complete denial. I just talked to her on the phone yesterday, and she still hasn't scheduled the surgery to remove the tumors—there's more than one now. She can't really afford much either, though, I guess. Plus, she's only taking medical advice from Ma."

"Jesus."

"She doesn't know when she's coming back," I say. "We might have to live with Dad and his woman forever."

Of course on TV the main character always survives the big battle just at the moment you think they're about to fail. Like when Buffy's Mom dies, and then Buffy dies, and then just when you think the show can't get any darker, Buffy comes back to life.

Sasha doesn't say anything. I move closer to her, but she just looks away at the waterfall, picks up a stone to flick on the water and makes it skip. I want to know if Sasha's still in there. Or does she just look like Sasha with someone else's thoughts stuck inside?

"She's doing it. She's really leaving," Sasha finally says. "I mean, maybe that's good. Dad left us first, so I guess she thinks it's her turn now. At least it means she won't be sulking around here all day, carrying on about how he sucked the life out of her."

"C'mon, Sasha, you're not even upset about this? I mean aren't you at least mad that she'll probably be gone for your graduation?"

Sasha shrugs.

"Whatever you say, Sasha. I know you miss her. And I know she misses you. So do I, by the way." I say this last part under my breath so that she can't tell how much I mean it.

"She didn't even take Kayla with her?"

Her question ignores my big attempt for the heartfelt and the direct, and I'm hurt. I shake my head.

"I'll talk to Dad about babysitting a few days this week. And I'll call Mom. Try and talk some sense into her. That is if she'll answer the phone. Her goodbye to me was pretty weak, even for Mom. I'll have to rub it in her face when she's back."

"Oh c'mon, Sasha. You know she's never coming back."

We're both quiet for a moment. Sasha takes my hand in hers. She gives me a look like she's scared. Somehow seeing Sasha show a feeling like fear makes me feel worse, and so I have to take my hand away.

"So what should we tell Kayla happens to Anansi when she gets sick?" she asks.

I smile. "Well, maybe she goes to that beach in Mayaro and asks for the river God."

"Goddess," she says. "Her name is Mama Dglo. Her hair is a wave, which means that it can't be touched."

"On top she's a woman."

"With huge-ass tits."

We giggle.

"Down below she's a snake. Her tail is somewhere around fifty feet long."

"Except she's got a dick and a pussy so she can switch back and forth. First the master and then the slave."

"Stop perverting the story, Sasha. This is supposed to be making me feel better."

"Well, it's making *me* feel better," she says and laughs. Then, "Okay, okay. So Anansi comes to the ocean wanting to be healed."

I go on: "She stands at the edge of the beach singing, 'Help me spirit, Mama Dglo. Rid me of darkness in your castle below.'"

"The ocean parts, and she emerges, coils around Anansi's legs, and carries her down to her palace."

"Washes her down with salt."

"Her skin gets soft like a sea stone."

"Combs her hair with gold."

"So it grows back from the chemo."

"Takes a look in the mirror and her insides come out."

"Till they're well again."

. . . . . . . . . . . . .

Back at the new house, Dad dances in the kitchen, making the dark wood and marble counter seem just a little lighter. I look around for Adaliz, but thankfully, she isn't there. Dad is dancing by himself to Toots & the Maytals. A pot of Trini-style callaloo bubbles on the stove.

"This is a song from way back to my childhood," he says.

"Yeah, I know, I love 'Bam Bam'!"

"The original!" he says. "This was the first song to win the Independence Festival Song Competition. It came out when I was six years old—four years after we became independent."

Dad stamps his feet and waves a dishrag in the air. I try to remember the last time I saw him dance.

"I didn't think you liked Trini callaloo, Dad."

"Thought it might be time to try something new."

And I start to wonder if maybe this is his way of saying that he misses my mother.

Dad keeps singing along to his music as he cooks, and I realize I can't remember the last time I saw him in such a good mood. Then again, there's been a lot of changes with Dad lately. Like I also can't remember the last time I saw him with a cigarette. This pisses me off. Like maybe it was Mom that put him in a bad mood because she was always pushing people away. She pulled her hurts inside herself till they became outside hurts: headaches, nausea, cancer.

I want to tell him that Mom still needs him, that she's scared, that she's doing something really stupid by leaving us for Ma, who we barely even know, in Trinidad, for God knows how long. But before I can say any of this, Adaliz walks in with their child.

"Dinner smells delicious," Adaliz says.

I try not to roll my eyes.

"It's callaloo," I say. "From my mother's country."

Adaliz blushes and Dad clears his throat. "Why don't you go set the table, Zora?" he says.

By the time I do, everyone else is downstairs, and we all sit down around the stewed chicken, white rice, and callaloo with Kayla scarfing down everything in sight and Madeleine swishing her food around her plate in circles.

"So, how's school?" Adaliz asks me. "Your father tells me you're at the top of your class. That's marvelous."

"Following in her father's footsteps of course." Dad beams and clasps his fingers into his wife's fingers right there on the dining room table.

And then it's almost as if another Zora is sitting at the table—a warrior like Buffy, Anacaona, and Mama Dglo mixed into one—while the real me just watches. I want to say something polite, but my body won't let me.

"Did you know about Mom?" I say. I know she must have said something to him before she left and dumped us on him and his new wife.

"Zora, why don't we talk about this later?" he says.

"And what about them?" I say, pointing to Madeleine and Adaliz. "Do they know?"

I half expect Dad to reach over so he can slap me across the face for my bald-facedness, but he doesn't. Instead, he just gives me a look, says, "Why don't we try that again?"

"It's okay," Adaliz says to him and puts her hand on his shoulder. "I'm sure this is a very hard time for them with their mom away and all."

"Oh, so you do know," I say, looking directly at her.

Dad puts his fork down, more confused than angry—like he senses there's another Zora at the table too. "Zora, what exactly has gotten into you?"

I sigh, drop my fork onto my plate, and let the words unfold. "Guess I'm just nauseated from the sight of you making eyes at your woman like you're at the freaking prom. Meanwhile Mom's probably gonna die soon, and you'll be too busy with your new wife to even bother showing up at the funeral."

Dad doesn't say anything this time. I don't know if I've ever seen his face look like this before—not angry, not violent, but something else altogether.

"I'm sorry," I say. I leave the table before I can see his face change into anything else.

. . . . . . . . . . . . .

I run into my room, throw on the yellow head wrap Mom left before she went away, grab *The Anansi Stories*, and run straight out the downstairs entrance without anyone noticing. When I get to the park, Sasha's sitting in the same place I left her hours ago.

"Sasha," I say, a little scared of what I might be interrupting.

She's hunched into a shell, head stuck between her knees. "What now, Zora?" she asks. When she finally looks up, her eyes are puffy and red.

I sit beside her on the grass, unsure of where to start. I decide not to ask her why she's crying. "I brought this," I say instead, pulling *The Anansi Stories* out of my book bag and placing it right on her lap.

She says nothing.

"There's a spell," I continue, "to save Mom." I open the book to the chapter on Mama Dglo. "So we can bring her back to us."

She pauses for a moment, wipes her eyes. "I'm listening," she says.

"So according to the book, all we have to do is find ocean water, wear the colors of the sun, and then ask Dglo to come to us."

"Oh is that all?" she says.

I ignore her and point toward the lake. "So I'm thinking we can use the water from over there for ocean water."

"Okay, you know that's not the ocean, right?"

"And then I brought Mom's head wrap we can use for the colors of the sun," I say, pointing to the yellow scarf on my head.

"Lord, Zora, do you really think this will work?" She looks at me.

I close my eyes and think about Mom and her hands turning to tissue paper, her gums turning black. I think about having to live in this house forever with Dad's new wife. "We have to try," I say.

Sasha looks at me and sighs. "I know just the place," she says and gets up.

I follow her down a path with too many trees and not nearly enough lighting.

"Umm, where are you taking me, Sasha?" I say, after a few minutes of walking through branches in the almost dark.

"What, are you gonna charge me with kidnapping too?" she says with a smile.

I laugh, but I feel a little nervous about how late it's getting and the fact that we seem to be the only people walking down this path.

"Sasha?"

"Hmm."

I try to think of how to form the words for what I've been feeling. "It's just . . . things will be different now. I don't know what's gonna happen when you go off to college. Maybe things won't be the same between us." Things haven't been the same for a while, I want to say, but I don't.

We don't say anything for a while, just walk over dead leaves and branches in silence.

"Well maybe I won't get in anywhere, and I'll have to join a commune," she says.

"Sasha!" I smack her on the shoulder playfully.

"I know, I know. I'm scared too."

I say nothing and just walk next to her, listening to her breathe in time with the cicadas crying all around us. I can barely see anything, but I can tell she's still not looking at me.

"Hey, Sasha?"

"Mm-hmm."

"Maybe you could take me with you to college next year."

"Yeah, okay," she says and turns to me, finally. "I'll miss you," she says. It's the nicest thing she's said to me all year.

And that's when I notice that the path we were just on has completely disappeared. We look like we're in the middle of a freakin' forest.

"Okay, but seriously, Sasha, where the hell are you taking me?"

"We're already here," she says with a smile.

And I look up to see that we're standing in front of a damn cemetery.

"Trust me, Zori, if the spell's gonna work—it's gotta be here. I came here once with Shay and it was . . ."

"Creepy?" I say, looking at the stone sculptures beyond the gates.

"I was gonna say mystical, but okay," Sasha says and shrugs before climbing over the fence.

"You know, mystical's just the PC term for creepy, Sasha," I say as she helps me over.

When I get out to the other side, it's actually beautiful. There are blue irises and purple azaleas all around us as well as a stone unicorn surrounded by forest animals.

"Oh my God," I say.

"Don't say it."

"It's—"

"Don't say it."

"It's our country, isn't it?"

"I knew you would say it."

"Well, it is, isn't it?"

Sasha rolls her eyes. "Yeah, and look—there's Anansi," she says, and I scream at the big hairy spider crawling our way. "Relax." She laughs. "Look at the water."

I do and it's beautiful. The lake is usually green with algae, but with the sun setting, the water looks almost golden. There are black swans swimming around the lake, and I realize that I've never seen a black swan before.

"I guess it doesn't really need to be ocean water, does it?"

"Guess we're about to find out." She shrugs. "So what are the words?"

"Help me spirit, Mama Dglo. Rid me of darkness in your castle below."

"Shouldn't we be standing closer to the water or something?" she says.

We walk over and look at the lake. We say, "Help me spirit, Mama Dglo. Rid me of darkness in your castle below."

There is a group of swans circling around one green spot in the middle, and I wonder if it's Dglo about to emerge with long green locs and a giant snake tail.

Sasha takes my hand, and we say it again. I take a deep breath.

"Help me spirit, Mama Dglo. Rid me of darkness in your castle below."

We say it louder this time. I try to feel the presence of all the ancestors and magic and hopeful thoughts in the world. I close my eyes and do the sign of the cross just for good measure. We say, "Help me spirit, Mama Dglo. Rid me of darkness in your castle below."

As I close my eyes, I imagine a giant tidal wave coming up, a giant snake tail smashing the grass. But I open my eyes and see nothing.

We stand there for a moment looking at the swans flapping their wings, looking for food.

"So, what's supposed to happen?" she says after a moment.

"It doesn't really get into that," I say, feeling deflated.

She pauses. "You feel any different?"

"Not really."

"Yeah, me neither." Silence and then: "Hey, I've got a story for you."

"Hit me," I say.

"Okay, so this one's not for Kayla, all right?"

"All right."

"This one's for Mom, okay?"

"Got it."

She goes: "Okay. So Anansi goes to the river and asks for Mama Dglo. Says, 'Help me spirit, Mama Dglo. Rid me of darkness in your castle below.' And Dglo's like, 'You sure you know what you'd be giving up? Once I do this, I can't undo it.' Anansi's like, sure I'm sure. So then Dglo's anaconda tail comes up and snaps Anansi's ovaries out from under her. And Anansi's like, 'But why my future children? Why would a woman—even a half a woman, do this to another?' And Dglo goes, 'Did you really expect to get your freedom with those things holding you back?'"

. . . . . . . . . . . . .

When I finally get back to the house that night, it's late and the house is quiet. When I walk into my room, Dad is waiting for me. He's sitting on the bed, staring at his knuckles.

"Hey, Dad—I'm sorry about before, I was—"

Dad waves his hand to stop me.

"First off, I already knew about your mother," he says.

I'm a bit thrown off by this. I was expecting a beating or a lecture. Certainly not a story about Mom.

"I tried to schedule her an appointment to run some tests when Kayla was first born. She wouldn't hear of it. You know your mother, once she puts her mind to something . . ." His voice is losing steam. He picks up Kayla's rag doll and drops it on the floor, not angrily, but more defeated-like. "I realize there's a lot you might think you know about me and your mother, but there's also a lot you don't know."

I stay quiet.

"You might have been too young to remember this, but many years ago your mother took off with you and Sasha to see her mother right be-fore she passed. I couldn't take off work at the time. You two were only supposed to be gone for a week. By the third week, I panicked. Couldn't get anyone on the phone to give me an answer. Six weeks later I get a call from Ma that you girls were never coming back."

I think back to my memory of us at the beach with Ma when she protected us from drowning. Were we really there that long?

"For you this was just a summer vacation," Dad continues, "but I honestly didn't know if I'd ever see you girls again. I was worried sick, not sure what was wrong with my wife or when you all were coming back. I was worried for the two of you. Before she left, she kept saying she was possessed. She thought that was why she couldn't sleep at night. Why she wasn't eating. Before she died, your grandmother used to say that Ma practiced Obeah, Devil stuff. I was scared for you. Also for your mother. Do you understand what I'm trying to say?"

Then Dad looks pleadingly at me for support.

I can't help but think of the time I thought I might be possessed by that demon that one spring, and I wonder if this is how Mom felt—like some being had taken control of her feelings and actions. And then I have another thought: what if it was us that made her feel possessed by the Devil or some other evil spirit, us that made Dad angry and them angry at each other. I start to feel sick.

At this point, there's a knock on the door. It's Adaliz. Her face is like a graveyard.

"Sorry to interrupt," she says. "Your great-grandmother called. It's about your mother."

Her voice hesitates. I feel my heart stop.

"What happened?" I say.

"She had a seizure and hit her head," she says, shuffling her feet nervously. "She's unconscious, Zora." She looks at me now, and for once there is no smile lingering on her lips. "Ma's taking her to the hospital. I thought you should know."

My father reaches for my hand. I lean over the bed and throw up.

# CHAPTER 9

# The Human Origins of Beatrice Porter and Other Essential Ghosts

Arima & Mayaro, Trinidad & Tobago
January 1975–1976

LET ME TELL YOU A STORY. NOW THIS ONE LET'S CALL THE origin. I cannot tell you what this story will give you. Only that this is how it begins.

Now let's just say there was a spider. Let's say she was a goddess who was stolen from the sky who then fell into the ground in pieces. Let's say she was transformed into a woman and then back into a spider into a line in your book into an absence on the page that the world cannot see. Let's say that without her we would never have even known that we existed.

See, what they won't tell you in school is that this whole world started with a spider. Only something so small and unassuming could have survived the heat long enough to travel the universe before it expanded into what you humans call the Big Bang. Only a creature that builds webs could make something as magnificent as the earth. Could crawl through cracks, crevices, sand, and rock—could birth roots, dirt, and oceans.

Some call this creature a trickster; others call her deceptive. Other folks simply call it survival. Let's call her Anansi. She is the god who exists to make a scene. She will weave you a story like she is weaving a web. She will have you start one place and end up at another, and you will have no idea how you got there. The place you get stuck is called the core. It is that place in the web where you are paralyzed, not knowing what's yet to come. She will ask you questions like an ancient call-and-response chant. She is still waiting for her answer. Here is an example. Please fill in your response below:

> *Why do we remember some stories more than others?*
>
> *And what happens to the ones that we forget?*

Let me tell you a story.

This one starts in 1492 with a man they call Columbus, who, like most symbols, started out as a tale. His story was dreamt up by the late great Washington Irving who tried to fabricate what might be the greatest creation myth of all time. A creation myth so powerful that now most Americans don't realize that Columbus never actually set foot in the United States of America.

Columbus told stories about the Caribs to the Spanish kings and queens in order to gain their trust and respect: "They wear human bones as trophies and drink the blood of their young," he would say until eventually earning the power to name the whole region after his own fear—calling them the Caribbean: Land of the Cannibals. And when it was finally revealed by scholars that the Caribs may, in fact, have never actually eaten the bones they allegedly took home as war trophies, that their name was, in fact, the Kalinago, it was too late. *Carib* was the only name that remained within the human imagination until they themselves believed that they were savage. Of course some say they should've just been grateful that Columbus went through the trouble of gifting them a name at all. I mean they could've all been known as "some land where some people died that had gold or something."

Let me tell you a story.

See once upon a time there was a woman. And this woman conjured stories from ghosts and gave them to her daughters. And this conjure woman's name was Beatrice. The daughters loved her stories, and when the woman died it was all that she left them. Little did they know that these stories had a life before them. That this book had a life before me. You see, I, Your Faithful Narrator, will always carry the burden of knowing how my stories will end. And I get a little worried because you are getting closer to the end of this tale, and I don't know that you'll like where you end up landing. Still, I'm hopeful that maybe as you're reading this you might try to save me—rip out my ending, write me something new and beautiful.

You see, when Zora's mother told her that she reminded her of the great chieftain Anacaona, she had no idea that this was not just a story. Sasha on the other hand has always suspected that their mother might be keeping something from them. After all, mothers don't beat you with a cocoyea broom followed by copious amounts of sobbing and prayers without a story. It is a story that Beatrice nearly took to her grave, although she did warn them: said that even though the magic's been white-washed into sin and though she's been taught that to be a good Christian mother she'll need to forget the calls of the Orisha, that one can still learn to see things, if they try.

And though I'm not sure that you've earned this, I will still tell you what happened the day Beatrice came face-to-face with the real-life Anacaona—someone who would change her life and her daughters' lives forever. Please pay attention for the quiz at the end of this chapter.

. . . . . . . . . . . . .

You see it all started in the year of 1975 in Arima, which was ten years after everyone started referring to Beatrice Dhawan as "Beatrice the Douen" and three months before she turned the tender age of sixteen.

. . . . . . . . . . . . .

For those who may be unaware, a douen is what is known as the ghost child—the consequence of losing your offspring before you've had the sense to have them baptized. Think the ghost twins from the American classic *The Shining* only their feet are turned backward and they wear straw hats big enough to swim in. Essentially, a ghost not to fuck with. Shout your child's name in a public place and the douen will call to them like they're their best friend and take them away forever.

.............

It was at this time that news started to spread that Beatrice's mother did dealings with the Devil—*She turn Obeah woman like she muddah. Mus' be why she husband leave she for a cocoa payol from Venezuela. Dat is why she always leaving town. De woman dealing with de Devil for true.*

What is also true is that Beatrice had turned quiet. Having children flee from her like she was diseased, she learned to take her lunch alone. Her former prefect friends from primary school, Catherine, Denise— even Mavis from down the road—were now afraid of her. At first she'd prop herself up in the schoolyard, enjoying sweet drink and stew pigeon peas. Days later she started setting an extra plate and an Apple J for Miranda, the imaginary friend she kept inside her head. People would catch them playing marbles, rummy, and all fours in the yard. Phrases like, "Gyal, like yuh gone mad" and "Matchstick stop playing wid yuh-self" were hurled at her on a daily basis. She paid them no mind. Poured Miranda another glass of Apple J and gave her some Smarties, which were taken from her Aunty Shirley's private refrigerator that very morning.

Lucky for Beatrice, her mother was busy playing mammy for some fancy white family in England when most of this foolishness had gone down and knew nothing about the allegations of being a Devil dealer nor did she know about her daughter's imaginary friend who drank all of Aunty Shirley's Apple Js. Without her mother around, Beatrice was left with her four older brothers and her Aunty Shirley—her only aunt who never had any children. Rumor had it that Aunty Shirley was barren like a desert and that the only reason Uncle Myron didn't leave her is that he didn't believe in divorce. Meaning she spent all her spare time in prayer or locked up in her bedroom while her husband spent his evenings spreading his seed to at least three underripe girls around the island. The six of them lived cozily together in her mother's three-bedroom house while her uncle Myron stayed in his and Aunty Shirley's one-bedroom shack across town on "business" four nights a week.

Beatrice's first tactic was to turn to her brothers for help with her "friend" problem (or lack thereof, as it were). Unlucky for Beatrice, her brothers were of little help. You see, young Matthew, Mark, Luke, and Zeke liked to spend their days by the river catching crawfish and roasting breadfruit, leaving poor Beatrice behind to sweep the cocoyea broom forty times across the yard, thirty times against the bathroom tile, fifty times across the carpet, as was required of her. "Yuh a real mad woman," Zeke said to her. And then the four of them howled like dogs before heading to the river, leaving Beatrice alone to steal Apple Js from her aunty Shirley's private refrigerator and cavort with jumbies.

. . . . . . . . . . . . .

From the looks of things, it was just an ordinary day. The sun beat down on the backs of women and children, so they held umbrellas to shield themselves from the sun while walking to their jobs or schools like always. Beatrice was in class, attempting to listen to Sister Agatha's boring history lecture.

"Who can tell me what this coming Monday represents?" Sister Agatha asked. She paced as she spoke, like she always did, walking up and down the aisles with her cane spinning around the air like a baton.

The class seemed distracted. A few of the girls were doodling in their notebooks or passing notes about the plan to break biche to watch the *Jaws* premiere at lunch.

"Is Discovery Day, Sister Agatha." This came from Anne.

"Anne, please tell the class what Discovery Day represents."

"Is a big festival we have up in Moruga dat time. Diplomatic people from Spain come and give speech. Dey have people dress up like Native and wear feathers and beads and paint dey body. Some dress up in long dress and stockings and thing, like the voyagers."

"That is correct, Anne. Glad one o you is paying attention."

Beatrice pulled her notebook over her face and rolled her eyes. "Teacher's pet," she whispered to herself. Beatrice imagined Miranda running out and stealing Sister Agatha's baton and dancing on the desks like a circus dancer. Sister Agatha's face would become a sunset, all cloudy and red. She imagined all the children getting up with her and dancing on their desks. A steel pan band would enter with some pan men, and they'd march just like that out of the classroom.

"What did I just say, Ms. Wilkes?" Sister Agatha's voice was like steel when she was angry: hard, but with a shine to it.

It appeared that poor Sharon had been caught mid-doodle, scribbling "I love Jeremiah" all across her notebook, when she heard Sister Agatha's baton smack Sharon's desk as a warning.

"That . . . that." She stuttered an answer.

"Speak up, Ms. Wilkes," Sister Agatha said. Sharon's face was frozen, knowing a wrong answer could mean a trip to the coconut grate later.

"That Christopher Columbus, Admiral of the Ocean Sea, taught us courage, perseverance, and integrity," Anne replied and smiled widely as Sharon's lips began to tremble.

Beatrice looked away as she heard the sound of Sister Agatha's cane meet Sharon's hands. She looked, instead, outside the window, wishing she could be outside playing with Miranda.

It was in this moment that she saw a woman sitting on the windowsill, holding a spider. The woman was very beautiful, with long, flowing dark hair and sharp brown eyes. She was wearing a shiny silvery pendant and a bag of arrows slung over her shoulder like an Arawak. Beatrice looked harder for a moment to make sure the woman's feet were not backward. They were not, but she sensed that the woman must be a jumbie on account of the red mark across her neck that looked like a hanging mark.

Startled, she looked away, back at her desk, and made the sign of the cross. She took a deep breath in and looked out the window one more time, but the ghost still sat there, waving at her. She looked around the classroom, but everyone else pretended to listen to Sister Agatha's anecdotes about Columbus while continuing to pass their notes.

Beatrice tried every rational thing she could think of to get herself to stop hallucinating and come back to earth: rubbing her eyes till they got red, pinching her forearms, clicking her heels, and blinking. But the jumbie and her spider didn't waver.

When class was over, the jumbie vanished, and Beatrice sighed, thinking she was safe. I mus' be going mad for true, she thought.

That is until she got to the courtyard and saw the Arawak-looking woman sitting in Beatrice and Miranda's usual corner. She was smiling mischievously at her, carrying her bag of arrows and spider in her hands.

"Chile, gi' me a sip o your Apple J, nah man," the jumbie said to her, stroking her spider.

Beatrice looked around the courtyard for help, but the other girls were all just sitting in corners, gossiping (probably about her, she suspected). No one else seemed to notice the jumbie.

"Ah got a little something for yuh, if yuh share," the jumbie said, her hand reaching out toward her Apple J.

Beatrice held her breath and gave her the bottle reluctantly, not wanting to vex a possible jumbie.

The jumbie guzzled down her Apple J in one gulp, wiped her mouth, and thanked her. Then she handed Beatrice the pendant she had been wearing.

"This fo' you to never forget that you's royalty," she said.

The pendant was even more beautiful up close. It was silver looking with a small turtle made of stone that sparkled like a diamond.

"Cyah take nothin' from strangers." Or jumbies, Beatrice wanted to say, but decided that might be rude.

The jumbie only shrugged. "Doh forget yuh history," she said. "One day yuh children will ask you."

Beatrice couldn't quite follow her meaning, but she'd heard that jumbies tended to speak in riddles. She shrugged and accepted the necklace from her peculiar jumbie but hid it away in her knapsack. Didn't want to have to answer any questions about it later.

"Call me Anacaona," the ghost said, walking away until she disappeared.

Beatrice went home that night, anxious. The feeling grew inside her stomach like a balloon. She sprinkled salt along her windowsill and in her doorway to stop the ghost from entering her bedroom.

A part of her wished that she could speak to her mother about all this, even if it meant getting a lashing. Though in truth, Beatrice had grown used to not having her mother around. There was a time that Beatrice and her mother were like white on rice. In fact, before Eislyn Anneca went off to London to become a nanny, one could say that Beatrice was her mother's favorite. As the only girl Eislyn Anneca ever birthed, Eislyn had dedicated her time to raising her in her own image: she dressed her daughter up for church in matching frocks and sun hats, which she sewed by hand while Beatrice stayed glued to her side. At other times, they would cozy up together in the hammock on their veranda, sip Apple J, and chat for hours. But Eislyn Anneca's time overseas playing mammy for whitefolks had hardened her.

That and the fact that whenever Eislyn Anneca looked at Beatrice's face, she saw Beatrice's father's face and his coolie stain that ran through her body like blood. She looked at Beatrice and saw the morning she caught her husband in their matrimonial bed performing cunnilingus on a red gyal she once shared her book of Psalms with at church. They had used the sheets she'd just washed, bent over on her knees scrubbing an ink stain through the washboard. Instead of matching frocks, now Beatrice received her mother's stares, locked in and cold whenever they exchanged looks.

Beatrice figured the next best option in sorting out her jumbie problem would be to speak to Aunty Shirley. Naturally, when Beatrice explained about the ghost who drank her sweet drink, Aunty Shirley had her concerns.

"Chile, yuh better stop yuh daydreaming before yuh end up mad and alone just like Ma."

Like the rest of her family, Beatrice was not permitted to see Ma. Folks in town referred to her as "De one who does deal, or Obeah woman."

Rumor had it that Ma had people who came to see her for ailments that the doctors couldn't cure: the burning pain that seemed to come from nowhere, the constant dull aching that started at the hips and just crept upward till it met the eye; the leg that wasn't broke, but couldn't quite move, the heart that wouldn't stop ache, the body that cyah get out the bed 'cept for rum. Who didn't call her Obeah woman called her the Healer. She who is greeted by Shakpana, god of smallpox, or she who walks closely with St. Jerome, the doctor of the church. She learned the art of healing and spell making from her great-grandmother who, rumor had it, once put a spell on her owner to get him to abandon his post long enough for she and his slaves to run free and join the Maroons. Now I bet you didn't know there were Maroons in Trinidad, but as a matter of fact, the Maroons could be found burning plantations and arming ex-slave militias in Trinidad, Haiti, Guatemala, Honduras, Florida, Virginia, and Louisiana alongside their infamous Jamaican counterparts. In Trinidad, the Maroons could be found setting up camp in Diego Martin in a marsh near Guayaguayare or escaping to Venezuela.

They were all destroyed eventually, of course, and I don't mean to alarm you, but you should know that as you're reading this, the blood from all of my bodies is soaking up the pages of this book. My tongue is being stapled to the shiny pages of Pearson-Prentice Hall's *The Caribbean: The Bold and the Beautiful.* If you look carefully through these pages, you will find absolutely no traces of blood. After all, they say the most horrific moments of our history get told to us as footnotes. Things that if you aren't looking, you would never see: the people who were swept up and made to keep quiet; the sizable chunks of my popped lung that are decorating the left-hand corner of this book.

The last time Beatrice saw Ma was at Aunty Clara and Uncle

Marvin's wedding. She must not have been more than five and she didn't remember much. But the story goes that only five minutes after cutting the cake, Aunty Clara had fallen down dead. Apparently, there had been a mark on poor Aunty Clara's breast for days on account of the fact that she had supposedly stolen Uncle Marvin from Aunty Clara's ex–best friend, Suzette, who had allegedly gone to an Obeah woman only two weeks prior to the wedding. Suzette never mention Ma by name, but the whole town did swear up and down that it had to be her. Ever since Aunty Clara's funeral, Ma had moved out of town and bought herself a magenta house by the beach in Mayaro to wait out her time as the Obeah woman, healer, or both.

And so Beatrice spoke to no one about her ghost acquaintance. But in the meantime, the jumbie kept appearing. Beatrice would find Anacaona sitting atop her classroom windowsill filing her nails, or hiding in the girls' locker room writing notes, or shuffling a deck of cards in the courtyard at recess so they could play all fours, sometimes whistling a strange-sounding song she called an areyto.

Now I'll admit that at first Beatrice found Anacaona and her hanging marks to be off-putting, but over time, perhaps out of boredom or desperation (as Miranda had long since disappeared, not being able to handle the competition of an actual jumbie) Beatrice began to confide in her new friend, filling her in on school happenings and all the most important gossip.

"Listen nah, yuh hear about how Erica who does act all high and mighty is going around wid some older fella from South in secret. Yes, and yuh know ah hear him married too, to some girl from Panama side no less. Like the girl have no sense atall, atall. So this chile better watch sheself next time she talk to me is all me o tell yuh."

Anacaona looked at Beatrice intensely as she spoke, never taking her eyes off her. "A man tried to make me his whore once, and I cut off his balls and fed 'em to my spider," she finally said. "She's a very adventurous eater."

And they went on like that for some time.

.............

Now if you're worrying about Beatrice's sad and lonely childhood, never fear. Because only weeks after our Beatrice found a friend in the dead spirit of Anacaona, did she make her first human friend—the notorious Aishani.

"Can I play?" Aishani asked her.

Beatrice looked up and around her before making her final decision. Sure, the rumors about Beatrice and her mother had gotten her ousted from most social circles for the time being, but most logical-minded people knew that Beatrice came from a good God-fearing family and that Eislyn Anneca, despite the rumors, was a force to be reckoned with.

Aishani, on the other hand, was the girl whose father was an alcoholic and ran off with some other woman, leaving her to be the school bastard. The same girl who had been forced to wear the dunce cap *six* times back in third form for falling asleep during exam week. Same girl it was said had been thrown out of the prestigious St. Elizabeth's for illicit behavior.

Beatrice shrugged. "I guess you can play." It might be nice to play with someone who was not a ghost.

Aishani just sat down and gestured toward the set of jacks Beatrice had in front of her. "What we playing for?" she asked.

"We not playing for anything. Girls not allowed to gamble."

Beatrice's face skin up at the sight of her. The belt around Aishani's trousers was missing, so that they hung baggy like a ruffian's. They'd probably make her kneel on the coconut grate for that later. She looked up to see if she could notice teeth sucking and rolls of eyes from the other girls, but they seemed to be paying her no mind.

Aishani only smiled. Even with her obvious attempts at obscuring herself, she could not get away from her girliness completely. Her thick unplucked eyebrows only brought out further the deep almond of her eyes. The unkempt clothes and strands of hair out of place only emphasized where they fell on her breasts, which seemed large for her age.

"Well, I was go'n let you win de first round anyhow, but all right," she said.

Aishani threw the jacks down with grace, her fingers opened wide. Her pickup routine was flawless—like the rhythm of a clock, she didn't miss a single turn. She leaned over to pick up her victory jack, and Beatrice could smell it: men's cologne.

"Dat Old Spice yuh wearin?"

"You like it?"

"No," Beatrice decided. "Old Spice is men's ting."

"And jacks is child's ting," Aishani retorted. "Why yuh tink de other girls look at yuh funny so?"

"My brothers taught me jacks."

Aishani smiled. "So yuh really tink yuh seeing jumbie for true?" She gestured toward the extra Apple J. "Or yuh just extra thirsty?"

Beatrice looked away, embarrassed. "No," she said, yet there Anacaona was, sitting atop the mango tree beside them.

"It's all right. Yuh doh have to explain. We all have our secrets."

"So why yuh get kicked out yuh last school?" Beatrice said, changing the subject.

"Why, what yuh been hearing?"

"That you does sleep in bed with de Devil."

Aishani laughed loudly and unladylike, holding on to her sides. "Depends on what you does call de Devil," she said.

Beatrice gave her a look but said nothing.

"So, there's a place I go sometimes. I think you would like it," Aishani said.

"You didn't answer my question."

Aishani shrugged and looked away. "Is a drumming group. All women. Inspired by de Black Revolution that dem tink dey shut down."

"I doh wanna get mix up in any kinda rough crowd, yuh hear."

"Nah, it eh nothing so. We just want to stand up for we-self. Over there is nobody to judge yuh—whether you seein' jumbie or"—she paused—"whether you a he-she like me."

Beatrice looked away embarrassed.

"It's okay," Aishani said. "I know you been thinking that all de while we talking. Ah doh feel ashamed."

Beatrice stared in disbelief for a moment, wondering what it would be like to not be ashamed of the things that people shamed her for.

But before she could contemplate this further, Aishani had pulled back her hair, thrown off her shoes, and climbed up the tree Anacaona was perched on to go and fetch a mango. Beatrice looked up at her new non-jumbie friend in awe. So did the other girls. She wanted to run away but couldn't help but stare. As Aishani climbed up, Beatrice could see the muscle in her legs flex, the round plushness of her buttocks. But as soon as Beatrice realized where her mind was headed, she quickly looked away. She looked around to see if the other kids were still looking, but they had gone back to playing all fours, rummy, and gossiping.

"Here. Take one." Aishani handed her a starch mango when she climbed back down. Her smile seemed to say that she knew what Beatrice had been thinking when Aishani climbed up the tree, buttocks stuck out all perky-like for the whole world to see.

Beatrice said nothing, but she well take the mango that Aishani fetch for her and hungrily peel off the skin. She could feel Aishani's eyes on her—watching her as she ate the meat in four large bites and sucked on the pit till it was dry. She tried not to feel self-conscious with Aishani's eyes on her, but at a certain point their eyes met. Aishani's stare was direct, but there was a twinkle in her eye—a slight arch of the eyebrow.

"Eh eh, but why yuh watchin me so? Why yuh doh just eat one yuh-self?" Beatrice asked, but Aishani only smiled and said nothing.

Beatrice felt the trickle of mango juice come down her lips to her cheek until her face felt sticky. And before she could move her finger to wipe it off, Aishani reached her hand to Beatrice's cheek, stroked the juice off her face, and licked her fingers slowly, one by one.

"Taste good," she said.

Beatrice felt herself start to sweat. She felt her heart start to thump. Her mind was racing to places she knew it was not supposed to go.

Now let me be clear, Beatrice was no stranger to what she called impure thoughts. Why just one month prior, she'd had one about Freddy Baptiste while watching him sprint the track field before he was chosen for Nationals. His shorts were tight, and she could see the shape and size of his man parts through the bright green nylon. But this felt different.

Now normally when these thoughts came over Beatrice, she'd say a prayer, and make a sign of the cross to put her mind to more pleasing matters in the Lord's eyes: last week's cricket match, for instance. But in this moment, it was not just the thoughts that were impure, it was the feeling between her legs, like the inside of the mango, soft and wet.

Now Beatrice would rather I didn't disclose this particular impure thought regarding Aishani in its entirety, and I do hate to quarrel with the dead, so instead, I will give you just a moment to let your imagination roam. Use the space below and come back when you are ready.

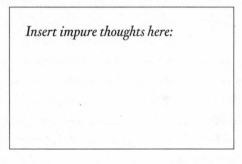

*Insert impure thoughts here:*

. . . . . . . . . . . . .

The next day when Beatrice returned to school, she wondered if people knew of her transgressions. She buried her head deep into her textbook, hoping the book would act as a shield so that no one could see into her head and read her thoughts. Every so often she would look up nervously, trying to read people's expressions, but they appeared to be paying her no mind.

Only the final time Beatrice looked up at the classroom windows, she found Anacaona sitting on the windowsill, grinning and stroking the spider in her lap, which seemed larger now. As Beatrice stared at the spider, she noticed that the eyes looked like human eyes, like a woman's eyes—and they appeared to be smirking. Frightened, Beatrice ran out of the classroom and hid in the washroom until lunchtime, hoping that Anacaona and her human-eyed spider wouldn't follow.

When Aishani came up to her at recess, Beatrice was startled.

"Gyal, like yuh seeing jumbie again?" Aishani asked. Only this time she sounded concerned.

Beatrice didn't answer.

Aishani put her hand on Beatrice's cheek and said, "Let we go somewhere, nah man."

She took Beatrice's hand and led her out of the school—in the middle of a school day no less. Beatrice was so alarmed by Anacaona's jumbie spider, she did not fully consider what she had agreed to until they were already halfway across town.

"Where yuh taking me?" Beatrice asked, now worried.

"Trust me." Aishani smiled, a bit too smugly (one might even say devilishly) for Beatrice's tastes.

"Lord, Jesus," Beatrice said, but she continued to follow the devilishly smiling Aishani into the unknown. In this moment, Beatrice Dhawan could have marched right back up to school, fumbled an apology, and possibly avoided a seat on the coconut grate. But she didn't. I guess you could say that the curiosity had overpowered her.

The two walked out hand in hand and headed down the road, took a taxi from over by the dial, up El Tucuche—the only mountain range rumored to still have words engraved by the Indians. It's the mountains where they say the ancestors still lie.

"Where yuh find this place?" Beatrice asked.

"People say this house was built by Black Caribs—descendants of the Arawak and the Maroons. Built out of dey sacred rock."

"Who tell yuh that?" Beatrice was incredulous.

Aishani shrugged. "What I can say is yuh cyah find houses like this in town."

Beatrice had to admit that this was true. The house also wasn't at all like the houses Beatrice was used to in Arima with the thick concrete walls and tin roofs, nor was it like the big houses her stush former prefect friends lived in, in Cascade, with their fancy driveways and cars. As she ran her hands up and down the side of the house, she felt thousands of seashells and stones that made up the exterior. The house itself seemed suspended in midair, like an illusion due to the wooden structure holding the house high aboveground. The dark green balcony stared down at them, appearing to sit atop a sea of clouds. Inside, the walls were etched with symbols like they learned in school about warriors like Anacaona and the stories about when she and her army went into battle.

"Now this is the place where the women come to drum." Aishani took her hand. "Come let me show you my favorite room," she said and led her into a room with six tassa drums and a few cymbals.

Aishani picked one up in the far-right corner and put it over her shoulder, picked up the stick, and began to play. The drum was so large it seemed to cover her entire torso down to her knees. She played slowly at first, tapping the stick against the head lightly and using her hand to bang the other side, swaying her hips from side to side. She picked up the pace, her hands flying wildly against the drum in both directions.

Beatrice had never seen a girl play the tassa drum before. As the rhythm quickened, Beatrice began tapping her fingers against her thighs, tapping her feet against the floor. Generally, Beatrice felt self-conscious dancing in front of strangers, but sooner or later and in spite of herself, Beatrice found herself dancing. Her legs moved in all kinds of directions at first, but they soon found their way to the beat. Her waist began to wine, moving in circles, her knees bent, her legs wiggling in place, her hands dancing about her body. When Aishani finished her number, Beatrice cheered.

"But where you learn to play like that?" Beatrice wanted to know.

"Where you learn to dance like that?" Aishani said, making Beatrice's cheeks burn with embarrassment. "I loved it from when I was small," she continued and sat down with the drum. "My daddy was a tassa player, and when he up and leave we, he leave me with he drum," she said, cradling the drum in her lap on the floor. "Mommy was fine to let me play while she was cryin' all around town 'bout leaving me to grow up without a father to claim my name, till I turn around thirteen. Then she worry. Say girls cyah play tassa. So I leave this drum here and meet the women. We go be the first all-girl tassa group in Trinidad."

Beatrice noticed that Aishani had put down the drum beside her and had moved closer toward her now. Beatrice felt her breath get short and heavy.

"Let me go," Beatrice said. "Cyah have Aunty Shirley worry."

Beatrice got up and straightened out her frock. She turned to head out the door, when she felt Aishani push her up against the seashell wall. Beatrice's first instinct was to run, but she found, against all logic, her whole body relaxing under the weight of Aishani's lips, her tongue. Her neck started to tingle. Her feet started to twitch. Her hands went limp.

We won't go into details here, but please take a moment to fill in the blanks below:

---

*How much can you remember about your first time?*

*And do you wish to remember it?*

*Does it replay itself in your mind without permission?*

*Would you wish it upon another?*

---

..............

After their afternoon in the dream house on the hill, Aishani and Beatrice could be found playing jacks together at lunch five days a week. They could even be seen walking home together holding hands or with Aishani carrying Beatrice's books.

As the girls' bond tightened, so did the gossip build and spread in all directions: *Eh eh, like dem eh have no brought-up-sy. And allyuh know dat St. Elizabeth's convent expel de little coolie bastard. Yes, m'dear, me hear dat ting will go around wid anyone—pipers, he-shes, no matter. Dat's right, me hear she a he-she.* And now she after Beatrice.

It was around this time that Beatrice was approached by Catherine and Denise.

"We just want to let you know because we know who your mother is, and we're concerned. You might want to steer clear of Aishani and she nasty business for a while. Come to church wid us dis Sunday. We know yuh muddah ent around to take you on these days."

"Steups." Beatrice sucked her teeth. "Jus' mind yuh business, y'hear?" It could be inferred that Beatrice felt like a real hot steppa just walking away from them like that, but her chest still tightened at the word "nasty" and wouldn't let up.

After school during their walk-home ritual, Aishani moved to hold Beatrice's hand, but Beatrice moved away.

"Not this time." Her body became stiff. She was thinking about what the girls said earlier. She was thinking about her mother.

"You lookin' sour. How 'bout I go and fetch you a mango from over dere so and sweeten you up?"

Beatrice forced a weak smile. Aishani held out a hand to link with hers, but Beatrice moved away. "Ah not sure ah can link yuh no more. De whole town starting to talk."

"People always go'n talk, Beatrice. Last week they called you a crazy jumbie lover, now dey saying something new. Since when yuh care?"

"I just . . . I doh know."

Beatrice tried to look at her feet so she wouldn't catch the disappointment in Aishani's eyes. But she could hear it in her voice.

"I see. Shoulda known I guess."

Beatrice could hear Aishani kicking the dirt as she walked.

"No, Aishani. Is not like that."

Beatrice looked up at Aishani to see her thick lips get stiff, her eyes become keyholes.

"No? Tell me, then, what is it like?"

"Is just . . ." The stammer in her voice got louder, more noticeable.

"But what? Suddenly I'm the strange one? Yuh tink they care about you, ent? Well, I really hope they do."

Aishani walked away.

Unfortunately for Beatrice, her attempt at severing the relationship with Aishani came too late. The news of their illicit friendship became the embarrassment of the whole of Arima. This also happened to be the week her mother returned from London. From the moment Eisyln Anneca's plane landed at the Piarco Airport, the news of Beatrice's new friend was coming at her from every direction: people approached her in line at the airport washroom, while waiting in line for the maxi, and while waiting in line at the bank before she even reached home. Eislyn Anneca was so upset, she and her four sons pooled money to buy Beatrice a one-way ticket to America. But not before teaching her a lesson.

. . . . . . . . . . . . .

The first thing Beatrice noticed when she got home was the smell of red lavender—the thing her mother used to cleanse the house of spirits. When Beatrice entered her mother's kitchen, Eislyn Anneca had her back turned to the stove, currying chicken. Beatrice felt a pang in her chest and put her hand to her heart. It was the first time she had seen her mother since last Christmas, almost a year ago.

"Mommy." Beatrice said the word so quietly, she wasn't sure her mother had even heard it. She put her hand out to touch her but pulled back before it could reach her skin. Her instinct was to run toward her, to scream her name out loud, but she knew better.

"Come," her mother said, not turning away from the stove.

As Beatrice drew closer, she saw that her mother's skin looked tired and older, with wisps of gray that weren't there before.

Her mother put a hand to her daughter's cheek and kissed her the way she did when she was young and waking up from a bad dream. She looked at her daughter's face, studying it as though she had never really seen it before.

Beatrice, too, looked up at her mother. Her eyes started to well up with tears she didn't know she had. She wanted to say, I'm sorry, Mommy. I need help. She wanted to say, Hold me.

"Mommy," was all she said.

Eislyn Anneca broke her stare and looked into her hands. She wiped a stray tear away from her cheek. "Get the switch," her mother said and walked out of the room. The chicken was simmering.

............

You see, it wasn't supposed to happen this way. The most unforgivable accidents often happen to those we love most of all. Her mother ordered one lash for every day she'd misbehaved while she was gone and a few more just for good measure.

Beatrice went out to the yard to fetch a limb from the tamarind tree, making sure it was not so small to get her extra licks for being smart, but small enough. The tree had been a member of the Dhawan family for years. Beatrice associated it with the joy in climbing to pick tamarind to boil for chutney or for throwing at teenage couples stealing kisses against their families' wishes. But it was also called the Beating Tree.

Beatrice dragged her feet slowly toward her mother, shaking from head to groin. Impatient, Eislyn Anneca met her outside to lash her right in their backyard. Her mother's face scrunched up tightly into a ball, her eyes barely visible, so that Beatrice could hardly make out the expression of pure rage written all over Eislyn Anneca's face.

Beatrice closed her eyes as her mother lifted her hand up high into the sky in anticipation of the first lash. It came down with the sound of a snap and a scream from Beatrice. Beatrice stood bravely, upright for the first few lashes before cowering onto the Beating Tree, hugging the trunk close for dear life. All one could hear in the house and down the block and through the neighborhood and throughout history was the sound of tree limb against Beatrice's back, her arms, her legs, the sound of Beatrice crying out, and the occasional, "Blasted child!" from her mother.

The sky started to break with rain, and Beatrice felt the brief relief of water against her back, underneath her wet blouse. Beatrice wondered if the heavens above were trying to show her sympathy pains through their crying, but the lashes only got stronger with dampness, making the switch denser, heavier. Beatrice could feel the welts forming on her arm, her back—the places where the branch met the skin.

The rain fell harder, and she could no longer tell whether she was still crying or if the sky was merely breaking down on her. She couldn't make out anything through the rain except the tree, which looked like a moving creature underwater—the branches dancing around like jellyfish.

After a while, the switch started to break in her mother's hands, but she merely blinked before picking up another switch to beat her with.

The sky became loud with thunder and Eislyn thought of the time (dinner) and the mouths to feed (four boys and her ungrateful sinful daughter). Her hand became heavy with rain, and she paused, looked up to the sky, cried, "God, grant me the serenity to save this child." She lifted her arm up high toward the heavens, holding the switch like it was her cross. And as she brought her arm down upon Beatrice's back for the grand final lesson, a thing happened like a miraculous domino effect: lightning struck a branch, which fell onto their telephone cable, which severed from their house, which caused a scene like a firework—like God's holy intervention.

"Oh, Jesus!" Eislyn Anneca screamed, looking at the flames on her house. It was a sight to see: a roving fire on a rooftop in the middle of a rainstorm. Eislyn Anneca abandoned Beatrice momentarily in order to scream to her four boys to run out of the house. Beatrice could barely make out the figures of her brothers running, but she could see the fire moving toward her.

Of course one would think that fire would have become mundane after 1.5 million years of making them. Yet humans never seem to stop staring at them. Beatrice was afraid of the fire, yes, but she was more afraid of her mother. Yet as she saw the fire dancing toward her, she thought she heard her mother scream for her to move, thought she saw in the distance a figure waving like a madwoman, while her brothers ran toward her. So Beatrice decided to let go of the tree and make her way to the fence where her family stood. Only, as Beatrice tried to move her limbs again, one single holy branch grazed her back with fire. The fire spread to her legs, to her throat, which tried to scream. A panic rose inside her.

I couldn't describe the pain to you if I tried. They say there is no worse way for a human to die than to be burned alive. Consider that a human body can burn for up to seven hours in its own fat. Consider that burning was a favorite pastime for whites to perform on Negro and indigenous bodies for centuries. Consider that we are still burning.

.............

It took twelve hours for Beatrice to regain consciousness. Her head was pounding. Her skin was searing. She struggled to lift her eyelids. By the time she did, the room blurred before her. After a moment or two, she was able to make out a table, two chairs, a creased mouth, and a furrowed brow that she took to be her aunty Shirley. Beside her was another shadow that she couldn't make out.

"Yuh mother not here," Aunty Shirley said. "It look to me like she couldn't quite bear the sight of yuh."

Beatrice tried to open her mouth to speak, and her throat burned like fire.

"She say it was the guilt. Seeing you with all them scars." Aunty Shirley moved closer to her, hovering a hand over her body, but not touching her. Like she fraid.

"Ah imagine it was also de shame. God have a way of striking down sin. Yuh mother house and all have to suffer too. Is so it go sometimes. Now de five of dem jam-packed like sardines in Myron and my own shack. Yuh see what does come from ungodly actions? Eislyn Anneca only daughter sinning with sodomite. Steups. Good thing yuh uncle Myron and me here to len' a hand. Now yuh brothers dem running 'round like chicken without head, trying to find a house for yuh family. Meantime, yuh muddah lock up sheself; say she doing penance; cyah help blaming sheself, and praying, too, for yuh salvation. How she go face de world after something like dat? De bes' solution, and we all agree, is to ship yuh off to yuh muddah cousin and she Yankee husband, in New York. Well, child, ah only hope yuh learn yuh lesson. Why it must take a ting like this to straighten yuh out, only God mus' know. If dis eh do it, yuh aunty Dorothy go know how. Yuh go have to watch yuhself wid she. She doh play joke."

Aunty Shirley moved to the window, muttering to herself intermittently. As Beatrice's eyes adjusted to the light, she noticed that the shadow she thought she saw earlier was only Uncle Myron standing in the corner, chewing tobacco, not saying a word.

Beatrice couldn't make out his face, except for his eyes: pupils black like Pitch Lake and breath that smelled like a bottle of Old Oak.

Beatrice opened her mouth to speak, but her throat still burned. "Water," was all she could make out.

"Water who?" Aunty Shirley sounded annoyed.

"Aunty. Please." Her voice was hoarse. She sounded like someone else.

"Maybe yuh shouldn't talk," Aunty Shirley said, her face scrunched up in concern.

A white coat, two eyes, and a mouth with too much lipstick entered the room. "How we feeling today?" the white coat asked.

Beatrice strained her mouth to open, but she couldn't get it to speak.

"She cyah speak, doctor," Aunty Shirley said. "Ah believe she want water."

"Of course yuh can't. I'll have de nurse bring you some right away." The white coat smiled.

Beatrice wondered if the white coat also smiled like this before telling her patients they were about to die.

"Your burns were severe. Praise God yuh muddah got yuh here when she did," the white coat said.

"Will the scars heal, doctor?" Aunty Shirley asked.

"The burns will heal, but the scars, well," the white coat began and then paused. "Well at least it didn't mess up yuh face."

Aunty Shirley covered a gasp with her hand.

Uncle Myron emerged from the corner to comfort his wife, putting a hand on her shoulder. "How much pain is she in?" He finally spoke.

"The morphine is just wearing off, so she's definitely in some pain, but don't worry, Beatrice." The white coat smiled again. "It's time for yuh next dose." The white coat took Beatrice's arm, and she felt a pinch before seeing the syringe, huge and white. She closed her eyes and winced for a moment. "Yuh should be feeling that in just a moment," the white coat said. "Or not feeling it ah should say." The white coat laughed lightly at her own joke. No one laughed with her.

"Well, ring me if you need me," she said to the room and then left.

Beatrice closed her eyes, waiting to feel a relief from the burning. But mostly, she wanted to know what her body looked like with all her scars. She was ashamed to have such a vain thought pop into her head. No thought about her health or how long her recovery period would be. No, her first thought was about what her body looked like under fire. No wonder God had struck her down.

Yet she couldn't help it. She imagined her body covered in scales like a dragon. She wondered if Aishani would ever look at her the same way. If she would ever be touched like that again by anyone. Of course, she would probably never see Aishani again anyhow. Soon she would be in America. She wondered how soon. She sighed and felt her rib cage, breaking-like.

Hours passed and Aunty Shirley and Uncle Myron watched her rest silently. Catherine and Denise paid their respects, bringing red and yellow hibiscus flowers. Her brothers brought her guava cheese and coconut fudge. At one point she thought she saw her mother with a priest, face puffy and red, hands wiping her eyes, covering her face inside someone else's chest. Beatrice reached a hand out to touch her mother's face, but in a moment she was gone.

It took Beatrice two days to realize her body was hooked up to IVs.

She heard words being spoken, tears being shed, but mostly she let her mind drift, thinking of the dream house in the mountains, how Aishani made her dance, how soft Aishani's lips felt against her neck, how her hands reached deep inside her, making her body explode like a firework.

At some point it seemed to be night. She could no longer feel the pain. Figured it must be the morphine. She seemed to be alone in the room, and yet she thought she saw the shadow again. Was it the drugs? Was it the Devil? Was it her jumbie?

"Anacaona?" she whispered aloud. It had been days since she'd been visited by her ghost, and although she didn't like to admit it, she was beginning to miss her.

"Shh." She heard a man's voice, rough like Brillo pad.

She felt something crawling over her body like a spider. It was a thing like fear. But then she felt a hand. The hand touched her leg and her skin prickled. She felt something wet underneath her panties. It was like what she felt that night with Aishani only this time she could see no face, no body attached to the hands that touched her. In the stillness of the dark hospital room all she could make out were his eyes, black as Pitch Lake.

"Shh," he said again.

> *Where were you the first time your body was taken?*
>
> *And where did you keep your insides hidden*
>
> *Away from being caught*
>
> *Inside somebody else's mouth?*
>
> *Did you let him swallow you whole?*
>
> *Or are you still being swallowed?*

Uncle Myron never came back to the hospital after that. And on the twelfth day, the white coat signed her discharge papers. The two weeks had gone by like a movie montage. She felt her mind behind a screen, her body being watched and prodded by others. Doctors had come in and out on schedule. Aunty Shirley sat in silence. Sometimes Beatrice's mother joined, dressed in black, the color of mourning. As though her daughter were already dead. The hospital staff wouldn't allow her to see herself in the mirror, her aunty Shirley made sure of this.

"Come. We already pack up yuh things," Aunty Shirley said, helping her into her oversized frock and sandals. The doctors had finally taken the bandages off her back. It was now that Beatrice noticed how tired Aunty Shirley's voice sounded. Lot of work defending a man you want to kill yet can't imagine living without.

When they got to Aunty Shirley's house, the first thing she noticed was that all the mirrors were covered up in sheets, just as they had been in the hospital, so she knew the scars must be bad. She imagined her skin had peeled off her body completely like a mango peel. Maybe she would spend the rest of her days walking around town wrapped in gauze like a mummy. There were four twin mattresses on the floor that the brothers must have been sleeping on. Beatrice was taken into a room with an ironing board and a clothesline and a small cot underneath.

"Make yuhself at home," said Aunty Shirley.

As Beatrice entered her room, she saw a figure from across the room that had to be her mother. Beatrice gasped, wanting to run to her.

"Doh trouble she now," said Aunty Shirley. "She's been through enough."

Her mother looked at her, her face bunched up in pain, her cheeks all puffy and red. Eislyn Anneca looked at her daughter long and hard.

"Mommy," Beatrice whispered.

But her mother just clucked her tongue and closed the bedroom door shut.

*What happens to the daughters who lose their mothers to heartbreak*
*To rape, to pages lost in memory?*
*And is it the same for the mothers who lose their daughters?*


*And what happens when those daughters become mothers*
*Who long for their mothers who were lost before they were born?*
*Who have daughters before they were ready to become mothers?*


*Who long for their mothers while their daughters long for them and may die*
*Never knowing their mothers' absence was written into their history.*

The next few weeks were a blur. Beatrice spent most of her time in bed, still hearing the tassa rhythm in her ears, the smell of Old Spice lingering in her mind, the sound Aishani made when making love to her like a howl and a whimper all at once. The nights were mostly quiet other than the few times Uncle Myron came to visit. He'd sit on the edge of her bed, stroking her leg, saying in a soft but coarse whisper, "Yuh perfect, yuh know that," before pushing her head into his lap.

One night Beatrice tried to fall asleep in her cot, only she couldn't. She felt seasick, like she was lost at sea on the ocean, like she could tip over at any moment.

The seasickness had been coming back every night for two weeks straight. She'd been feeling something else too. Something alien that seemed to be growing inside of her. It didn't feel human. Was more like a spider crawling against her organs, expanding like a parasite, haunting her like a spirit. Plus, her period was late.

She looked out the window, and she finally saw her: Anacaona and her spider.

"Took yuh long enough," Beatrice said.

It had been weeks since she'd seen them.

"You know," Anacaona said, "I watched a whole village burn alive once."

"So where yuh been?" Beatrice asked.

"You see"—Anacaona continued to ignore her—"before that man revealed himself to me as a traitor, Columbus had offered me a ride on his boat. I'd never been on a boat built for bloodshed before. Of course I didn't know that blood was the boat's purpose at the time. But years later I would see ships just like these carrying bodies stacked on top one another like decks of cards."

As she was speaking, Anacaona had slipped inside the window and began walking toward Beatrice lying still in her cot.

"Of course, I would be dead by then. But in my last moments on his blood boat, all I could tell was how the wind felt against my skin. I remember I was surprised by how fast we were moving. So fast my hair hit my face like a whip."

At this point, Anacaona was sitting beside Beatrice on her bed. She put her cold ghost hands on top Beatrice's bare belly. But on her belly, the hands didn't feel cold. They felt the way her mother's hands felt when she was young, and she would rub her belly down with Vicks when she was sick.

"Actually I could tell one more thing," Anacaona continued. "I could tell that the bright red cross painted on their sail seemed somehow ominous. Later on, the red was what we used to know they were coming. You could spot the burning red cross from a hundred kilometers away."

At this point, Anacaona's spider had crawled in through the window too. Beatrice's whole body stiffened as the spider crawled toward them on her cot. But Anacaona kept talking like she didn't even notice.

"When I returned from my boat ride with Columbus, his general had already made plans to burn my army alive. He gathered them together for a conference meeting and then he lit the whole building on fire. There were 81 men and women and about 112 of their children inside. But—and here's the thing about fires," she said, her eyes sparkling like lightning—like she could still see the flames.

"Once you start one fire, you're bound to start another. This general was no different. The twinkle in his eyes grew big like the stars as the flames danced around him. He was mesmerized. And who could blame him? After a while, the sound of the screaming man on fire became like a song to him. The man's flesh in flames, a part of the dance. Soon enough, he rounded up his men to join in the fun, and then they all came around on horses to light up our streets, our baby bedrooms, our schools, our prayer rugs.

"I came back to shore, and all I could smell was this stench. It was like nothing I had ever smelt before. But I would come to know the smell of burning human well. I didn't think it possible, but it was worse than the odor of pigs they brought that killed our villagers. It was a stench that wafted all the way to shore and lingered in the ocean for months. You see, burning is what you do to a spirit that can't be tamed. There are books full of stories of burning women. I wish yours wasn't one of them."

Anacaona smiled at Beatrice. The spider was now at the edge of the bed, beside them. Beatrice wanted to run but couldn't.

"Years from now, you'll barely remember this moment. The burning will be like a dream, a hopeful story you tell your children when they feel lost at sea."

The spider was on Beatrice's bed. She tried to inch away, but Anacaona kept stroking Beatrice's belly with one hand before picking up the spider with the other.

"Leave with us tonight," Anacaona said finally. "It isn't safe for you here anymore." And just like that, she got out the bed and crawled back out the window like a spider.

Her limbs grew long as the spider's legs. The spider's eyes grew wide like Anacaona's, and Beatrice wondered, in that moment, which one was which.

For a moment Beatrice lay in bed, paralyzed. But soon enough, she heard the twist of a doorknob, and the smell of chewing tobacco and dark rum.

She didn't know if it was real or an imagining, but Beatrice leapt out of bed in that instance like she'd never been burnt. She jumped out the ground-floor window and followed the two ghosts into the cane fields.

.............

Beatrice didn't know where she was going until she arrived, and then it all made sense. There was an ivory-white gate before a magenta-colored house. This was Ma's house. She had no idea how she found it, seeing as Ma's house was at least an hour away from Aunty Shirley's by car. But sure enough, Beatrice stood in front of it not knowing whether or not to enter. After all, this was the woman rumored to have aided in the murder of her aunty Clara—who practiced the Devil's magic on strangers and called it medicine. But this was also her grandmother. The woman who, before she was banished from the rest of the family, would watch over her when her mother was away. Who boiled water for Milo and told her stories about the spider-god they called Anansi.

The gate to Ma's house was locked. Anacaona walked right through and waved. Beatrice took in a deep breath and put her hand to the other side of the gate and pushed the gate lock open.

"Yuh late," Ma said as she opened the door. She was smaller than Beatrice remembered. She was more beautiful than she remembered too. Like Snow White from the fairy books: with skin black like the panthers, lips purple like calla lilies, and hair white as cotton fields. On top of her hair was a white scarf studded with flowers.

"Was expecting you hours ago. Only jumbie does travel this time o night. Come in, come in," she said, ushering Beatrice through the door, impatiently.

Inside the house was a table filled with flowers and candles and bottles of lotion. The table was flanked by cocoyea brooms. The white walls held paintings of what looked like African goddesses. As Beatrice looked closer, she noticed that the wallpaper had the same engravings she had seen in the dream house with Aishani.

Inside, Ma was boiling something on the stove. Stirring a large pot of liquid with a strong smell of spices her nose couldn't place.

"Sit," Ma said, and Beatrice sat.

She wondered how Ma knew she was coming when she herself did not know until she arrived in front of her house. Perhaps she was under a spell like Aunty Clara, and she'd be dead in two weeks.

"Yuh pregnant," Ma said. This wasn't a question.

"I think there's a demon inside me," Beatrice said by way of explanation.

"Yuh mean de baby or de thing yuh take to be sinning?" Ma said, not looking at her, but continuing to stir the pot with a wooden spoon that looked too big for her.

Beatrice shrugged, unsure. She'd heard of morning sickness before, but this sickness came at all hours. Whatever was growing inside her didn't feel human. It felt like Brillo pad and smelled like rum. It felt the way she imagined the Devil would feel if it were growing inside her.

"A baby not a demon, child." Ma stopped stirring to look straight at her. "Ah take it yuh not keeping it."

Beatrice felt her eyes well up with tears just then. After all, God only gave His children so many chances. How many times would she need to be struck down before it was too late?

Ma walked out the room in this moment, and Beatrice wondered if she'd left her to be alone with her sins. But she returned only a moment later with a towel and a bucket.

"Hush, hush, child," Ma said and placed the towel on Beatrice's face. The towel was hot and soothing.

Ma's eyes seemed softer now than they had been a moment ago.

"Yuh know what happens to a forest after it get burn down?" Ma asked her.

And Beatrice shook her head, no.

"Dey say sometimes when de earth burn is when it most fertile," Ma said, pausing to add some herb Beatrice had never seen before to the pot as she continued stirring. "You see sometimes a forest seem healthy.

It seem green. But underneath all dat green, de root rotten, de trees diseased. Sometimes de only thing to cure it be de fire. After fire, de dead root turn to ash, and de dead earth see sunlight for de first time all season and then come back to life."

Ma then lights a long white candle and hands it to her. Beatrice had no idea what Ma was talking about, but she did remember her mother once saying to her that her Ma was mad cuz she always spoke in riddles like the jumbies.

"Wha' yuh mean, Ma? Wha dis candle for?" Beatrice asked.

"It mean that new life will always move toward light. Yuh see, you m'dear are on your way to America—the land where nobody know dey own history. Nobody gon' trouble deyself about yours. Trust me."

Beatrice stared at the candle, the yellow melting into the white. She didn't want to go to America to live with her mother's cousin whom she'd never even met, or attend high school with a bunch of Americans who would make fun of her accent and have no idea how to play all fours.

"Now I eh calling mehself a seer, but ah can bet yuh future will have plenty love. I have a feeling yuh gon' have daughters and dat dey will tink you are magic. Dis is all dat matters in de end."

Ma turned off the stove and ladled the hot liquid into a tall wooden mug.

"But what dat mean, Ma?" Beatrice asked again.

"Hush yuh mouth and drink."

Ma handed Beatrice a mug of something the color of mildew.

Beatrice shook her head at the stench of the thing. "That ting smell like some Obeah business."

"And what yuh know about all o dat?" Ma asked.

Beatrice shrugged. "My mother tell me is like Devil dealing."

Ma slapped her leg, howling with laughter. Like an animal, Beatrice thought.

"Look, child. People like to talk. And talk does bring talk. I eh no Obeah. But let me tell you, Obeah is Obeah. Is Shango. I am Orisha. And eh not'ing Devil-like 'bout me." Ma took Beatrice's hand in hers.

"Orisha is the only religion we ever have to make it through bondage. Is where we go when we give up on de thing de white man put in we body they does call medicine. Dat all magic really ever is."

"Will it kill my baby?"

"Thought yuh said it was a demon?"

But Beatrice didn't answer.

"What you want me to say? Is called an abortion," Ma said. "It won't be pretty. You want to keep dis baby? You let me know."

But Beatrice knew that she didn't.

"Look," Ma said, "sometimes a baby born of rape feel like a parasite. Is de body's way of getting the hurt out. Drink dis," she said, bringing the mug closer. "Sit in de bucket and wait for it to fall out. And doh look inside de bucket once it come pouring, mind yuh. Like I said, it won't be pretty."

Beatrice put the candle down and sat in the bucket with just a towel covering her privates. She took a sip of the hot mildew-looking substance. She puckered her lips. The thing tasted like what she imagined poison would taste like. Then again that could've just been her guilt. But she imagined the tea swimming inside her, killing everything in there till there was nothing left of her but a scaly red dragon skin.

"It bitter like gall, eh? I know, chile," Ma said and got up to pour the rest of the liquid into a jug. "It ha' to push a whole fetus out yuh nani. Cyah expect it to taste like Milo."

Beatrice looked aghast for a moment that Ma would cuss like that, but she wasn't seeming to pay her any mind, and so she shrugged and tried to take another sip. This time was even worse. She clutched her belly tight to try to keep from throwing up. "So what happens now?"

"We wait," Ma said.

"For how long?"

Beatrice was scared. She'd heard stories about abortions from the nuns at school—fetuses that looked like aliens, like they couldn't possibly come from a human body, with necks distorted, thin as chicken wire. The mothers that threw their fetuses in the trash were wicked, wicked creatures who deserved a fate worse than death and always wound up in Hell. But even as Beatrice continued to have these thoughts, she continued to drink the tea. She wasn't sure why, but the thought of carrying out a demon baby seemed more frightening than being sent to Hell.

"Let me tell you a story," Ma said.

Beatrice felt her stomach turning inside her like the tide. "Which story now, Ma?" Beatrice said, grateful for anything that might distract her from the pain.

"Ah ever tell you de story of Anacaona?" Ma asked, eyebrows raised almost mischievously.

Beatrice's stomach lurched in that moment. She didn't know if it was the tea Ma gave her or the fact that she was bringing up Anacaona—as if she somehow knew she'd been seeing her.

"We learn about her in school, Ma," Beatrice said, trying not to make eye contact. She didn't want to let on that she'd been seeing jumbie just yet.

"No, not that one," Ma said, looking away now to wash the pot the poison tea had been in.

"In school, dey only tell you some, not all—how she was the only female warrior chief and how she eventually get defeated by the Spaniards while she watch her village burn to pieces. But the real story is what happen afterward."

As Ma spoke, Beatrice's body began to cramp up. She felt herself bend over without permission. She felt her stomach slide up and down inside her. She tried not to look down into the bucket, but she could already feel it coming out: her baby demon. Ma put her arms around Beatrice to hold her steady.

"Squeeze my arm. And scream if you need to."

Beatrice tried to nod, but it was hard to ignore the pain. As though this time she were being burned from the inside. In her mind swirled images of Hell: red spirals that went on forever, trapping her down there in that burning place.

"So what happen next?" She needed to be thinking about anything but the demon falling out her body. She squeezed Ma's arm tight, and Ma winced a little but kept going.

"You see after dey burn down Anacaona village, she get vex. Only forty people not dead yet out of seventeen hundred who she gather in her own home. Dem forty who never fight a day in dey life. A spider was there too. Anacaona go back to the colonel general who say he will spare the rest of she people if she come willing as his personal concubine. Now Anacaona was a looker. But she damn sure not going to be anybody's jagabat. Still, she need to think about her people, her villages—fifty-three other villages, in fact, all across the Caribbean."

Beatrice screamed. The pain was searing now. The blood rushing out like a waterfall.

"Breathe in," Ma said. "Breathe out."

Beatrice breathed.

"Close your eyes."

Beatrice breathed in and out three more times.

"So what happen next?"

"Well," Ma said, "see at first she pretend to say yes to de colonial who want to take she for whore and dey prepare a nice peaceful celebration. She come onstage to perform for dem an areyto. Now in English, areyto mean poem—really is more of a story. One dat have dancing and singing. Usually some magic. To tell de truth, nobody knows what was in de story she tell de colonials dat day. When dey killed her and she people, dey never bodder to write anything down. But one person survived. He travel on turtle and make he way out of Haiti after it burst in flames and come to what we now know as Trinidad.

"But dis is how I hear de tale: Anacaona gets on that stage and start her areyto. She open her mouth to sing, and everybody fall under she spell. Each and every one of them colonials' mouth drop open. All o dem went back and revisited dey childhood as she telling story about alligator and de seal. She ha' dem transfixed for nearly forty-five minutes, singing, shaking she hips, belting out verse, weaving story, until finally dey wise up to what happening. But by then it all too late.

"De forty people she gather get a hold o' the colonials' guns and ambush de men right there and then burn up dey ships. Who dey shoot and miss, run, but dey eh run far. You see de spider Anacaona bring was very peculiar. Dis spider make a web no man alive could get out of. De web go 'cross all de windows and all de doors. And so each man who run, run right into she web. And de more each man fight de web, de more him get stuck—de more him get taken up higher toward de ceiling. But de man who try to make Anacaona he whore, she deal with personally. She walk right up to him, shaking and writhing in de spiderweb while she take she wooden macana out she skirt to he balls. She slice them right off like meatballs, bobbing on de floor."

At this point, Beatrice's bucket was full. She imagined seeing her baby's demon head all caved in, its arms and legs all twisted. But all she saw was endless blood and something grayish inside. She felt something else in her stomach and threw up.

"Come," Ma said and carried her to the washroom. Beatrice wondered how her grandmother, the size of a baby kangaroo, could carry a fifteen-year-old girl, but she was too weak in the head to question anything.

Ma turned on the hot water and put Beatrice in the tub. The water was calm and warm like childhood.

"Sit in here awhile," Ma said. "You'll soon start to feel better." Ma walked to the washroom door like she was ready to go.

"But Ma," Beatrice said, and Ma stopped in the doorway. "At the end of de story, don't dey kill her? Don't dey kill dem all?"

Ma sighed. "Oh dey kill she all right. When dey come back for de rest of de Indians, dey deal with dem proper. Every last one o' dem dey shoot, except Anacaona. Dey save she to hang instead."

Beatrice thought about the rope marks around Anacaona's neck. "So why you tell me this story eh, Ma?"

Ma shrugs. "Some say she does return to help women in dey time of need. I thought it was fitting."

Ma smiled when she said this, and Beatrice knew she must've known she'd been seeing her.

"Dere are some, though, who doh believe da' is how de story go," Ma continued. "Who say if is true, how come it eh written in de history book. And to tell de truth, who's to know? None o' we was there. All I know is somebody been telling dis story for de past four hundred and seventy-six years. What more truth you need dan dat?"

Ma turned toward the door to leave again.

"Stay in here as long as yuh like. Yuh have a big day ahead of you tomorrow. Ah spoke to yuh mother so ah know to take yuh to de airport come morning," she said.

Beatrice sighed. She wanted to see her mother. It was hard to imagine that tomorrow she would be in America. Where would she go to get curry? Or would she be forced to eat hot dogs instead? Would the air be soft and wet like Arima? Or bright and sharp like Times Square? And most importantly, would there be jumbies?

Years later, Beatrice's daughter Sasha will sit at home wondering at what point her mother decided not to abort her. The thought had come after many years of hearing her mother call out to God to save her from her life. If you were to see Sasha's mother huddled on the ground crying night after night to be saved, to be magicked, asking God, "What have I done to deserve this life?" you, too, might shudder and wonder why her magic never came.

It's true that when Beatrice was pregnant with Sasha, she went to Coney Island to look for Anacaona, Mama Dglo, or anyone who could save her. She didn't find any of those things, but she did find a man named Dr. Levi Straub who told her he could assist and that her husband needn't find out. He did anyway, of course. Drove up to the place and dragged her right back home. This was the first strike in their marriage. It landed on the bridge of her nose, breaking it so that it looked like the letter *M*.

But eventually, Beatrice got out of the bath. She stood up slowly, holding on to the walls to steady herself. When she got out, she stood in front the first mirror she had seen since she'd been struck down by God. She touched her face, her breasts, her belly that lay still without a fetus and stared at the glass. She did not look nearly as scaly as she felt. Until she turned around and noticed her neck, her back, her shoulder blades. The scars looked a bit like the Picasso paintings she saw in her art class: so many overlying shapes and shades of red, blue, and black.

When Zora first saw the scars on her mother's back as a child, she recalled that they did not look at all to her like a painting. But more like the backs of slaves she saw in her history books whose whippings and welts and burnings created backs just like her mother's. And yet when Zora writes about this in her journal for the book she eventually writes, she will describe the scars like paintings.

"Not so bad," Beatrice said to the mirror. And she smiled for the first time in weeks.

Years later, when Beatrice beat her daughter with the cocoyea broom after finding her in the study with another girl, she would say, "In my day, families got lit on fire for lesser sins."

Sasha thought this to be a figure of speech until she remembered her mother's back.

............

On January 15, 1976, Beatrice took the window seat on her very first commercial aircraft to the United States of America. She looked out her oval window as the plane taxied around the parking lot, waiting for the wheels to disappear and the plane to take off.

The flight attendant came around to make sure her seat belt was securely fastened while another woman took out an air mask that was supposed to prevent you from dying if the plane went down.

"Be sure to secure your own mask before attempting to help others," said the woman.

Beatrice began to tune out her words. She took out the book from her carry-on that Ma had given her as her going away present.

"Don't forget yuh history," Ma had said. "One day yuh children will ask you." And Beatrice tried to remember where she'd heard this phrase before.

She ran her hands over the red leather covering, the engraved gold lettering that spelled out the words: *The Anansi Stories.*

As she opened the book, she swore she heard a thousand whispers all at once. She put her hand to her neck and felt the pendant that Anacaona had given her. She never did see her again, at least not in life. She felt the plane speeding up and held tightly to the arms of her seat. She watched herself rising above the Caroni buildings, above the clouds into nothingness. She closed her eyes and tried to imagine herself reborn. She imagined she found someone who loved the scars on her skin and made them seem beautiful. She imagined this person taking her hand and walking her through America: giving her her first American hot dog and showing her where not to go to avoid pickpockets or where to avoid INS. She imagined telling stories to her children about Anacaona, Nanny, Anansi. She imagined her children living in a world without ghosts, without violence, without death. She imagined that she'd hold them when they cried, that she'd tell them she'd never leave. She'd tell them that until they knew it to be true. She'd say, "I came to America so that I could hold you." She opened her eyes and stared at the sky. It had never looked so bright, so blue. She stared until the plane landed in America, waiting for signs of change.

# The Quiz at the End of the Chapter

1. *Choose the description that fits best.*

A ghost is:

a. A word that lives at the tip of your tongue; a hole you swear you'd fill if you could only find it again.

b. A memory lingered you cannot touch; a wound that leaves no scar except in memory: a haunting, a rape, a people's history erased; something not legitimized as real; a folktale; a legend.

c. A language called a dialect; a language swallowed by cowboys.

d. Something you won't believe in until you're given no other choice; when your only weapon lies in the imagining.

e. A people who exist only in stories like the time Beatrice won a school contest by peeling a mango with her bare toes—inside the skin was plump and perfect; like the time her husband beat her so bad she had raised marks up and down her sides like rows of violet—she felt the bruises inside long after they faded—like once the cancer came, the hair became a memory—the wig she bought a ghost of her former self.

f. None of the above.

2. *Which tool is most needed in reviving a ghost from the dead?*

a. Salt.

b. Cocoyea broom.

c. Forgiveness.

d. Stories.

3. *What is the best method for reviving a mother's ghost once she's long since passed?*

a. Retrace all the steps you could have taken to prevent her death: called more often, made her favorite tea, not left when things got too hard and you wanted to start your own life.

b. Keep her in a journal all to yourself. Write down everything you remember before you forget and she becomes an absence and not a ghost. New memories appear on the page each day: the Tina Turner wig you bought her to make her feel young again when her hair fell out, the coral eye shadow you bought her to take attention away from her fake teeth that she never wore.

c. Write down her name each morning and say it out loud: Beatrice. Like a mantra, a prayer.

4. *This is the sound a word makes as it breaks out of existence:*

a. *Sshhh*: as in a wave, like a lullaby, soothing until it washes her body out of sight, out of memory.

b. *Clack*: as in whips cracking on backs till all language is lost, like a mouth sewn shut, there's many screams, but all you hear is silence.

c. \_\_\_\_: as in nothing.

# PART III

---

# BEATRICE

# CHAPTER 10

# Lost in Her Story

*Sasha/Ashes*

Tunapuna & Mayaro, Trinidad & Tobago
April 2005

SO I'M SITTING AT THE BOOTH IN MAGENTA LOUNGE WONDER-
ing if she's into me. You can never tell with these white girls. She tries to
read me by scanning for my eyes underneath my baseball cap. She says
her name is Silke.

"So Ashes—that's a girl's name, right?" she says.

"You tell me." I smile, not ready to give up the game quite yet.

"You're a girl," she decides. "You have a woman's smile."

I smile back at her shyly but decide not to answer the question.

See as a girl, I'm a rebel, sharp-tongued and confident. Or at least I
had my phase. As a boy, I'm shy—the nicest boy you've ever dated.

I decided to take her out to Magenta because it's a mixed bar—
meaning that it's not exclusively gay but it's pretty accepting. We specif-
ically didn't call it a date. I honestly wasn't entirely sure if she was gay
or just curious. And at this point, I still don't know which one she wants
me to be: butch lesbian or pretty boy. Between my mother's eyeliner and
the sock in my crotch, I have to admit to myself that I look like a bit of a
gender fuck. A pretty good one, I'd say, but still a gender fuck.

"You know, I never knew there were so many lesbians in Trinidad,"
she says. "I'm sorry, that's a stupid thing to say." She blushes and her
freckles light up like a diagram of the solar system.

"No." I smile. "It's not stupid at all."

The music playing is jolting the nerves that my beer quickly tries to soothe. It's pretty dark except for the dim red lights overhead that give the cue to the crowd to move as they please—fearlessly. Even still, there are at least twenty to thirty jammed in the corners, waiting to be asked to dance. The timid crowd makes me wonder if I'm the only queer out tonight.

But this girl is definitely flirting with me. Every few minutes she puts her hand across the table and lets her fingers linger beside mine. Of course, straight girls do this sometimes.

When I first got to Trinidad, I never would've had the nerve to walk into a bar in my mother's country with a sock in my crotch. Back then my mother called me every day worried sick. I couldn't tell if she was more worried for me or for her. The last thing she asked me was who I really had in mind when I told her I'd come back here to help her: "Help me?" she kept repeating as though I was actually trying to kill her—not drop out of college to be by her bedside like a nanny for half the year. But in a way she was right. I didn't come here for her. In fact I'd barely gone to visit her since I left her and Ma's place to go and be on my own.

Silke whisks the red hair out of her face and puts it behind her ears when she speaks.

"Why do you do that? I love your hair," I say and hold my fingers near her forehead for just a moment.

"Seriously? I hate my hair. Leave it for a day and it starts looking like this." She holds up a greasy-looking strand for me to see. And then she smiles.

But is this a flirty smile? I can't tell—she hasn't shown any teeth yet. Of course sometimes the teeth imply a forced politeness. She's so subtle it's confusing. Probably just wanted somebody to pay for her food. Though we've already been here an hour and she's gone through three Caribs, which she paid for herself. She didn't offer to pay for mine.

I'm sorry, I want to say. I wish I could be better at this. My feelings for you are stuck inside me somewhere, waiting to feel less stuck. I also want to tell her that her hair is like the falling of leaves. It suits her face, which is pleasantly uncomplicated. Her nose is the perfect shape, though you barely notice it at first, especially under the bar lights. But when she leans into me, I wonder if I can fit that nose into a box and give it to somebody, like earrings.

"So what are your plans for the rest of the weekend?" she asks.

"I don't know. I have to go see my mother in the morning." I regret the words as soon as they leave my mouth.

"Your mother lives here? Oh so, you're like from here from here," she says.

"Yeah, I mean she is . . . she just moved back here a year ago and when I don't visit she gets . . ." But I can't quite finish the sentence and settle for looking down at my lap and peeling the label off my Carib bottle.

"So does your mom know?" she asks. "About you, I mean?"

I can't help but snort into my beer at that. "I guess you could say that."

Right before my mother left for Trinidad, we had a fight. We always fought, of course, but this one felt like the kind of fight that could end us.

I was sitting in Dad's old study when it happened, which had become the room designated for irrelevant objects: Dad's old fax machine that didn't work, a typewriter, Mom's broken lamp. I had gone in there with Mel.

Mel was the kind of pretty that could get away with anything: four different tattoos on her back and shoulders, multiple piercings all the way up her earlobes, another ring around her eyebrow, and seafoam-green hair.

"So how many?" Mel asked me and threw her head back, staring up at the ceiling in that seemingly effortless way white girls do sometimes.

"You've asked me this before, you know." I remember trying to make my voice sound confident and carefree like hers, but it was pretty obvious I was stalling.

"Yeah, and you didn't answer me the first time either."

She pulled off her scrunchie and ran her fingers through her hair.

"Three," I said, avoiding her eyes.

"Oh yeah?" she said and put her face close to mine. I could smell the cherry Now and Later on her breath. "Then why'd you hesitate?"

"Come here," I said and ran my hand through her seafoam hair. It moved through my fingers like ocean waves.

"No, you come here." Now she was on top of me on the floor. "Stay," she said, before taking off her shirt.

She wasn't wearing a bra, and so her chest bounced out her Gwen Stefani T-shirt like tennis balls. She lifted up my shirt with her hands and placed her fingers over the ACE bandages wrapped around my chest. I flinched, then tried to relax. But then she came toward me and proceeded to take off my shirt. I tried hard not to clench my jaws, but when she moved her hands to unwrap the ACE bandage, I panicked. I stopped her from moving any further by holding on to her wrists.

"Wait—" I said.

Her eyes widened up at me in suspicion. "What?"

"It's just . . ." But I couldn't finish the sentence.

"I knew it," she said.

I let go of her wrists and looked away. "Look, just don't tell anyone, okay."

She started laughing and punched my arm playfully. "Oh my god you're like a dude. Like no one cares, okay?"

"Don't say that."

"Don't say what? Look, being a virgin just isn't that big a deal."

"No, not that. The part about me being a dude. I don't like that."

"Oh," she said and brought her lips closer to mine. "Well, you're like a nice dude if that helps."

"It doesn't."

She turned my head to face hers. "Well, I like you, whatever you are."

"I'm just me. Ashes," I say. I was feeling defensive, but I was also feeling her eyes on me. They were intense and making me dizzy.

And that's when I heard the footsteps.

"Shit."

"Is that?"

"My mom. Yeah. Hide!"

Mel was scrambling to gather her shit, and I was trying to push her into a corner before Mom could see her.

But before I knew what to do, the door crashed open, and Mom was standing over me with the cocoyea broom. Her eyes were swirling fire like the Devil himself.

"Mel, run!" I said.

Mel looked at me terrified like she didn't know what the fuck to do.

"Get this girl out of my sight," Mom said. Her voice was a low growl.

Mom lifted the broom in the air, and I crouched into a ball on the floor to protect my face.

Thwack. I could feel the spiny branches grazing my back.

I looked up to see Mel running out the door, screaming like a white girl in a horror movie. Her tennis ball titties were bouncing around, flying up and down as she was running.

Mom was screaming words in between her thrashing.

"Doh."

Thwack.

"Bring."

Thwack.

"Sodomite."

Thwack.

"In."

Thwack.

"My."

Thwack.

"House."

Thwack.

I could feel my skin ripping apart beneath the broom. I felt my back ringing with pain. I didn't want to give her the satisfaction of seeing me cry, but I did anyway, silently and in my hands. I think it was more from the embarrassment than the actual hurting.

And then a funny thing happened. She fell to the ground beside me. I looked up to see her sobbing into her knees.

"Mom?"

"Forgive me," she said, looking nowhere in particular. I wasn't sure if she was talking to me or to God.

"Forgive me," she said again. "Forgive me, forgive me, forgive me."

Silke is staring me down right now like I'm the alien from those Sigourney Weaver movies, and I realize I'd been blanking out again. A thing I've been doing a lot since I left school last year.

"You all right?"

"Sorry," I say. "I don't really like talking about my mom."

"Then why'd you bring her up?" she asks and laughs.

"I dunno."

"It's cool," she says. "I mean, I guess I should've figured it would be a touchy subject. Being from the Caribbean and all. I heard they wouldn't even let Elton John in."

I feel my body tensing as she says this. I want to tell her that I feel more at home in my queerness here than I ever did in Brooklyn, but I just shrug and look back down at my drink. "Well, I don't know, I guess sometimes the thing you don't want to talk about is the thing that ends up coming out, right?"

"Yeah," she says. She chugs her drink and sets it down on the table. "So this was nice. We should do it again sometime." She places her fingers tentatively on her empty bottle.

"Yes." I place my hand firmly on top of hers. Her fingers feel cold from holding beer bottles all night. "Let's."

She smiles but stands up from her chair. "Well, I should get going. It's getting late," she says.

I follow her out, imagining everything: the smell of her face on my bedsheets when she leaves, her voice before coffee. I imagine it to be low and soothing like a bull underwater or airy, perhaps, like a wind instrument.

"So, how are you getting home?" I say.

She laughs. "I've been living here for three months already. Don't worry about me. I travel a lot."

"Right, of course, I mean, if you'd like to do this again—"

"I'll call you," she says. "Have a good night." She doesn't smile as she leaves.

I reach into my pocket, pretending to look for my keys and not at her leaving me. I realize I forgot to pay for my last Carib, but I leave the patio anyway and keep walking. I try to keep my eyes on the Avenue so that I can't see the look on the midnight crowd of people moving from place to place as they mercilessly judge the way I just threw myself at a white woman.

Tonight the air is cool and lit with stars. The moon is full and bright. I realize as I'm digging in my pockets that I still can't find my keys. I keep staring at the moon, and I can't tell if it's because I'm wasted or what, but the moon and the stars seem to be morphing right in front of me. One star above looks like it has legs and crawls across the sky like a giant spider.

I take a deep breath and try to focus, but my heart won't stop pounding. Damn, keep it together, Ash.

When I look back up at the sky, the spider-star is gone. I'm sitting on the sidewalk, holding on to my chest, when I see my mother. I'm twelve years old with a fever of a hundred and one. I've never been this sick before. Mom's sitting over me rubbing Vicks VapoRub into my back. Some nights later she finds me lying in bed feigning sickness, telling her I gotta stay home from school today. Of course she always thought I was doing it just so I could skip and well, she wasn't completely wrong about that. But it wasn't the only reason. Thing was, whenever my mom watched over me she was different. Like suddenly she was this cartoon fairy godmother who'd switched places with my real mom and would sing me songs and tell me stories and call me her little baby girl.

"You know what happens to girls who deceive dey mothers because dey want to stay home and be lazy?"

"No, what happens?" I'd said, but in my head I was rolling my eyes.

"Well, dey get turned into spiders. Just like Anansi."

"That's not how Dad tells it. He says that—"

"Who telling you dis story? Me or Dad?"

"Sorry, Mom."

"Okay, then."

She got out the Vicks VapoRub and told me to lie on my stomach.

"See de story go that Anansi was born a god. Girl didn't know how good she had it. Was spoiled just like an American child. Had nothing to do all day but sit up in de clouds telling fool-fool stories to de other godchildren."

"Really, Mom?" I rolled my eyes for real this time. Mom's stories always had to have something about the child being spoiled and learning her lesson the hard way.

"Yes, really. Don't interrupt."

"Sorry, Mom."

"Anyway, de point is that dis child had an easy life. In fact, she only had one task—one task alone—which was to compel de Rain to fall every morning inside de cloud forest. Tell de Rain a story about itself, and it will always fall de way you want it to."

Her hands massaged into my back. They felt nice and soothing like they could put me right to sleep.

"Mmm-hmm," I murmured.

"But of course, knowing Anansi, she get bored. Decide to change up de story. Telling Rain tall tale about some terrible monstrous spider that threatened to stick her in its web and drink her blood slowly and for hours so that even Lion and Tiger grew frightened. Needless to say, Rain wanted nothing to do with dat forest. Anansi tell dis story so much dat de godchildren grew scared of dis forest for true. What Anansi also knew was that in dis forest lived many spiders and one in particular dat stayed perched on top de trees day in and day out. It was just an ordinary spider, but she appeared so big and wretched in people's minds with its bloodsucking ways dat de spider from their minds is de only one dey could see."

"But why would the spider—"

"Steups. You want to hear de story or not, child?"

"Sorry, Mom."

"Like I say, sooner or later when de trees in the forest dry up and die, Anansi muddah ask, Anansi: 'What happen to Rain?' Anansi answer: 'Well, didn't yuh hear? Rain fraid the evil spider that sits up on the treetop.' Anansi muddah waste no time. She went straight over to Rain, demanding an answer. Rain say, 'Yes, me fraid. Who eh go fraid the Spider Anansi say is giant and eat other children? Even godchildren like we.'"

At this point I had relaxed and felt my body drift into dreamland.

"Now Anansi muddah get suspicious. She goes to the forest sheself to look upon the spider they calling giant, evil, monstrous. And lo and behold, what yuh think she found? It was just an ordinary likkle ting. Not even a poisonous likkle creature neither. Like a regular Daddy Long Legs–looking spider.

"Well, Anansi muddah get so vex with she chile's foolishness that she hit Anansi with she lighting rod, and *pam!* Anansi body get split into two. Then *pam!* She two selves get split into two again and then *pam!* Two again! Until she was left with one body and eight legs. With no more superpowers, she wasn't allowed to sit in the sky with the other gods and was instead banished to live with the humans as an ordinary spider on earth. As a spider and not a god she had no more powers except for one—she could make anyone get lost in her story."

I take a deep breath, stand up, and decide to walk over to Bacchanal because it's the only club I've ever been to where you can see the moon from inside its walls. I look up at the sky for the spider, but it's nowhere in sight. Tonight they're showing a late-night flick about being gay, being Christian, and then dying for it in the Bahamas.

"Why dey always mus' make de Caribbean seem like cesspool for backwardness and homophobia?" a woman turns to me and says.

"Right?" I say. "But I guess it's good they're saying something."

"Mmm-hmm." She looks at me incredulously.

"What's that supposed to mean?" I'm aiming for flirtatious, but I'm still slowly entering reality, trying to reabsorb the world around me. I don't know how I'm coming across.

The woman has long thick locs that are wrapped up in a headdress and a nose ring that accentuates its size: proudly taking up half of her face.

"It mean yuh sound like Yankee."

"My mother's from here," I say defensively.

She laughs. "So yuh one of those, ent?"

"One of those what?"

"One of those who muddah get slack, and get dropped off stateside when dey was young and make dey children lose dey whole culture. I like to call those halfies—watered-down Caribbeans." Yet she says this with a smile. "But at least yuh cute," she says and tips her drink toward me.

Yet she has a point. I still prefer risotto to pelau, I don't care who wins the next Soca Monarch, but still, I feel attached to my watered-down identity. I want to explain that being half of every culture, even the one you grew up with, can do wonders to your self-esteem, make you feel like you don't exist, that not knowing your history eats away at something inside you like a parasite.

After the movie, I ask if I can buy her a drink. She says her name is Candace.

Her smile is promising: a wide grin showing a slight overbite she clearly isn't ashamed of. And then someone else walks in and sits across the bar from us that looks exactly like Shay. The woman wears a Knicks cap, low above her eyes that look like Shay's eyes, which are the deepest of brown. I once thought I could live inside those eyes.

And now I see Shay the last time he visited about a month ago. He goes by "he" now. When I last saw him, his grandmother had just died of leukemia. His girlfriend had dumped him right before that. I told him to come and stay with me for a week, get his mind off things, and he did.

We'd been drinking beers by a waterfall—almost like we were back in Prospect Park, only thing is, this waterfall was real. We had to hike up a mountain to get to it.

"You know, back when my grandma first got sick, my ex—she was like this great escape," he said, taking a long swig of beer. "Like suddenly, I could put all that shit about my grandma—the standing around waiting for her to fucking die, feeling like I should be saving her, feeling guilty for having days that aren't totally about her—knowing she doesn't get to have those days anymore—I got to put all that into my ex because at least I knew *she* wasn't gonna die."

"That's pretty fucked up," I said, and he laughed.

"Well, how are you doing with waiting for *your* mom to die?"

"It fucking sucks, you're right."

"You get tired of waiting."

"So fucking tired."

"It's like you just want to get to the part where you can mourn and just be sad already. The waiting for it feels like the hardest part."

"Is it?"

"No, the dying sucks ass too," he said, and I laughed.

"So you ever have the dreams?" I ask.

"The one where you save her or the one where she says goodbye?"

"Both. Except I never save her. I always think I'm going to, and she always slips out right before I wake up. That bitch always dies on me."

We laugh before looking at each other awkwardly, looking down at our own bodies, trying to get out of the moment. I wade into the water and try to think of a way to change the subject.

"So here's a story for you," I said. "Once upon a time there was this spider sitting on death row. But when the COs come to put her ass in the electric chair, she crawls right into the throat of the chick in the next cell. Poor chick wakes up telling stories she didn't know she had. People started saying she was possessed, but they were missing the point. Because—and see here's the thing about stories—sometimes when you really believe it, the story comes to life," I said and dove down into the water.

"You should be a writer," he said when I emerged.

"Nah, Zora's the writer," I told him, catching my breath. "I just tell stories."

"I mean, yeah, you don't write them down like your sister. It's more like a performance. You're like a story conjurer or some shit."

"Story conjurer," I repeated. I liked the sound of that.

I look up now to realize that Candace has left the table to go talk to another girl. I see her whisper something into the woman's ear, while darting her eyes nervously in my direction.

I decide to leave at this point, feeling embarrassed, and head back out to Murray Street. Outside, people are singing calypso because it's too late to be playing music on the loudspeaker in the streets. People are dancing to the singing, to the drumming on their knees, on cardboard, and empty beer bottles. I buy another Carib and drink it outside on the curb so I can watch and get lost in the crowd.

I stay there until I realize I still can't find my keys, and I know if I ring the bell at my apartment at this hour, my roommate will flip. She still thinks I'm loose because I don't have a man yet show up at all hours of the night.

I keep walking till I get to the docks. There are boxes upon boxes of unshipped cargo and cranes that look like robotic creatures in the dark. All I can hear is the ocean tide pulling in and out and the cars driving by in the distance. I lean against the pier and watch for a moment, transfixed by the waves crashing onto the docks, when I think I see something: a spider crawling out from the sky, walking on top the ocean. I blink, thinking it will disappear again, but it keeps moving, walking across the water as though it's ice. I feel the blood in my body get cold, and so I run, and run, and keep running, until I realize I've run all the way to the hospital where my mom is.

I don't know if they'd let me in at this hour, but there's this rumor that if you go to an emergency room, they can't kick you out, even if you're just sitting on the floor. When I enter, the hospital is like any other: an aroma of hospital food, air-conditioning, and air fresheners that makes you forget the smell of death underneath you. There are names being called by the nurses. People waiting to be seen, arguing with the lady behind the counter about how it's taking so long and how they've been here all day, like she gives a shit. Saying things like, *Lady, ah could die in here.*

I go up to the counter and talk to the nice-looking lady with a braided bun and diamond-studded earrings. "I'm here to see Beatrice Porter—I mean, Dhawan. Miz Beatrice Dhawan, my mother," I say. The nice-looking lady furrows her brow at me.

"Yuh must be Sasha," she says.

"I'm her daughter," I say.

The lady clicks her tongue and looks away at her computer. "Yuh muddah checked out three days ago."

I feel myself getting dizzy. I hear a lady screaming next to me that her boyfriend is having a seizure. She's saying she told them this would happen. That they've been waiting to be seen all day. I watch one of the nurses trying to calm her down and then another nurse come in with a stretcher.

"She did ask for yuh. Several times. Two days ago. Mrs. Andrews checked her out."

I feel a knot growing inside my throat.

"You let Ma take her?" I say.

"Her grandmother, yes," she says.

"Did she tell you that she's 106 years old?"

I feel my voice getting hot. A security guard looks over at me, like he's worried I'm about to pop.

The lady must've sensed my heart sinking because she finally says, "Take the maxi outside. Tell them yuh going Mayaro. Yuh will have to switch in Sangre Grande. Make sure de driver knows so he can let yuh know when yuh reach."

As I get into the maxi for Mayaro, I start to panic, realizing I never removed the sock from my crotch. I cross my legs to the side and carefully slip my hand into my pants when the passenger next to me isn't looking, then pull the sock out over my waist band. I look out the window and see people selling coconut water in between the bacano trees. As I look closer, I see something crawling up one of the tree trunks. Is it the spider? I look again and the spider is gone.

An hour later, the driver waves to me that we're at my stop, and so I get out of the second maxi, trying to remember where to go next, but I feel the sock crumpled in my hand and feel a pang in my stomach. Walking down the road, I think I see my mother. It's the last time I saw her at Ma's. She's convulsing like the girl from *The Exorcist*. I remember staring at her like I was paralyzed, until Ma ran in and started yelling, "Why yuh ent tell me yuh muddah was having seizure?" She pushed me out the way and started clapping her hands and speaking in tongues until her body stopped shaking. Ma placed a hot towel on my mom's forehead as she lay still, her eyes closed shut.

"Why was she shaking like that?"

"Doh worry, child," Ma said. "Seizure is normal for yuh muddah condition."

"I wish she would—"

"If you had come to the last appointment with us, yuh would know how low yuh muddah chance of survival is right now. Doh stress she. And if yuh doh know how to do that, well," she said and wrung out the towel into a bowl. The water looked a yellowish brown.

I haven't been back to see her since.

I'm so deep in thought, I don't notice a man wearing too much cologne has started following me.

"Yuh here alone?" he says to me. From where I'm standing, I can smell the rum.

I shrug.

The man sucks his teeth. "Yuh too pretty to dress like a man. Make yuh look like a bulla man." He pushes past me and walks off around the corner.

As he leaves, I feel my body sinking into the ground. I try to think about how my body is my body and nobody else's, even when it is forced into someone else's gaze. I try to think safe thoughts. I try to imagine my mother, imagine Zora in my mind for a moment, holding their arms out toward me. But I see nothing.

I open my eyes again to see a spider. It looks the size of a large raccoon and walks toward me like it knows me. I stare at it, thinking I should run, but my body feels frozen. I think maybe this is fate. After all, it's already come after me twice. Besides, a spider seems an easier way to go somehow. Less messy, no props needed.

Now the spider is only a few feet away. As it gets closer I feel my heart leave my chest. I close my eyes and count to one hundred, waiting for death. I feel nothing. I open my eyes, and the spider is just standing in front of me, watching. I look into its eyes—all twelve of them. They blink. I didn't think spiders knew how to blink, but the more I stare at them, the more they look like eyes I've seen before, the more they look almost human. The spider crawls away.

As I get up, I feel my legs aching, realizing I've been up all night. The walk to Ma's takes about twenty minutes. It's not yet 7:00 a.m., but Ma is an early riser. The sun is peeking out over the houses on the block that look like little red clay pots. I can hear the singing of trogon birds in the trees. On the way to Ma's, I stop to buy a bouquet of hibiscus—my mother's favorite flower because it's both beautiful and edible.

Ma is standing at the doorway, face crinkled into a frown. She's wearing a long flowy white dress that matches her white satin head-wrap. She looks at me for a moment, noticing the way my hair is shaved to the scalp, the eyeliner smeared under my lids, my bandaged chest, and straight-legged jeans. Her eyes are looking at me all steady-like. It's unnerving.

"Yuh looking more like him every day," she says.

"Who?"

"Yuh father," she says and starts to walk inside. "Glad yuh could finally fit us into yuh busy schedule. She been asking for yuh."

"My mother never asks for me," I say, looking away from her.

Ma just sucks her teeth and goes back to folding the pile of clothes on the table beside her. "She resting dere, down de hall," she says.

Ma's house creeps me out. There always seems to be more shadows than people and sounds I can't make out. I take a deep breath and enter Mom's room.

"I hate yuh hair," is the first thing she says.

"I thought maybe we could be twins," I say, moving my hand lightly across her newly shaved head. "Besides, wasn't it you who told me that a woman's hair is not what makes her beautiful?"

I go to the table beside her bed to rest her flowers in an empty glass of water.

"Sometimes I wish I never tell you these things."

"Too late for that, Mom." It takes a lot of effort to smile as I speak.

"And I can smell the beer on yuh breath from a mile away."

"I just had a few drinks with a friend is all," I say. But my head is still pounding, and I feel nauseous. I sit next to her on the bed so I don't fall over.

"I worry about you here. It's not like the States. They not so accepting."

"You know, the buggery law was brought here by the British, so it's technically them who are unaccepting," I say. I notice that her skin seems dry, which it never did. And thin.

"Well, I'm glad you finally decide to pay attention in school," she says. "Yuh bring the dhalpuri like I ask you?"

"I brought you flowers, Mom."

"Well, I doh know what good flowers is if I dead tomorrow. Bring flowers to de funeral. Allyuh know Ma hand too shaky dese days to cook a proper roti."

"It might be time for you to stop being so picky, Mom. Focus on lighter things."

"So how's yuh father?" She smiles like a mischievous little girl.

"*Lighter* things."

She groans as she tries to turn herself over.

"What's wrong?" I say, putting my hand on her shoulders.

"Doh worry with dat, child." She waves me away.

"Mom."

"Just be a useful child, and pass meh my medicine from on top Ma cabinet for me, please. I tiyad."

"Is this medicine something the doctor gave you or something Ma looked up on magicmama.com?" I say.

"Steups. No questions for meh, please, nah man. I tell yuh I tiyad. Just pass it for me, please."

"Did the doctors tell you to leave the hospital, Mom?"

As I get up to pass the bottle, the nausea gets worse. I hope I won't throw up.

"Let meh tell Ma to make yuh some tea."

"I don't need tea."

"It's a special tea. It will help with yuh hangover."

I open my mouth to protest but decide against it. "Thank you, Mom," I say. Once I get the tea from Ma, I feel better. "Thank you," I say again.

"I didn't come all de way home to use de white man's medicine, Sasha."

"Mom."

"I worry about you, you know."

"Yeah, you're one to talk."

I lower my head into my mug so she can't see my fear.

"I was so worried de day I call to tell yuh about how de surgery went. Yuh never come. Was a time yuh would've come and see me right away."

"Was a time I wouldn't have had to. We would've been together. All of us."

"Well, yuh know what I always tell allyuh children. If ah going to die, it won't be in America. I won't die in the cold."

I can't help but laugh.

"What's funny?" She looks up at me angrily.

"I won't die in the cold," I say and look at her. "Damn drama queen." And we both laugh.

I want to say something to let her in, to let her know what I'm feeling, but I just squeeze her arm instead. She puts her fingers to her temples and closes her eyes.

"Mom?" She looks weak. It's scaring me.

"Sasha," she says and puts her hand on mine. Her voice is fading. Her hand is shaking. Her eyes are to the ceiling, trying to ignore the pain. "Tell me something nice," she says.

"Okay," I say and sigh. "So there once was this girl named Anansi."

"No, no. Not that one."

"And Anansi was always being told by her mother that she was nothing but a sinful, lazy, good-for-nothing daughter."

"Steups."

"But what nobody seemed to realize was that she had the whole sky down on lock."

"On lock?"

"Yeah. Under her spell. She could control the Rain fall based on how she made it feel each day."

"Hmmm."

"She tell Rain a story to make her feel good—make her feel important and shit—it would fall all normal-like. But tell Rain the wrong story, and well—"

"This not how de story supposed to go, Sasha."

"Who's telling the story, Mom? Me or you?"

"Steups."

"But one day she goes too far. Has Rain scared to fall down for days. Shit's not supposed to be this way."

"Sasha, tell de story proper, nah man."

"So now the trees are gone, and Anansi is in some real shit."

"Oh lawd, Sasha, this is not how de story—"

"But rather than get caught she figured out a trick. See, people like Anansi always getting tested by they enemies. People always wanna see Anansi suffer. Figure she has life too easy. But what they don't see is she's smarter than all the rest of them knuckleheads. See she's got this superpower where every time someone swings at her, she splits her body in half. She be in two three places all at once. Learning everybody's secrets. Now normally she was able to come back together into her true form after the chasing of her enemies was over. But not this time. Nah, this time Mom was out to kill. And so when her mom comes swinging at her, her body stay split. That shit split eight different ways. She was the strangest-looking spider the world had ever seen. Like a fucking elephant—"

"Sasha!"

"Sorry, Mom—like an elephant-sized spider with eyes that make you feel like you're frozen stiff. Now Anansi remained a spider for the rest of her life. Banished by her mother. Hiding inside cobwebs, under doors, on top of ceilings. Poor thing lost all her powers except for one—she could make anyone get lost in her story."

I look at Mom waiting for her to say something, but she's quiet, narrowing her eyes at me.

"Well, you lost me for sure," she says finally.

I start to laugh. "What? You didn't like it?"

"No. Now let me tell you how de real story go."

"I know the story, Mom, I was just—"

"I listened to you, now you listen to me."

"You didn't listen to me. You interrupted me every chance you—"

"Listen to de story."

"Go ahead, Mom."

"Thank you. Okay, so there once lived a girl named Anansi."

"Uh-huh."

"Only she wasn't a girl. She was a god."

"Sigh."

"She was the only god in the sky who knew how to convince the Rain to fall when land was dry. De only one who knew how to stop de hurricane from drowning her village. She was a powerful, beautiful trickster of a god."

"Okay, now we're talking."

"She had an ego though. And boy could she lie!"

"And here it comes."

"And yet still . . . this child *lived* to please her mother. Could do her mother no wrong. Did all her chores and all her brother's chores too."

"Sounds about right."

"In fact, she only ever made one mistake in all her life. She reach about fifteen years old when she fell in love with a wrong one. Her mother was so furious, she took a rod of lightning and broke her in two and then in two again and then in two again until she was nothing but a pile of ash."

I look at her now. In all her years telling this story, she never sounded so serious.

"Mom?"

"She was nearly burned alive for her sins," my mother continues. "She never see her family again."

I look at her again. The oblong scars along my mother's back and shoulders are peeking out of her T-shirt.

"Is that how you got your scars?" I ask, a little scared. She'd never told any of us the story. We learned after the first few lashings never to ask again.

Mom shrugs. "Families have been burned alive for lesser sins."

"Okay, Mom, you're scaring me again."

"Still . . . knowing me?" she says and stretches her feet out long. "I wouldn't change a thing."

I look at her, perplexed. "You could've left him you know." I look away while I try to get the right words out. "We would've come with you—I would've come with you."

Mom sighs and takes my hand. "Ah not talking about yuh father, child." She pauses, looks at the back of her hands. "Besides," she continues, "who would I be without you children in my life?"

"You could be happy, Mom."

But Mom only shrugs. "You know," she says, "sometimes I do wonder what my life would've been like if I'd never met your father."

"And?" I say.

"I probably would've been just as miserable," she says.

"Well, that's depressing," I say, and we both laugh.

"Sasha," she says. And then she looks at me for a moment, with eyes like she used to—like maybe, just maybe, I could still be her little baby girl. "Take de trash out when you leave for meh, please. Ah tiyad."

And as I walk out the living room, I see it next to the paintings in the corner: a spiderweb hanging from the ceiling. I blink and swear I can see my mother's body lying in the web. She's lying there wrapped in silk, and I honestly can't tell whether she's alive or dead. Her eyes look to me now like a doll's eyes—like they're still and made of glass. I grab for the web, and her body disappears. Now I feel my own body disappear into the web. I hear Ma call out my name, asking me what's wrong, telling me to lie down. She sounds so far away. And as I close my eyes, I swear I can feel my mother's hands on my back, rubbing in a bottle of Vicks.

# CHAPTER 11

# Dglo

*Zora*

Brooklyn, NY
Tunapuna & Mayaro, Trinidad & Tobago
May 2005

ABOUT A WEEK AGO I WOKE UP TO AN EMAIL FROM MY MOTHER that read like this:

*Hello Zori,*

*Bought you a ticket to Trinidad. Arrives in Port of Spain at the end of this week. Please let me know if you did not receive your e-ticket. Try to pack lightly.*

*Love, Mom*

I called her first thing in the morning, all groggy-eyed and frog-voiced. "Did someone die?"

It was an honest question.

"Steups." I heard my mother suck her teeth loudly on the other end. "Why you asking chupidness so early in the morning, nah man?"

"Because I just woke up to find out I'm going to Trinidad at the end of the week."

"And isn't it you who been asking and asking me how come I don't send for you to come and visit me and yuh sister as yet?"

"Yeah, I know, but—"

"So now that I get the ticket, you eh want to go."

"You know you're acting kinda nuts, Mom, I'm not gonna lie."

And she was. The last time I went to Trinidad I was still young enough to sleep with my Addy doll.

"Look. Save your questions for when you get here for me please. It's better if you don't know."

"Don't know what?"

I could hear her sighing loudly on the other line. "It's yuh sister. She needs our help."

"What kind of he—"

"See you next week."

And then she hung up.

In between then and now, I've gotten snippets with slightly more information. See, according to Mom, Sasha's more or less gone off the rails and has apparently shaved her head and spent every night wandering through Port of Spain drunk. She said that Sasha was gonna end up just like Uncle Zeke who was an alcoholic until he walked into a crane and wound up in a coma for six months. He came out of the coma and is fine now and just went back to managing his construction firm last month. But still, Mom says, he could be dead.

And to be honest, I don't really want to go. I mean it's not like me and Sasha have been particularly close lately. Me and her used to talk maybe once or twice a week when she was away for college, but once she left for Trinidad, it was more like once a month and then it was not at all. I'm trying not to hold it against her, considering it basically sounds like she was having a nervous breakdown or whatever. But there's a part of me that feels pissed at her like how she promised that nothing would change between us, and now I have to hear about her nervous breakdowns and alcoholic tendencies from Mom.

But if I'm gonna be totally and completely honest here, the real reason I don't want to go to Trinidad right now is that Jay Robert Ellison asked me out on a real official date two weeks ago—five weeks before the prom—which I know, I know, nobody really cares about prom except for on TV, but since I have to go anyway, it'd be nice to have a date.

See the way it goes in my head is that he walked me home from school and suddenly there were flowers in his hand, not that he bought at a store, but like he picked them from the Botanical Gardens in their rose garden cuz he's a rebel—of course he's not really a rebel, cuz he's captain of the basketball team—but in my head he's sometimes a rebel who steals flowers to give me on dates—and as he's telling me this story of how he stole these flowers for me, he says, "I stole them for you because I want you to wear them as a corsage for our most formal date," and then we kiss like it's the movies and there's a sunset and a horse, or like we're Buffy and Angel the first time they kiss in Buffy's bedroom right before she finds out he's a vampire. It's perfect.

But here's what actually happened: see, Ashton—aka the Vulture—comes up to me all smug-like after school in her pink Pumas and cherry lip gloss with her arms crossed and goes: "So here's the deal. Jay says he wants to take you to prom. He's giving you till the end of the day to respond. Otherwise he's going with Meredith. Let me know what you decide."

And then she walks away. Just like that. I was humiliated. I figured we were already an item and therefore going together and possibly on our way to getting married, and here he was with a contingency plan—and no flowers, stolen or otherwise.

But of course I said yes. I mean it's not like I get asked out very often. Especially not by guys like Jay Robert Ellison. As in Jay Robert Ellison who finally got braces and never got called Rabbit Tooth again. As in Jay Robert Ellison who got into UCLA on a basketball scholarship but is choosing to go to Howard instead—as in Jay Robert Ellison who secretly writes poetry. He tells me I am the only person who has ever read his poetry. And yes, I know this is a thing he is probably saying to get me to like him better, and it's working. He showed me one after school last week. It was about trying to break free of society's expectations and how he learned to love rather than tame the Black male beast within. It wasn't very good. But he read it so earnestly and nervously, I felt like I was seeing a part of him that no one else had ever seen before. Except for his ex, probably. She's probably seen that part of him among other parts that I don't like to think about very often.

Today he decided to walk me home from school. He asks if he can hold my jacket. It had been unseasonably cold all last week, but it's finally feeling like spring again, and like an idiot I chose to wear my North Face bubble coat—just in case.

"So . . ." he says, when we get to the front of the house, a smile finally emerging at the corner of his lips.

"I can't invite you in."

"Why not? Your parents home already?"

"No, but my sister's bus will be here any minute. I'm on babysitting duty until my stepmom gets home."

"So what you're telling me is that no one's home," he says, smiling.

"They'll be home any minute," I say again.

"So I'll only stay a minute."

I give him a look but unlock the door anyway.

"Just tell them I had to use the bathroom," he says and walks right past me inside my father's house. Bold as fuck, I think, but I follow him and lock the door.

"Damn, nice crib," he says as he walks around, eyeing my walls.

Adaliz has been on the art collecting hunt lately. There's a giant bird sculpture that she said she got from her trip to "Africa." The glass eyes of the bird look as though they're peering right through you. Jay seems transfixed just eyeing the thing.

"Creepy, right?" I say to him.

"Nah, you serious? This is great. House is like a museum and shit." And then he turns around and looks at me and I wonder what he sees.

"Yeah, my stepmom's loaded," I say and begin nervously tugging at my braids.

"Why do you always play with your hair like that? You look great."

He doesn't wait for an answer though. He takes my hands away from my braids and places them inside his. His hands are large and warm. He leans in, and I can feel it coming: I feel it on my cheek, my neck, my lips. His kisses don't feel sloppy like the other boys' before him. I can feel his lips more than his tongue, and it feels nice and tender. I feel his weight pushing me toward the leather couch in my living room, his hands tight around my waist. And of course now that his hands are finally where I want them to be, I feel my own hands sweating.

I try to decide whether I want to be led to the couch or not. I feel like I need to savor the kiss before other things happen—things that I imagine happen on couches. In the movies, the kiss on the couch always signifies that something more than kissing is on its way—but it's too late—already we're on the couch.

Now I'm thinking about things like how Mom always said to stay away from athletes because girls will do anything for them, and after a while they start to expect things. Like what if he expects me to go down on him or something, and I don't know how, or I say no and then he kills me.

And as though he's reading my mind he goes, "You okay?"

"Sure, sure," I say, but my hands are shaking.

"You sure you're sure?" he says with a smile.

"Yeah, I mean, I think, I mean . . . I dunno." I'm worried that if I tell him what I'm thinking, he'll think I'm crazy and decide to go to prom with Meredith instead.

"What's wrong?" he asks and then he strokes my cheek with his hand.

"I guess I just wanted you to know that like . . ."

"Yeah?"

"That I—I just don't give head . . . like not at first . . . just so you know."

He narrows his eyes, furrowing his brow, and just stares at me for some time. "What?"

"I just thought I should tell you that, you know, because you're a jock or whatever."

He looks at me real serious for a moment before his mouth cracks into a smile. "You've never done this before, have you?" he says.

I turn away from him, embarrassed, but he puts his arms around me.

"It's cool," he says. "I'm not in a hurry."

And then he takes the remote beside him and switches on the TV.

It's then that I hear the familiar key jingling in the doorway, and already I know that it's too late for me.

Jay and I instinctively move away from each other on the couch when I hear the sound of Sebastian barking, the high-pitched chattering of Kayla, Madeleine, and Adaliz, who is looking at me, arms crossed, lips pursed. I grab the remote to switch off the TV. I feel my stomach sinking.

Sebastian runs up to Jay excitedly. Jay puts his hand out for Sebastian to sniff like a pro.

I put my hands in my lap to appear more ladylike. Jay gets up to introduce himself.

"Hi, I'm Jay. I go to school with Zora," he says, and I can tell by the sudden shift in his voice and stature that he's had a lot of practice convincing parents of his gentlemanly nature.

"It's nice to meet you, Jay. You must be the prom date."

I look away when she says that. Of course she'd try to humiliate me.

"Ooh, Zora's got a boyfriend!" Kayla taunts.

"Zora's boyfriend! Zora's boyfriend!" Madeleine chimes in.

"How's it going, ladies?" he says to them, and the girls start giggling as though even at four and five years old they already know what it means to be in his presence.

"Girls, go upstairs now, please," Adaliz says. "I'll call you down when dinner's ready."

They follow instruction, but not without making kissy faces all the way up the stairs, shouting, "Zora and Jay sitting in a tree, K-I-S-S-I-N-G!" as they exit. Sebastian pants up the stairs behind them.

"It's nice to meet you, Mrs. uh . . . Porter?" Jay says, unsure if she has the same last name as me. He extends his hand to shake hers.

"You can call me Addy," she says, taking his hand.

I sigh in relief. White Mom is playing it cool. She'll probably want to talk after. Feign slight concern about having boys over but really just use it as a reason to make us have a long conversation intended for bonding. Whatever. So long as Dad doesn't find out.

"Very nice to meet you, Mrs. Addy," he says. "I better get going." He starts to gather his things.

"Come for dinner sometime, won't you, Jay? I'm sure Zora's father would love to meet you."

I give her a look that I know I could never give to my mother, but she merely walks him to the door like she doesn't even notice.

"Well, I guess it's a good thing I had to take Sebastian to the vet today or those poor girls would've been waiting by themselves for God knows how long," she says when he leaves.

"Jay just walked me home," I tell her. "He was just saying goodbye since I'm not gonna see him for a while. I was going to pick them up right as you guys came in."

"Zora, you know your father doesn't want you having boys in the house."

"You're right, I'm sorry. I should've been more responsible."

She pauses, then invites me to sit on the couch with her. "So," she says, and I see the smile coming and I know what's about to happen. "Tell me everything."

I tell her the things I know she wants to know, like the fact that he's an athlete who also writes poetry and about how much he liked all of her African artifacts. I think about how this conversation would go if my real mom was here right now. Probably less of a conversation and more of the feel of her belt against my back, the tears burning my cheek, and then only after I'd proven that I understood the dangerous predicament I'd put my family and myself in—leaving my sisters to be kidnapped for trafficking at the bus stop half a block away from our house, being alone with a boy I barely knew when God knows what could have happened to me—then and only then would she wrap a blanket around me, put a kettle on for Milo, and tell me a story about Mama Dglo—the infamous Mother of the Water who warns foolish little girls of the boys who will say anything to trick them into giving up their bodies and sell them for gold. *These bodies get found at the bottom of the ocean where the scuba tourists in Tobago go,* Mom would say.

"Be careful," is all Adaliz says after I've told her everything. "He seems like a heartbreaker."

"I know," I say. But he's *my* heartbreaker.

I replay the scene of our first kiss moment in my head: his tree bark eyes, his hands over mine, his soft tone when he asked if I was okay, and the moment he held me close, arms around me tight like a blanket.

............

Mom picks me up at the airport in Port of Spain and I'm surprised. And also pissed. Why wouldn't Sasha come to get me? I mean I know Mom says Sasha's going through it right now, but it's not like she has terminal cancer.

"Yuh losing weight," she says to me.

"Yeah, you're one to talk, Mom."

Mom's wearing a red dress that I can tell she wore to dress up for me. It's long and flowy and beautiful, but she's so thin now, she looks lost in it, like the dress is swallowing her whole. Her arms jut out of her sleeves like chicken bones. She's wearing too much makeup, and the sun hat she wears falls over her face, making it hard to see the expression in her eyes.

"I know, I know, ah look horrible, ent," she says, and I realize that I've been staring. Under her hat, I can see that most of my mother's hair that once met the middle of her back is now missing.

"I've missed you, Mom," I say, and when I lean in to hug her, I'm surprised at the tears falling down my cheek and onto her red balloon dress. "I know I should've called more. I—"

"I know, I know, Zori," she says, "but we don't have time for all o dat right now."

"Time for all of what?" I say, looking for the answer in her eyes, but she looks away and starts walking toward the exit.

"Come. Let's go for the maxi."

The airport is smaller than I remember, the air much hotter. I was expecting it to feel the way it does in those commercials—a nice summer breeze, with whitefolks in bikinis sipping their mojitos. But this heat is so aggressive it's suffocating.

"Was it always this hot?"

"Global warming," she says, still walking. "And you brought too much luggage. That's why yuh hot. You look like yuh planning to move in along with yuh sister."

We get to the maxi stand and wait for it to fill up. I want to ask so many questions, but there are too many people—talking on the phone to relatives, talking loudly to the person next to them about the latest news story, looking silently ahead. I look at my mother sitting next to me, hands clasped like in church. I wonder about all the worries clouding her mind that she's probably not telling me.

"So how bad is she?" I ask, wanting to break the silence.

"Bad," she says, not looking up. "Last time I go to check she, is like she forget who raise her, using all kinda brazen language. Steups."

"Well, she was always like that, Mom."

"No, Zori." Mom looks up at me now; her eyes are stone. "She's a different Sasha from the one you knew. People saying she might be possessed."

"What people?"

Mom shrugs.

"And hear what else. Sent yuh aunty Shirley who live that side to check she. She get no answer, but she say she could hear her voice— talking to sheself."

"How do you know she was—"

"Refusing to come to the door for she aunty Shirley, can you imagine?"

"Yeah, I can imagine her doing that." And I could.

"Thing is," Mom continues, "she say there was a smell."

"A smell?"

"A smell."

"A smell like what?"

"Like filth."

"Are you sure she was in there?"

"Oh, she was there," Mom says. "But this is why I bring you here. She listen to you. Ah swear, Zori, sometimes is like yuh the older one. Together we going to talk some sense in her."

But I wasn't so sure. Fact is that lately I haven't been thinking about Sasha much at all. Stopped worrying about her as much after she told me she was leaving college for Trinidad in a text message. All it said was: *Leaving this place for a while. Need to get away from all this white shit and get back to the important things. Gonna stay with Mom for a while. Come and visit sometime. I'll call you when shit starts to settle down.*

But she never did call.

"So when are we going to the beach?" I ask.

Mom gives me the stink eye but says nothing.

I sigh and look out the window. The air smells sweeter than it did in Brooklyn: like fruit and sea salt. There are people selling bananas, mango, and chennette on the sides of the roads and the mountains encircle us like hugs. In the cab, I take out my journal and write: *Once upon a time, a girl ~~sucked at writing~~ fooled herself into thinking she had something important to say until they laughed at her and she stayed quiet forever.*

We get to a busy intersection and stop.

"At the corner, driver," I hear Mom say. "We're here," she says to me.

Outside of Sasha's place, the apartment complex looks like a small yellow house with a fairly well-kept yard aside from the metal junk lying in the corner. Across the street is a house covered by mango trees. There are chickens perched idly in the treetops. I never knew until this moment that chickens could fly up that high.

My mother knocks on the front door. Nobody answers. We walk around to the back of the yard and come in through the kitchen entrance.

Something in my stomach starts to turn. All I can smell is rotting food melting in the heat. Sasha's kitchen is filled with maggots and flies eating her leftovers from the pots and pans filling up her sink.

I feel like I might throw up. As we walk into the living room, there are piles and piles of empty pizza boxes from Mario's and empty bottles of Stag and White Oak covering the ground. I pass the bathroom and see clumps of hair and a dirty hair clipper lying on the peeling linoleum on her fake tile floor.

I wonder at this moment what happened to her roommate. Did she leave at the first sign of chaos, or did she try to find out what was wrong before giving up?

There's a light coming through the door of what looks like Sasha's room. Her bedroom door is shut, and I'm afraid to enter—afraid that maybe some evil spirit has taken her place.

I look at Mom now, not sure what to do next. She motions for me to knock, and I do so, tentatively.

"Hey, Sash? It's me, Zora," I say.

No answer. I open the door, slowly, cautiously, as though a ghost might appear on the other side and try to possess me too.

Sasha is lying in her bed, watching *Grey's Anatomy*. She looks up from the TV to see me and Mom in her doorway.

Her face brightens, and she gets up to give me a warm and too-tight embrace. "Hey, sis," she says, "you made it." The hug feels unnatural. "Mom was all like, 'Zori's too busy, Zori has prom and shit,' but I knew you'd come." The cheeriness in her voice is overwhelming and catches me off guard. Her bald head makes her look like a stranger.

"Yeah, well of course," I say, stumbling to find the words. "Didn't you hear us knocking?"

Sasha just shrugs and points to her television set. "Had to catch up on my shows before you got here. I know you're always up-to-date. Didn't want you ruining the season finale for me."

"I didn't watch it," I say.

"You should," she says. "You'll never guess what happens to Derek and Meredith."

I don't know what to say so I just keep staring at her, waiting for it all to make sense.

"I'm sorry I couldn't come and get you from the airport," she says, her eyes drifting away as she speaks.

Aside from the forced cheeriness, her voice sounds almost the same, but her eyes, always watchful, look lost and empty. She looks over at me, but in a way like she can't really see me anymore—as though *I'm* the ghost. Then she looks past me and stares into the cracks in the wall, at the ants marching toward the food on the floor—at the beetles watching the ants, stalking their prey.

"Sasha," I say, looking around at the apartment. I'm not sure how to verbalize what I'm feeling.

"I know, I know, the place is a shithole," she says. "I tried to clean it before you came, I really did, but . . ." And then she looks away again, not finishing the sentence.

Mom puts a hand on my shoulder now. "Okay girls," she says. "It's time to go."

"Where are we going now?" I ask.

I'm eager to get the hell out of Sasha's maggot- and ant-infested apartment.

"To the beach," Mom says. And I can't tell if she's just messing with me or not.

They both start for the door as though this all makes perfect sense.

"Don't ask questions now, Zori," she says before I can say anything, and keeps walking.

We take the maxi to Sangre Grande, and Sasha is staring out the window, looking transfixed.

It's a strange thing seeing someone you've known your entire life, someone you knew so well they were like a body part, and having no idea what to say to them.

After about twenty minutes, I try to break the silence: "So . . . what does happen to Derek and Meredith?"

Sasha looks back at me, wide-eyed. "You won't believe it," she says. "That motherfucker's still married."

"Seriously?"

"Yup. His wife's a doctor too. Beautiful. Redhead. Seems like trouble."

"Well, I never liked him anyway."

"Yeah, I kinda think the people who say they do are just pretending."

I smirk, when Mom shouts, "Right here, driver!"

Sasha looks startled.

"Sasha?" I say.

But she looks back out the window as though she sees something there besides the cars whizzing past us on the highway, the mountains beyond.

"There's nothing there, Sasha," I say, but she just shrugs and puts on her headphones like I'm not even there. I take out my journal and write: *Once upon a time, a girl had a sister who took a trip inside herself several years ago and has yet to be found. If you look, you may find her evil clone asleep in her bedroom or if not, you may find her trying to wake up while watching* Grey's Anatomy *or if not, you may find her trying to fall asleep with a bottle of Stag and an Old Oak. The girl tries to be sympathetic while trying not to shake her sister back to life, even if it kills her.*

We get into three other maxis, lugging my giant suitcase around into each one. In the last maxi, we go through an endless grove of trees: coconut, breadfruit, and bacano—all tall as giants. We pass women selling coconut and mango and pommecythere until we wind up at a house in Mayaro.

The house is nicer than I expected: a magenta-colored beach house with white pillars and a large gate right on the main street. Mom tells us as we're getting out that this is Ma's old house. She died about a month ago at 106 years old.

"You knew about this?" I whisper to Sasha, lugging my suitcase from the maxi.

"Mom's trying to get the Devil out of me," Sasha says as though this is a totally normal thing for her to say.

"What?"

"Remember that time you thought you had demons in your walls?"

"You know those weren't really demons, right?"

But Sasha shrugs and follows Mom inside. I mean, she walks like Sasha, talks like Sasha, but this definitely is not Sasha. I start to imagine there really is a demon inside of her—a dark red cloud, eating away at her arteries, her brain, until there's nothing left. I close my eyes and try to force the image of the Devil outside of my brain. But when I open my eyes, I still see it: the shape of the Devil.

I take a deep breath and walk inside, afraid I might find skulls and cauldrons and dead chickens as I enter. Instead there are candles and stones, cocoyea brooms and statues of saints. On the walls are portraits of women, all Black and majestic, standing in rivers, oceans, forests, under moonlight, and watching us. Each one has a name plaque underneath it: Yemayá, Oya, Oshun.

"The Orisha deities," Mom says, watching me watch Ma's paintings.

"What's happening to this house now that she's gone?" I ask.

"She left it to family," Mom says. "I is the only one who really come to maintain the thing. We'll see how long it last."

"Are you sure you should be doing that—you know, given your . . . ?" But I can't finish the sentence.

Mom waves my question away and beckons to me and Sasha to follow her to a small bedroom with a bed that reminds me of a giant coffin, with its red velvet sheets and its weirdly hexagonal shape. There's a lacy black canopy tied to the bedposts that look like horns. In the corner of the room is a table with a yellow lace tunic lying on top of it. Mom instructs Sasha to put on the yellow tunic before leaving to gather the materials for the beach.

I use the moment to get my calling card from my suitcase and dial Jay's number, but nobody answers. I call again. No answer. I try again. Still no answer.

"Do you see that?" Sasha says. She's staring at a crack in the wall, unaware of what I'm doing.

"What?"

"Never mind," she says and continues to stare as though being transported somewhere.

I sigh and put the phone down. As soon as I do, the phone rings. "Hello? Jay?" My hand is shaking.

"It's Zori Bear!"

It's Dad. I try hard not to sound disappointed. "Hi, Daddy."

"Did you forget you had a father, Zori?"

He sounds like he's in a good mood. "Sorry, Daddy. We've just been . . ." But I don't know how to say what I'm feeling.

"And who is Jay, exactly?"

"It's no one—"

"I'm listening."

"A friend of Mom's," I lie.

"I see. Well, how are those two doing? Hope they're not driving you too crazy. I know how those girls can be."

"No, they're not . . . they're just . . ." I try to think of something to say to prove him wrong, but my mind is blanking.

"Hang in there," he says. "You'll be home soon."

"We're having a good time, Daddy," I try.

"Look. I can only stay for a minute. Have to run into a meeting, you know how it is. Talk soon."

"Bye, Daddy." I hang up.

I look over at Sasha, but she's still just staring at the wall. I decide to make another attempt to talk to her. "So what do you think this is for?" I say, pointing to the tunic. "Your coming-out ball?

"Dglo," Sasha says. Her voice is hollow like an echo. "We're calling Dglo."

"Sasha," I say, "what's wrong with you?"

"Help me with my clothes," she says, struggling to zip it from the back.

I sigh and walk over to help her fit the yellow tunic over her body.

"Let's go," Mom calls out.

We both turn around.

"To the beach?" I ask.

"To Dglo," Mom says.

. . . . . . . . . . . . .

We get to the beach at sunset. The sky is orange and red. It always is at sunset, of course, but right now I feel like it might be showing its anger in solidarity with the rest of us.

Sasha sits at the edge of the shore in her yellow lace tunic. Beside her, Mom lays out the mirror, golden comb, and yellow candle from Ma's house, then wades in, peering deep into the ocean. She's listening for something. "What do you hear?" she asks us.

The water rocks back and forth at a slow, uneven pace. The waves crash the way they always do, revealing shells and small fish underneath as they push and pull. I listen for a few moments, trying to hear something else, something magical—and then I do—it's something like the sound of sighing muted by water.

"It's Dglo, isn't it," I say.

Mom nods. "You can tell she's here when the water looks more green than blue," she says.

Indeed, the water seems to have changed from a clear sky blue to a deep mossy green. I always thought the change of the ocean colors was just something the ocean did, the way a wave always has to crash. But now I wonder, how many times have I swum among the infamous Mama Dglo?

"So what do we do now?" I ask.

"Once upon a time there was a girl," Mom says, her voice calm and heavy as the ocean. "She was tired of being broken in. But she wasn't born tired. See, the girl didn't know it, but she had magical powers. For she had the ability to communicate with the goddesses."

I look at Sasha, who looks out at the water, watching a spot in the distance where the ocean looks like a lagoon, a deep green circle that keeps getting larger.

Mom looks at me to continue. I feel hesitant. I think of the last time Sasha and I tried to call Mama Dglo to heal Mom, and now here she is, thin and dying. And yet on the beach today, she looks beautiful. I still don't know if this will help Sasha but decide to go along with it anyway.

"Men didn't like that she had this gift, and so they tried to break her," I say. "One smashed her face wide open with a sledgehammer. The gashes in her face like cracks in the earth. One day, she'd had enough. The girl climbed to the highest cliff and looked out at the sea. She said, 'Help me spirit, Mama Dglo. Rid me of darkness in your castle below.' And then she jumped high into the air, preparing herself for flight. Preparing herself for death."

"And as she jumped, she heard a sound," Mom says, taking my hand. "At first it sounded like thunder: loud and crushing. But it wasn't thunder."

As we tell the story, the tide is rising steady and fast, the sound like a heartbeat.

"No," I continue, "because as she plunged into the waters, she felt something coil around her legs, taking her deep down under. Her body guided this way and that. She thought, 'maybe this is death.'"

"But it wasn't death," Mom goes, "because when she opened her eyes, she saw Mama Dglo sitting before her."

The waves crash hard against our feet. I wonder if we should move away from the tide, yet Sasha seems transfixed by the waves. I move to hold her hand. The water starts to hush in time with the story, after every beat as we alternate the telling.

"Half of her, a beautiful woman with locs as long as the tallest tree," I say.

Shhhh.

"But the other half was a snake—a deadly anaconda, not to be messed with," Mom says.

Shhhh.

"'Am I in Hell?' asked the girl, still believing she was dead."

Shhhh.

"Dglo laughed a great belly laugh and the ocean rocked like a toy boat."

Shhhh.

"'This is the ocean,' answered Dglo."

Shhhh.

"The darkness is the place inside yourself you cannot see."

Shhhh.

"Some people call it Hell, while others call it heartbreak, like a pain you cannot place or name."

Shhhh.

"'But who are you?' asked the girl."

Shhhh.

"'My name is Mama Dglo.'"

Shhhh.

"'I am the protector of the forests, the keeper of the seas.'"

Shhhh.

"'Like the Devil for those who try to test me. I come to wreak havoc against those who disrespect the waters.'"

Shhhh.

"'But they also call me the healer and occasional vengeance seeker for those they call broken. Usually girls like you are the ones that get thrown away.'"

Shhhh.

"'Sometimes men find themselves at the bottom of the ocean, never to return, and this is why. The question for you, little girl, is what do you want?'"

Shhhhh.

"I want to live," says Sasha. Her voice cracks when she says this.

I'm so distracted by Sasha, I don't notice the giant tidal wave growing upward toward us like a moko jumbie. In the moment before the wave crashes, I think I see something: a glimmering underneath the waters—like the scales of a green tail. And then I feel the crash. I feel myself tumbling. I move my arms wildly. I don't know how it's possible that I got moved so far out into the ocean when we were sitting on the sand, but I can't feel the surface. My feet can't feel the bottom. I start to panic.

In the story, this is where I am supposed to be saved by Dglo, taken down with her into her palace. I open my mouth to scream, but all I do is swallow more water. Finally, I feel something grab my hand, pulling me onto its back. I can feel myself being carried.

My mind drifts to a memory. I'm floating inside a canoe and arrive at a place I can't name. All of us are in it together, Sasha, Dad, Mom, and me floating somewhere that feels familiar though I can't say why exactly. I want to open my eyes, but I'm afraid of the snake-woman-goddess who must be carrying me. She lets me go, and I feel myself sink into sand. A hand caresses my face, and I open my eyes to see my mother sitting above me. I don't know whether it's because I'm so out of breath or because of the glare of the sun, but my mother has never looked so beautiful.

"You carried me?" I ask, but she only smiles and looks away at the ocean.

I sit up finally, looking around at my surroundings. I see Sasha lying in the sand, eyes closed, body limp, mounds of seaweed wrapped around her legs, her face, her torso.

"Sasha," I whisper. I run to her, hovering over her, looking for signs of life. "Sasha," I say again and fall on top of her.

"Come, let her breathe, child," Mom says, pushing me away, but then she falls on top of her just the same, and we all lie there together in a heap on the wet sand.

After a few moments, Sasha flutters her eyes open and starts coughing up water.

"Are you okay?" we ask.

She nods and we help her sit up.

"Did you see her?" I ask once she's up.

"Leave her be," Mom says. "She needs time to process."

"I didn't see her," Sasha says after a pause.

"Oh," I say, disappointed.

"But I did *feel* something," she says. "It's hard to explain. It felt like a memory, like Mom putting me to sleep when I was little or something. I don't know. I felt safe, though. It was something like safety."

I wonder if she saw the canoe, but I decide not to ask this out loud.

"You are safe," I say, although I don't know that I believe this. In a week, I'll be gone. Away from her again. I can't protect Sasha any more than I can protect myself. And there is something chaotic and scary about knowing that—that as much as you might love someone, they are more or less on their own.

..............

We get back to Ma's old house so Mom can start dinner.

"I'm gonna take a shower," Sasha says.

But instead of walking toward the shower, she just stands there in the middle of the room, looking dazed. I wonder how much the beach trip helped—if it helped at all. I wonder why the thing that carried me in the ocean today felt nothing like my mother.

"Help me out these clothes," she says.

I walk over to her and unzip her wet yellow tunic. But instead of taking it off, she sits on the bed, making the mattress damp and sandy. I sit next to her anyway, trying to think of what to say, trying to remember what it was like to never have to think of what to say when I was with her. Looking at her, I can't help but notice that she looks so strange underneath all that flowy yellow, like it doesn't belong. But I also can't help but notice how beautiful she is with her bald head and her bright yellow tunic like the sun.

"Sasha," I try one more time, "tell me what's wrong."

"I want to tell you," she says, looking at me from the bed, "but I can't. Not yet."

We sit there in silence a moment.

"So let's just say there was a spider," I say, "and the spider's been possessed by the Devil."

"Or maybe she got trapped inside that wall," Sasha says, pointing, and I think of her eyes earlier—transfixed to the wall where beetles and ants marched out from the cracks.

"Maybe she calls on someone to help her—a woman by the name of Dglo," I continue.

"Dglo hears the spider struggling inside the walls and so she smashes them open with her tail."

"She crawls out into the wild. She finds her web inside the forest. She's home free."

"Home free," Sasha repeats, pulling at the ends of her tunic. "You ever wonder what was really in those walls when we were little?"

"I seem to remember you thinking they were pigeons," I say.

"Yeah," she says, "but then at a certain point, we realized it was just some people fucking." She pauses. "And then . . ." Her voice falters.

"What?" I ask.

"Well, lately I keep seeing these—these spiders."

"Spiders?"

"Yeah," she says. "Sometimes I think it could be Anansi."

"What do you mean? You think it was Anansi inside those walls?"

"I don't know," she says. "It's just a feeling I have."

I stare at her a moment. "I didn't know you still believed in all of that."

"You don't?" She looks at me, surprised.

"The last time I tried believing, Mom left," I say. "And so did you, if I recall."

"I know," she says. "I'm sorry."

"And besides, our spell never worked. Mom will be—"

"I know," she says. "You ever see her in your dreams?"

I know without her saying so that she's talking about our mother. "Every night."

"You ever save her?" she asks.

I think about her skin crinkling like tissue paper in my hands but say nothing.

"Me neither," she says. "Not once."

"Honestly, I don't know how you do it, Sash," I say, moving closer to her on the bed.

"Do what?"

"Stay here, knowing that she's just going to die," I say and move to help her pull off her tunic, which she tugs at like it hurts.

"That's the thing," she says. "I'm here, technically, I guess, but every time I try to be with her I just feel—"

"Scared?" I ask.

"Lost," she says, "like I'm not really here." She lies on the bed shivering without the tunic on, and I move to bring her a towel and her Hilfiger hoodie.

"Like sometimes I'll be sitting by the window, reading a book, smoking a blunt or whatever, and I think to myself, what would it feel like to fall?"

I look out at the chickens in the trees outside the window and picture them falling. "You mean like if you jumped?" I say and move closer to her to make sure she doesn't.

"No, not jumped. Fall." I hear the sound of her voice cracking. "I don't know," she says. "Maybe it'd feel good to fall."

I put my hand on her face and stare her down. "You better not, Sasha."

"Okay," she says and moves my hands away.

I grab her hand and hold it tight. "I'd die for you, you know that right?"

"I know."

"I'd kill for you, too, you know."

"I know."

"All my life spent in solitary and all of eternity spent in Hell just for you."

"Yeah, yeah, Zora, okay."

"You ever die and I'm bringing you back, just so I can kill you my-self. You remember that."

"Okay, okay. Got it," she says, throwing her hands up in surrender, and then she leans her head into my chest. I rub my hand across her bald head. It feels strange and waxy. "I'm really glad you're here, Zori," she says.

I start to smile, until I feel her breath, harsh and deliberate, letting me know she's still in pain. I feel her tears travel down my neck, wetting my shirt.

"I'm so scared, Zori."

And then I can't help but cry, too. We stay there like that, until Mom comes in. She looks at us crying for a moment, and I think she's gonna say something. But she just climbs on the coffin-shaped bed next to us and starts to cry with us. We cry until the whole bed is wet to the touch as though there's a puddle forming beneath us. I put my hand in-side our puddle, and it feels almost like the ocean, warm and salty.

. . . . . . . . . . . . .

Hours later, I wake up, and tiptoe to the living room, leaving Mom and Sasha sleeping next to me. There is a bookshelf with candles and flowers surrounding it where Ma kept her books on the Orishas. I scan the titles, but they all look like typical medical books: *Gray's Anatomy*, a few physicians' manuals, some books on herbs. Nothing about magic. And then I see on the table an open book with dog-ears and underlining in pen. The book has that old book smell like my mother's Bible and my father's copy of Melville stories. I turn it to see the cover and it says *The Anansi Stories* in large gold lettering, the book that Sasha and I fought over when we were little. The last time I remember reading it was when Sasha and I tried and failed to save Mom from cancer. I never saw the book again.

"I see you found yuh favorite book," Mom says, startling me.

"Where'd you come from?"

"Yuh know, yuh should really ask before going through Ma's things. She was always very particular."

"Well, I don't think she'll mind, you know, all things considering."

"Don't disrespect the dead," Mom says, taking the book from my hands and putting it back on the shelf. "They have a way of knowing."

"Did Sasha steal our copy and bring it here?" I ask, picking up the book again.

Mom shrugs. "God only knows."

Inside, there's an illustration of Mama Dglo wrapping a man's legs in her tail and bringing him to her mouth in the middle of the ocean.

"Does Sasha look any better to you?"

Mom puts her hand over mine and squeezes it. "How can you expect to use the magic when yuh eh have no faith?"

"I have faith."

"Steups. Doh lie to me, child."

"Well . . . I just don't know if all this magic stuff is really working . . ." I try not to stare at her bony arms, which seem to lose more flesh by the hour.

"Medicine and magic are not de enemies yuh make them out to be, Zori. Is your country teach you that."

She walks to the stove and turns it off at the sound of bubbling. When did she get up and begin cooking? The smell of herbs fills the room. She ladles something into a bowl and pushes it toward me. "Come. Yuh never eat yuh dinner."

I see a gruesome-looking cow heel swimming in the bowl, and I groan. "Mom, you know I don't eat that stuff anymore," I say. "Besides, since when do you eat meat?"

"Just say God is love, and eat the food."

I sigh, and begrudgingly put a tiny bit of liquid on my tongue.

"Hmm," I say. It tastes like pepper and thyme.

"Is good, ent?"

"It's not bad," I concede.

She sits down next to me with her bowl of cow heel soup.

"Ma take me to the hospital sheself just last year. I was in the hospital mus' be two months doing chemo. You'd know that if you ever come to visit," she says in between sips.

The words sting. "It'd be easier to visit if you never left."

I feel guilty, saying these things to my mother who's probably going to die soon, but I say them anyway. "You shouldn't have left me with them." Meaning Kayla and Madeleine and the woman who isn't my mother.

Mom sighs and puts down her spoon. "Hard to stay in a place after it kills your spirit. Besides, your father needed you. From the sounds of things, his time with you has been good for him. A chance for him to start over and be the father he wanted to be before . . . well, you know." She pauses and looks away for a moment. "I'm happy for him. Kayla and the halfling. They need you too."

"Don't call her halfling, Mom," I say, but I can't help but smile a little in spite of myself.

"Yuh know, the red-skin gyal."

"It's Madeleine, Mom. Her name is Madeleine."

"Yes, she. I'm glad she have she father. I'm glad you have him too."

I say nothing.

"Just have a likkle faith, Zori. It mightn't look it, but I've been feeling better since I first went to Ma. In three days, I'll go to the doctor to see if Ma's treatments make the cancer shrink. If it don't, well—"

"I don't want to lose you, Mom." I want to be angry, but I can't help but feel the tightness of tears rising in my chest again.

She puts her arms around me. "Mothers never die," she says. "The story go that children love to resurrect us in they stories."

. . . . . . . . . . . . .

I walk into the bedroom, and Sasha's still fast asleep. I get into my bed next to hers and watch her chest rise and fall. She looks so peaceful in this moment. I close my eyes and try to sleep, too, but I can't. There are too many thoughts whirring through my brain, so I log on to my laptop and open my Myspace page. There's a message from Jay. He sent me the music video for Tupac's "Dear Mama," with a message that said: "Hope this brings a smile to you and your mama's face."

I start to blush just reading it.

Now I scroll through his page and see a photo of him with his hands up after scoring in the last game against Wingate. Maybe he's out celebrating. I try to think of something cute and positive to send him to rival the Tupac video. And then I see something else. It's a photo of Ashton with her vulture wings all over Jay's beautiful torso. The caption reads "Me and this sexy chocolate after the big game."

I feel nauseous.

I look over at Sasha and decide to wake her. "Sasha," I whisper. No answer. "Sasha!" I say louder.

She rustles a little and then glares at me. "This better be good," she says finally.

I take my laptop and sit on the edge of the bed next to her.

"Look," I say, pointing to the photo.

She rubs her eyes and yawns before peering into the screen. "That Ashton?"

I nod.

"Ashton who made fun of you when that kid threw that spit wad at you in the fifth grade?"

"Yup."

"The Vulture, Ashton?"

"That's the one."

"Then what'd you expect?" she says and turns on her side to go back to sleep.

"Sasha!" I say, nudging her. "I need your help."

She rolls over and looks at the photo again. "So should we kill him?"

And I laugh. "No, Sasha. It's not even like that. I mean we weren't official or anything."

"So what's the problem?"

"Well, he did ask me to the prom."

"I see," she says.

"So I guess I figured we were bound to be official eventually."

"Doesn't sound very official," she says.

"Sasha!"

"Okay, okay," she says, sitting up. "But seriously, Zori. What do you even like about this guy? I mean I think I get the physical appeal," she says, looking him up and down, "but other than that, he looks like a bit of a douchebag if you know what I mean."

"Well . . ." I try to remember what I told White Mom, but now those reasons feel too silly to repeat to Sasha. "He just makes me feel special is all," I say.

"Hmm," she says.

We sit in silence like that for a while until I break it with: "So today at the beach with Dglo, did you like—see a canoe or something?"

She doesn't say anything for a while, seeming deep in thought. "I saw Mom. She was rubbing Vicks VapoRub on my back and telling me a story like when I was little."

"Mom, huh?"

"Yeah," she says, "it's kind of like the happy memory I go to sometimes. Maybe the canoe is yours."

Which is when I remember the canoe I tried to build for Dad to take him and our family to a place far away from our troubles in Jamaica. I'd almost forgotten that place.

"Sasha," I say, "I haven't been able to write, you know. Since you left."

She looks at me.

"I keep writing the same line over and over again."

"What line?"

"Once upon a time, a girl."

"Well, that's your problem," she says. "There's two of us."

"You can't leave me," I say. "Never again."

"Okay," she says, even though we both know that in a few days, I'll be gone. Now she takes my hand in hers. "Once upon a time, there were two sisters torn apart by history," she says.

"And brought back together by stories," I continue.

"And when these sisters tell stories, weird shit starts to happen."

"Spiders appear on windows."

"Snake-women create tsunamis."

"And mothers die."

. . . . . . . . . . . . .

I take my laptop out into the living room and let Sasha sleep. I have a new message. It's from Jay. It says, "Hey, don't know why Ashton posted that photo. You know how she can be. We was just playing around. Don't take it too serious. Saw you called. Was out celebrating with my boys. Message me if you still awake."

I stare at the message for a while, trying to figure out how to respond. It's what I would've wanted him to say and yet reading the message now, over and over again, I feel nothing: not relief, not joy, just a numbness crawling over me and spreading. I stare at the message until my eyes start to glaze over from the glare of the computer screen. I delete the message and close the laptop.

I take out my journal and write: *Once upon a time, the girl had a sister, who in fact, does get found. The sister wakes up one day and travels the ocean to Mayaro and cries till she can feel her feet again. She cries till Mama Dglo appears at her window from her tear river and then disappears again into the waves before the girl can notice. She cries until she owes $15,000 of water damage for the hardwood floors. She cries until she gets a subpoena floating into her bedroom about the money she owes the provincial government and half her neighbors for the flood damage. Her neighbors sing outside her house chanting songs for her to get better, telling stories about Anansi's spider legs becoming human legs, becoming tree stalks, saying that anything is possible.*

CHAPTER 12

# The Anansi Stories
*Sasha & Zora*

Brooklyn, NY
Mayaro, Trinidad & Tobago
October 2005

## Sasha

SO LATELY I'VE BEEN NOTICING THIS STRANGE THING HAP-
pening where every day for the past month or so, my room has felt just
a little bit smaller. But not just felt. Is. Like the air is tighter. Stuffier.
Like my window that used to take up half my room is now roughly the
size of a door. But whenever I go to get the tape measure, it swears it's
still the same size.

I've been staying with Mom in Ma's old house ever since Zora left in
May. Since then, I've been sleeping in the room Ma used for her clients
while my mother sleeps in Ma's old room. I didn't want her to sleep in
there—in the room where Ma died, but the bed in my room is shaped
basically like a coffin, and the walls are the color of ashes, which somehow seems worse.

I stretch, half asleep, to look out the window. The neighbor's rooster
that sometimes wanders into our yard is still crowing at 10:00 a.m. He's
been at it since four. Even with my window shut and my factory fan
on blast, I can still hear him, ringing in my ears like a bell. I open the
window and yell at the bird to shut the fuck up. He stops crowing for a
moment and looks back at me, startled. Well, thank God, I say and start
to pull the sheets back over my head.

But just as I get my body settled back into sleep, the crowing starts again. I walk back over to the window, swinging my fist in the air and threatening to make him into curry. He glares right back at me, beak pointed up to the house like a weapon. He opens his beak and crows. It sounds like a word—only it can't be. Until I hear it again. "Dead." The word is clear and vaguely human. I shut the window and run out the room.

"We have to get out of this house," I say to Mom over breakfast.

I made her a veggie omelet like she asked, but she picks at it with her fork and stares at the floor.

"I was talking to Aunty Shirley," I continue. "She said we can go stay with her. Said she'd help cook you meals from your childhood and everything."

"Steups," Mom says and drops her fork onto her plate. "Aunty Shirley cyah cook for shit."

The sound of the word "shit" on Mom's tongue prickles my skin.

"Mom." I take her hand. "You know, I really don't think it's healthy you sleeping in Ma's old room."

Mom looks at me, finally, her eyes cold and firm. "I'm dying, Sasha. Nothing healthy about it," she says, plopping a wad of egg into her mouth. "Besides. You know what the doctors said. They say that—"

"Don't," I say and take her plate.

I let the hot soapy water fill the sink and spill onto the floor. Mom says nothing and just watches the suds sink into wood.

I carry Mom to the bathroom to bathe her like I've had to do every day for the last two weeks since she came back from the hospital. She feels like a cat, soft and limp. She collapses in my arms like a folding chair.

"Water's cold," she says as I lift her into the tub.

"The water is warm, Mom."

"I'm cold," she says and reaches for the nozzle. I stop her hand.

"Wait, you might have a fever. Let me go get the thermometer."

As I get up to go, Mom grips my arm stronger than she should be able to at this point.

"Don't," she says. Her eyes look scared. Feral. Like the thing inside my mother has gotten her eyes too.

"Aunty Shirley will pick us up tomorrow," I say, trying to force a calm into my voice. "She's making curry."

"Doh make me go," she says.

She says this like she is a child. She says this like I am her mother.

"Mom, what's wrong?" I kneel back down beside her and move the sponge across her back in a circle.

"Doh make me go," she says again. Her voice splinters.

"Mom," I say, but she grips my hand again.

"Tell her ah sorry. Ah sorry for what I did to God and the family."

"What the hell are you talking about, Mom?" I drop the sponge in the water and let it float.

"Please doh make me go, Ma. It's cold in New York."

I put my hand on her face. The doctors said it was normal for Mom to get confused about things now that the tumor had spread so far across her brain. They said she might see things she shouldn't be seeing. They didn't say she would be time traveling.

"Ma's dead. She died six months ago, remember?" I say. "I'm your daughter. Sasha. And nobody's making you go back to the States."

Mom's face scrunches up now into a knot. "I thought yuh said yuh go help meh get rid of that demon thing," she says. "Ah too young to have a child."

I stop and breathe hard into my hands.

After the bath, I put her to lie in my coffin bed for her nap to get her out of Ma's room and all that ghost energy. As she sleeps, I lie next to her, holding on to bones. She doesn't hear me cry.

Suddenly it's an hour later, and I'm exhausted, but still I can't sleep. I get up and look out the window, but the rooster is gone. I put my hands over the walls and feel the engravings of the Garifunas—what my mother still calls the Black Caribs, what my father still calls the Maroons—that built this house, at least according to Ma. As I walk across the room, I feel it—this something else, creeping across the room like a shadow. As soon as I walk in front my bookshelf, I see it: *The Anansi Stories*. The book stares back at me from the third shelf as though its cover were a face.

I take the book off the shelf and open it. It flips open to the chapter entitled "The Conjurer."

It says, "To conjure is to create something out of thin air or maybe to imagine." Says "A conjurer is someone who can make a thing appear—a thing that logically shouldn't exist."

Underneath is one of those photos where it changes if you bend the page or hold it under the light. Below the picture, it says "Or does it just make you think it appears?"

## Zora

"Good morning, Gatsby-ites!" says Professor Dawson. "And welcome back to Advanced Fiction!" He says this at the beginning of every class. Professor Dawson looks like a cherub when he speaks—all blond-haired with red cheeks shaped like onion bulbs on his face. His hands wave about like an orchestra conductor directing the class to light up just like him, and I'm worried he might try to make us dance on our desks like we're in *Dead Poets Society* or something.

"Today I have only one question for you," he says, rubbing his hands together in anticipation of something. And then he closes his eyes, his lips spread out like a watermelon slice: "Who lights your literary fire?"

The class perks up at this question with excited murmurs and giggles. My stomach immediately turns into knots. Truth be told, I can't remember the last "smart adult person" book I've actually read this year. And already I can tell that the man doesn't exactly care for my writing. The last two stories I gave him came back to me all in red.

"So who would like to start?" he asks, and I look deep into my notebook so that he can't possibly call on me.

Of course Tommy, our resident Lit-Bro, has to answer first. "James Joyce," he says, tipping his Yankees cap toward the rest of the class knowingly. Professor Dawson nods back in approval.

Corinne, who always looks like an extra from *The Craft*, with her plaid skirt and too much eyeliner, claims Sylvia Plath as hers. Well, duh, I mumble to myself. But also I wish I'd thought of that. I've actually read Sylvia Plath.

I look over pleadingly at Jasmine, the one other Black girl in our class, for support. She wraps her long Aaliyah-length hair through a ballpoint pen as she smiles at me. She raises her hand tentatively: "Toni Morrison," she says. Professor Dawson beams. My stomach sinks.

As more and more hands are raised, I get nervous, knowing that it's coming to me soon. The rest of the class names all the major *C*s: Chaucer, Chekhov, Carver, but my mind is still a blank. The last thing I remember reading from cover to cover was the latest edition of *Cosmo* featuring Mariah Carey wearing fishnets and the cowboy boots I wish I had.

I realize in this moment that the entire class is looking at me, waiting for me to say something brilliant.

"And you, Zora?" Professor Dawson looks at me curiously. "Who lights *your* literary fire?"

"Well," I say, feeling my palms start to sweat. "Lately, I've been feeling pretty inspired by Sarah Michelle Gellar in *Buffy the Vampire Slayer.*"

Other Black Girl shakes her head in utter disapproval. It's our first midterm season and already I've been dismissed by my one classroom ally.

Professor Dawson clears his throat. "Thank you, Zora," he says.

I spend the rest of the class with my head down, not speaking, while he gives an impassioned speech about all the ways we will continue to grow and inspire one another, even ourselves.

After class, I try to run out without making eye contact with anyone, but he stops me.

"So, Zora I wanted to talk to you about your last piece," he says to me. His voice is dry and unreadable.

The last story I submitted was about a town taken over by vampires until one girl gets chosen to save it—until, of course, she realizes she is transforming into a vampire herself.

"You know that my course is usually not open to freshmen." He goes on. "But the story you sent to be considered for this class was so moving, I thought I should make an exception."

"Oh?" I say, blushing in spite of myself.

"And then I read more of your work."

"Oh."

"Now I could just tell you that your stories this semester have been derivative and unimagined, which would be true and quite possibly too generous."

His voice escalates from dry to the level of disappointment usually reserved for black sheep family members.

I stand there waiting for more.

"But more than that," he continues, "I can't help but feel like this isn't really the story you want to be telling."

"What is the story I want to be telling?" I wonder.

"You tell me," he says, handing me back my story. "Now this one scene between the girl and her mother"—he points to my typed pages all marked in red—"now that was interesting."

"Oh," I say. The scene in question is a fictionalized account of the night before my mother left for Trinidad. Only in the story version, the two are fighting because the girl has just discovered that turning into vampires is a gene passed down to her from her mother's side, like werewolves.

"Why not start there?" Professor Dawson says. "Uncover a family secret. Document what you're seeing. I'm sure you must have more stories about your family, being from the Caribbean and all."

"We all have stories," I say, and I start to push my pen open and closed in my hand until it stabs me hard in my palm.

"I want to see something real in your next story. I want to *feeeel* something," he enunciates. "That is your next assignment from me."

I leave feeling hot and agitated.

I get back to my dorm and sit on my bed, staring at the empty walls I never bothered to decorate that make the room look like a concrete box. I take out my pen and journal. I write: *There once was a girl ~~who woke up one day to realize she was a vampire slayer and so she staked her professor to death.~~ The girl had a mother who left her to die in ~~Trinidad and so she fed her to a vampire just so that she could bring her back to life again.~~*

Lord. I'm so gonna fail this class. But to be honest, writing just hasn't been the same for me lately. Like I thought I would be happy to be away from Dad and White Mom and their spawn for a while, just focusing on me and my own thing, but I haven't really been able to focus on much lately. It's been five months since I came back from Trinidad, four since I graduated high school and ended things with Jay Robert Ellison, and two since I left Brooklyn to end up in bumblefuck nowhere upstate.

I get up to go look at the one photo I have on my desk. It's me and Mom taken maybe a few hours after I was born. I look like a giant wet mouse, but Mom? She looks good. Her skin is this golden color that seems almost unreal to me because of how vibrant and shiny it is. Her black hair winds around her neck down to her waist and makes her look like a princess.

This morning I got a text from Sasha. It read "Last night I had to carry Mom to and from the bathroom like she was a fucking child. She felt like a cat. It was disgusting. I know you just started school and all, but I really think you should come down here."

I take out my journal and write: *There once was a girl whose mother had sealed her fate with death. One day her cells began to deteriorate until she was nothing but atoms.*

I turn off my phone and let my journal drop to the floor.

## Sasha

When Mom comes to, I'm in the middle of rolling a blunt on the floor. I usually wouldn't do this with Mom sleeping only four feet away, but considering she didn't even know who I was an hour ago, I'm feeling a bit ballsy. Besides—I don't want to leave her alone in this room with the Anansi book watching us like that.

"I told you never to bring that Devil weed in this house, Sasha," she says, sitting up. Her face has her usual scowl, so I know she must be feeling better.

"Oh, so you remember who I am now, huh?" I say, still rolling.

"What foolishness that now?"

"Never mind, Mom." I realize it isn't worth it to upset her right now.

"Yuh not smoking that in here," she says.

"You know, I actually brought this for the both of us."

I can tell by her face she's pissed she's not strong enough to get up and box me over the head anymore.

"No, seriously, Mom, it'll make you feel better," I say as I take my lighter from my pocket.

"Watch yuhself, yuh hear." Her finger points toward me as a warning.

"You know, Mom, there are actual studies written by scientists that say that marijuana is one of nature's greatest painkillers."

"Lord Father, if yuh light that Devil stick up in here—"

But before she can finish her sentence, I've already lit the blunt and taken my first exhale.

"Well, I feel much better now, thank you." I smile and start walking toward my mother very slowly.

"Get that thing away from me, Sasha." Her arms are crossed, and she looks out the window.

I sit down on the bed next to her.

"Lord Father," she says, looking up to God.

"Look, Mom, all I'm saying is it's really not so different from all those herbs Ma had you drinking in your teas. I'm pretty sure one of them had shrooms in it."

"Give me that thing," she says and snatches it out my hand. She looks like she's going to throw it out the window for a moment, but then she looks at the blunt, puts it to her lips, and breathes in.

I look at her startled. I didn't actually think this would work.

"How do you feel, Mom?" I say, still staring.

"Steups." She sucks her teeth and then starts coughing uncontrollably.

"Mom, are you okay?"

"Just remember." She sips on her glass of water. "This never happened," she says, before taking another hit.

I laugh. "Copy that." But I can still feel *The Anansi Stories* watching me from the bookshelf.

"So, Mom," I say, "what happens to Anansi after she becomes a spider?"

Mom exhales a ring of smoke. "You know what. She becomes the keeper of stories."

"But after that. What happens after?" I'm feeling anxious.

"What always happens. She becomes too powerful for them." She passes the blunt to me.

"I thought you said her only power was telling stories," I say between puffs.

"Exactly. Nothing more dangerous than a story with an owner that no one can touch," she says. "Pretty soon, every woman who tried to tell her story had her tongue cut out."

"Cut out?"

Mom nods. "But they could never kill her. Slaughter, maybe, but never kill. No, her ghost leapt from she throat before her last breath was taken to form a book," she says, pointing to my bookshelf. "Some say, she still waiting for someone to bring she back."

I look at her, put the blunt down. "So, what are we waiting for?"

## Zora

I decide to go home for the weekend to clear my head, but I end up getting off at my old stop first—the one we lived off before Mom left for Trinidad. As soon as I get out the subway station, I feel relieved by the loud music on the streets, the grandmas looking me up and down for wearing a crop top on the subway in the middle of October. And also,

I'm starving. I walk down Flatbush to Ali's—the spot my Mom used to take us to, and I immediately feel nostalgia for everything: the people selling snow cones on the sidewalks, the dollar vans whizzing past me like they're in a car chase scene, when I see something else. Right where Ali's used to be stands a wide glass structure with bright pink lettering. It reads JANE'S COFFEE SHOP across the front. I stand in front of the glass a moment until a woman with a stroller impatiently pushes past me through the front door. I step inside and see a flock of people laughing with the barista—a round tattooed woman with half of her blond hair shaved. I recognize no one in the shop, and yet they all look like they've been drinking lattes here for years.

"Can I help you?" the woman asks me.

I run out without saying a word and walk four blocks to the next closest roti shop. I shake off the image of the bright pink lettering, the half-shaven blond.

I pay for the doubles and walk outside to take my first bite. Maybe it's because I'm so hungry, but something about these doubles tastes just like the summer Mom took us to Trinidad when we were little. When we arrived at the airport that summer, I remember my mom's whole face lighting up like the sky. She'd practically skipped all the way down to the doubles stand before buying us both two with slight pepper. And then she took her first bite, closed her eyes, and said, "I'm going to die here." She licked her fingers and lips, then smiled and said, "What a fête that will be."

I walk across to the other side of the park and end up in front of the house. As I stand there, I feel suddenly unsure of whether or not to go in. But Dad opens the door before I even ring the bell.

"Zori!" his voice booms, his arms extend toward me.

"You startled me," I say, slightly shaken.

"Spending too much time upstate, I see," he says, chuckling. "Becoming a scared suburbanite already."

He looks older. His skin looks thick like leather. His beard is shaggy and gray.

When we hug, I smell his Old Spice and Hugo Boss cologne, and I realize how much I've missed him.

"Oh, Zora, you're here!" says his woman, and she reaches to grab me too.

I try not to cringe too noticeably as we embrace. You would think that with me having lived with them for two years, I'd be used to her by now. But I notice myself stiffening every time she gets close.

As I look around, I notice that the living room has turned into a real-life museum. In addition to Adaliz's glass bird sculpture, there is now a large black Egyptian cat figure guarding the entrance to the kitchen and a maternity sculpture from Ghana.

"Another trip to Africa?" I smirk.

"You should go with her next time, Zora. You're always talking about wanting to learn more about your history."

I turn to look back at the black cat so Dad can't see me rolling my eyes.

"So where are Kayla and Madeleine anyway? It's way too quiet in here."

"Oh they're at a sleepover," Adaliz says. "We didn't know you were coming until we got your text an hour ago. They would've loved to see you, I'm sure."

"But we're making your favorite for dinner," Dad says.

"Leg of lamb!" says his wife. "You still like lamb, don't you?"

"Sure, I like it." I shrug. It isn't my favorite, but I decide not to correct them.

We sit at the table, which looks longer than I remember—like the Romans could eat here with us.

"So, do you guys know what happened to Ali's?" I ask as Adaliz serves me a hefty portion of lamb and mashed potatoes.

"Oh yes, your favorite roti shop lost their lease," Dad says.

"So sad." Adaliz shakes her head.

The inside of the lamb is beet red. As I cut into it, the blood makes a circle around my plate.

"But the new coffee shop is great," Dad says, mixing the lamb with his mashed potatoes until they turn pink. "Their coconut lattes are out of this world. You have to try one before you go."

"How'd they lose their lease?" I ask.

"Couldn't keep up, I suppose." Dad shrugs between bites of red lamb. "And it's sad, yes, but there are other roti shops. I see this as a win for the old neighborhood. I mean just think, if it had been there when we moved, we could've made double on the old apartment."

The sight of the red lamb is starting to make my stomach turn. I push the food around my plate and hope they won't notice me not eating.

"Yes," Adaliz agrees, "I hear they're opening a new Mexican spot too. The same owner as the guy who opened El Toro down the block from us."

"Well, that is good news," Dad says, a trail of blood trickling down his cheek. "Have you been to El Toro? They have this roast duck taco— you have to try it, it's to die for."

"I haven't," I say and gulp down my glass of water.

"You haven't touched your food," Dad says, pointing a bloody fork at me.

"I'm sorry," I say, "I'm not really feeling that well. I think I should go lie down."

"Of course, Zora. You need your rest," says Adaliz, her hand rubbing my father's shoulder.

"Yes, we'll catch up in the morning, Zora. I have quite the day planned for us."

After dinner I go into my room and rest on my old bed. I can hear Dad and his wife laughing together and possibly dancing in the kitchen.

I look at my phone and see I got another text from Sasha. It says "Mom's not doing well. Don't think she'll make it to Christmas. Please just come. Or at least write me back."

I start to write: "Sorry for my delay, but I think I may be drowning in something." I erase the text and put down my phone. I take out my journal instead. I write: *There once was a girl who had a father who was a brilliant painter. A painter who tried to cover a white house black but ran out of the color toward the end of the paint job. Even if he were to buy more paint for the house, he'd still have this feeling that the black was never supposed to be there to begin with. A true artist would never be able to live inside that house.*

## Sasha

We sit in the yard under a silk-cotton tree. Ma once told me that she planted this tree when she moved to this house, in order to communicate with the dead. You can see silk-cotton trees in pictures alongside most of the stories in our Anansi book. Apparently, this is the place where the ghosts come out to play.

I gathered the candles, salt, and copy of *The Anansi Stories* before wheeling Mom out in her wheelchair. The sun sits smack in the middle of the sky, beaming at us.

Mom directs me on proper setup from her wheelchair, like it's her throne.

"This salt looking more like square than circle," she says, pointing to the ground.

"What are you talking about, Mom? This is definitely a circle."

Mom bursts into laughter then. "Watch she come back as a soucouyant to come and bite you up in yuh sleep," she says, slapping her thighs.

I guess the weed finally kicked in.

"All right, Mom. Just help me with this ritual. You know you're the only one who knows how to do these right."

"Guess yuh shoulda think of that before you drug up yuh muddah, ent," she says, still laughing.

I can't tell if I'm more amused or horrified by the sight of my mother this high.

"You're right, Mom. I'm sorry." But then I laugh with her in spite of myself.

I light the candles in a triangle inside the salt circle and then open the book. We read the lines together in unison.

"On average, an ordinary spider lives for only a year at a time," we begin.

"But this was no ordinary spider."

"No, this was the one they called Anansi."

"One day it was a spider."

"And on the next day he turned into a man."

"And on the next day a woman."

"And on the next day a ghost."

"And on the next day a story."

"And on the next and final day, she was a spider again."

"And it was in this way that she never died."

We blow out the candles, and I dig a small hole with a hand trowel to bury the book while Mom fans herself with a washrag.

"Watch we bring back Dracula instead, ent?" Mom says, howling.

I look at her, not knowing how to respond.

"You hear me, Ma?" she says, yelling into the ground. "We bringing him back! He might just make a good boyfriend for Sasha."

"Mom!"

"Okay, maybe for Zora, then," she says, still laughing.

As her laughter subsides, I try to bring her back to the task at hand. "So, what happens now?"

"We wait," she says.

"How will we know if it works?"

"We'll know."

And then it occurs to me: my mother is high. I can ask her anything I want.

"So, Mom?" I say after a moment.

"Hmm."

"When are you going to tell me who your family nearly burned you alive for?" I say, covering the hole back up. "You know, the wrong one you say you fell for who wasn't Dad?"

"Steups," she says and closes her eyes.

I stare at her till she opens her eyes. "It was a woman, wasn't it?"

I don't know when I realized it, but every child learns at some point that there is only one type of love that families tend to burn their children alive for.

Mom looks away from me quickly, and I know that I'm right. "What does it matter now?" Mom shrugs.

But it does matter.

"What starts with fire ends with fire," she says finally. "Makes no difference in the end."

"You should've told me," I say.

"I was trying to protect you."

"You didn't," I say.

We sit in silence in this knowledge for a moment, the sun creating rain down our backs.

"Maybe you could still find her," I offer.

"Steups."

"No, seriously. I can do some digging around. Ask around by your old high school."

"It's too late for that," she says, and we're silent again. The air thickens around us.

"So," I say, finally, "you ever watch *The L Word*?"

We get to the part where Jenny watches Shane fucking some girl in Bette and Tina's pool, when Mom has had enough. The weed must've worn off, because she makes us watch three episodes of *Touched by an Angel* as penance.

"I'm gonna make a snack, Mom, do you want anything?"

"Popcorn," she says.

I go into the kitchen and open the cabinet to where the popcorn is kept and jump back. Inside the cabinet are roaches crawling over the knives and forks. I run to grab the Raid and inch my way back to the army of pests colonizing our kitchen cabinets. I squint my eyes, nozzle pointed down when I notice something—the roaches have eight legs. I open my eyes and look. These aren't roaches at all. They're spiders.

Spiders of all sizes and levels of hairiness. Spiders crawling around the sink. Spiders climbing up the refrigerator. Spiders creeping up the kitchen closet door. Spiders crawling out from the cracks in the walls. I drop the Raid in my hand and listen to it clatter on the floor.

"What was that?" Mom calls out, but I can't open my mouth to respond. I hear my mother hobbling toward me in the kitchen.

"What nonsense," she says and then puts a hand to her lips. "Lord Father, have mercy," she gasps when she arrives. "She's here."

## Zora

I wake up early, and my body feels like lead. Last night I woke up to images of my mother. I got to Trinidad just in time to see her die. I got to Trinidad just in time to save her. She looked like Goldie Hawn in *Death Becomes Her*—alive but with limbs falling off her body. Her skin smelled like sewage.

I open my laptop and type "spells that cure cancer." Every time I look for spells, they seem to be a bust, and yet searching for them still seems better than thinking about the alternative. On witchbaby.com, I find one that says I need to slaughter a baby goat and rub its blood on my feet. Magic Mama says to find stones from every ocean and take them to the tallest mountain at sunrise.

"What's happening here, Zori?" My father is standing over my bed and the laptop that is currently filled with incriminating magical spells. I look sheepishly from my laptop screen to my father's concerned expression and then down at my floral comforter.

He comes to sit beside me. "I was wondering why you didn't touch your food last night."

I want to tell him about all the blood on the lamb, but I decide not to bother. "I'm trying to find a spell," I say.

He looks at me curiously.

"It's for Mom," I add.

"I see," he says, and takes the laptop from me so that I have to look at him. "You know," he says, putting a hand on my shoulder, "you could write your own spell."

I look at him, confused.

"They say stories make the best incantations," he says.

"See, that's the thing," I say, "I haven't been able to write any stories lately. At least not any that anyone wants to read."

"Well, I'm sure that's not true."

"My professor called my last story derivative."

"Sounds like an idiot," Dad says, and I imagine him marching down to my school and making Professor Dawson's red bulbs glow with embarrassment like Christmas lights.

"I mean it was basically a rip-off of *Buffy the Vampire Slayer*, so he may have a point," I say.

"I see," he says.

"I'm worried I may have lost the writing spirit, Dad."

"You know," he says, pulling at the grays of his beard, "that happened to me once."

I look at him. Since he married his new wife, he hasn't told us many stories. Kayla and Madeleine have had to rely on me, instead, to scare them out of running off and accidentally coming up against the Rolling Calf.

"My father never wanted me to tell stories. And then he died." His voice feels strained now, as though he isn't sure he should keep going. "He wanted me to join him in the bauxite factory, but no—I had to be a writer. The day before he killed himself, he told me I should've become a tailor because I could create lies out of thread. Sometimes I still think about that."

I realize in this moment that I never knew how my grandfather died. I want to ask him why Granddad killed himself, but I decide against it.

"Granddad called you a liar?" I ask instead.

"He called me a lot of things," he says. The creases in his face seem thicker now, as though they're hiding stories he may die never telling.

I want to say something corny but true, like, I always wanna hear your stories. But the words get stuck. I move to put a hand on his shoulder, but it wavers in the space between us.

He smiles. "When I told your grandmother I was coming to America to write, she laughed in my face. And then she begged God to let her join her husband along with her favorite son—the one who could sprint from our house to Small Ponds in under fifteen seconds and lift fifteen-pound sacks of rice over his head like bags of cotton candy. She died before I could see her again." His voice falters. "Then again, perhaps she was right," he says, "because eventually, those stories . . . they just stopped coming."

"Well, maybe we could write one together," I say.

His smile fades. "We'll see," he says, getting up. "Oh, and I almost forgot." He hands me a blue box. "This came for you in the mail. It's from your mother."

I open the blue box, and inside is the turtle pendant Mom wore when she left for Trinidad—the one I found on Anacaona's neck in *The Anansi Stories.*

"She always said this necklace is what gave her her stories. I thought it was nonsense at the time, but who knows . . . maybe it will help."

When he says this, his eyes look lost in memory, and I wonder if he misses her.

"Dad," I ask, "when did you stop?"

"Stop what?"

"Loving her."

Dad sighs. "I didn't." He sits down again and extends his arm toward me. "It's just . . . well, it's really something, you know, trying to watch the person you love suffer like that. After a while they either have to change or someone has to leave so you don't have to watch them anymore. This is a fact. This is just what happens. Something you may wind up dealing with if you ever get married."

His voice is rough. Unstable. I worry it might break. That the image we have of him: stone wall and standing, will shatter, and all we'll be left with are the feelings we never knew he had.

"I'm not saying I was right. I know I wasn't. But loving a woman like your mother was never easy."

"You should tell her that," I say.

He smiles and gets up to leave the room. "Come," he says, "I'll make us breakfast."

"I'll be down in just a minute," I say.

I put the necklace on and feel the metals cool my neck.

I write: *There once was a girl whose father's skin was thick as leather. The creases were from being worn out, from trying to hide his expressions. The man's hands were made to choose between mining bauxite for aluminum where his father first lost the will to live or staying home to care for his mother's unable body. Her body broke from walking four miles a day taking care of someone else's children and tripping and falling in the river. Sacrifice is going to town to sell your clothes, books, and food until you have enough money to come to America and become a writer. Sacrifice is not having enough money to see your mother before she dies alone in her rocking chair. Sacrifice is leaving your mother knowing that she is drowning because you want to save the fire that lives beneath your breath and come to America.*

I get a text from Sasha: "You're dead to me."

## Sasha

By the time Aunty Shirley shows up with an empty maxi she rented, the spiders have created colonies in every room of the house. My mother and I held each other tight on my coffin bed all night, unable to sleep.

"What happen to allyuh?" Aunty Shirley asks, hands on hips, demanding an answer.

"Didn't get much sleep," I answer for us both.

"Yuh cyah be keeping yuh mother up at all hours like that no more, Sasha. Yuh remember what the doctor said."

"Now look who doh want to listen to de doctor," my mother says, nodding her head in my direction.

"Of course, Aunty Shirley," I say. "I won't."

"Well, let we go, nah," she says. "Beatrice, you wait here, we'll carry yuh things into de maxi for yuh."

As I wheel Mom out into the maxi, I whisper, "What do you think will happen if we leave the spiders here?"

My mother beams up at me from her wheelchair and says, "I think I'm really going to enjoy my time in America."

"What?" I say.

"Thank you, Ma," she continues, "for making me go. It'll turn me into a good woman, I promise."

And then she squeezes my hand.

"Mom," I say, sternly at first, but soften when I see her face. I squeeze her hand back. "You're welcome," I say.

And then the three of us pile into the maxi and drive off into the sunrise.

## Zora

After breakfast, my father and I spend the day together at Coney Island. When he leaves, I decide to spend some time walking the boardwalk before making my way back upstate. The air is crisp and salty.

As I walk, I see a flock of seagulls picking at leftover hot dogs in front of me. As I pass them, the seagulls stop and look at me for a moment. Their eyes turn from devouring the hot dogs to my Old Navy jean jacket. I walk faster past the birds and stop a few yards ahead to buy some funnel cake. In line, I see a man with a snake around his neck walking by, and I shudder. I hate when people take their giant snakes for walks in the city. I close my eyes and open them again and breathe a sigh of relief as the man has long since passed. But as I watch him walk away, I notice that his snake has wrapped around the man's neck to look back at me, its unblinking eyes are steady. I leave without buying the funnel cake and sprint all the way to the subway station.

On the train, I push my head into my knees, trying not to feel the eyes of the subway car, watching me. I start to shiver and hold my breath, hoping I'm just imagining things. I pull out my phone and decide to text Sasha. I write "I'm so sorry, Sasha. Something strange has been happening lately. I keep feeling like something's watching me. Either that or I'm just losing my mind. I love you. And yes, I'll be there for Thanksgiving."

She writes back immediately: "It's time to come home, Zori. Thanksgiving is okay. Next week would be better. Please bring Kayla."

I put my phone away and pull out my journal. I write: *Once upon a time there was a girl. And this girl had the power to keep people alive through her words. The girl told herself that she would save her mother from skin cancer, and so it came to be that she would never die. They say the girl's mother had skin that was like the paint that runs in all different directions and spills on the floor but somehow manages to come out just right. Her family didn't understand this and grew frustrated with trying to make sense of her colors. Sacrifice is letting her family set her on fire in order to make sense. Sacrifice is finding the strength to fly to America in burnt skin. To become untouchable. Sacrifice is finding someone, even if that someone is a man like the wounded writer who, in spite of everything, is her mother's savior because he loved the shades the scars made across her back and didn't want her to be alone in America.*

# CHAPTER 13

# Instructions for Communicating
# with Dead Mothers

Mayaro, Trinidad
December 2005

SO THEY GET TO THE VIEWING, AND SASHA CAN'T HELP BUT notice that her daddy looks like he just swallowed a whole gallon of thunderstorm. She's upset that she's looking at him now instead of at her mother, wondering if anybody's noticing that she's looking at him now instead of at her mother—and of course she's relieved that he's given her the opportunity to take a break from her. She also can't help but look at his wife. Nigel's woman is always prettier than Sasha wants her to be. She can see that the woman took the time this morning to press her hair down and to curl her daughter's head into perfect brown ringlets while she let her husband come to embarrass them all in his untucked button-down. Not that it'd be like Nigel to let a woman make him do anything—let alone dress different. But still. Dad's woman and daughter are holding hands, which Sasha has to admit is sweet in a way—and perhaps she should stop calling them Dad's woman and daughter (she should) since she knows their names, but she can't help pretending that she doesn't.

Zora, on the other hand, is not at all surprised they decided to come. She tells Sasha it's good that they want to make peace with the dead. After all, with Adaliz awkwardly trying to be the supportive second wife and Dad not quite sure how he should be acting, it was up to Zora to spend the last few days guiding Kayla and Madeleine through the socially acceptable childhood displays of grief until Aunty Shirley finally arrived to take over. Thank God Kayla decided to cry with Aunty Shirley instead—who is doing much better now (praise God!) that she started taking up embroidery and not taking any crap from men like her good-for-nothing ex-husband who rumor has it was done in by his twenty-four-year-old assistant three years prior.

Aunty Shirley says she was shocked: both at herself and everyone else in attendance who cared a lick about Beatrice Porter and didn't have the nerve to chase Adaliz out. It's true. The fact is, Adaliz Austerlitz has been wanting to meet their mother for a looong looong time.

Sasha and Zora get in line to pay their respects. Sasha looks at Zora to see if she's looking at Dad's woman too, but she's just looking down at her own hands. The turnout is pretty good considering how highway-robbery-like the flight rates have been with it being right smack in the middle of holiday season and all. Of course, not everybody was able to make it. Uncle Zeke and Aunty Alicia in Florida, for instance, couldn't afford a last-minute ticket to Port of Spain with her being on disability after the accident (understandable). Cousin Crystal and Jackie are finishing exams in school.

Their father is shaking now. Zora can't quite see the tears, but there's a noticeable quiver running through the man—like he's trying to keep himself from losing it. And then it's time for them to go look at their mother again. Now that there are only two people in front of them, Zora prepares her face to carry the appropriate amount of sadness. She's careful to put a Kleenex to her nose and eyes in case she's not able to cry or look at the body directly. She reaches for Sasha's hand, and Sasha squeezes back. They lock eyes and nod, agreeing to take a deep breath in.

Now they decide to look: their mother's wearing an ankle-length grandma dress in white that she would hate, but it's the only one that would cover up all of her scars. The makeup artist put six layers of concealer and three layers of blush on her to make her look more human. Zora puts out a tentative hand to touch her mother's cheek.

"Steups."

The sound comes from the coffin. They look at their mother's lips, which even through the lipstick look like rubber. Still, no woman the sisters have ever met had been able to successfully master the art of hissing disappointments at her children the way Beatrice Porter could. Zora whispers, "Were Mom's lips like that when the woman did her makeup?"

And it's true. Mom's lips are noticeably pursed into a state of utter disgust. They look at each other a moment. They start to walk away.

Zora breaks the silence: "Yuh mean to tell meh that allyuh couldn't find no dress to show off meh figure?" They burst into laughter. Mourners around them look politely offended. The mourners have to be polite. After all, it's not their mother in the coffin—maybe the girls' laughter is masking their tears? Sasha continues to conjure her mother: "What if that cute nurse Terry comes to pay his respects? What then?"

The sisters take their seats to watch what happens next. Nigel comes up with his wife and child. Adaliz is the first to say goodbye to Beatrice. She moves her hand tentatively toward their mother with gloved fingers. Of course, just as Adaliz Austerlitz's hand moves toward the coffin, the lid with its Christmas-green-colored lining begins to wobble before falling shut with a clatter. Nigel's wife lets out a gasp and moves her hands quickly out of harm's way. The people behind them jump, and the ones sitting down stop crying and look up attentively to see what's going on.

Their father—after attending dutifully to his startled wife, leaves the child with her to reopen the coffin along with some of the pallbearers. Sasha and Zora take one last glance at their mother before leaving the place. They find Mom's body looking dead as usual. They make their way through the crowd, passing their father on the way to the house their mother lived in before dying. Beatrice never did believe in wakes, so it will just be the two of them until their father comes back with the family from their beach trip.

"They came all this way; they might as well see what all the fuss is about," he'd said, meaning the Caribbean Sea, which is much warmer than the Isar River that his wife is used to in Munich.

. . . . . . . . . . . . .

They get back from the funeral to find their mother sitting in her rocking chair. The sisters can't explain this to you if they tried, but today their mother looks more beautiful than ever. Her skin, which had been dry and loose on the hospital bed, is now well-oiled and perfumed—like she's about to get onstage to play mas. She's gotten all her hair back on her head. Like the hair she had as a teenager, like the manes from a pack of panthers falling on all sides of her body. Her eyes are the only things that give away the fact that she's a corpse—they don't blink. The sisters never saw their mother young and in action. But they had heard stories.

"What took you?" Beatrice says.

"We just finished burying you, Mom," Sasha says.

"For so long?"

They shrug and sit at the table.

"How yuh father look?"

Neither of them is prepared to answer.

"He bring he woman?" she asks before letting out a loud "Steups."

"She's not so bad, Mom," Zora says.

Sasha rolls her eyes.

"Yes, I saw her. I only asking to see what allyuh have to say about she anyhow. I doh know who she feel she is letting she halfling daughter come round *my* dead body in she cheap old-time-ish shift dress."

"Maybe they were trying to make amends," tries Zora.

"Probably get she dress from Kmart, looking like an old granny and ting."

"Mom!" the sisters exclaim simultaneously.

"All right, all right," Beatrice says with a smile. "I bring a friend I want to introduce to allyuh children anyhow." They look to see where their mother has pointed: two long legs climb through the window and land on the floor. Her sheer-colored miniskirt reveals the flex of her hamstring muscles. Her skin is the color of chili powder lit ablaze under the dining room lights.

"Nice legs," Zora says and snickers—catching Sasha in the act of her ogling.

"Please, be respectful, girls," Beatrice says. "Besides, Sasha, she's much too old for you."

"Don't worry about me, Beatrice," the woman says. "If I could take on a homicidal Spaniard with too much chest hair, I'm sure I can handle your daughter." She smiles at Sasha, making her blush like crazy. "Though, you are something, I must say."

Sasha looks down bashfully at her own sweating hands.

It was Anacaona. In the flesh.

She takes Sasha's hand and kisses it.

Even Zora admits it: the woman looks great for 539. Her long hair is thick as rope and wraps around her thighs. Her calf muscles pulse like she's done a lot of running in her day.

"Anacaona's been trying to convince me that you'll be safe here," Beatrice says to Sasha. "I guess yuh could say that ah coming around to the idea of yuh being with women," she continues.

"Well, that's good because when you're ready, I'd like to introduce you to this new girl I'm seeing."

"Figures for you to introduce me to yuh girlfriend after ah dead."

"Let's sit outside." Anacaona attempts to change the subject. "This table smells like the stand I get hanged on. Mus' be made from the same wood."

"Walnut," Beatrice says. "Dark enough to absorb up to seventeen bodies of blood without leaving a mark—blend right in."

The four crowd around a small table in the garage to avoid the walnut wood in the kitchen. Beatrice doesn't want to be seen outside, though Anacaona assures her she won't be. Anacaona says, "African people forget how to fly, and yuh expect dem to see jumbie?"

Anacaona's patois is very good. She speaks eighteen different languages so that she can comfort the weary and spy on all her enemies regardless of her location.

"Pam!" Anacaona slams a 6:6 next to Zora's 3:6. The legs of the table shake so much with every play that they have to move Sasha's glass of water to the floor.

Beatrice wanted to play rummy, but the girls insist on dominoes—
the pieces are too thick for the ghosts to cheat.

Beatrice coughs again. She's still getting used to her ghost voice.
Every once in a while, she coughs up a piece of her lung and then orders
Zora and Sasha to clean it up for her.

They don't realize the day has turned to night until Nigel walks
through the door with Kayla who has fallen asleep in his arms. Nigel
told his wife and child to wait for him at the hotel so he could talk to his
family, and they understood.

Now Nigel looks at Beatrice. Beatrice looks at Nigel. Zora's worried he's become a scared nonbeliever after spending so much time with
whitefolk. But he puts Kayla down and then comes toward her, extend-
ing his hand like he wants to shake it—like they're doing a business deal.
And then the unexpected happens: he takes her hand and kisses it.

"You look beautiful," he says.

Beatrice blushes the way only ghost-women can—her whole body
fills with the holy glow. You can see the static running through her hair.

"Well, Nigey, it's been a long time," she says. "I see yuh bring yuh
women with she cheap dress to meh funeral."

Nigel clears his throat, looks down to the floor, looks like he just
might apologize. "I brought you some tamarind balls," he says instead,
pulling out the sugar-covered peppery sweets from his pockets.

"Steups," she says. "When we were together, yuh never eat a tamarind ball a day in your life."

"That's why I brought them," he says. He comes closer to her, still
holding the bag of sweets toward her as a peace offering. For a while, no
one is sure whether the late great Beatrice Porter will budge. But eventually her lips begin to smile, her arms reach in his direction.

The embrace is long. A few tears from Beatrice. Sasha looks away in
disgust before she can see whether or not her father has shed a couple.
When she turns back, he's smiling.

"Ready to get yuh ass whooped in dominoes?" Mom asks.

Anacaona pulls out a seat for him and Kayla. And they go on like that with their game.

"Will you be leaving anytime soon, Mom?" Zora's the first to ask. Sasha picks up a waking Kayla and covers her ears, afraid of what her answer might be. Anacaona fans herself with a dishrag in anticipation of Beatrice's response.

Mom puts down the dominoes and takes Zora's hands. "Child, where yuh think I going? I've got everything I need right here."

The sisters smile at this. They begin to cook dinner so the parents can talk.

The sisters decide on pelau. Sasha and Zora cut up the pumpkin and the coconut while Kayla stirs. Anacaona leaves eventually and then it's just us: Sasha, Mommy, Daddy, Kayla, Zora, and me. It's the first time we've eaten together as a family in years.

And I have to admit that it's nice just watching them the way I used to. I think about them all as children, the games we used to play, the stories we told. The way they'd reenact me and read me aloud like there was no one else in the world.

You see, the funny thing about stories is that we want them to end with a sprint into the sunset, an evil stepmother getting what's coming to her, a true love that never fades, a mother who comes back from the dead. But also, we don't want stories to end. Especially when they're our stories. After we die, we want to live forever in the moment we love the most. We want the moment to be replayed over and over again until our record player breaks, but it can't break because this is forever. And we don't want to be aware that we are living in forever because it's the thinking about forever that makes us all want to die in the first place.

You see in a way I, Your Faithful Narrator, have constructed the ending I want for my own life. I want you to be hopeful when this book ends so that I can be hopeful too. I want you to finish reading this book thinking, maybe people change, maybe people aren't born evil.

Maybe the isms and the bullshit are enough for even the best of us to go batshit crazy and Doc Ock/Bane on the whole world.

But I don't want to lie to you. Tales have to end somewhere, though some never do. Trickster tales, in particular, tend to end where they begin. Like one day, Anansi walks into a house looking for a glass of water. An old man waits in the doorway not saying a word. "Trouble you for a glass of water?" Anansi asks. No response. "Trouble you for a glass of water?" he asks again. Still nothing. Anansi goes inside, drinks the man's water. Sees that the man's still standing there, so decides to take some food too. Decides to come back the next day. Takes some more food. The man still says nothing. Comes back on the third day and brings his daughter. "For your hospitality and for allowing me to eat all of your food," he says, "I've decided to give you my daughter's hand in marriage." The man says nothing. Anansi shrugs his spider legs. Comes back the next day. Smells something baking in the oven. "Mmm. Smells like black pudding," he says to the man. "She always knew how to cook."

He calls for his daughter. No answer. He opens the oven door. Pulls out the pudding with his daughter's wedding ring sticking out at the top. "Where's my daughter?" Anansi demands. "Dinner," the man says, pointing to the dish. Anansi drops the dish and jumps up and down in protest. "After everything?" he says. "I give you my daughter and you turn her into food?!" "I'm Death," says the man. "I thought you knew."

Anansi realizes what he's in for. He runs to his house to tell his wife and other children. They climb up the ceiling to make a family web, knowing that only spiders can penetrate it. Still, Death comes knocking on their door. Death enters their house with a burlap sack, ready to take Anansi and his family. One by one, Anansi's wife and children fall into the sack. All except Anansi. Anansi jumps on Death's head, temporarily blurring his vision, giving him enough time to get away. Anansi spends his days having Death always three feet behind him. Whenever Death gets close, he creates another web. When you see a spiderweb on your kitchen wall, know that it is Anansi's, that he is still trying to get away from Death.

Let me tell you a story.

You see, day was I was called a god, prayed to by children, by mothers, by those who felt broken or numb. Some days I would travel to earth gathering stories, sharing secrets for battle, for spell-making, for love-making. In this time, when a person died, they told their stories through me. As if the more stories they told, the stronger I became.

But just as they came for Anacaona and her villagers, they also came for me. First, they pulled me from the sky and made me into a spider. They thought that this would crush me. Of course the tricky thing about spiders is that we can be everywhere, watching you from your windowsill while you sleep, from your very own pillow you keep so nice and neat. What they didn't know was that I was also a lagahoo, a shape-shifter, a magician, a Maroon, and a mother. I was everywhere there was a story. Children would grow up saying my name until they got too old, and the name would get lost at the tips of their tongues.

It's funny, really. Not so long ago, I wanted you to save me. In a way I guess you could say I started believing in the stories that others were inventing about my very existence. The ones that say I'm still being chased by Death—they're still hunting me. They realize there is nothing more dangerous than a story with an owner that no one can touch.

Yet now that she has saved me, buried me in the earth so that I might breathe again, I realize I've forgotten something. Because what happens to the stories that get killed? That get buried and erased?

Oh, honey, didn't you hear?

We always come back haunting.

# ACKNOWLEDGMENTS

First and foremost, I would not be here without my parents. Thank you to my mother, who read me stories and books almost every night before bed, including my favorite of hers, "Boyie, Lynette, and the Lagahoo."

Thank you to my father, who used to tell us stories as children about the Rolling Calf and Anansi the spider, including one that appears in this book, where Anansi cuts off a piece of his buttocks to feed to his family.

My parents blessed me with my love for storytelling and folklore to the point where I was telling stories before I learned to write. You also modeled what it means to dream for the impossible and to never stop fighting for myself and for those whom I love.

Thank you to the stories that gave life to this book, many of which have no known author. The ones that do and appear in some form in this book came from *Anansi the Spider Man* by Philip M. Sherlock, *Caribbean Folk Legends* by Theresa Lewis, and the website anansistories.com by Michael Auld. Most of them come from my ancestors, who died never getting credit for their work. Thank you to Nanny, Anacaona, and all the many ghosts that make my existence possible.

Thank you to my creative and brilliant siblings! Thank you to my sister Kendra aka Kenny Bear aka Chicken, with whom I wrote my first stories about the fairyland Ivclonia and who has been helping me to draft this book since its inception in 2004. Thank you, Kenny, for also sending a copy of *The Last Unicorn* to me in Virginia at a time when I felt like giving up on my writing.

Thank you to my sister Carrie, who always answers my calls and first taught me to dance, and who helped me with so much of the Jamaican dialect in this book.

Thank you to my brother, Paulie, who is always available to brainstorm and bounce ideas off of and who has been a huge supporter of my work! Thank you for your imagination, your stories, your heart.

Thank you to Tumi, who I know will be reading this book from beyond. Thank you for your passion, your love, for Audre Lorde, and your infectious laughter. I love you and miss you more each day.

Thank you to *Calyx*, *Callaloo*, and *Ploughshares* for first publishing versions of what would are now chapters 1 to 3 of this book, respectively.

Thank you to my teams at Catapult Books and Serpent's Tail. Thank you especially to Megha Majumdar, without whom I would never have realized the potential of what this book could become. You have made me a better writer, and you did it all with such brilliance, compassion, and patience. Thank you to the rest of my editorial team at Catapult: Alicia Kroell, Laura Gonzalez, and Laura Berry. Thank you to the marketing team, Alisha Gorder, Rachel Fershleiser, Megan Fishmann. Thank you to Sara Wood for the exquisitely beautiful cover design you created. Thank you to my Serpent's Tail team: Hannah Westland, Mehar Anaokar, and anyone else I've missed.

Thank you to my agent, Laura, for believing in me and working with me through countless drafts till we got to this point. Thank you also for your friendship, your insight, and your wit.

Thank you to Darin Quan for taking beautiful photos of me for my book. Thank you to Kevin Tinsley at Cheese Slice Films for your amazing work on my very first promotional video.

Thank you to all my friends and family in Trinidad, who gave me the inspiration to turn these many stories into a novel. Thank you, Aunty Marcia for allowing me to live in your home for the first two months I stayed in Trinidad. Thank you to Aunty Anette who has taken me into your home so many times since.

Thank you, Akeila, Stephanie, Josimar, and Armando for long drives to the beach, nights out dancing, and so much food.

Thank you to my grandmother, Evelyn who loved stories and romance and always made the best pepper sauce. I love and miss you so very much.

Thank you to Aunty Patsy, Colin, and Andrew, who are no longer with us in body, but whom I can still feel in my spirit.

Thank you to my cousins in Trinidad, Andel, Roniel, and Ariel.

Thank you to the community of women who helped raise and shape me into the person I am today along with my parents. Thank you to Aunty Angela, Aunty Joycelyn, Aunty Jackie Reid, Aunty Collette.

Thank you to Kathy Martino, for saving my life in more ways than one, and to the entire RC community.

Thank you to my friends and chosen family, without whom I might not be here today: Cassie, Emily Nora, Jasmine, Alexis, Karolin, Shanon, Rahson, Jeremy, Joel, Lindsay, and Sara. Thank you to Haley, Pooja, and Kedon for the many years of laughter, conversation, and joy that have turned my life around.

Thank you to all my grandparents, both living and passed, Gertrude, Wray, Kenny, and Evelyn. To my many aunts, uncles, and cousins who have been supporting me since day one.

Thank you to my work children, nephews, and nieces throughout the years: Naomie, Dai, Khea, Karencia, Eugena, Kia, Enya, Malik, Tony, Khadajah, Angie, Emmanuella, Wasun, Migos, and so many more.

Thank you to my many, many writing mentors throughout the years, without whom I surely would've given up on this book. Thank you to Anna, my fourth-grade teacher, who helped me with my very first stories in her class and who has always believed in me.

Thank you to my high school mentors, who stopped me from failing out of school and were always a shoulder to cry on: Mr. Streep, Mr. Thayer, Mr. Laybourne, Mr. Turner, Mr. Rosenbluth, and Bayard.